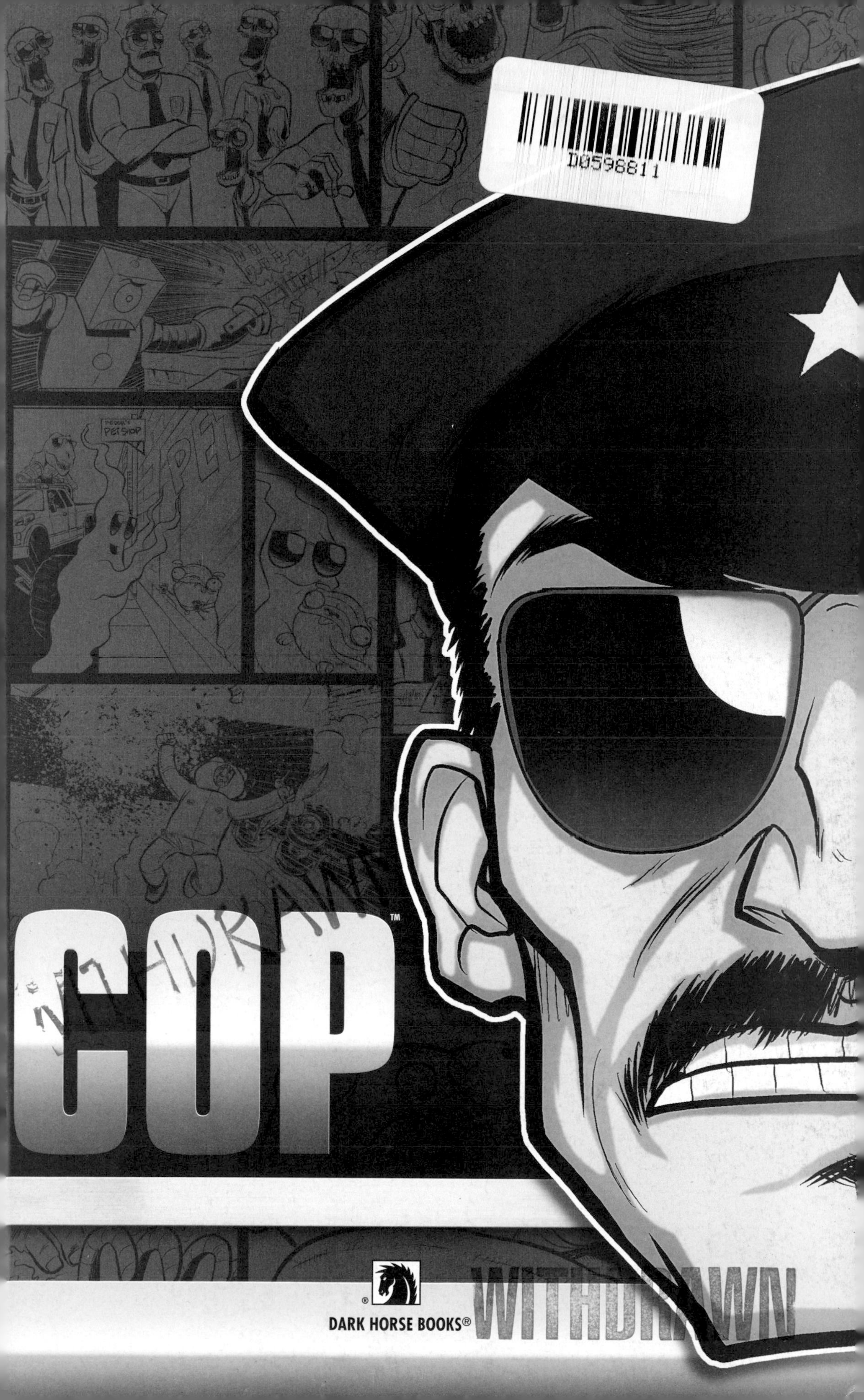
COP™
DARK HORSE BOOKS®

MALACHAI AND ETHAN DEDICATE THIS BOOK TO EACH OTHER

Publisher MIKE RICHARDSON

Editor SHAWNA GORE

Associate Editor RACHEL EDIDIN

Designer ETHAN NICOLLE

NEIL HANKERSON Executive Vice President · TOM WEDDLE Chief Financial Officer · RANDY STRADLEY Vice President of Publishing ·
MICHAEL MARTENS Vice President of Business Development · ANITA NELSON Vice President of Business Affairs · MICHA HERSHMAN Vice
President of Marketing · DAVID SCROGGY Vice President of Product Development · DALE LAFOUNTAIN Vice President of Information
Technology · DARLENE VOGEL Director of Purchasing · KEN LIZZI General Counsel · DAVEY ESTRADA Editorial Director · SCOTT ALLIE Senior
Managing Editor · CHRIS WARNER Senior Books Editor · DIANA SCHUTZ Executive Editor · CARY GRAZZINI Director of
Design and Production · LIA RIBACCHI Art Director · CARA NIECE Director of Scheduling

AXE COP Volume 1

Published by Dark Horse Books
A division of Dark Horse Comics, Inc.
10956 SE Main Street
Milwaukie, Oregon 97222
darkhorse.com

Visit axecop.com

First edition: December 2010
ISBN 978-1-59582-681-7

3 5 7 9 10 8 6 4

Printed by Transcontinental Gagné, Louisville, QC, Canada.

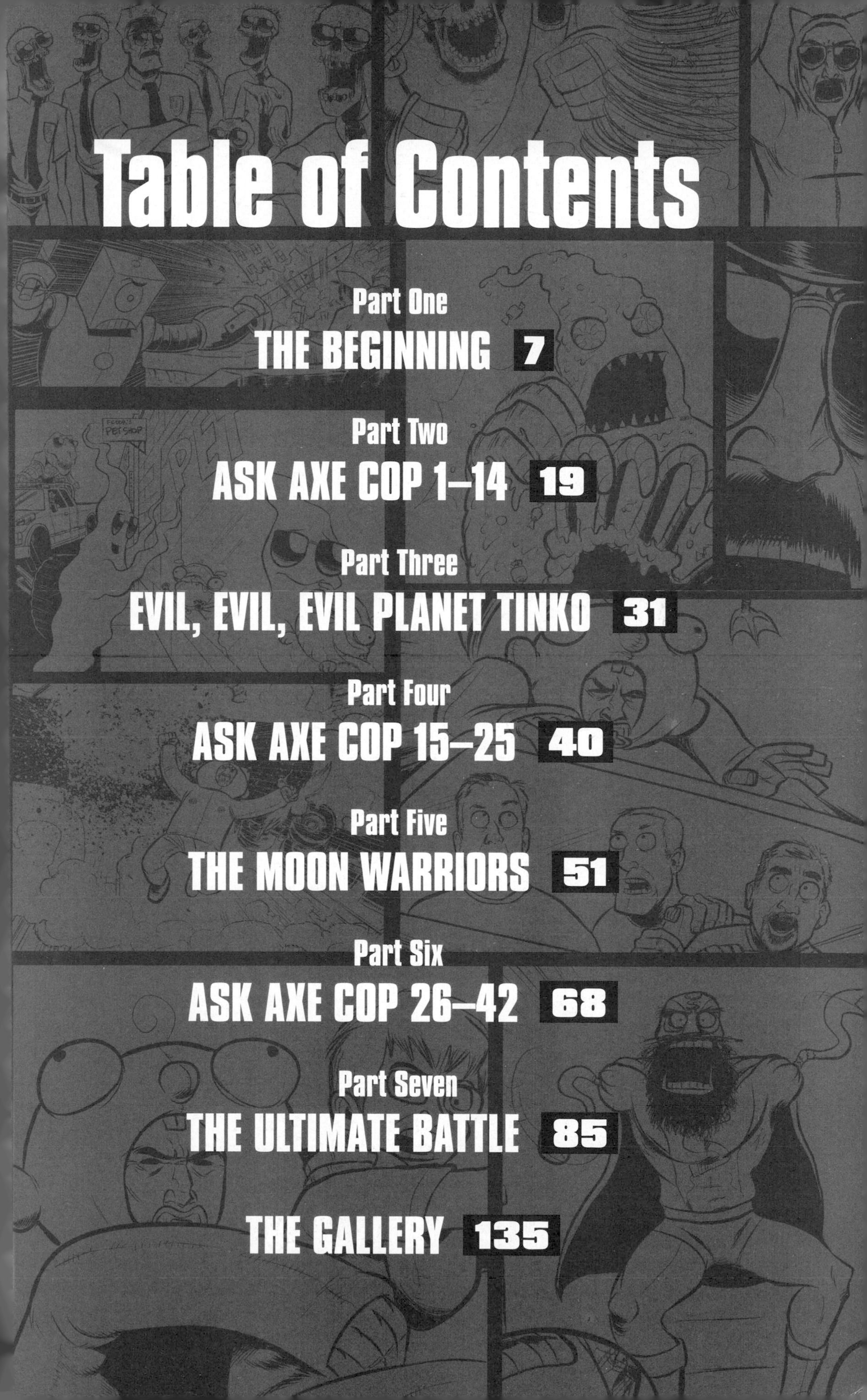

Table of Contents

Axe Cop: A Foreword of Sorts

By Kevin Murphy

"If this is the best of all possible worlds, what are the others?" —Voltaire, *Candide*

Okay, what on Planet Poop is going on here? An avocado for a superhero? A good guy who kills unicorns? An axe-wielding, uniformed cop hero with a wakka-chikka moustache who routinely endangers babies and wants to sleep with Abe Lincoln?

You have stumbled, or deliberately plunged, headlong into the world of *Axe Cop*, sprung fully formed from the Olympian mind of young Malachai Nicolle and brought to the page by his brother Ethan. In its first meteoric year of online publication, it's garnered, and I believe this is accurate, eleven jillion followers. This includes me, and it's the first comic series I've read completely and from the beginning, ever.

First, you should know that I have never been faithful to comic books. Growing up, I only read them when I was sick, or bored, or when I didn't have a recent copy of *Popular Science* or *Mad* magazine around. Superhero worlds seem overly bound with rules and conditions. Imaginative, sure, but so damn-blasted serious. But I get over the novelty of it quickly and look at the thing as story. Funny as it is, it's not *Peanuts* funny. People die in Malachai's story, lots of 'em: the innocent, the wicked, the young, the old, the cute, and the ugly. Immediately it evokes one of my favorite sci-fi novels, Harry Harrison's *Bill, the Galactic Hero*, a tale of a big, affable lug with two right arms who battles all manner of creatures with all manner of armaments in the name, at least vaguely, of Us. I'm also reminded obliquely of Ursula Le Guin's novel *The Lathe of Heaven*, in which an impressionable fella, name of George, finds that his dreams change the real world, and as his dreams become crazier, so does the universe at large. The more he tries to fix it, the crazier it gets.

But now I risk getting smacked repeatedly with this very book to say that the ecstatic, violent, giddy, metamorphic mess that *Axe Cop* is summons into my skull memories of reading *Candide*, a story in which people walk the jewel-lined streets of El Dorado, believe they can control earthquakes, and routinely run each other through with swords, a story which never ends up where we think it ought, and yet also a story in which the hero learns from his beleaguered tutor that, though the best of all possible worlds may seem like, well, as Malachai might imagine it, a planet made of dung populated with an army of turds, you can always move on to the next world, though you'll probably find the same thing holds true there.

And here's the real trick to it—Malachai accomplishes all this without a conscious hint of satire, not a whit of irony, not a gram of snark, and Ethan works hard not to impose such on his panels. It's the pure-light-spectrum view of a kid who's pretty new to the world, and just trying to keep it interesting, to surprise himself, to wring out as much fun as can be wrought. I think he's constructed the world's biggest, coolest sandbox, and, as you'll remember always happens in the sandbox, he's become part of the story.

Ultimately it's good guys versus bad guys, though you don't always know which is which, so you can only try, ask for help when you need it, don't take anything at face value, and always be ready for battle. Already that's more story than I've seen in any Michael Bay movie. See, I think Malachai, with the help of his brother Ethan, already has the chops to make a dandy action movie. That is, if they would let him, and if he doesn't grow out of it.

Part One: The Beginning

Episodes 1–5 and episode 0

Axe Cop started by accident during my 2009 Christmas visit to see my family. My time with my (much younger) siblings is always an escape from everyday life . . . They demand so much attention that I am usually either drawing them something, watching a movie with them, or sleeping. I never really try to work when I visit them—which is fine, because I don't travel all that way just to work.

During play time with my (then) five-year-old brother Malachai, he invited me to play "Axe Cop" with him. He had a plastic toy fireman axe, but he didn't want to fight fires; he wanted to chop off the heads of bad guys. I joined him, because the moment he said "Axe Cop" I got this visual in my head of a square-jawed eighties cop holding a red axe and using it to fight crime. As play time progressed, we teamed up, and he became Flute Cop (after grabbing the next thing he could find that could possibly harm someone off of his pile of toys . . . a plastic recorder) and headed out to find dinosaurs. The whole time, in my head I was thinking, "This could be a funny comic . . ." At first I resisted the urge to make *Axe Cop* into a comic because I just wanted to be lazy . . . Then I decided to just draw a one-page comic as quickly and sloppily as I could stand. This was just for family anyway.

I went on to draw four *Axe Cop* episodes during that visit, with Malachai guiding the story as I asked him questions to fill in plot holes. My eyes were bloodshot from laughing so hard at some of the things we came up with. The entire time I drew them I laughed, sometimes until I cried. But I figured it was all coming from my love of my little brother. I had no idea these seven or eight pages of comics would become the most well-known pieces of work I had ever created and within the next month or so would dwarf everything else I had done in the comics industry to the point of making it all look very insignificant.

There are six episodes in this section. Episodes 1–4 were all written and drawn at my parents' house in Washington with Malachai. These were never really intended to be anything more than something for friends and family to laugh at. We also wrote episode 0 while I was there and I drew it when I got home. Episode 5 was the first episode done over the phone with Malachai. This set of comics was the first to appear on the *Axe Cop* website. I had thought about getting into webcomics, and I figured these would be good to use to test out functionality and presentation. I thought a few people might find them cute, but two days after the site went live on January 25, 2010 (a month after we had created *Axe Cop*), it literally became my job overnight.

—Ethan

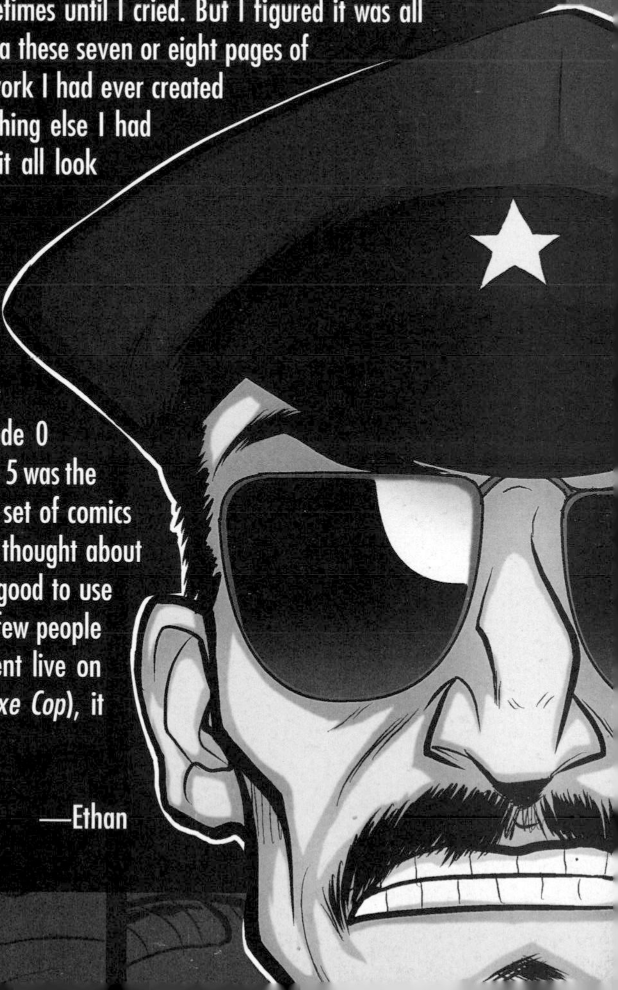

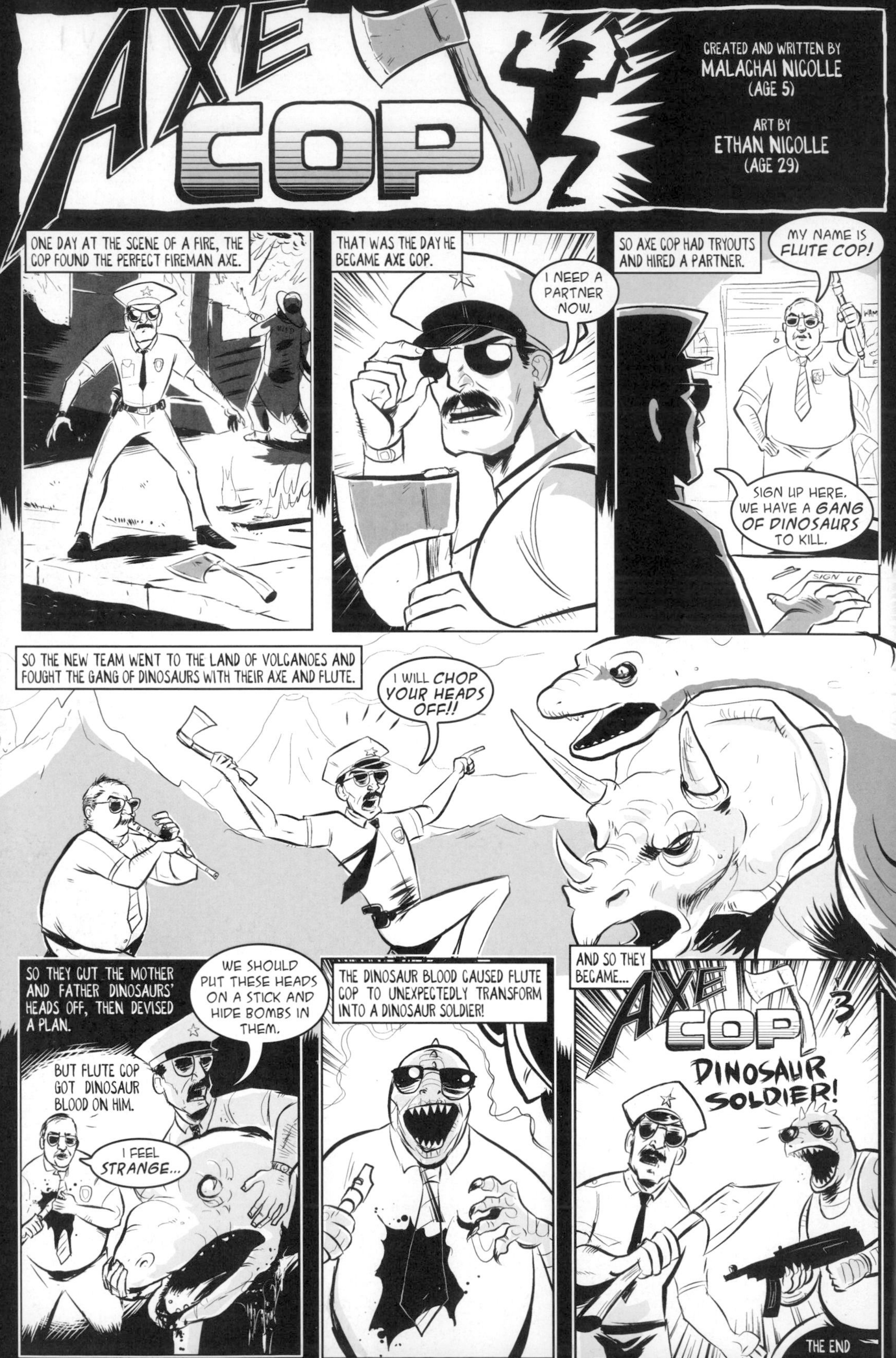
AXE COP
CREATED AND WRITTEN BY
MALACHAI NICOLLE
(AGE 5)
ART BY
ETHAN NICOLLE
(AGE 29)
ONE DAY AT THE SCENE OF A FIRE, THE COP FOUND THE PERFECT FIREMAN AXE.
THAT WAS THE DAY HE BECAME AXE COP.
I NEED A PARTNER NOW.
SO AXE COP HAD TRYOUTS AND HIRED A PARTNER.
MY NAME IS FLUTE COP!
SIGN UP HERE. WE HAVE A GANG OF DINOSAURS TO KILL.
SIGN UP
SO THE NEW TEAM WENT TO THE LAND OF VOLCANOES AND FOUGHT THE GANG OF DINOSAURS WITH THEIR AXE AND FLUTE.
I WILL CHOP YOUR HEADS OFF!!
SO THEY CUT THE MOTHER AND FATHER DINOSAURS' HEADS OFF, THEN DEVISED A PLAN.
WE SHOULD PUT THESE HEADS ON A STICK AND HIDE BOMBS IN THEM.
BUT FLUTE COP GOT DINOSAUR BLOOD ON HIM.
I FEEL STRANGE...
THE DINOSAUR BLOOD CAUSED FLUTE COP TO UNEXPECTEDLY TRANSFORM INTO A DINOSAUR SOLDIER!
AND SO THEY BECAME...
AXE COP
DINOSAUR SOLDIER!
THE END

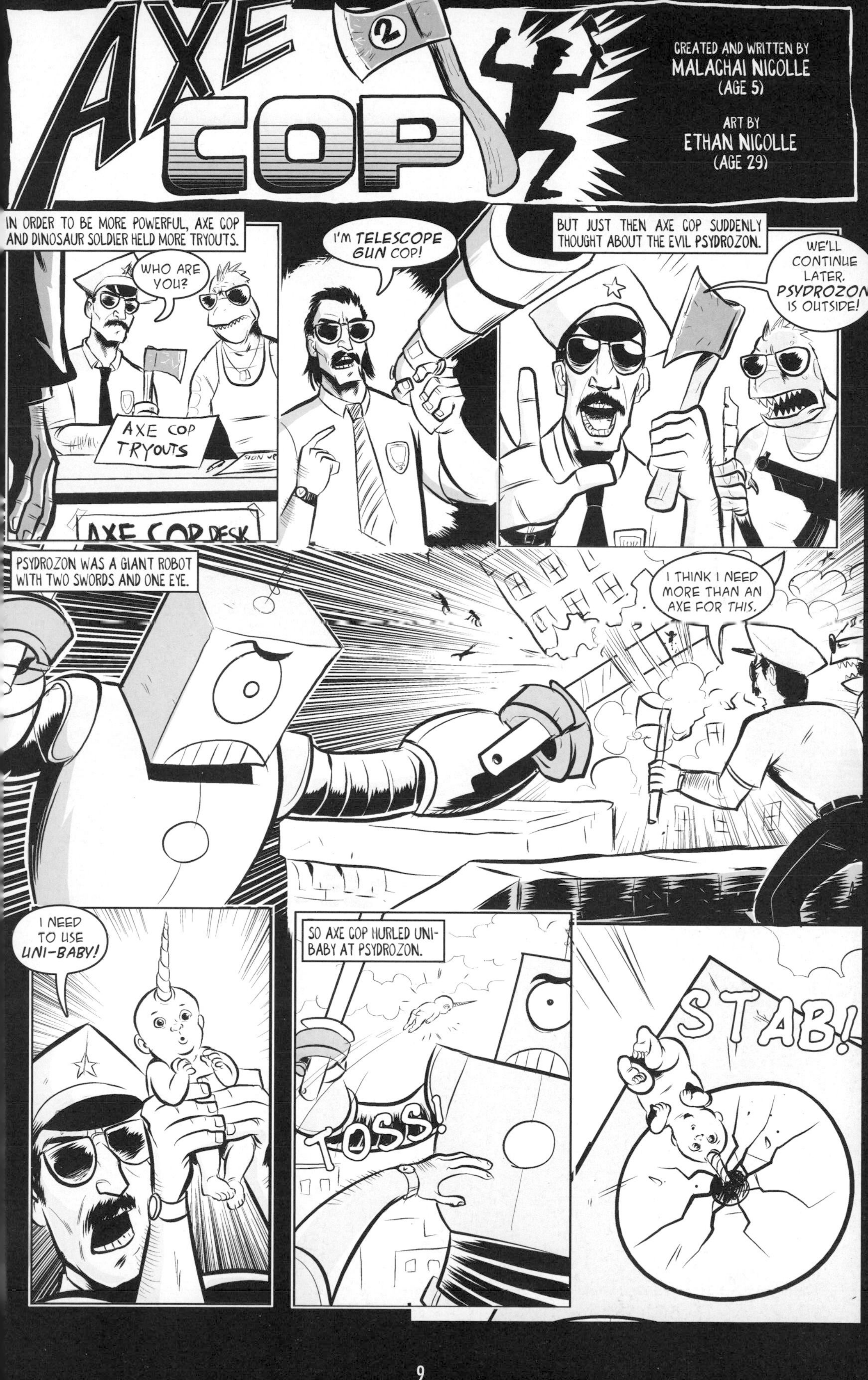
AXE COP 2
CREATED AND WRITTEN BY
MALACHAI NICOLLE
(AGE 5)
ART BY
ETHAN NICOLLE
(AGE 29)
IN ORDER TO BE MORE POWERFUL, AXE COP AND DINOSAUR SOLDIER HELD MORE TRYOUTS.
WHO ARE YOU?
AXE COP TRYOUTS
AXE COP DESK
I'M TELESCOPE GUN COP!
BUT JUST THEN AXE COP SUDDENLY THOUGHT ABOUT THE EVIL PSYDROZON.
WE'LL CONTINUE LATER. PSYDROZON IS OUTSIDE!
PSYDROZON WAS A GIANT ROBOT WITH TWO SWORDS AND ONE EYE.
I THINK I NEED MORE THAN AN AXE FOR THIS.
I NEED TO USE UNI-BABY!
SO AXE COP HURLED UNI-BABY AT PSYDROZON.
TOSS!
STAB!

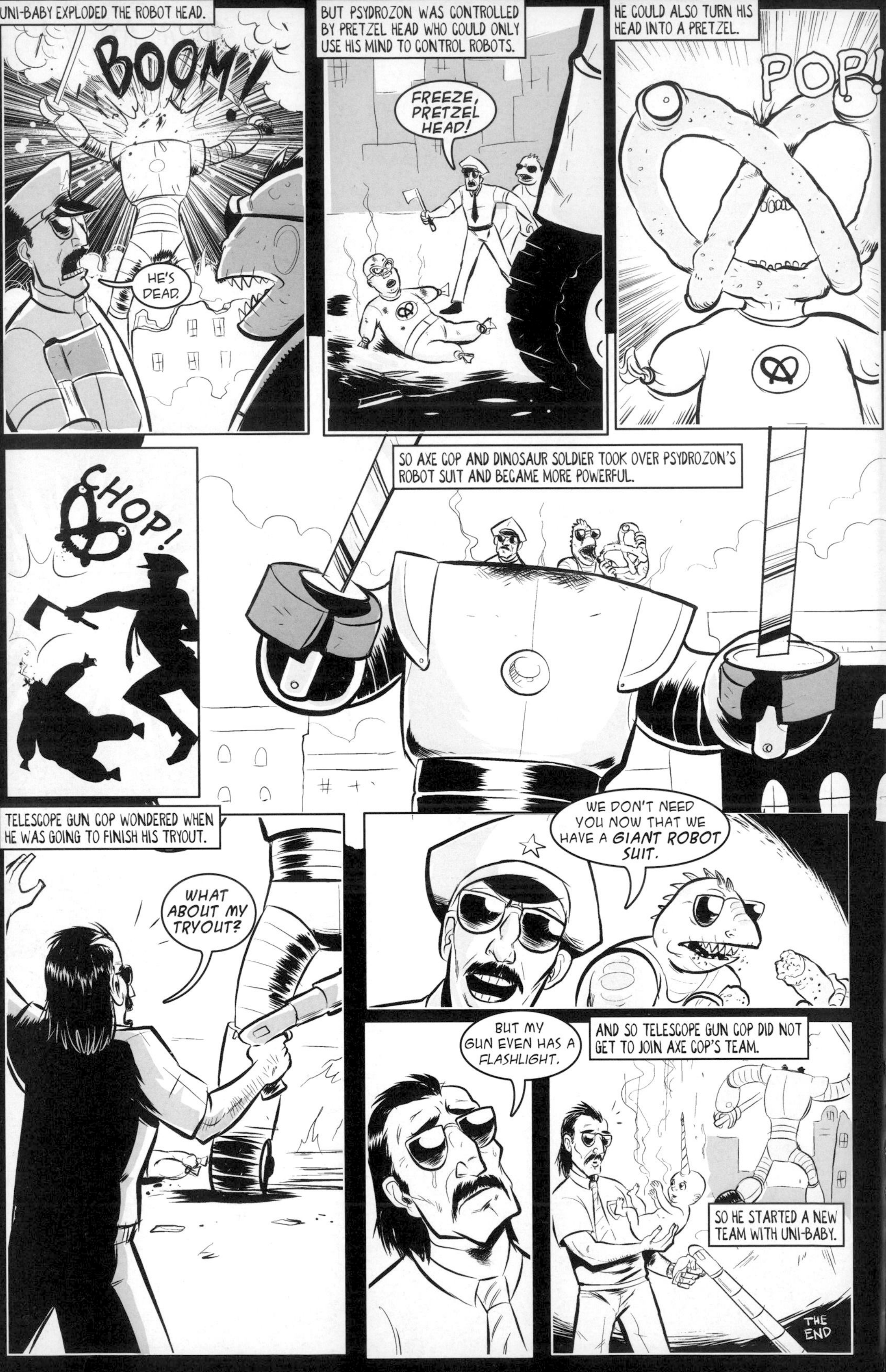
UNI-BABY EXPLODED THE ROBOT HEAD.
BOOM!
HE'S DEAD.
BUT PSYDROZON WAS CONTROLLED BY PRETZEL HEAD WHO COULD ONLY USE HIS MIND TO CONTROL ROBOTS.
FREEZE, PRETZEL HEAD!
HE COULD ALSO TURN HIS HEAD INTO A PRETZEL.
POP!
CHOP!
SO AXE COP AND DINOSAUR SOLDIER TOOK OVER PSYDROZON'S ROBOT SUIT AND BECAME MORE POWERFUL.
TELESCOPE GUN COP WONDERED WHEN HE WAS GOING TO FINISH HIS TRYOUT.
WHAT ABOUT MY TRYOUT?
WE DON'T NEED YOU NOW THAT WE HAVE A GIANT ROBOT SUIT.
BUT MY GUN EVEN HAS A FLASHLIGHT.
AND SO TELESCOPE GUN COP DID NOT GET TO JOIN AXE COP'S TEAM.
SO HE STARTED A NEW TEAM WITH UNI-BABY.
THE END

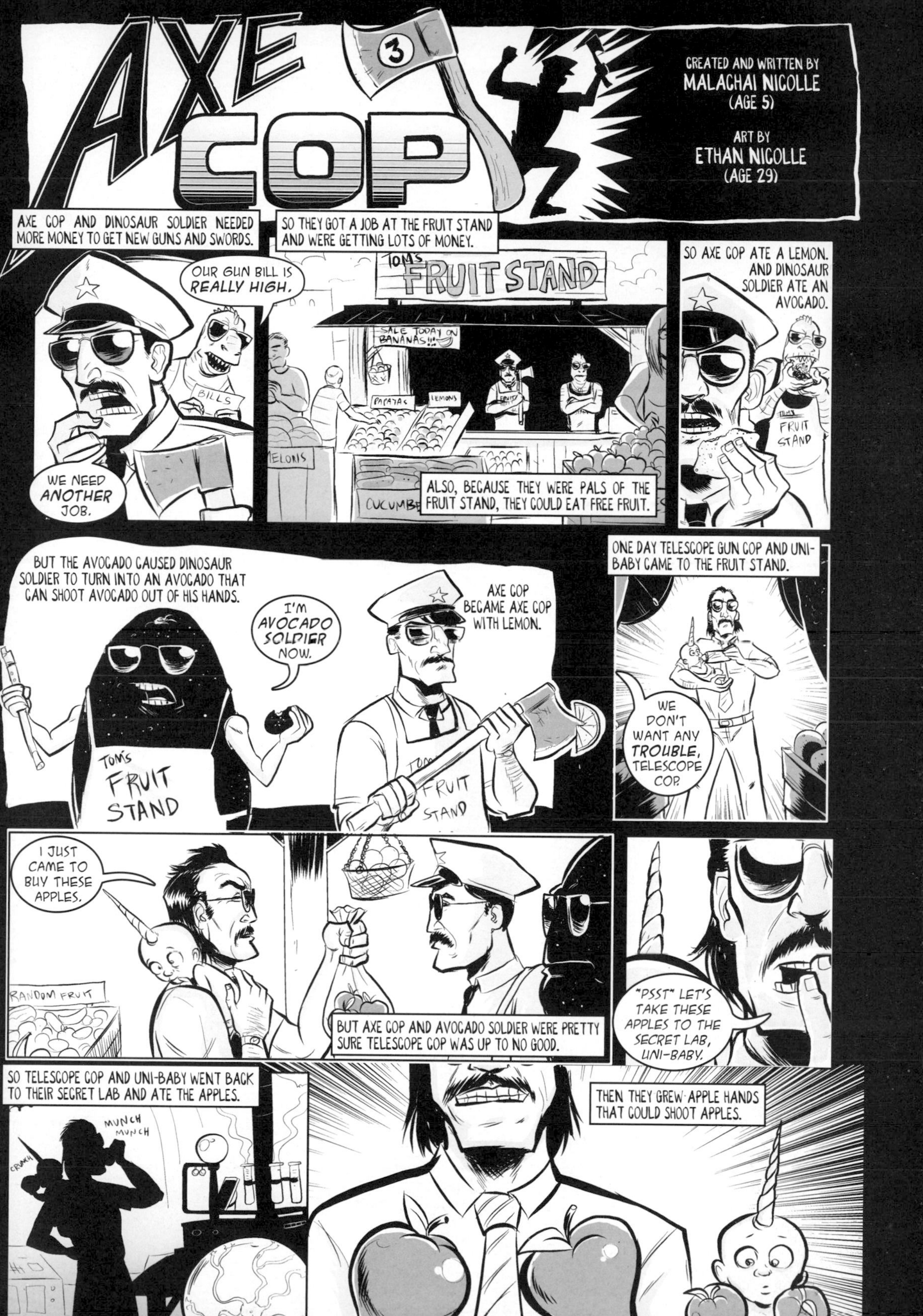
AXE COP
3
CREATED AND WRITTEN BY
MALACHAI NICOLLE
(AGE 5)
ART BY
ETHAN NICOLLE
(AGE 29)
AXE COP AND DINOSAUR SOLDIER NEEDED MORE MONEY TO GET NEW GUNS AND SWORDS.
OUR GUN BILL IS REALLY HIGH.
BILLS
WE NEED ANOTHER JOB.
SO THEY GOT A JOB AT THE FRUIT STAND AND WERE GETTING LOTS OF MONEY.
TOM'S FRUIT STAND
SALE TODAY ON BANANAS!!!
PAPAYAS
LEMONS
MELONS
CUCUMBE
ALSO, BECAUSE THEY WERE PALS OF THE FRUIT STAND, THEY COULD EAT FREE FRUIT.
SO AXE COP ATE A LEMON. AND DINOSAUR SOLDIER ATE AN AVOCADO.
TOM'S FRUIT STAND
BUT THE AVOCADO CAUSED DINOSAUR SOLDIER TO TURN INTO AN AVOCADO THAT CAN SHOOT AVOCADO OUT OF HIS HANDS.
I'M AVOCADO SOLDIER NOW.
TOM'S FRUIT STAND
AXE COP BECAME AXE COP WITH LEMON.
TOM'S FRUIT STAND
ONE DAY TELESCOPE GUN COP AND UNI-BABY CAME TO THE FRUIT STAND.
WE DON'T WANT ANY TROUBLE, TELESCOPE COP.
I JUST CAME TO BUY THESE APPLES.
RANDOM FRUIT
BUT AXE COP AND AVOCADO SOLDIER WERE PRETTY SURE TELESCOPE COP WAS UP TO NO GOOD.
PSST LET'S TAKE THESE APPLES TO THE SECRET LAB, UNI-BABY.
SO TELESCOPE COP AND UNI-BABY WENT BACK TO THEIR SECRET LAB AND ATE THE APPLES.
MUNCH MUNCH
CRUNCH
THEN THEY GREW APPLE HANDS THAT COULD SHOOT APPLES.

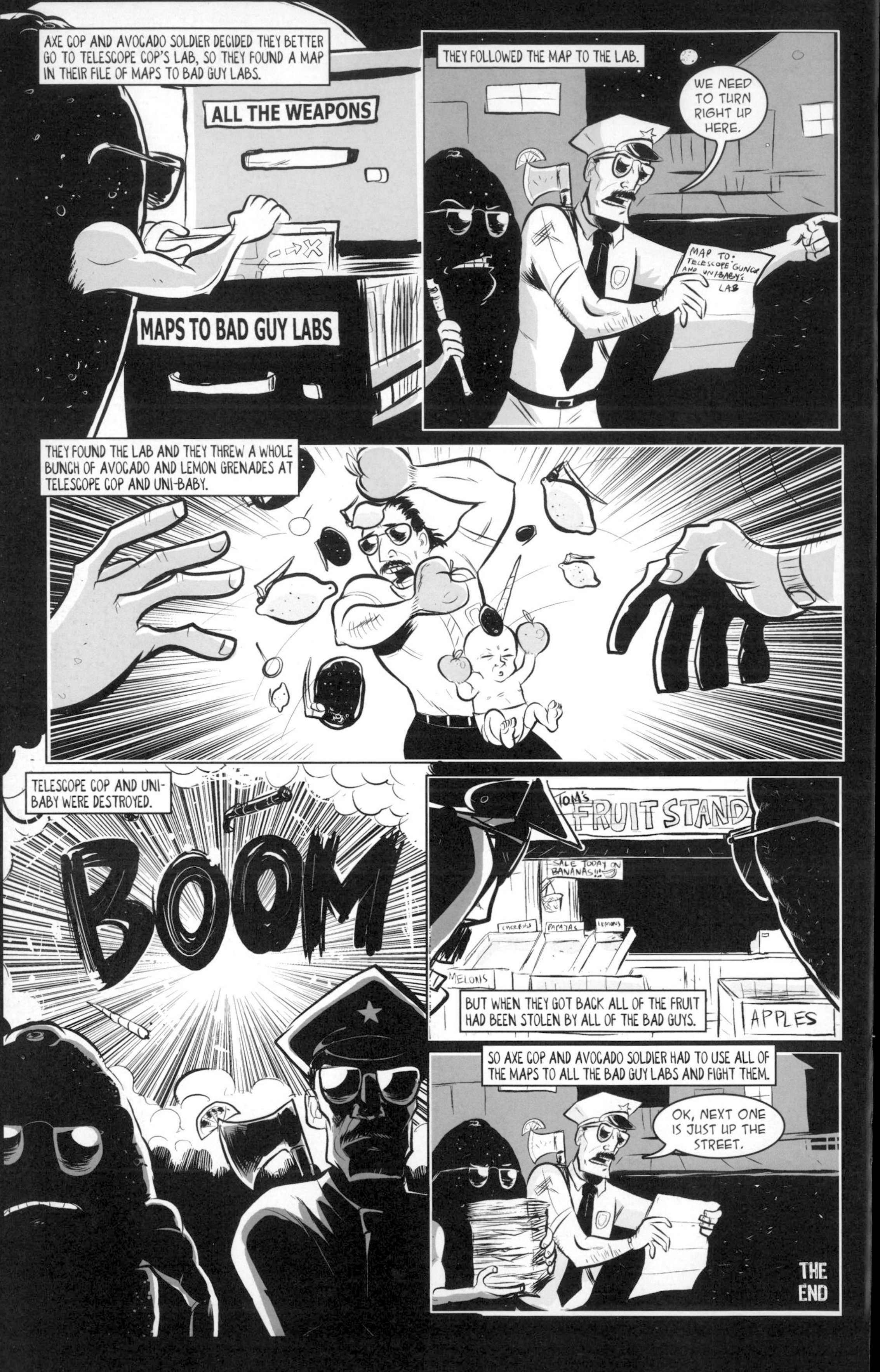
AXE COP AND AVOCADO SOLDIER DECIDED THEY BETTER GO TO TELESCOPE COP'S LAB, SO THEY FOUND A MAP IN THEIR FILE OF MAPS TO BAD GUY LABS.
ALL THE WEAPONS
MAPS TO BAD GUY LABS
THEY FOLLOWED THE MAP TO THE LAB.
WE NEED TO TURN RIGHT UP HERE.
MAP TO: TELESCOPE GUNCE AND UNI-BABY'S LAB
THEY FOUND THE LAB AND THEY THREW A WHOLE BUNCH OF AVOCADO AND LEMON GRENADES AT TELESCOPE COP AND UNI-BABY.
TELESCOPE COP AND UNI-BABY WERE DESTROYED.
BOOM
TOM'S FRUIT STAND
SALE TODAY ON BANANAS!!!
CHERRIES
PAPAYAS
LEMONS
MELONS
BUT WHEN THEY GOT BACK ALL OF THE FRUIT HAD BEEN STOLEN BY ALL OF THE BAD GUYS.
APPLES
SO AXE COP AND AVOCADO SOLDIER HAD TO USE ALL OF THE MAPS TO ALL THE BAD GUY LABS AND FIGHT THEM.
OK, NEXT ONE IS JUST UP THE STREET.
THE END

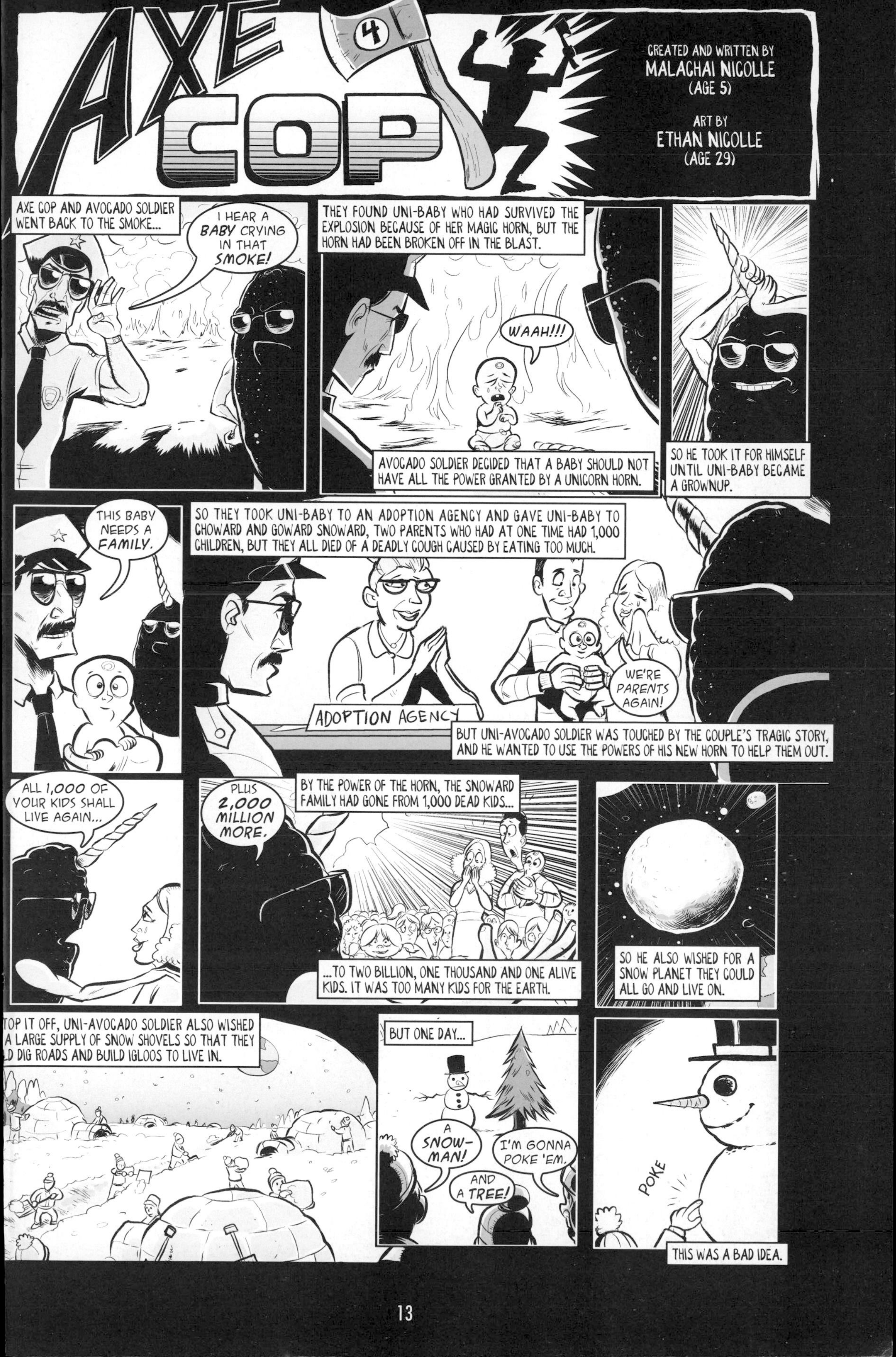

AXE COP
4
CREATED AND WRITTEN BY
MALACHAI NICOLLE
(AGE 5)
ART BY
ETHAN NICOLLE
(AGE 29)
AXE COP AND AVOCADO SOLDIER WENT BACK TO THE SMOKE...
I HEAR A BABY CRYING IN THAT SMOKE!
THEY FOUND UNI-BABY WHO HAD SURVIVED THE EXPLOSION BECAUSE OF HER MAGIC HORN, BUT THE HORN HAD BEEN BROKEN OFF IN THE BLAST.
WAAH!!!
AVOCADO SOLDIER DECIDED THAT A BABY SHOULD NOT HAVE ALL THE POWER GRANTED BY A UNICORN HORN.
SO HE TOOK IT FOR HIMSELF UNTIL UNI-BABY BECAME A GROWNUP.
THIS BABY NEEDS A FAMILY.
SO THEY TOOK UNI-BABY TO AN ADOPTION AGENCY AND GAVE UNI-BABY TO CHOWARD AND GOWARD SNOWARD, TWO PARENTS WHO HAD AT ONE TIME HAD 1,000 CHILDREN, BUT THEY ALL DIED OF A DEADLY COUGH CAUSED BY EATING TOO MUCH.
ADOPTION AGENCY
WE'RE PARENTS AGAIN!
BUT UNI-AVOCADO SOLDIER WAS TOUCHED BY THE COUPLE'S TRAGIC STORY, AND HE WANTED TO USE THE POWERS OF HIS NEW HORN TO HELP THEM OUT.
ALL 1,000 OF YOUR KIDS SHALL LIVE AGAIN...
PLUS 2,000 MILLION MORE.
BY THE POWER OF THE HORN, THE SNOWARD FAMILY HAD GONE FROM 1,000 DEAD KIDS...
...TO TWO BILLION, ONE THOUSAND AND ONE ALIVE KIDS. IT WAS TOO MANY KIDS FOR THE EARTH.
SO HE ALSO WISHED FOR A SNOW PLANET THEY COULD ALL GO AND LIVE ON.
TOP IT OFF, UNI-AVOCADO SOLDIER ALSO WISHED A LARGE SUPPLY OF SNOW SHOVELS SO THAT THEY D DIG ROADS AND BUILD IGLOOS TO LIVE IN.
BUT ONE DAY...
A SNOW-MAN!
I'M GONNA POKE 'EM.
AND A TREE!
POKE
THIS WAS A BAD IDEA.

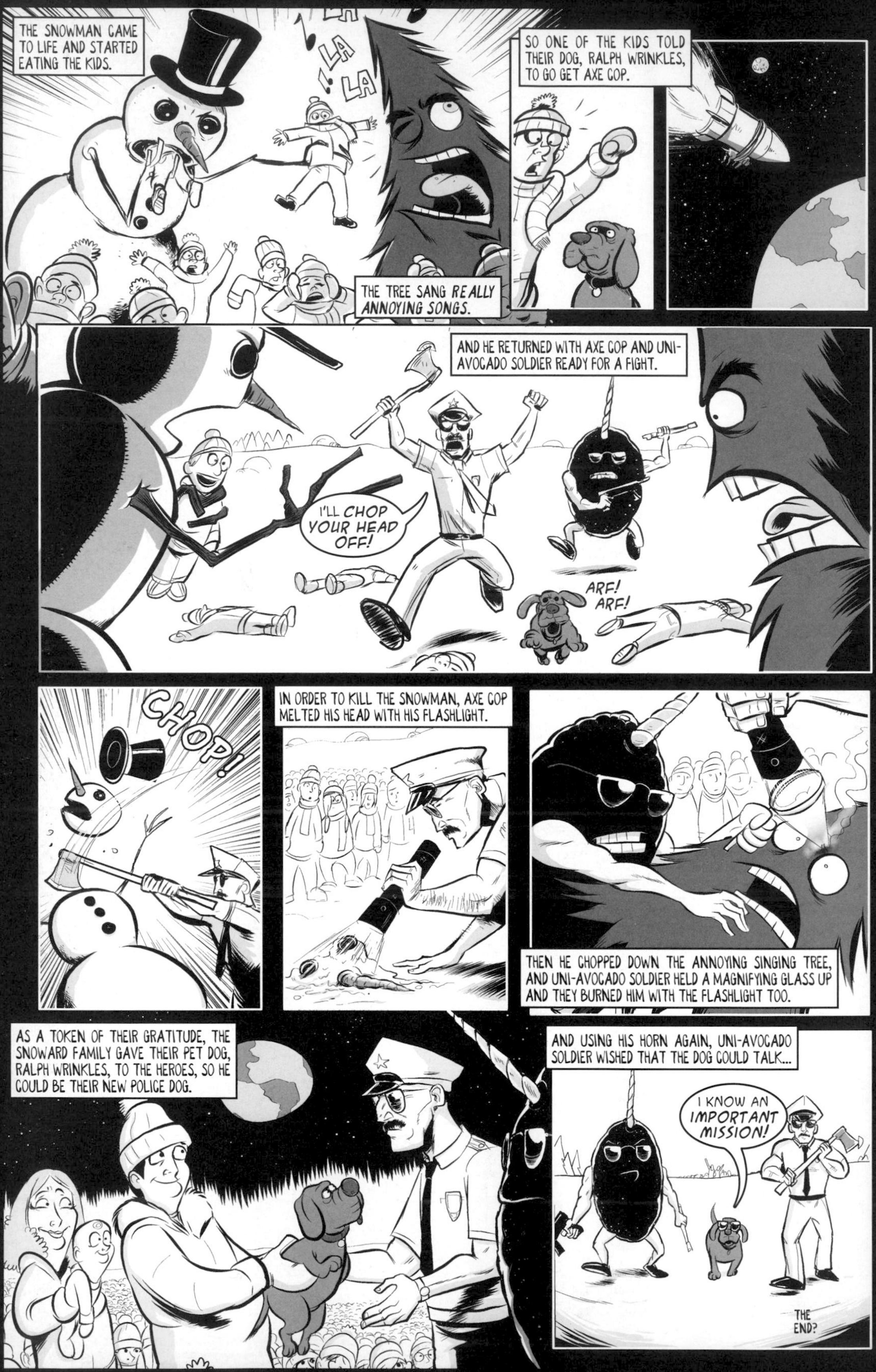
THE SNOWMAN CAME TO LIFE AND STARTED EATING THE KIDS.
LA
LA
LA
THE TREE SANG REALLY ANNOYING SONGS.
SO ONE OF THE KIDS TOLD THEIR DOG, RALPH WRINKLES, TO GO GET AXE COP.
AND HE RETURNED WITH AXE COP AND UNI-AVOCADO SOLDIER READY FOR A FIGHT.
I'LL CHOP YOUR HEAD OFF!
ARF! ARF!
CHOP!
IN ORDER TO KILL THE SNOWMAN, AXE COP MELTED HIS HEAD WITH HIS FLASHLIGHT.
THEN HE CHOPPED DOWN THE ANNOYING SINGING TREE, AND UNI-AVOCADO SOLDIER HELD A MAGNIFYING GLASS UP AND THEY BURNED HIM WITH THE FLASHLIGHT TOO.
AS A TOKEN OF THEIR GRATITUDE, THE SNOWARD FAMILY GAVE THEIR PET DOG, RALPH WRINKLES, TO THE HEROES, SO HE COULD BE THEIR NEW POLICE DOG.
AND USING HIS HORN AGAIN, UNI-AVOCADO SOLDIER WISHED THAT THE DOG COULD TALK...
I KNOW AN IMPORTANT MISSION!
THE END?

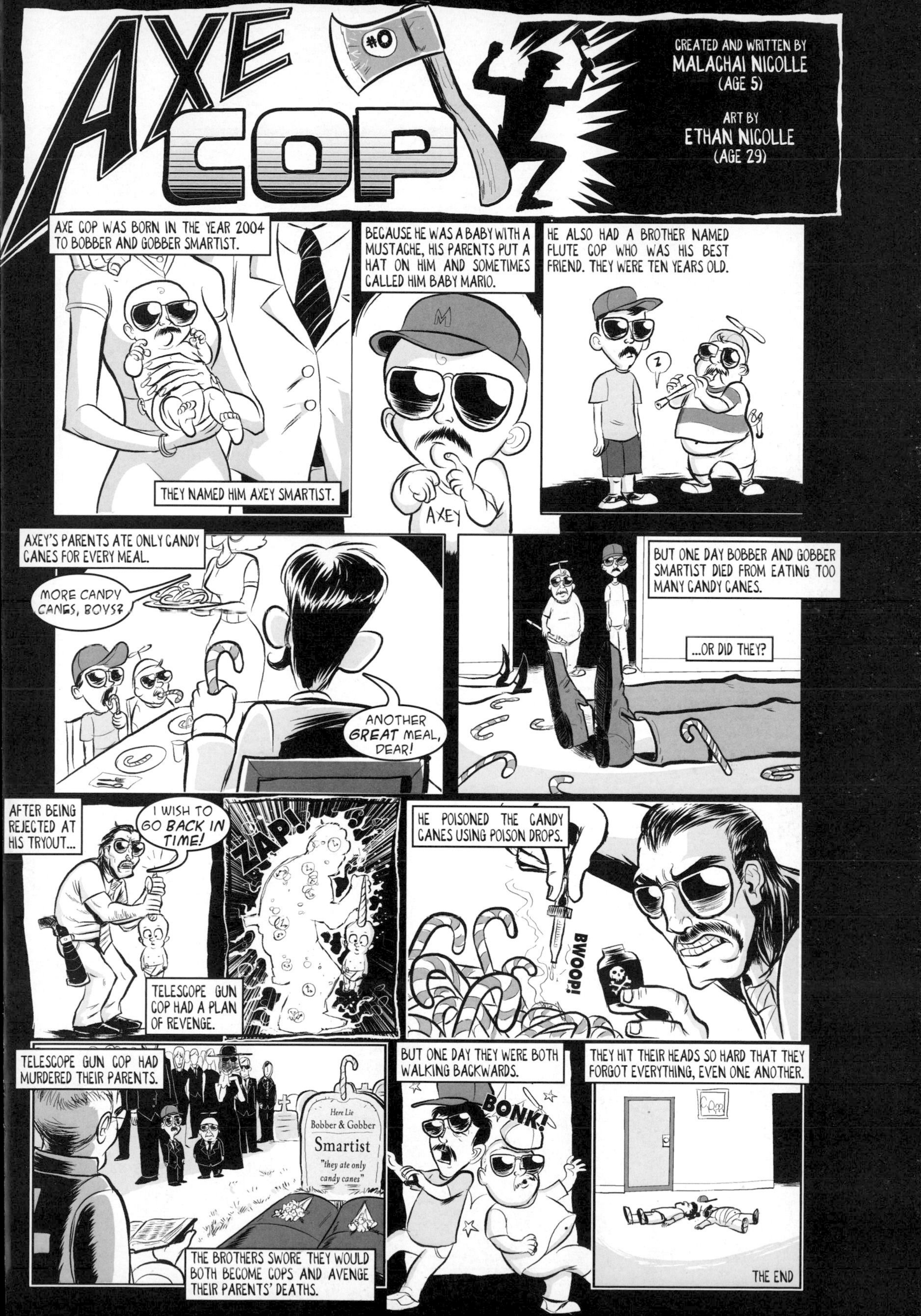

AXE COP
#0
CREATED AND WRITTEN BY
MALACHAI NICOLLE
(AGE 5)
ART BY
ETHAN NICOLLE
(AGE 29)
AXE COP WAS BORN IN THE YEAR 2004 TO BOBBER AND GOBBER SMARTIST.
THEY NAMED HIM AXEY SMARTIST.
BECAUSE HE WAS A BABY WITH A MUSTACHE, HIS PARENTS PUT A HAT ON HIM AND SOMETIMES CALLED HIM BABY MARIO.
AXEY
HE ALSO HAD A BROTHER NAMED FLUTE COP WHO WAS HIS BEST FRIEND. THEY WERE TEN YEARS OLD.
?
AXEY'S PARENTS ATE ONLY CANDY CANES FOR EVERY MEAL.
MORE CANDY CANES, BOYS?
ANOTHER GREAT MEAL, DEAR!
BUT ONE DAY BOBBER AND GOBBER SMARTIST DIED FROM EATING TOO MANY CANDY CANES.
...OR DID THEY?
AFTER BEING REJECTED AT HIS TRYOUT...
I WISH TO GO BACK IN TIME!
ZAP!
TELESCOPE GUN COP HAD A PLAN OF REVENGE.
HE POISONED THE CANDY CANES USING POISON DROPS.
BWOOP!
TELESCOPE GUN COP HAD MURDERED THEIR PARENTS.
Here Lie
Bobber & Gobber
Smartist
"they ate only candy canes"
THE BROTHERS SWORE THEY WOULD BOTH BECOME COPS AND AVENGE THEIR PARENTS' DEATHS.
BUT ONE DAY THEY WERE BOTH WALKING BACKWARDS.
BONK!
THEY HIT THEIR HEADS SO HARD THAT THEY FORGOT EVERYTHING, EVEN ONE ANOTHER.
THE END

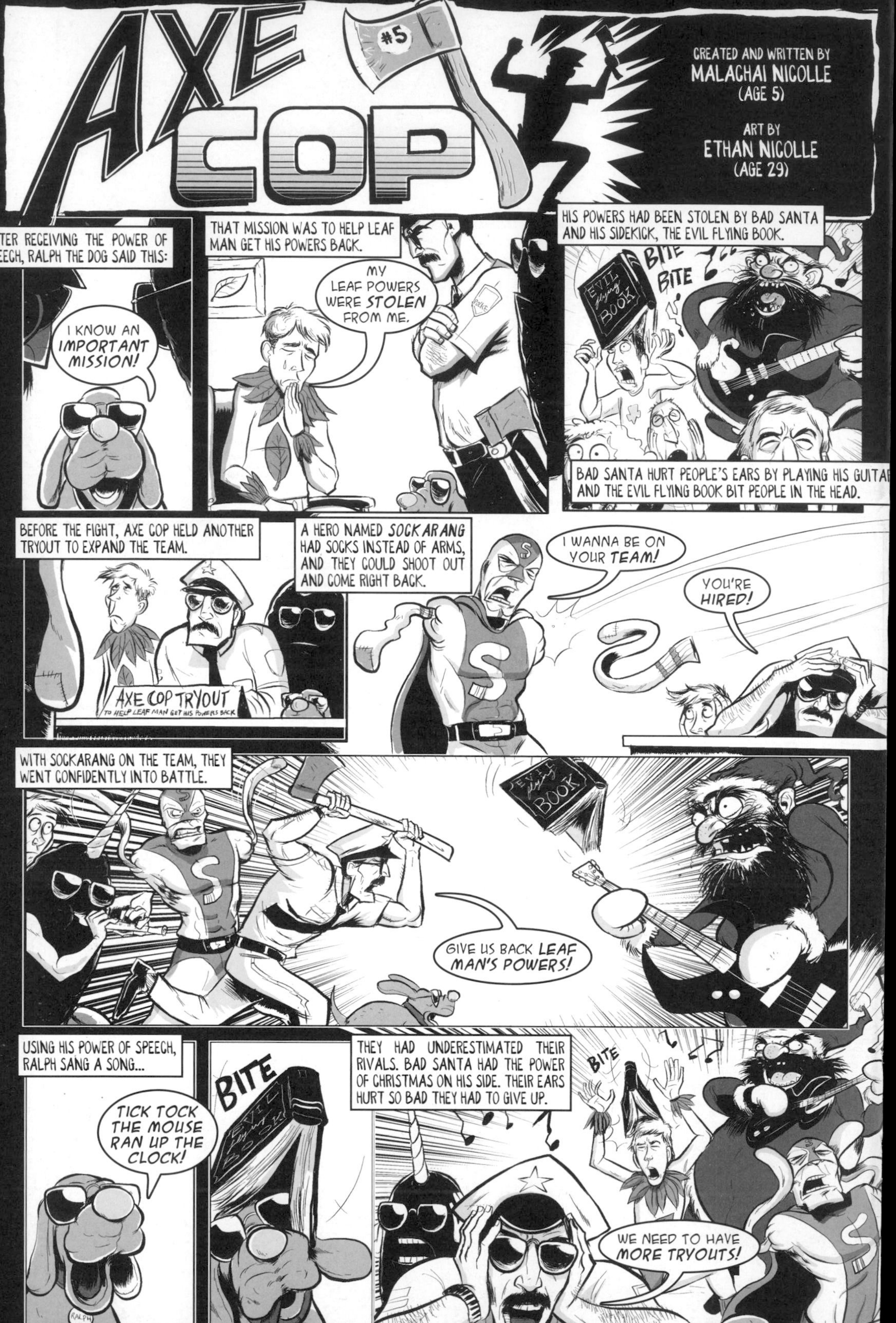
AXE COP
#5
CREATED AND WRITTEN BY
MALACHAI NICOLLE
(AGE 5)
ART BY
ETHAN NICOLLE
(AGE 29)
AFTER RECEIVING THE POWER OF SPEECH, RALPH THE DOG SAID THIS:
I KNOW AN IMPORTANT MISSION!
THAT MISSION WAS TO HELP LEAF MAN GET HIS POWERS BACK.
MY LEAF POWERS WERE STOLEN FROM ME.
HIS POWERS HAD BEEN STOLEN BY BAD SANTA AND HIS SIDEKICK, THE EVIL FLYING BOOK.
EVIL flying BOOK
BITE
BITE
BAD SANTA HURT PEOPLE'S EARS BY PLAYING HIS GUITAR AND THE EVIL FLYING BOOK BIT PEOPLE IN THE HEAD.
BEFORE THE FIGHT, AXE COP HELD ANOTHER TRYOUT TO EXPAND THE TEAM.
AXE COP TRYOUT
TO HELP LEAF MAN GET HIS POWERS BACK
A HERO NAMED SOCKARANG HAD SOCKS INSTEAD OF ARMS, AND THEY COULD SHOOT OUT AND COME RIGHT BACK.
I WANNA BE ON YOUR TEAM!
YOU'RE HIRED!
WITH SOCKARANG ON THE TEAM, THEY WENT CONFIDENTLY INTO BATTLE.
EVIL flying BOOK
GIVE US BACK LEAF MAN'S POWERS!
USING HIS POWER OF SPEECH, RALPH SANG A SONG...
TICK TOCK THE MOUSE RAN UP THE CLOCK!
RALPH
BITE
THEY HAD UNDERESTIMATED THEIR RIVALS. BAD SANTA HAD THE POWER OF CHRISTMAS ON HIS SIDE. THEIR EARS HURT SO BAD THEY HAD TO GIVE UP.
BITE
WE NEED TO HAVE MORE TRYOUTS!

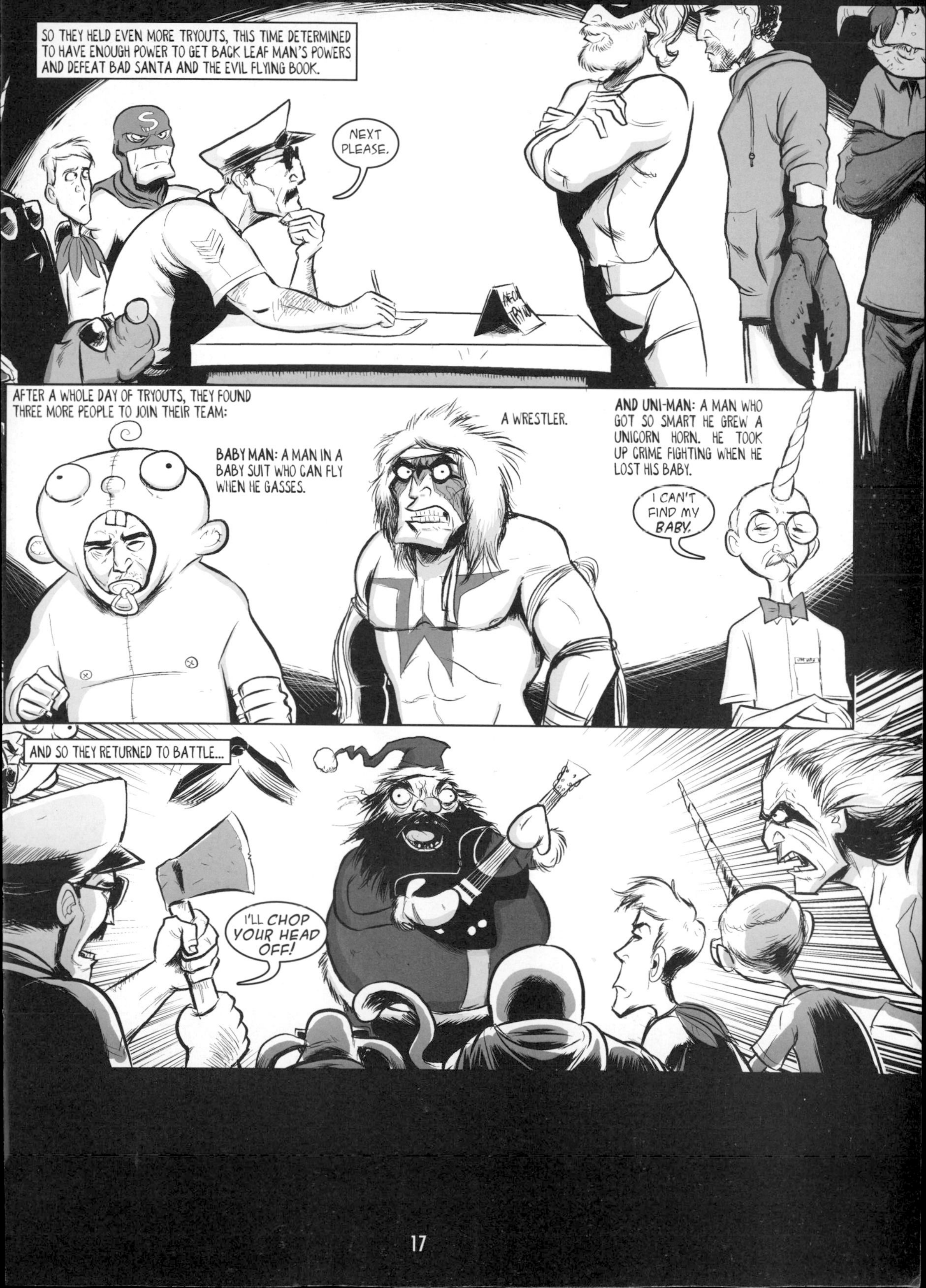
SO THEY HELD EVEN MORE TRYOUTS, THIS TIME DETERMINED TO HAVE ENOUGH POWER TO GET BACK LEAF MAN'S POWERS AND DEFEAT BAD SANTA AND THE EVIL FLYING BOOK.
NEXT PLEASE.
AFTER A WHOLE DAY OF TRYOUTS, THEY FOUND THREE MORE PEOPLE TO JOIN THEIR TEAM:
BABY MAN: A MAN IN A BABY SUIT WHO CAN FLY WHEN HE GASSES.
A WRESTLER.
AND UNI-MAN: A MAN WHO GOT SO SMART HE GREW A UNICORN HORN. HE TOOK UP CRIME FIGHTING WHEN HE LOST HIS BABY.
I CAN'T FIND MY BABY.
AND SO THEY RETURNED TO BATTLE...
I'LL CHOP YOUR HEAD OFF!

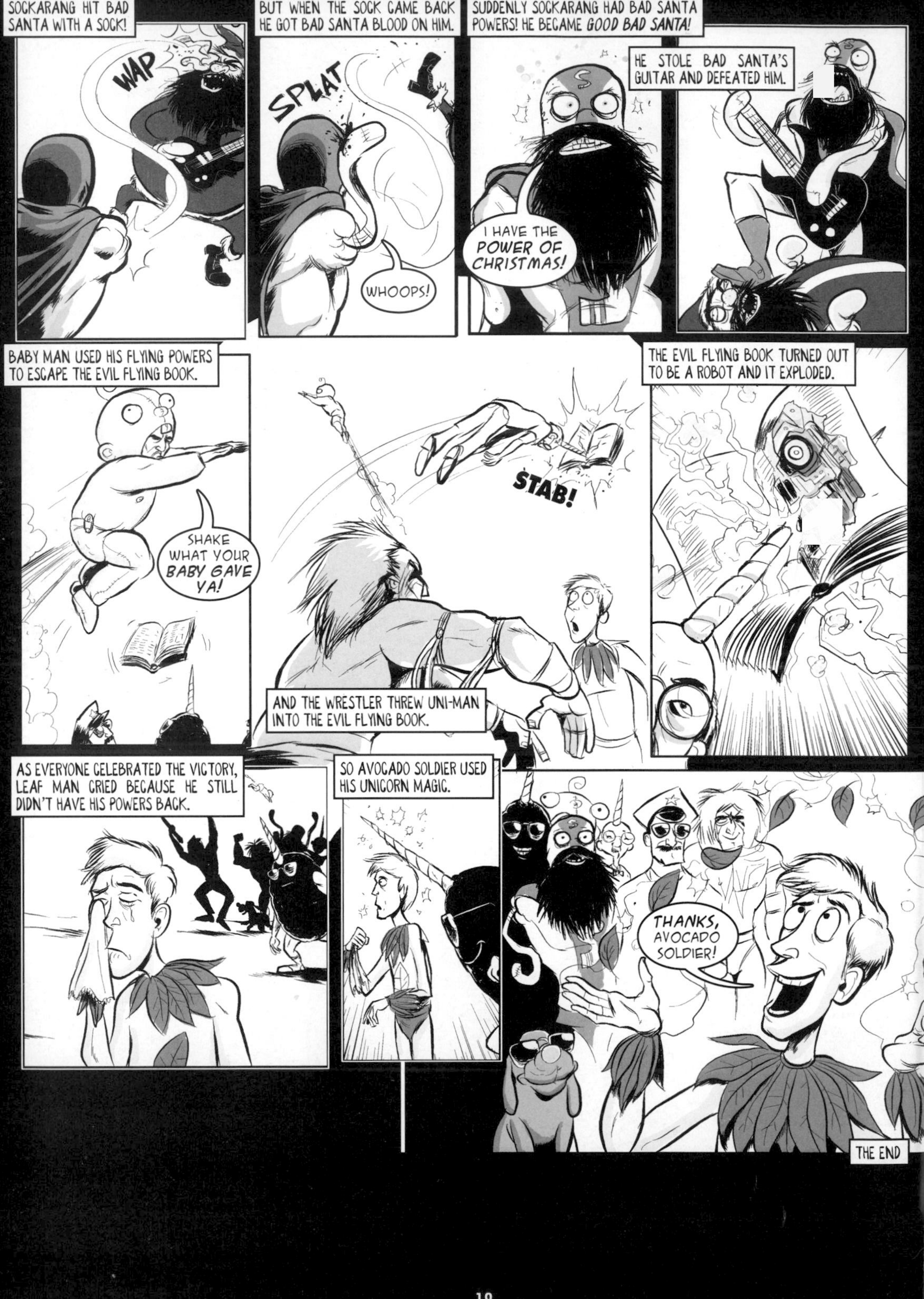
SOCKARANG HIT BAD SANTA WITH A SOCK!
WAP
BUT WHEN THE SOCK CAME BACK HE GOT BAD SANTA BLOOD ON HIM.
SPLAT
WHOOPS!
SUDDENLY SOCKARANG HAD BAD SANTA POWERS! HE BECAME *GOOD BAD SANTA!*
I HAVE THE *POWER OF CHRISTMAS!*
HE STOLE BAD SANTA'S GUITAR AND DEFEATED HIM.
BABY MAN USED HIS FLYING POWERS TO ESCAPE THE EVIL FLYING BOOK.
SHAKE WHAT YOUR *BABY GAVE YA!*
STAB!
AND THE WRESTLER THREW UNI-MAN INTO THE EVIL FLYING BOOK.
THE EVIL FLYING BOOK TURNED OUT TO BE A ROBOT AND IT EXPLODED.
AS EVERYONE CELEBRATED THE VICTORY, LEAF MAN CRIED BECAUSE HE STILL DIDN'T HAVE HIS POWERS BACK.
SO AVOCADO SOLDIER USED HIS UNICORN MAGIC.
THANKS, AVOCADO SOLDIER!
THE END

Part Two: Ask Axe Cop

Ask Axe Cop Questions 1–14

Ask Axe Cop started after I'd decided to make an *Axe Cop* website. We created an e-mail submission page where people could send us questions to ask Axe Cop. I figured if the real process of creating *Axe Cop* comics was to ask Malachai questions and get him to complete a story, then why not try having him answer random questions disjointed from a plot just to see Axe Cop's take on various predicaments, and to get his opinions and explore his world a little more.

When Axe Cop's site went live I got a handful of questions to pick from so I started to make short episodes of Ask Axe Cop. The idea was for these to create more content for me to put up that wasn't an entire page. Of course, they ended up becoming as much work as a page most of the time, but it was worth it. Once the site went viral, questions for Axe Cop were coming in so fast that I had to give Axe Cop his own e-mail account. In no time there were thousands of questions to choose from.

Many have said that they think Ask Axe Cop is even funnier than the main story line, and I think I agree. The bizarre and hilarious answers that have come out of these strips are pure gold and we never would have got them if we hadn't asked.

—Ethan

ASK AXE COP
Q1.
Dear Axe Cop,
I'm having an argument with my dad. He says that spicy food is great, but I can't stand the stuff. Am I a weenie or is he a jerk?
—Sean
LISTEN. JUST EAT A PEANUT BUTTER AND JELLY SANDWICH WITH YOUR DAD'S HEAD ON IT BECAUSE I AM PRETTY SURE YOU'RE A ZOMBIE HEAD EATER.
PEANUT
-AXE COP

Ask Axe Cop #1 was a bizarre beginning. Malachai had a tough time understanding this question. He had never heard of the insult "weenie" and he didn't really even get what he was being asked so finally he just assumed the kid was a zombie and told him to eat his dad's head on a sandwich. Malachai's mom was not incredibly thrilled with this one.

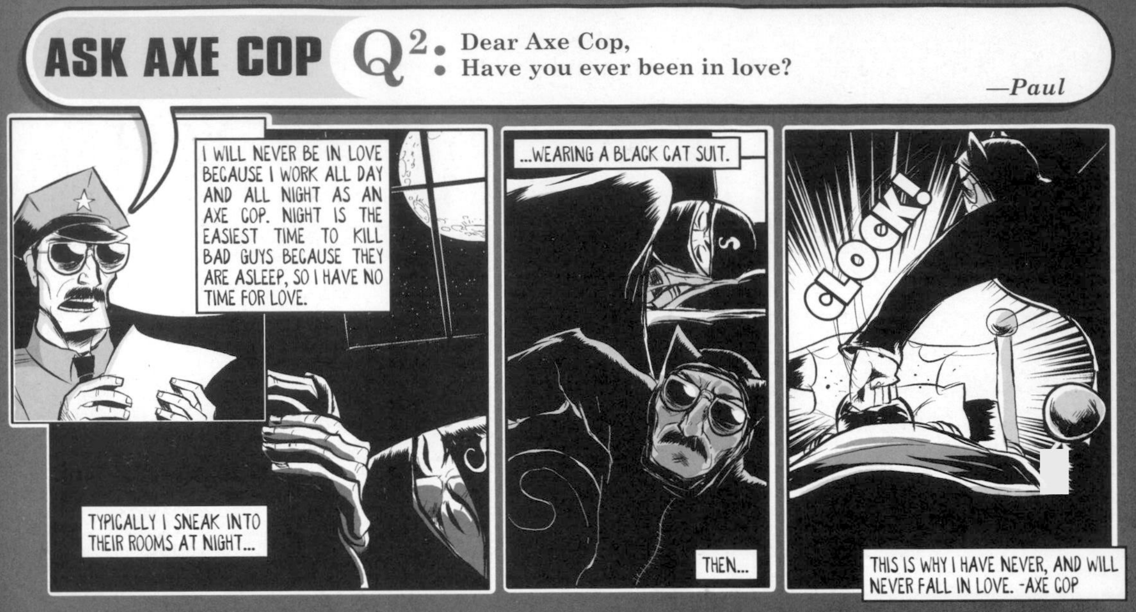
ASK AXE COP
Q2: Dear Axe Cop,
Have you ever been in love?
—Paul
I WILL NEVER BE IN LOVE BECAUSE I WORK ALL DAY AND ALL NIGHT AS AN AXE COP. NIGHT IS THE EASIEST TIME TO KILL BAD GUYS BECAUSE THEY ARE ASLEEP, SO I HAVE NO TIME FOR LOVE.
TYPICALLY I SNEAK INTO THEIR ROOMS AT NIGHT...
...WEARING A BLACK CAT SUIT.
THEN...
CLOCK!
THIS IS WHY I HAVE NEVER, AND WILL NEVER FALL IN LOVE. -AXE COP

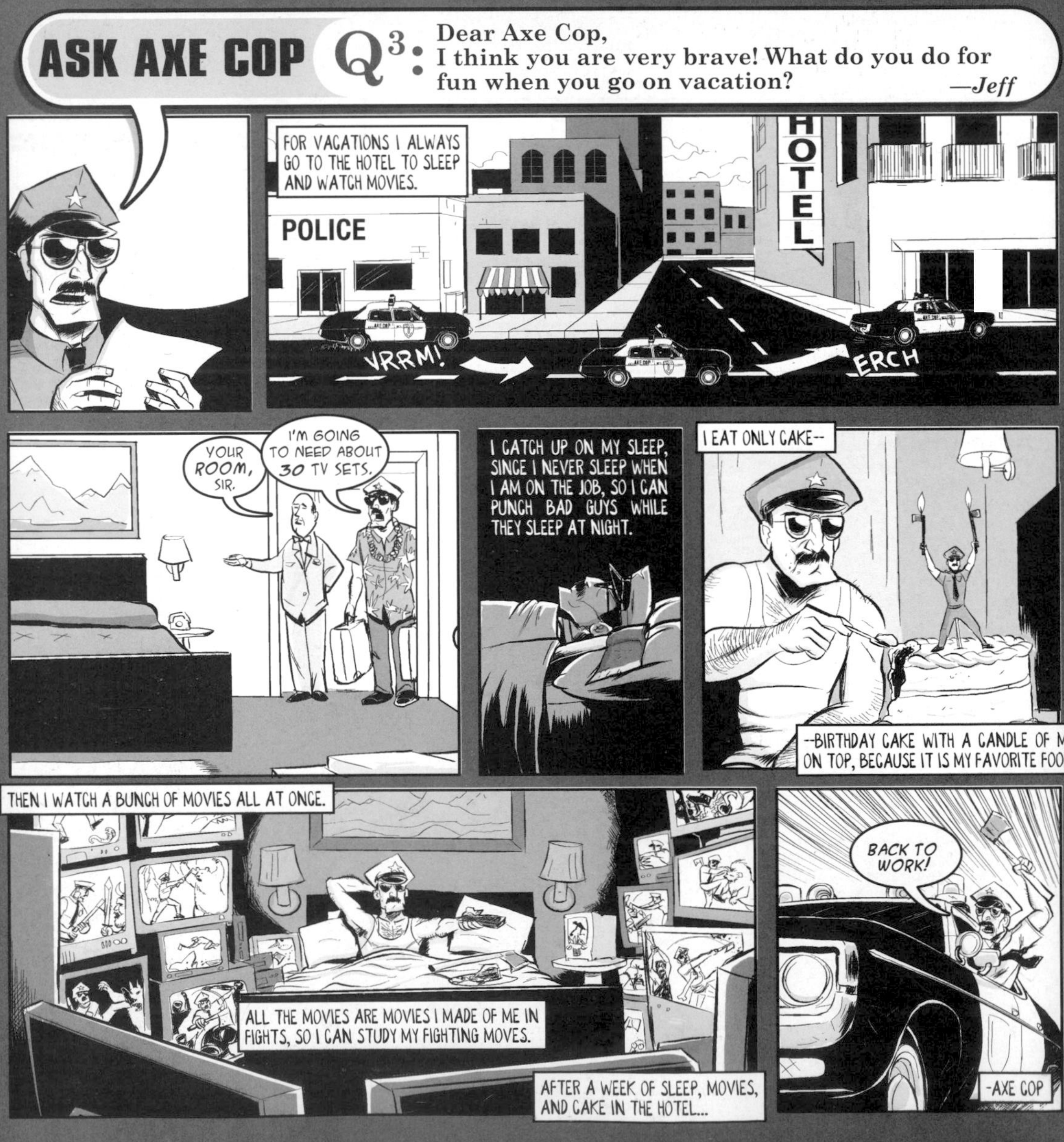
ASK AXE COP
Q3: Dear Axe Cop,
I think you are very brave! What do you do for fun when you go on vacation?
—Jeff
FOR VACATIONS I ALWAYS GO TO THE HOTEL TO SLEEP AND WATCH MOVIES.
POLICE
HOTEL
VRRM!
ERCH
YOUR ROOM, SIR.
I'M GOING TO NEED ABOUT 30 TV SETS.
I CATCH UP ON MY SLEEP, SINCE I NEVER SLEEP WHEN I AM ON THE JOB, SO I CAN PUNCH BAD GUYS WHILE THEY SLEEP AT NIGHT.
I EAT ONLY CAKE--
--BIRTHDAY CAKE WITH A CANDLE OF ME ON TOP, BECAUSE IT IS MY FAVORITE FOOD.
THEN I WATCH A BUNCH OF MOVIES ALL AT ONCE.
ALL THE MOVIES ARE MOVIES I MADE OF ME IN FIGHTS, SO I CAN STUDY MY FIGHTING MOVES.
AFTER A WEEK OF SLEEP, MOVIES, AND CAKE IN THE HOTEL...
BACK TO WORK!
-AXE COP

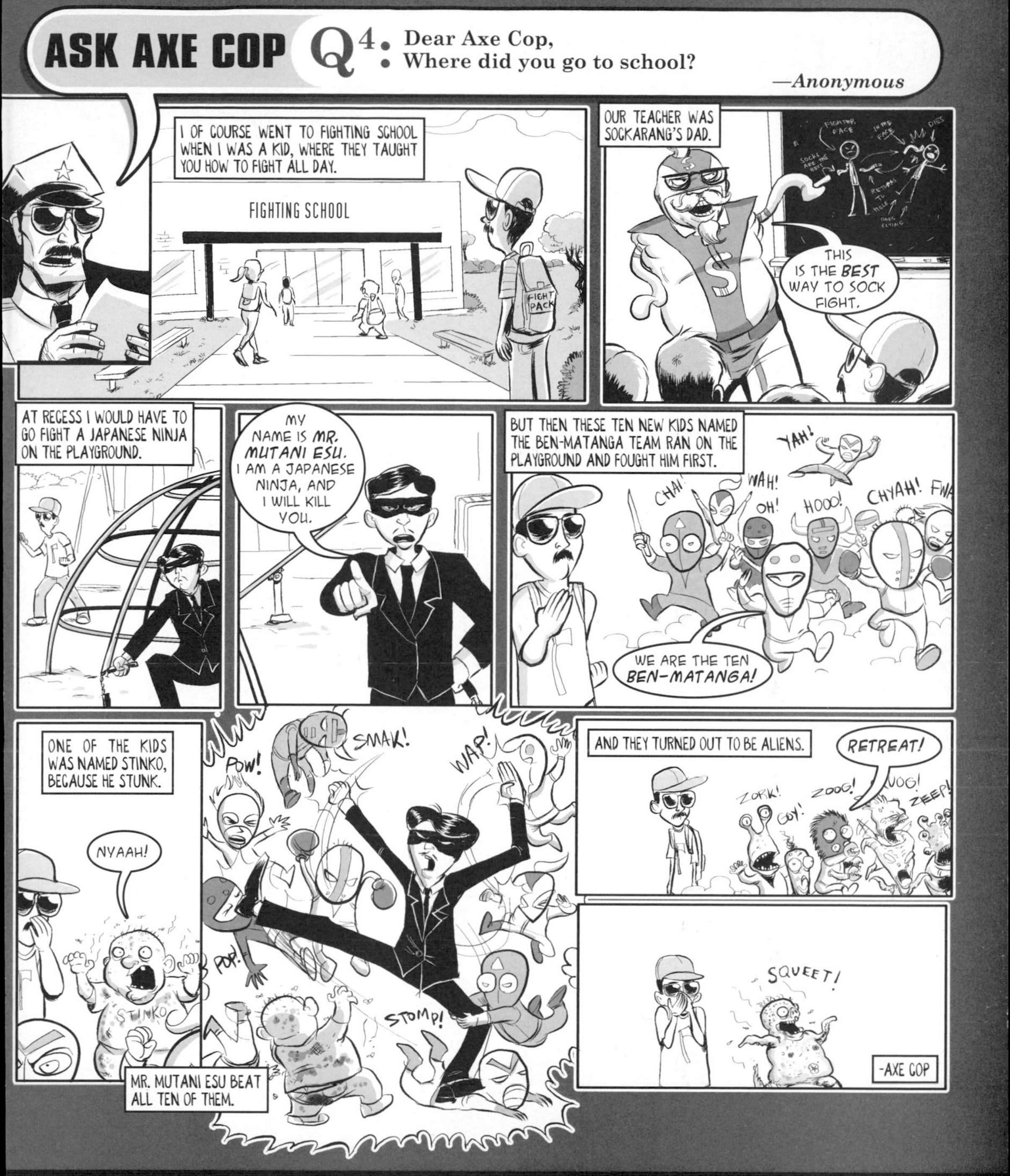

ASK AXE COP
Q4: Dear Axe Cop,
Where did you go to school?
—Anonymous
I OF COURSE WENT TO FIGHTING SCHOOL WHEN I WAS A KID, WHERE THEY TAUGHT YOU HOW TO FIGHT ALL DAY.
FIGHTING SCHOOL
FIGHT PACK
OUR TEACHER WAS SOCKARANG'S DAD.
THIS IS THE BEST WAY TO SOCK FIGHT.
AT RECESS I WOULD HAVE TO GO FIGHT A JAPANESE NINJA ON THE PLAYGROUND.
MY NAME IS MR. MUTANI ESU. I AM A JAPANESE NINJA, AND I WILL KILL YOU.
BUT THEN THESE TEN NEW KIDS NAMED THE BEN-MATANGA TEAM RAN ON THE PLAYGROUND AND FOUGHT HIM FIRST.
YAH!
CHA!
WAH!
OH!
HOOO!
CHYAH!
WE ARE THE TEN BEN-MATANGA!
ONE OF THE KIDS WAS NAMED STINKO, BECAUSE HE STUNK.
NYAAH!
STINKO
POW!
SMAK!
WAP!
POP!
STOMP!
MR. MUTANI ESU BEAT ALL TEN OF THEM.
AND THEY TURNED OUT TO BE ALIENS.
RETREAT!
ZORK!
GOY!
ZOOG!
NOG!
ZEEP!
SQUEET!
-AXE COP

Ask Axe Cop #2 was very memorable for me because it made me realize this "Ask Axe Cop" thing really was going to work. While working on it, I would laugh so hard that if I tried to talk I would go into this girly squeal. This is also where the truly insane side of Axe Cop started to come out. The guy sneaks around at night in a black cat suit and kills bad guys in their sleep. Some heroes might see that as sort of cheating, but Axe Cop likes to keep things simple and efficient.

Ask Axe Cop #3 remains one of the funniest answers yet. Our family doesn't have the kind of money it takes to really travel. We never flew on planes; we just seemed to drive to a hotel somewhere and do stuff in another town. Malachai's concept of a vacation really is just going to a hotel, and the coolest part is watching TV because he doesn't have cable at home.

▲ **Ask Axe Cop #4** came out of Malachai's desire to include his favorite cartoon, *Ben 10*, in an *Axe Cop* strip. I kept having to tell him to change stuff so that it was his idea and not someone else's, and that is where we got the *Ten Ben-Matanga*. Even though they appear to be bad guys, Malachai insists that they are good guys (well, except for Stinko).

ASK AXE COP Q5:

Dear Axe Cop,
How did you become a cop? Was the training hard??
—Anonymous

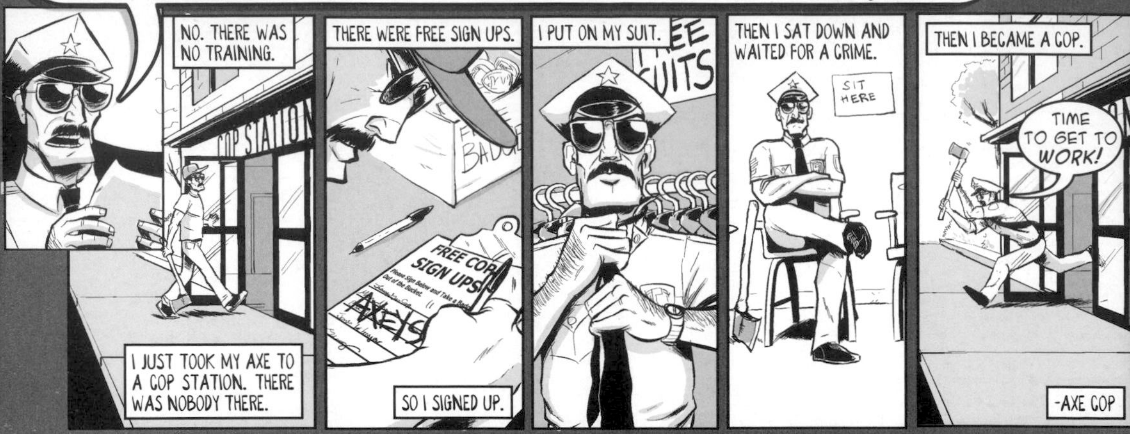
NO. THERE WAS NO TRAINING.
COP STATION
I JUST TOOK MY AXE TO A COP STATION. THERE WAS NOBODY THERE.
THERE WERE FREE SIGN UPS.
FREE COP SIGN UPS
AXEY
SO I SIGNED UP.
I PUT ON MY SUIT.
FREE SUITS
THEN I SAT DOWN AND WAITED FOR A CRIME.
SIT HERE
THEN I BECAME A COP.
TIME TO GET TO WORK!
-AXE COP

Ask Axe Cop #5 was Axe Cop's first glaring plot hole. Since Axe Cop is depicted finding "the perfect fireman axe" at the scene of a fire, you would assume that he did not have one before he became a cop. This was my fault. Malachai never specifically said he had his axe here. However, if we view this axe as a *normal* axe, it could follow that the "perfect" axe he finds later is the one that replaced it and really made him decide to fight crime. It can still work. You would assume a guy named Axey would own an axe anyway.

Ask Axe Cop #6
I got a lot of these questions where someon would present some weird situation wit some sort of evil animal. Malachai ofte chose to poison them. This episode cracks m up because it is so dark. Also, this is where th beloved "Secret Attack" line first appearec

ASK AXE COP Q6:

Dear Axe Cop,
If dirty apes took over the world, what would you do to stop them?
—Anonymous

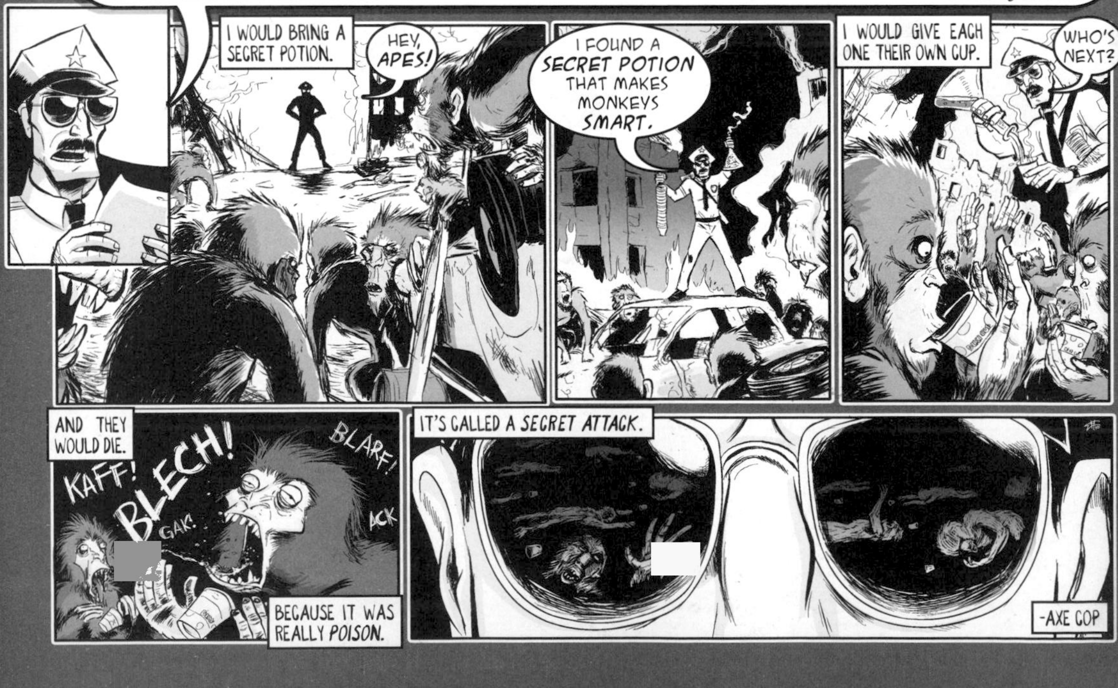
I WOULD BRING A SECRET POTION.
HEY, APES!
I FOUND A SECRET POTION THAT MAKES MONKEYS SMART.
I WOULD GIVE EACH ONE THEIR OWN CUP.
WHO'S NEXT?
AND THEY WOULD DIE.
KAFF!
BLECH!
BLARF!
GAK!
ACK
BECAUSE IT WAS REALLY POISON.
IT'S CALLED A SECRET ATTACK.
-AXE COP

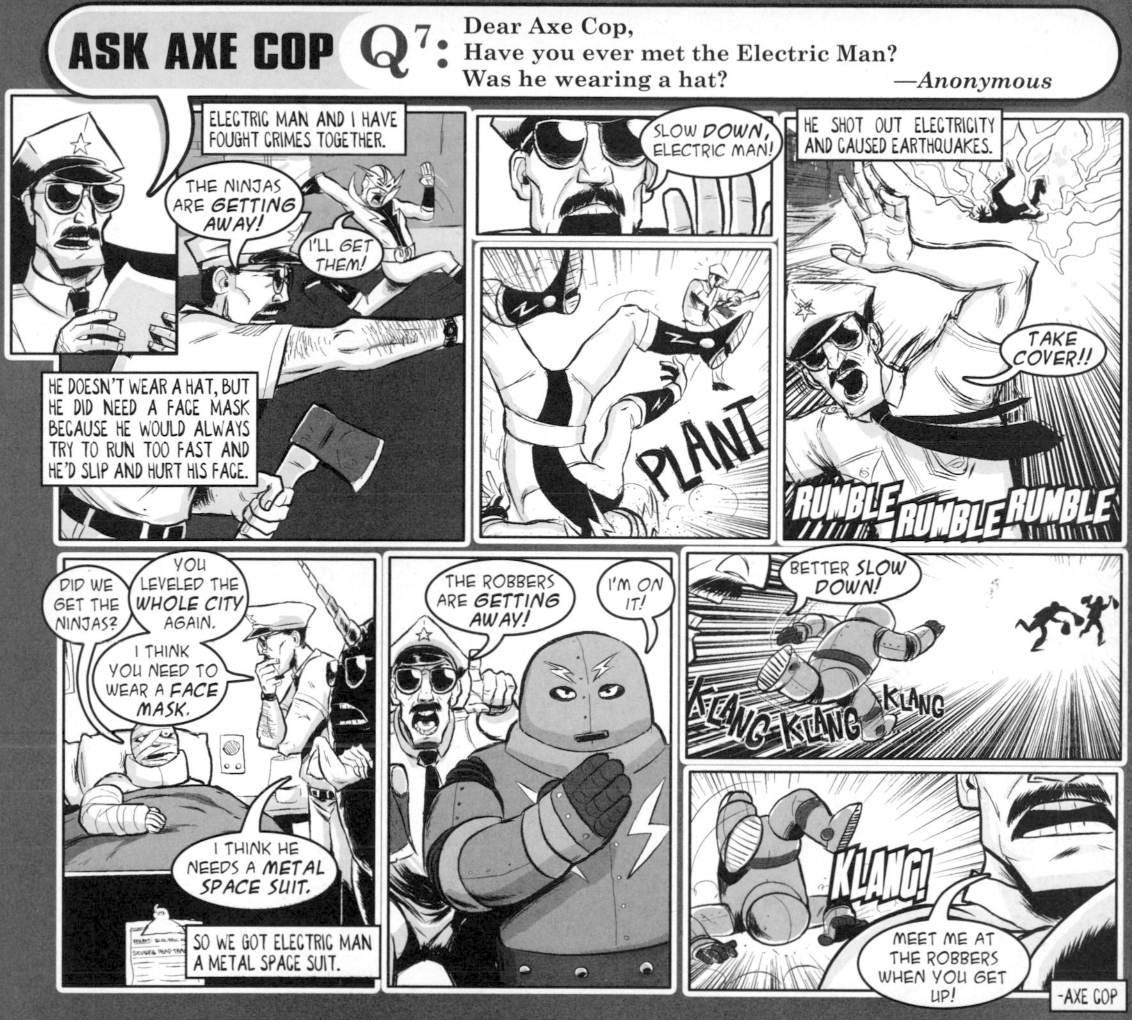
ASK AXE COP
Q7: Dear Axe Cop,
Have you ever met the Electric Man?
Was he wearing a hat?
—Anonymous
ELECTRIC MAN AND I HAVE FOUGHT CRIMES TOGETHER.
THE NINJAS ARE GETTING AWAY!
I'LL GET THEM!
HE DOESN'T WEAR A HAT, BUT HE DID NEED A FACE MASK BECAUSE HE WOULD ALWAYS TRY TO RUN TOO FAST AND HE'D SLIP AND HURT HIS FACE.
SLOW DOWN, ELECTRIC MAN!
PLANT
HE SHOT OUT ELECTRICITY AND CAUSED EARTHQUAKES.
TAKE COVER!!
RUMBLE RUMBLE RUMBLE
DID WE GET THE NINJAS?
YOU LEVELED THE WHOLE CITY AGAIN.
I THINK YOU NEED TO WEAR A FACE MASK.
I THINK HE NEEDS A METAL SPACE SUIT.
SO WE GOT ELECTRIC MAN A METAL SPACE SUIT.
THE ROBBERS ARE GETTING AWAY!
I'M ON IT!
BETTER SLOW DOWN!
KLANG KLANG KLANG
KLANG!
MEET ME AT THE ROBBERS WHEN YOU GET UP!
-AXE COP

Ask Axe Cop #7

I love this episode simply for the fact that you have a superhero who gets so excited to chase bad guys that he runs way too fast and face plants every time. I am sure this comes from the constant caution from adults to "slow down!" when Malachai, or any kid, is being too rowdy. It's only logical that some adults need to be told this too. Slow down, Electric Man!

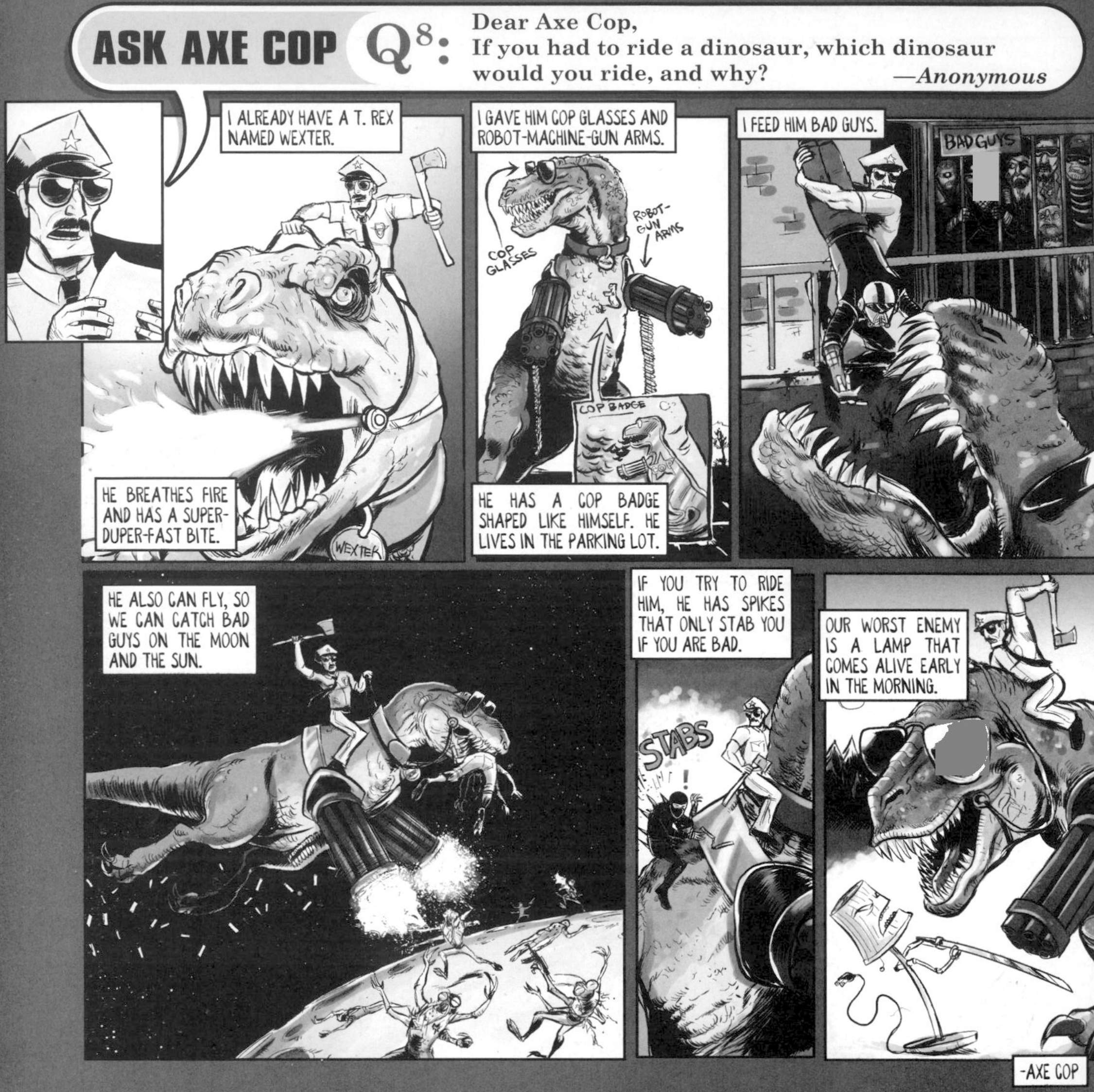
ASK AXE COP
Q8:
Dear Axe Cop,
If you had to ride a dinosaur, which dinosaur would you ride, and why?
—Anonymous
I ALREADY HAVE A T. REX NAMED WEXTER.
HE BREATHES FIRE AND HAS A SUPER-DUPER-FAST BITE.
WEXTER
I GAVE HIM COP GLASSES AND ROBOT-MACHINE-GUN ARMS.
COP GLASSES
ROBOT-GUN ARMS
COP BADGE
HE HAS A COP BADGE SHAPED LIKE HIMSELF. HE LIVES IN THE PARKING LOT.
I FEED HIM BAD GUYS.
BAD GUYS
HE ALSO CAN FLY, SO WE CAN CATCH BAD GUYS ON THE MOON AND THE SUN.
IF YOU TRY TO RIDE HIM, HE HAS SPIKES THAT ONLY STAB YOU IF YOU ARE BAD.
STABS
OUR WORST ENEMY IS A LAMP THAT COMES ALIVE EARLY IN THE MORNING.
-AXE COP

Ask Axe Cop #8

This answer became one of the most famous *Axe Cop* strips, especially the image in panel four where Axe Cop is riding his *T. rex* to the moon to kill bad guys. It has to be one of the most manly images ever created. The moment Wexter was created he became Malachai's favorite. I think he may have become everybody's favorite. He just added a whole new level of awesome to the *Axe Cop* universe. He sure is a pain to draw though.

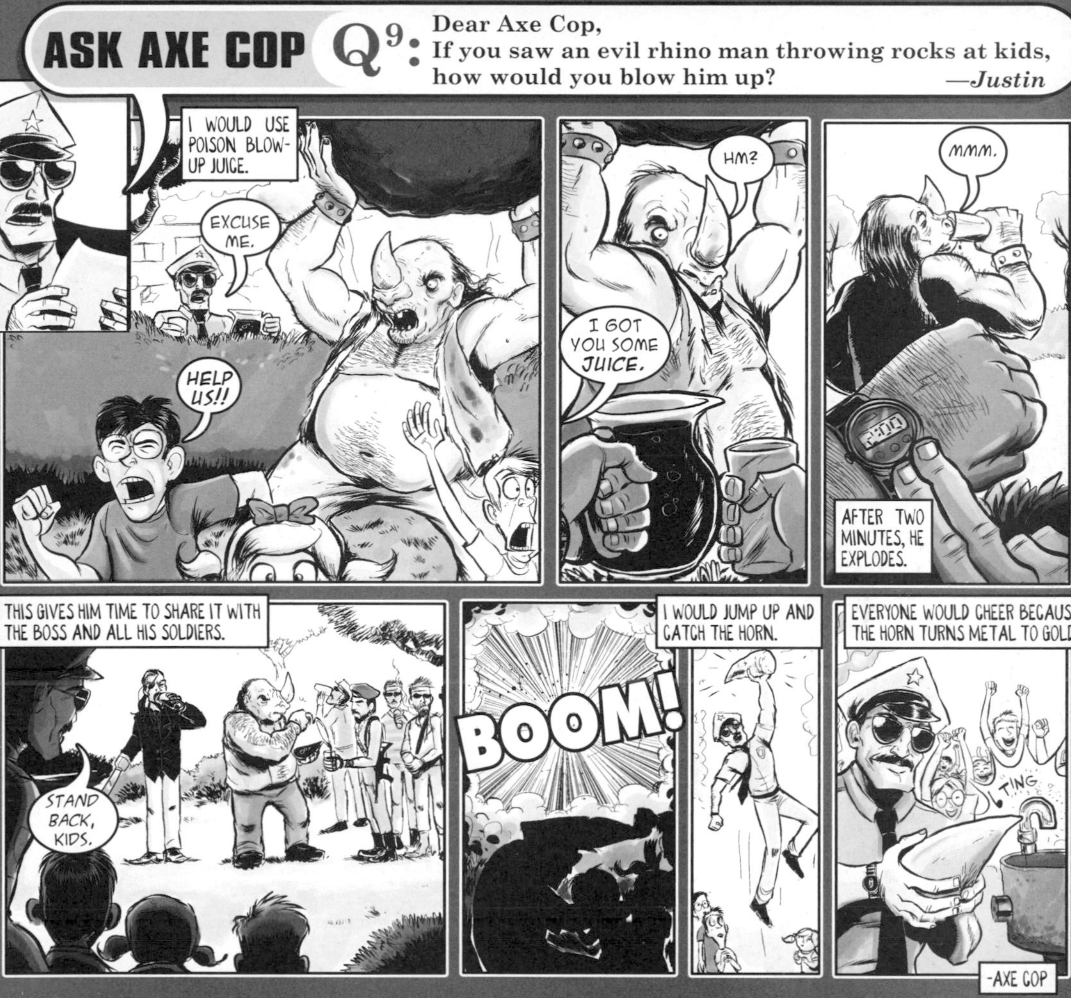
ASK AXE COP
Q9: Dear Axe Cop,
If you saw an evil rhino man throwing rocks at kids, how would you blow him up?
—Justin
I WOULD USE POISON BLOW-UP JUICE.
EXCUSE ME.
HELP US!!
HM?
I GOT YOU SOME JUICE.
MMM.
AFTER TWO MINUTES, HE EXPLODES.
THIS GIVES HIM TIME TO SHARE IT WITH THE BOSS AND ALL HIS SOLDIERS.
STAND BACK, KIDS.
BOOM!
I WOULD JUMP UP AND CATCH THE HORN.
EVERYONE WOULD CHEER BECAUSE THE HORN TURNS METAL TO GOLD.
TING
-AXE COP

Ask Axe Cop #9

Once again, Axe Cop uses poison to kill the bad guys. One consistency in the *Axe Cop* universe is that bad guys are pretty stupid. I generally have to really work with Malachai to make bad guys any sort of challenge because he doesn't see the point of making them hard to defeat. Axe Cop is also very thorough in that he poisons *and* explodes his enemies. This episode feels like one of those G.I. Joe "Knowing is half the battle" shorts, and that is probably what I love most about it.

On a side note, Malachai was not happy with Rhino Man being fat. I figured the character design was up to me, but I guess I was wrong.

ASK AXE COP
Q10:
Dear Axe Cop,
Would you ever consider running for president?
What would your platform be?
—Matt
I WOULD ABOLISH THE WORD "PLEASE" FIRST THING.
ANYONE WHO SAYS "PLEASE" GOES TO JAIL FOR 100 WEEKS.
I WILL CHOP YOUR HEAD OFF
I WOULD BE MAGIC. I COULD DO ANYTHING.
I'D GIVE ALL MY MONEY TO THE POOR: $100.
CHOP
I WOULD MAKE A BOMB THAT ONLY KILLS BAD PEOPLE.
BOOM!
SOME BAD GUYS WOULD ESCAPE TO A BAD GUY PLANET THE DAY I TOOK OFFICE.
BUT I FILLED THEIR PLANET WITH BOMBS.
CRUST
MANTLE
BOMBS
BAD GUY PLANET
THEY WOULD ALL BE DESTROYED.
I'D GET REALLY BORED.
-AXE COP

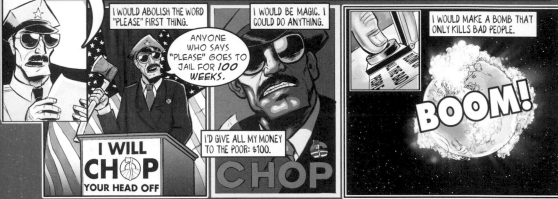

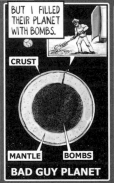

Ask Axe Cop #10

Another very memorable episode. The Obama rip-off Axe Cop poster in panel two became an iconic Axe Cop image. It is so cool that even Roy from *The IT Crowd* has it hanging in his apartment.

Ask Axe Cop #11

This episode turned out to be one of my favorites. Malachai's initial answer to the question was pretty minimal, so I had to dig up other things he had said at other times and piece it together. Malachai never really explained what a psychic move is, so I went with the telekinetic neck snap.

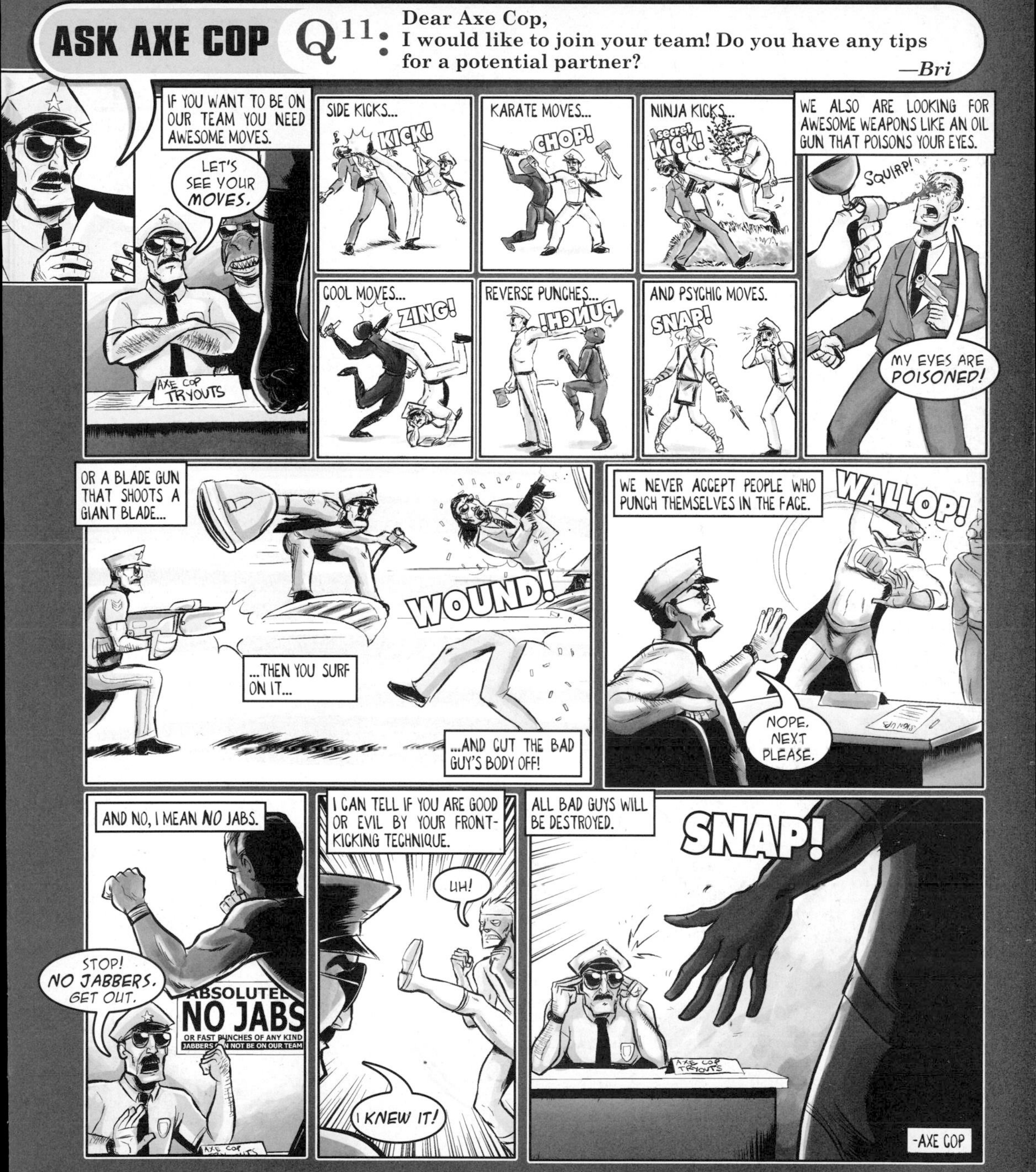
ASK AXE COP
Q11: Dear Axe Cop,
I would like to join your team! Do you have any tips for a potential partner?
—Bri
IF YOU WANT TO BE ON OUR TEAM YOU NEED AWESOME MOVES.
LET'S SEE YOUR MOVES.
AXE COP TRYOUTS
SIDE KICKS...
KICK!
KARATE MOVES...
CHOP!
NINJA KICKS...
secret KICK!
COOL MOVES...
ZING!
REVERSE PUNCHES...
PUNCH!
AND PSYCHIC MOVES.
SNAP!
WE ALSO ARE LOOKING FOR AWESOME WEAPONS LIKE AN OIL GUN THAT POISONS YOUR EYES.
SQUIRP!
MY EYES ARE POISONED!
OR A BLADE GUN THAT SHOOTS A GIANT BLADE...
...THEN YOU SURF ON IT...
WOUND!
...AND CUT THE BAD GUY'S BODY OFF!
WE NEVER ACCEPT PEOPLE WHO PUNCH THEMSELVES IN THE FACE.
WALLOP!
NOPE. NEXT PLEASE.
AND NO, I MEAN NO JABS.
STOP! NO JABBERS. GET OUT.
ABSOLUTEL
NO JABS
OR FAST PUNCHES OF ANY KIND
I CAN TELL IF YOU ARE GOOD OR EVIL BY YOUR FRONT-KICKING TECHNIQUE.
UH!
I KNEW IT!
ALL BAD GUYS WILL BE DESTROYED.
SNAP!
AXE COP TRYOUTS
-AXE COP

ASK AXE COP   Q12: Dear Axe Cop,
Have you ever fought Chuck Norris?
—Steph
(and basically everyone on the Internet)

YES. HE WAS TAKING HIS POODLE FOR A WALK AND WANTED TO FIGHT ME.

HEY, AXE COP! YOU'RE GOING DOWN. I'M CHUCK NORRIS. I KNOW KARATE!

YOU DON'T HAVE A PET!

GRRARR

I HAVE A PET.

HIS NAME IS WEXTER. HE BREATHES FIRE AND HAS A SUPER-DUPER-FAST BITE.

CHAR!

HUP!

BACKFLIP!

HA! YOU MAY HAVE BURNED MY POODLE, BUT YOU MISSED ME AND BURNED YOURSELF TOO!

I DON'T HAVE TO WATCH OUT FOR FIRE. IT JUST TURNS ME INTO...

AXE COP FIRE

SCORCH!

I ALMOST FORGOT...

... TO CHOP YOUR HEAD OFF!

CHOP

THEN UNI-AVOCADO SOLDIER USED HIS POWERS TO TURN CHUCK NORRIS'S BLOOD INTO ROBOT BLOOD BECAUSE IT GIVES WEXTER DOUBLE ENERGY.

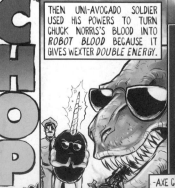

-AXE C

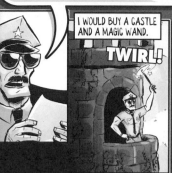

ASK AXE COP
Q13: Dear Axe Cop,
If you were rich, what would you do?
—Anonymous
I WOULD BUY A CASTLE AND A MAGIC WAND.
TWIRL!
I WOULD WISH FOR ALL THE BAD GUYS ON EARTH TO DIE.
THEN I'D WISH FOR ALL ALIENS...
...TO TURN EVIL...
...THEN DIE.
ONCE ALL THE BAD GUYS WERE DEAD, I WOULD SLEEP ALL YEAR.
EXCEPT I WOULD WAKE UP JUST ON MY BIRTHDAY.
THEN I WOULD FLY ON MY BROOM AND GIVE EVERYONE IN THE WORLD A WII CONTROLLER.
(I'M A GOOD WITCH.)
THE WHOLE WORLD WOULD PLAY AGAINST ME ON THE WII.
AXE COP WINS AGAIN!
...AND I WOULD NEVER LOSE.
-AXE COP

Ask Axe Cop #12

One of the most common questions sent in was "Have you ever fought Chuck Norris?" Malachai had no idea who Chuck Norris is, so I just said, "He's some guy who knows karate." I suppose you could accuse me of getting a little caught up in *Axe Cop* as a meme when I indulged in the question, but Chuck Norris or not, this episode introduced Axe Cop Fire, and for that we will be forever grateful.

Ask Axe Cop #13

Malachai has never heard of Howard Hughes, yet amazingly Axe Cop practically became Howard Hughes once he got rich. Axe Cop sleeps for an *entire year* once the bad guys die . . . that's how hard he works. He is also a witch, by the way.

Malachai asked me if aliens are bad, and I said some are probably good. To be thorough, he decided to make them all bad before he killed them. I'm not sure where Malachai stands theologically, but if I had to guess, I'd say he's a Calvinist.

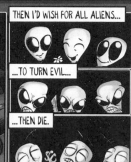

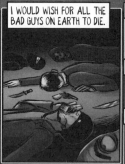

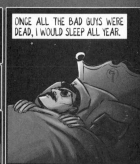

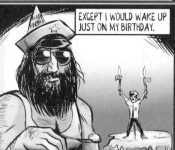

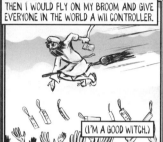

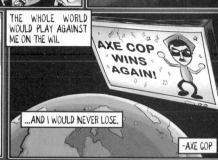

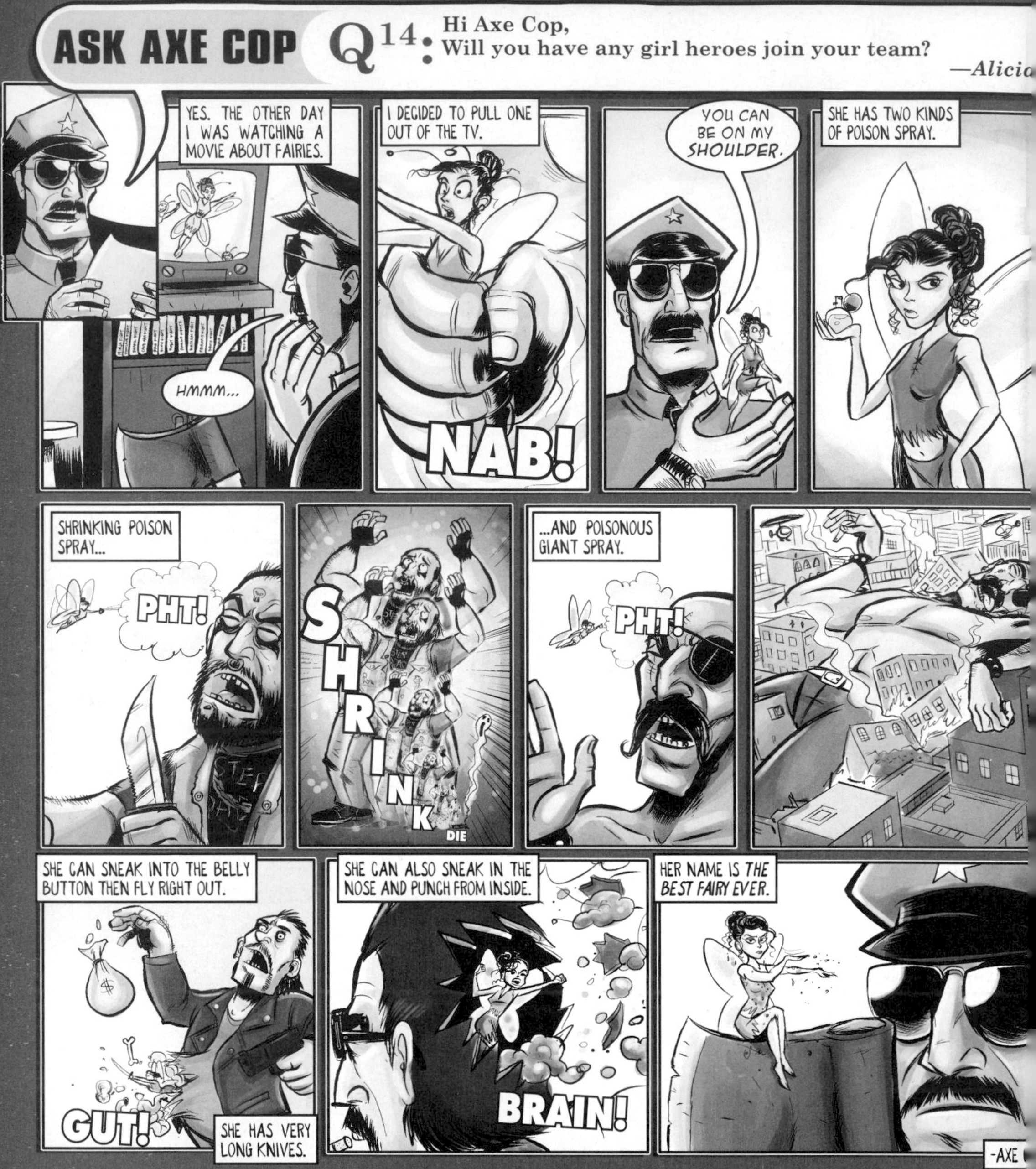
ASK AXE COP
Q14: Hi Axe Cop,
Will you have any girl heroes join your team?
—Alicia
YES. THE OTHER DAY I WAS WATCHING A MOVIE ABOUT FAIRIES.
HMMM...
I DECIDED TO PULL ONE OUT OF THE TV.
NAB!
YOU CAN BE ON MY SHOULDER.
SHE HAS TWO KINDS OF POISON SPRAY.
SHRINKING POISON SPRAY...
PHT!
SHRINK
DIE
...AND POISONOUS GIANT SPRAY.
PHT!
SHE CAN SNEAK INTO THE BELLY BUTTON THEN FLY RIGHT OUT.
GUT!
SHE HAS VERY LONG KNIVES.
SHE CAN ALSO SNEAK IN THE NOSE AND PUNCH FROM INSIDE.
BRAIN!
HER NAME IS THE BEST FAIRY EVER.
-AXE

Ask Axe Cop #14

One day I called Malachai and he told me he had some new characters, but he needed someone to help him read them to me. He had a piece of paper with writing on it and he gave it to my dad, who started to read aloud: "A fairy who has perfume bottles . . . a princess . . ." There were details about clothing and jewelry and makeup. Obviously, older sister Megan was trying to sneak in on this *Axe Cop* action. I told Malachai to put it away; I wanted to hear his ideas. A month or so later I asked him this question and he said, "Yeah, remember the fairy?" I said, "No, I forgot. Do you remember?" He said he did not, so I told him to just make up a new, awesome one. The Best Fairy Ever was born.

Part Three:
Evil, Evil, EVIL PLANET TINKO!

Episodes 6–8

Once it became obvious that *Axe Cop* was something much bigger than just a small joke between family members, it was time to try to construct a longer story with Malachai. It wasn't hard. We had already started building such a complicated little universe that when I would get on the phone with him there was no way the stories would fit in only a few pages . . . and why not stretch it out? The first few pages were thrown together sloppily as a side note to my "real" comics "career." When we started working on this story together I knew I was now drawing for the biggest audience I had ever had, so I started to put more effort into the art without slowing down.

Each of the three episodes that make up this story line were three pages each, so it was a nine-page story. Episode 5 really is part of this story, though this also works as a sequel. It picks up where episode 5 left off, just after Leaf Man got his powers back.

This is also where I started to experiment with the storytelling. Uni-man tells a chunk of this story instead of a narrator. Some people complained this didn't feel like regular *Axe Cop*, but I think maybe they were forgetting that Uni-man and the narrator are still both coming from the same person. Uni-man's voice is Malachai's voice just as much as the narrator's is.

One of my favorite parts of *Axe Cop* is the way it exercises *my* imagination. Malachai usually gives me very bare descriptions. He uses terms like "bad guys" and "aliens" and "robots" generically, so that when it goes down on paper I have to come up with these things and give them character and detail.

The aliens of Planet Tinko are definitely an homage to the aliens in many of the *Far Side* comics, and the landscapes of Planet Tinko are a weak attempt at paying tribute to Bill Watterson's great Spaceman Spiff backdrops. *The Far Side* and *Calvin and Hobbes* scarred me for life in a very good way.

—Ethan

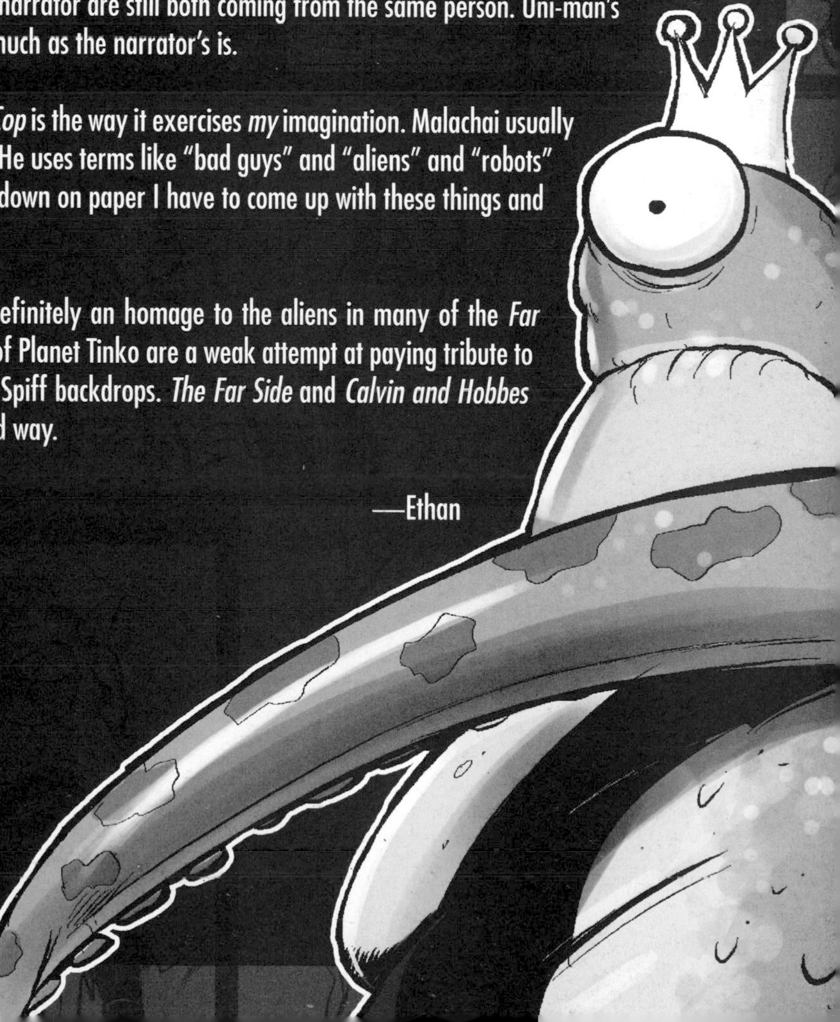

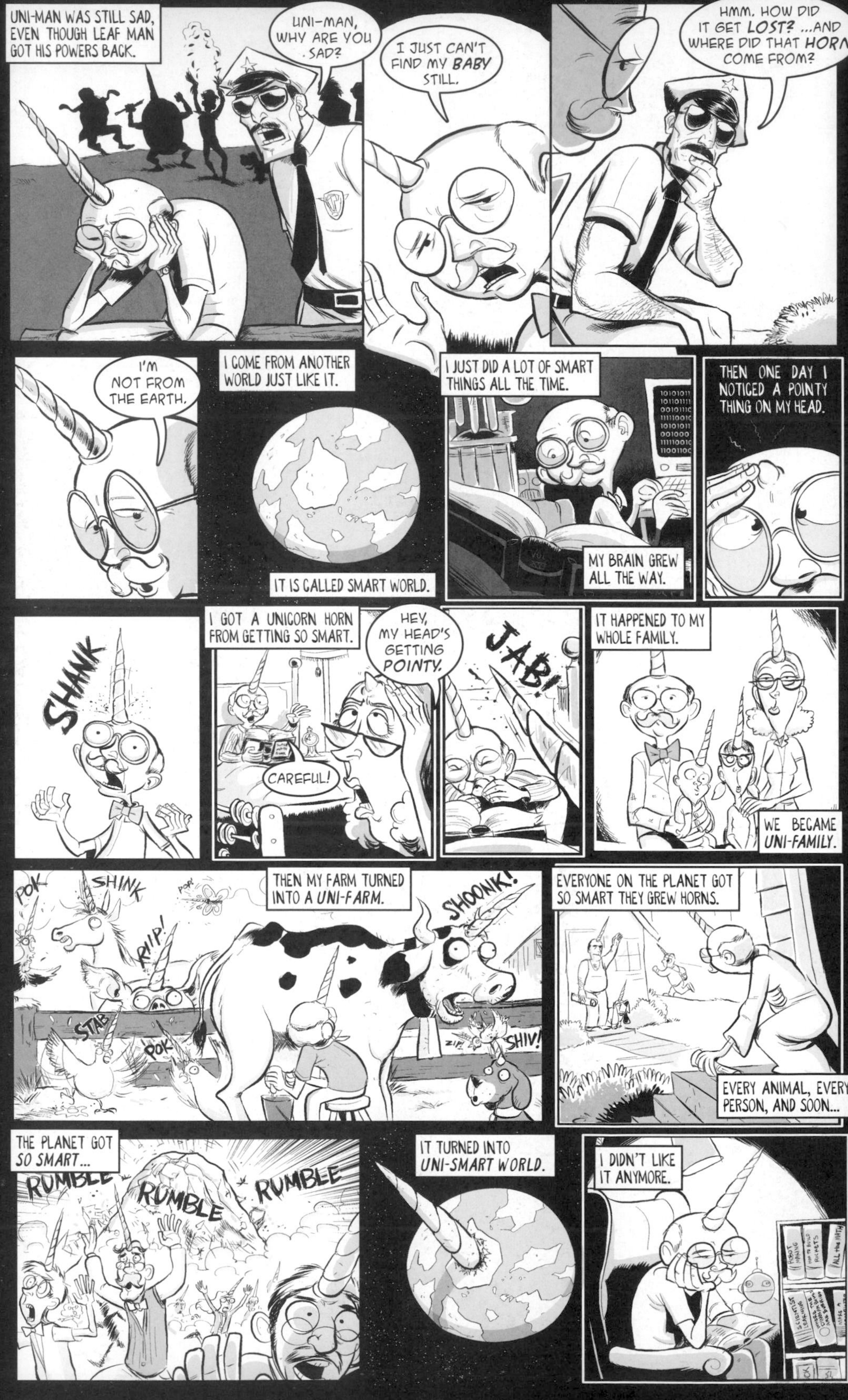
UNI-MAN WAS STILL SAD, EVEN THOUGH LEAF MAN GOT HIS POWERS BACK.
UNI-MAN, WHY ARE YOU SAD?
I JUST CAN'T FIND MY BABY STILL.
HMM. HOW DID IT GET LOST? ...AND WHERE DID THAT HORN COME FROM?
I'M NOT FROM THE EARTH.
I COME FROM ANOTHER WORLD JUST LIKE IT.
IT IS CALLED SMART WORLD.
I JUST DID A LOT OF SMART THINGS ALL THE TIME.
MY BRAIN GREW ALL THE WAY.
THEN ONE DAY I NOTICED A POINTY THING ON MY HEAD.
SHANK
I GOT A UNICORN HORN FROM GETTING SO SMART.
HEY, MY HEAD'S GETTING POINTY.
CAREFUL!
JAB!
IT HAPPENED TO MY WHOLE FAMILY.
WE BECAME UNI-FAMILY.
THEN MY FARM TURNED INTO A UNI-FARM.
POK
SHINK
POP!
RIIP!
SHOONK!
STAB
POK
ZIP!
SHIV!
EVERYONE ON THE PLANET GOT SO SMART THEY GREW HORNS.
EVERY ANIMAL, EVERY PERSON, AND SOON...
THE PLANET GOT SO SMART...
RUMBLE
RUMBLE
RUMBLE
IT TURNED INTO UNI-SMART WORLD.
I DIDN'T LIKE IT ANYMORE.
ROBOT MAKING
HOW TO BUILD ROCKETS
ALL the MATH

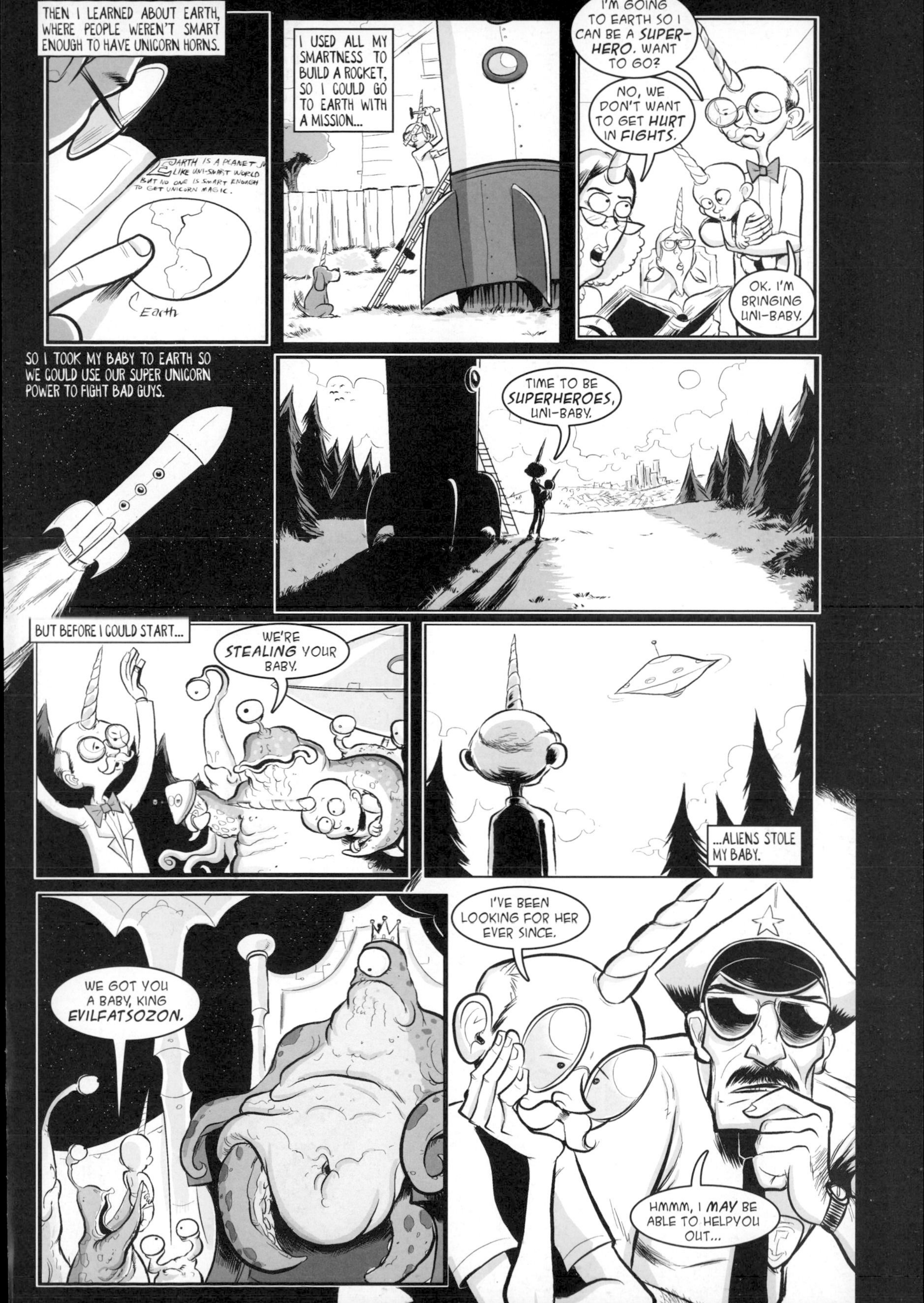

THEN I LEARNED ABOUT EARTH, WHERE PEOPLE WEREN'T SMART ENOUGH TO HAVE UNICORN HORNS.
EARTH IS A PLANET JUST LIKE UNI-SMART WORLD BUT NO ONE IS SMART ENOUGH TO GET UNICORN MAGIC.
Earth
I USED ALL MY SMARTNESS TO BUILD A ROCKET, SO I COULD GO TO EARTH WITH A MISSION...
I'M GOING TO EARTH SO I CAN BE A SUPER-HERO. WANT TO GO?
NO, WE DON'T WANT TO GET HURT IN FIGHTS.
OK. I'M BRINGING UNI-BABY.
SO I TOOK MY BABY TO EARTH SO WE COULD USE OUR SUPER UNICORN POWER TO FIGHT BAD GUYS.
TIME TO BE SUPERHEROES, UNI-BABY.
BUT BEFORE I COULD START...
WE'RE STEALING YOUR BABY.
...ALIENS STOLE MY BABY.
WE GOT YOU A BABY, KING EVILFATSOZON.
I'VE BEEN LOOKING FOR HER EVER SINCE.
HMMM, I MAY BE ABLE TO HELPYOU OUT...

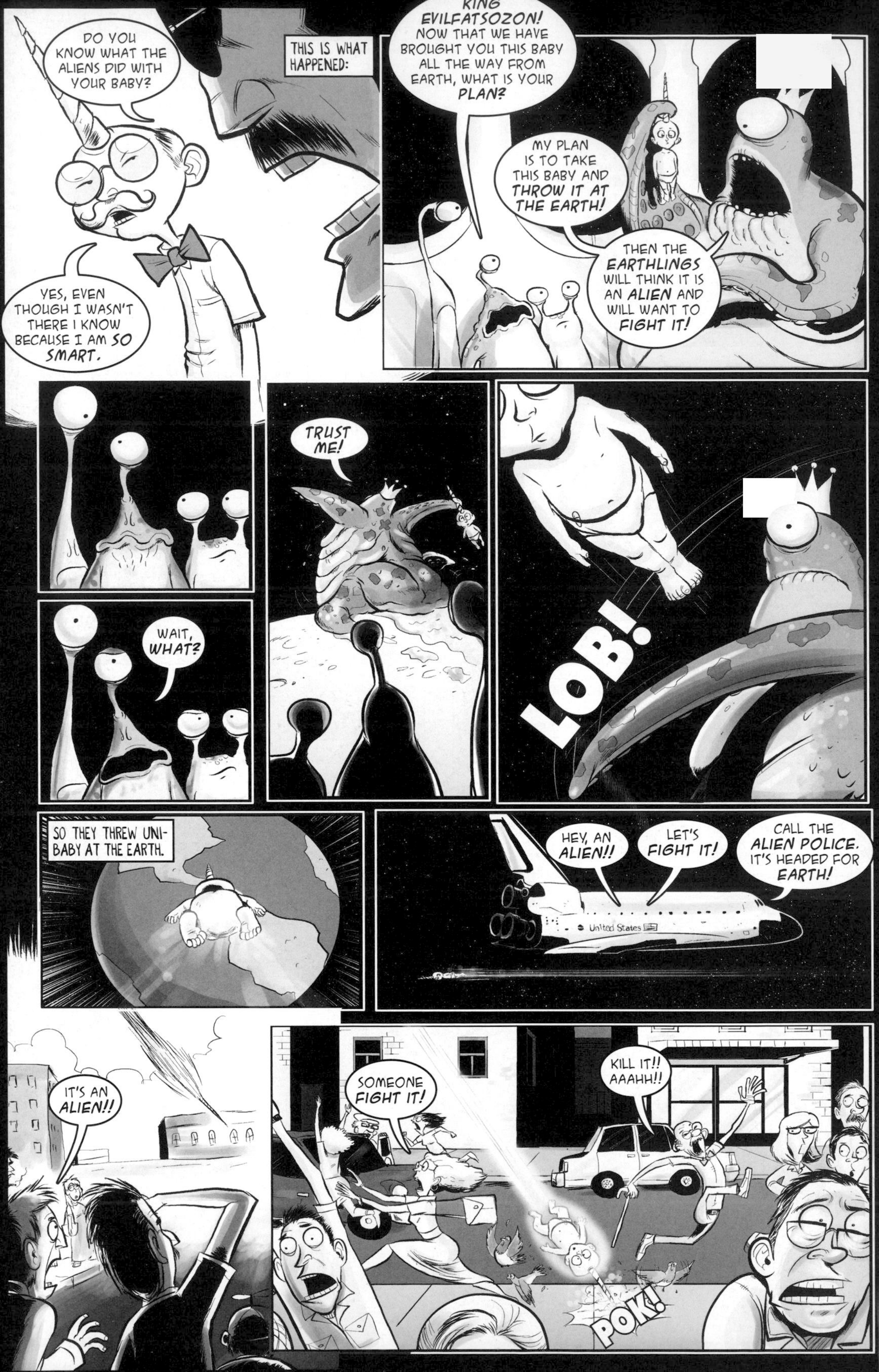
DO YOU KNOW WHAT THE ALIENS DID WITH YOUR BABY?
YES, EVEN THOUGH I WASN'T THERE I KNOW BECAUSE I AM SO SMART.
THIS IS WHAT HAPPENED:
KING EVILFATSOZON! NOW THAT WE HAVE BROUGHT YOU THIS BABY ALL THE WAY FROM EARTH, WHAT IS YOUR PLAN?
MY PLAN IS TO TAKE THIS BABY AND THROW IT AT THE EARTH!
THEN THE EARTHLINGS WILL THINK IT IS AN ALIEN AND WILL WANT TO FIGHT IT!
WAIT, WHAT?
TRUST ME!
LOB!
SO THEY THREW UNI-BABY AT THE EARTH.
HEY, AN ALIEN!!
LET'S FIGHT IT!
CALL THE ALIEN POLICE. IT'S HEADED FOR EARTH!
United States
IT'S AN ALIEN!!
SOMEONE FIGHT IT!
KILL IT!! AAAHH!!
POK!

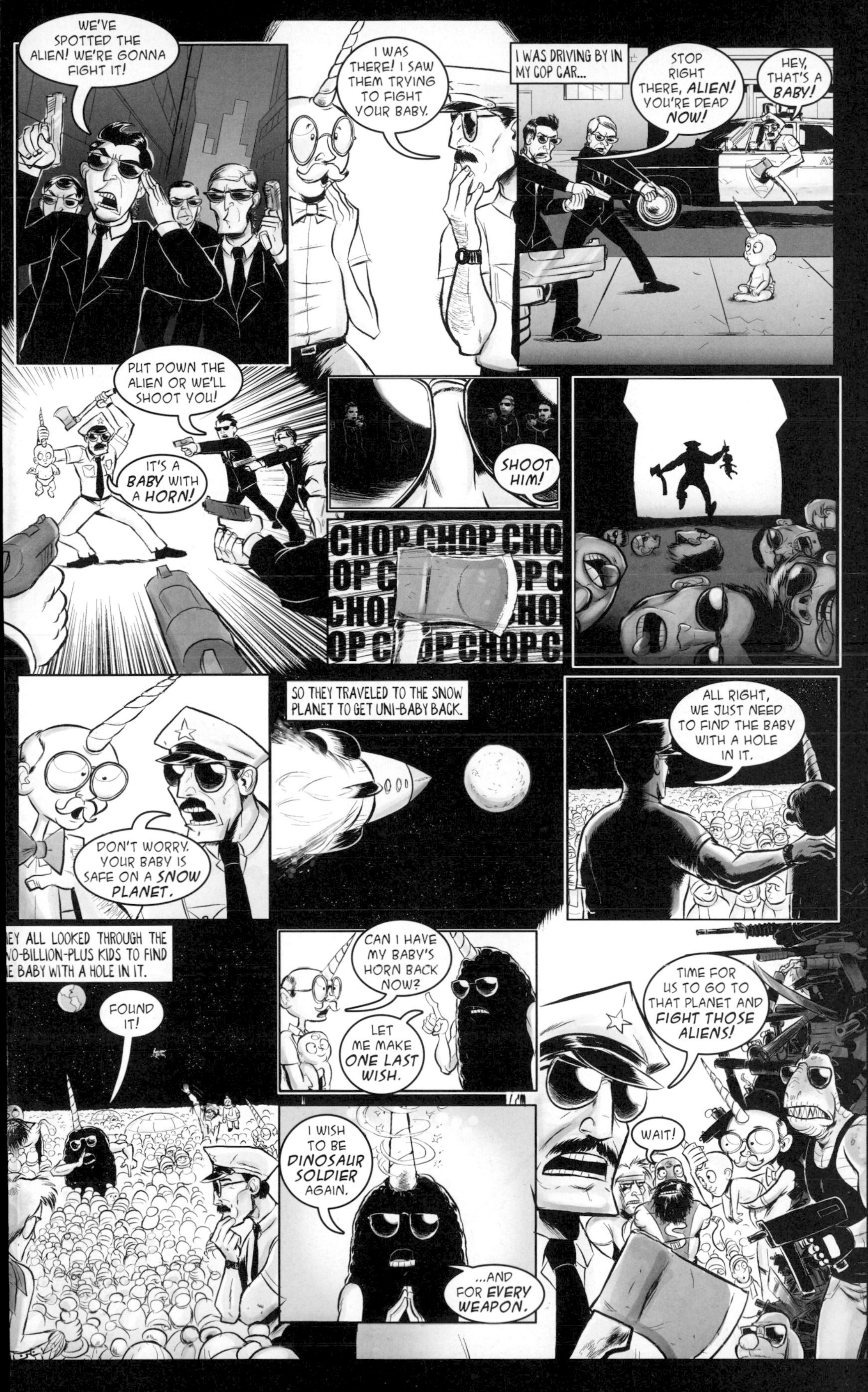

WE'VE SPOTTED THE ALIEN! WE'RE GONNA FIGHT IT!
I WAS THERE! I SAW THEM TRYING TO FIGHT YOUR BABY.
I WAS DRIVING BY IN MY COP CAR...
STOP RIGHT THERE, ALIEN! YOU'RE DEAD NOW!
HEY, THAT'S A BABY!
PUT DOWN THE ALIEN OR WE'LL SHOOT YOU!
IT'S A BABY WITH A HORN!
SHOOT HIM!
CHOP CHOP CHO
OP C
CHO
OP C
CHO
HO
OP C
OP CHOP C
DON'T WORRY. YOUR BABY IS SAFE ON A SNOW PLANET.
SO THEY TRAVELED TO THE SNOW PLANET TO GET UNI-BABY BACK.
ALL RIGHT, WE JUST NEED TO FIND THE BABY WITH A HOLE IN IT.
EY ALL LOOKED THROUGH THE
O-BILLION-PLUS KIDS TO FIND
E BABY WITH A HOLE IN IT.
FOUND IT!
CAN I HAVE MY BABY'S HORN BACK NOW?
LET ME MAKE ONE LAST WISH.
I WISH TO BE DINOSAUR SOLDIER AGAIN.
...AND FOR EVERY WEAPON.
TIME FOR US TO GO TO THAT PLANET AND FIGHT THOSE ALIENS!
WAIT!

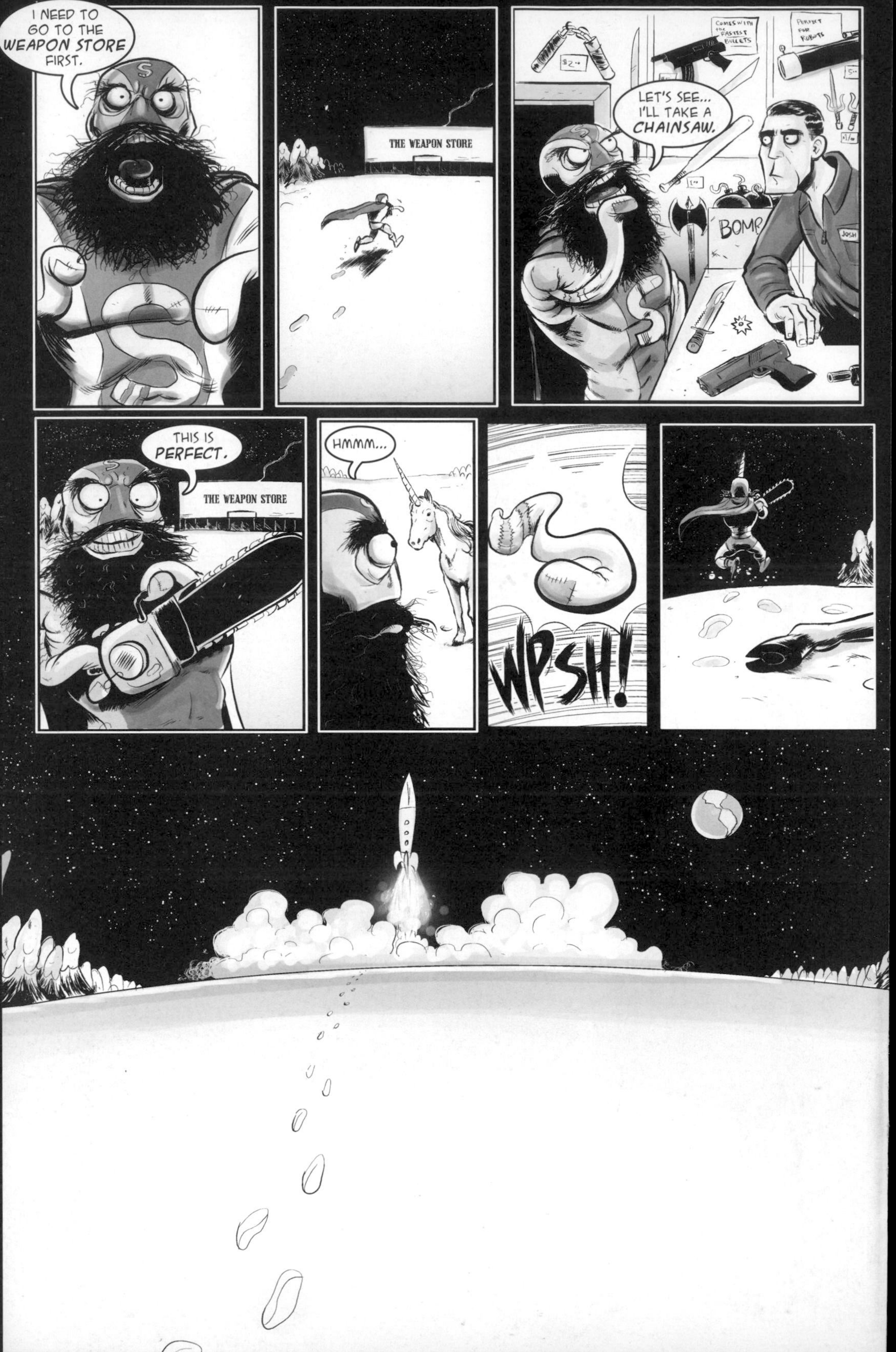
I NEED TO GO TO THE WEAPON STORE FIRST.
THE WEAPON STORE
COMES WITH the FASTEST BULLETS
LET'S SEE... I'LL TAKE A CHAINSAW.
JOSH
THIS IS PERFECT.
THE WEAPON STORE
HMMM...
WPSH!

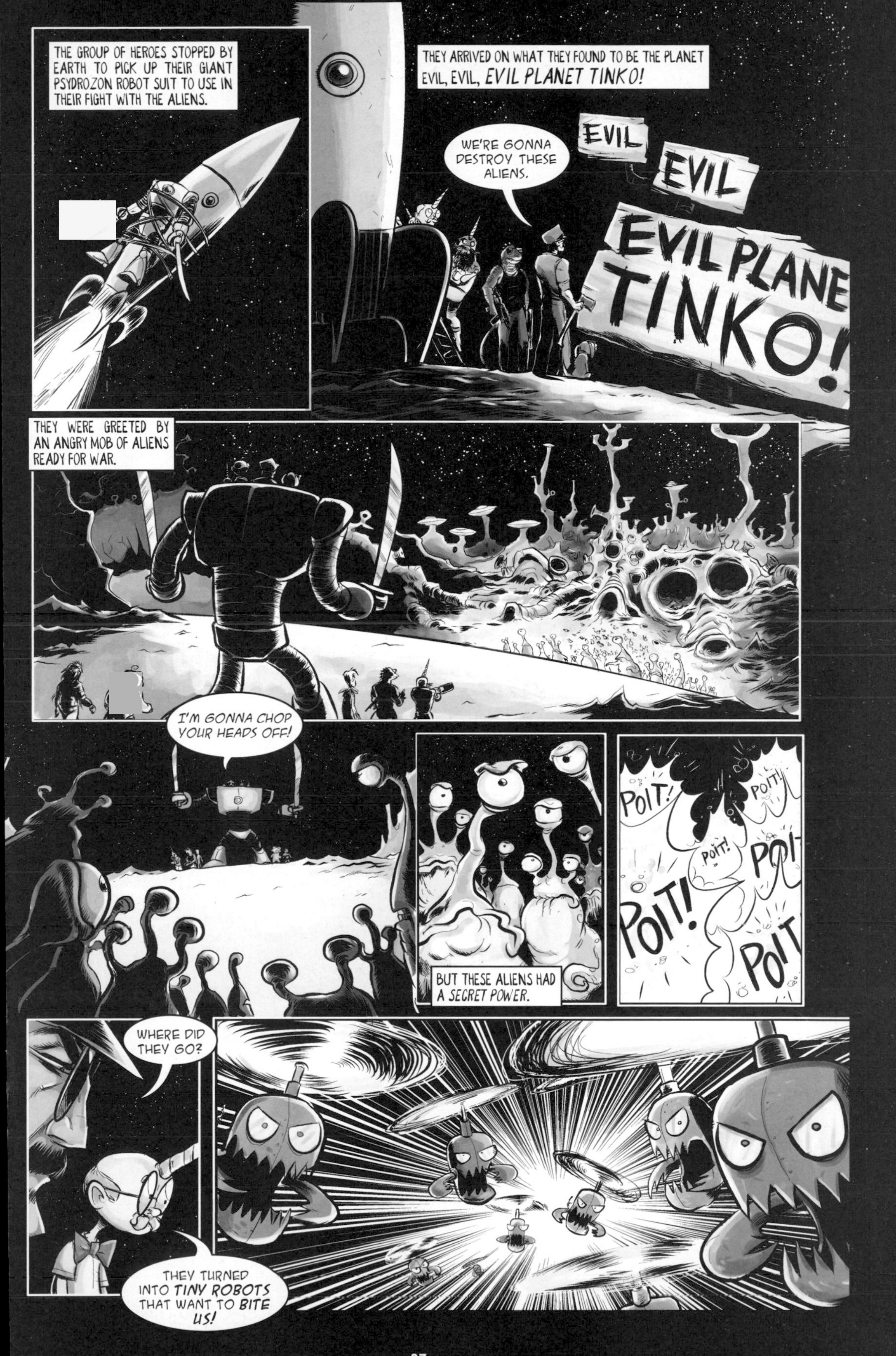
THE GROUP OF HEROES STOPPED BY EARTH TO PICK UP THEIR GIANT PSYDROZON ROBOT SUIT TO USE IN THEIR FIGHT WITH THE ALIENS.
THEY ARRIVED ON WHAT THEY FOUND TO BE THE PLANET EVIL, EVIL, EVIL PLANET TINKO!
WE'RE GONNA DESTROY THESE ALIENS.
EVIL
EVIL
EVIL PLANE
TINKO!
THEY WERE GREETED BY AN ANGRY MOB OF ALIENS READY FOR WAR.
I'M GONNA CHOP YOUR HEADS OFF!
BUT THESE ALIENS HAD A SECRET POWER.
POIT!
POIT!
POIT!
POIT!
POIT!
POIT
WHERE DID THEY GO?
THEY TURNED INTO TINY ROBOTS THAT WANT TO BITE US!

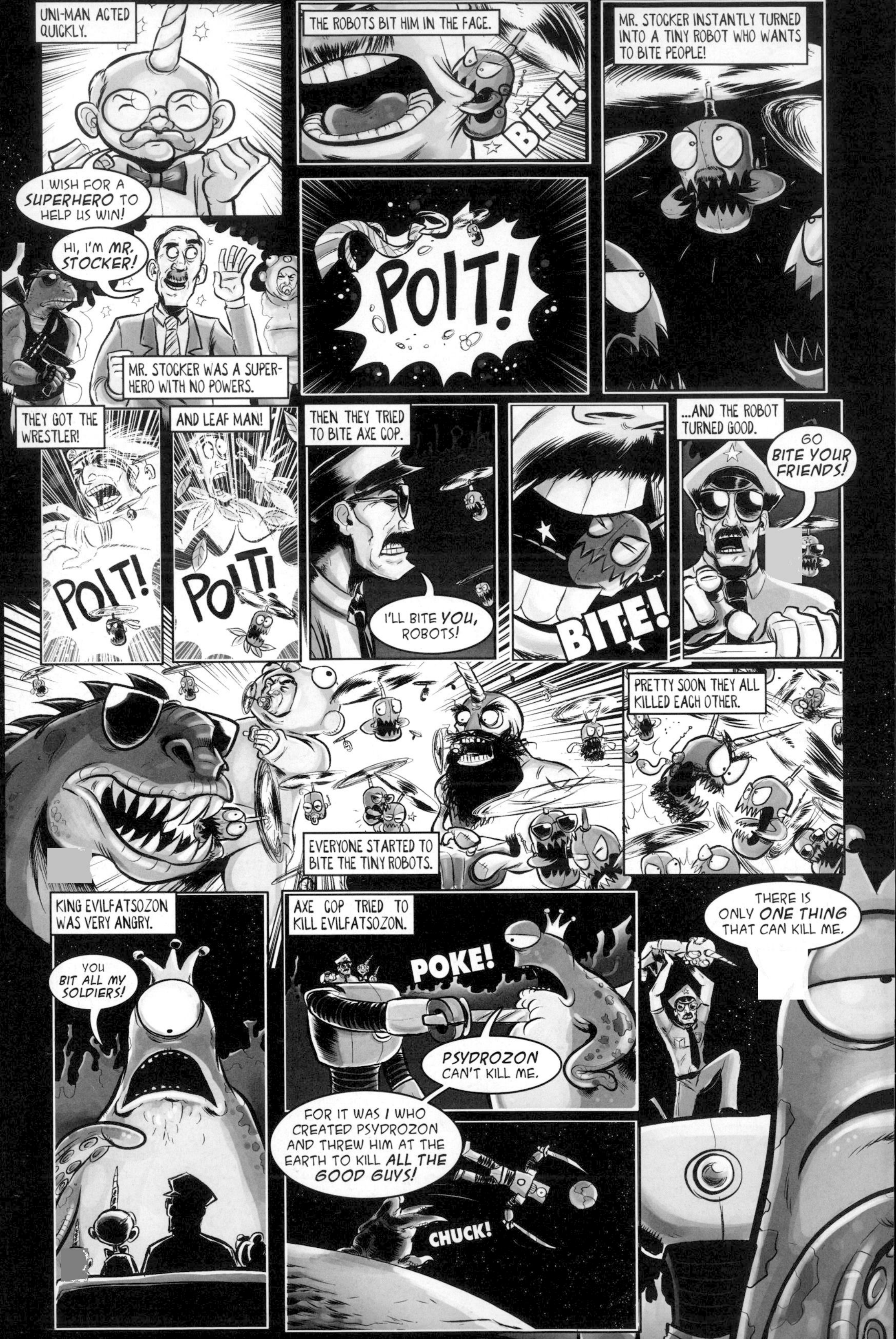
UNI-MAN ACTED QUICKLY.
I WISH FOR A SUPERHERO TO HELP US WIN!
HI, I'M MR. STOCKER!
MR. STOCKER WAS A SUPER-HERO WITH NO POWERS.
THE ROBOTS BIT HIM IN THE FACE.
BITE!
POIT!
MR. STOCKER INSTANTLY TURNED INTO A TINY ROBOT WHO WANTS TO BITE PEOPLE!
THEY GOT THE WRESTLER!
POIT!
AND LEAF MAN!
POIT!
THEN THEY TRIED TO BITE AXE COP.
I'LL BITE YOU, ROBOTS!
BITE!
...AND THE ROBOT TURNED GOOD.
GO BITE YOUR FRIENDS!
EVERYONE STARTED TO BITE THE TINY ROBOTS.
PRETTY SOON THEY ALL KILLED EACH OTHER.
KING EVILFATSOZON WAS VERY ANGRY.
YOU BIT ALL MY SOLDIERS!
AXE COP TRIED TO KILL EVILFATSOZON.
POKE!
PSYDROZON CAN'T KILL ME.
FOR IT WAS I WHO CREATED PSYDROZON AND THREW HIM AT THE EARTH TO KILL ALL THE GOOD GUYS!
CHUCK!
THERE IS ONLY ONE THING THAT CAN KILL ME.

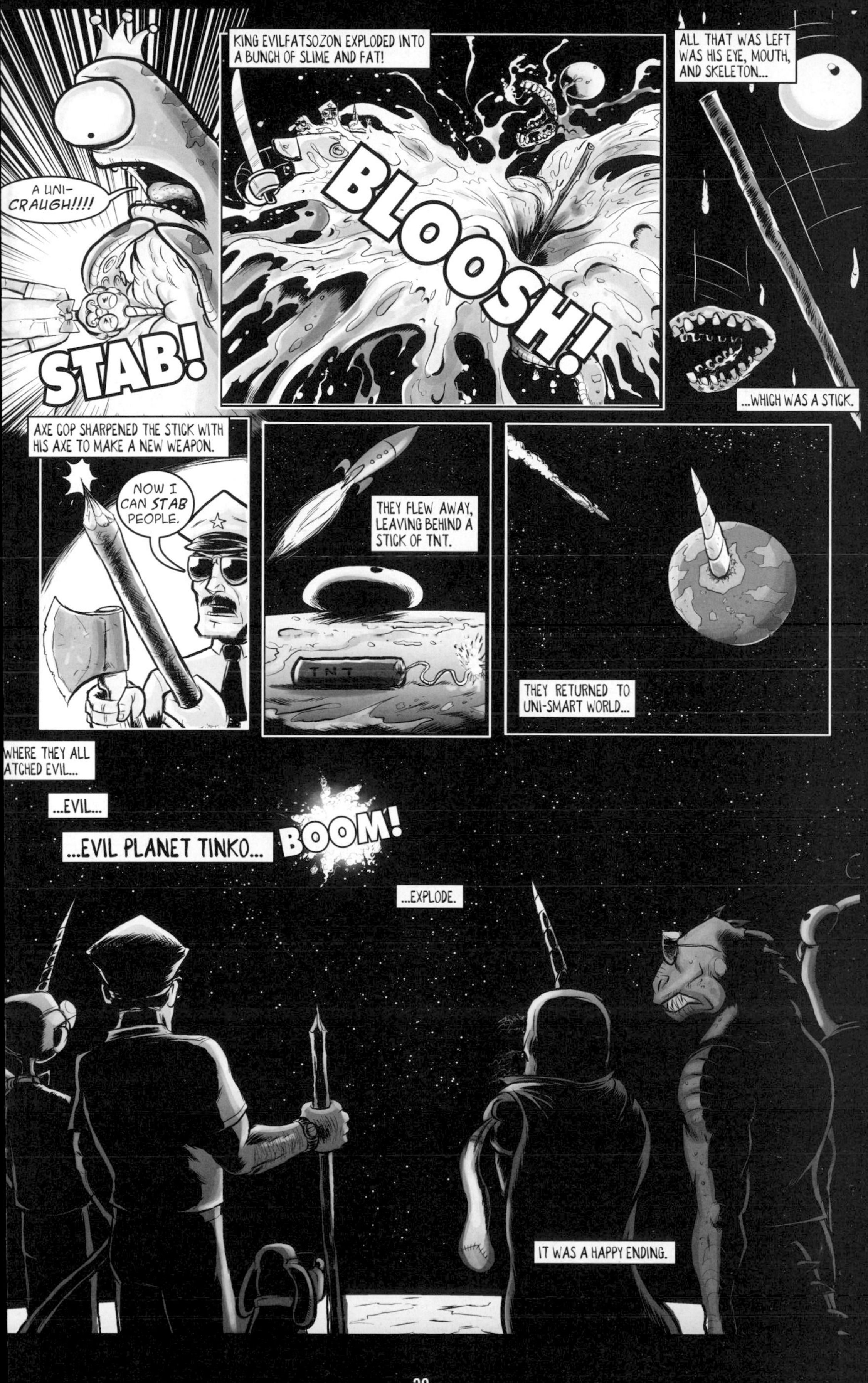

A UNI-
CRAUGH!!!!
STAB!
KING EVILFATSOZON EXPLODED INTO A BUNCH OF SLIME AND FAT!
BLOOSH!
ALL THAT WAS LEFT WAS HIS EYE, MOUTH, AND SKELETON...
...WHICH WAS A STICK.
AXE COP SHARPENED THE STICK WITH HIS AXE TO MAKE A NEW WEAPON.
NOW I CAN STAB PEOPLE.
THEY FLEW AWAY, LEAVING BEHIND A STICK OF TNT.
TNT
THEY RETURNED TO UNI-SMART WORLD...
WHERE THEY ALL
ATCHED EVIL...
...EVIL...
...EVIL PLANET TINKO...
BOOM!
...EXPLODE.
IT WAS A HAPPY ENDING.

Part Four: Ask Axe Cop

A Race with Puberty

Ask Axe Cop Questions 15–25

A few critics of *Axe Cop* said in reviews that Axe Cop would get old fast because he is one-dimensional and therefore there would never be any character development to keep people interested. They also complained he was too invulnerable and that the whole comic was based on absurdity alone. There is a lot of truth to all of that, but as we continued answering questions in the Ask Axe Cop comics it became apparent that character development was indeed taking place.

The first three questions in this section are some of my favorites because they contain a lot of raw humanity. Axe Cop makes a mistake and bursts into tears. Axe Cop would rather marry his best friend than some random woman. Axe Cop prays and asks God why he made sharks evil. They are bizarre, hilarious, and very, very true.

My fear that *Axe Cop* would grow stale disappeared with these episodes, replaced with a fascination and a desire to excavate as much of my little brother's imagination onto paper as I could.

My friend Doug TenNapel once told me that the reason he ended up having four kids (and wishing he'd had more) was because each time one was born it was so fascinatingly different than the last. Each was a reflection of him and his wife, and yet still totally unique, and each time he had a new kid, who he would get was totally unpredictable but always wonderful.

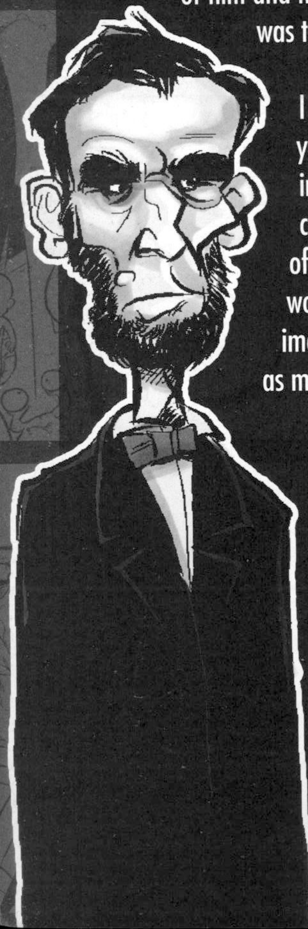

I started to see creating with Malachai in this way. You really never know what you're going to get with him, and the window of opportunity to explore his childhood imagination is slowly closing. He is rapidly changing, growing, and his outlook on life is constantly developing. The period of his life that could be called childhood is a tiny sliver of an entire life, and it will be gone in no time. Rather than fearing *Axe Cop*'s appeal would wear off, I began to realize that I was in the midst of building a monument to the imagination of a young boy in the form of an ongoing comic. I became determined to make as much as he and I could handle before puberty inevitably strikes.

—Ethan

Ask Axe Cop #15

One of my favorites. A shocker of an ending. So tragic and still so funny. Malachai came up with this scenario where Axe Cop killed a good guy on accident and sort of cornered himself. His only conclusion was that Axe Cop would cry if he killed a good guy. When he finished he said, "That was a sad one."

I have learned that I may actually have "mermaid wrong face syndrome." At Comic-Con someone said I always look mad, and I thought I was always smiling. I flexed my smile muscles and, sure enough, I was not smiling. I have since tried to retrain my face to smile correctly. I don't want to be mistaken for a bad guy.

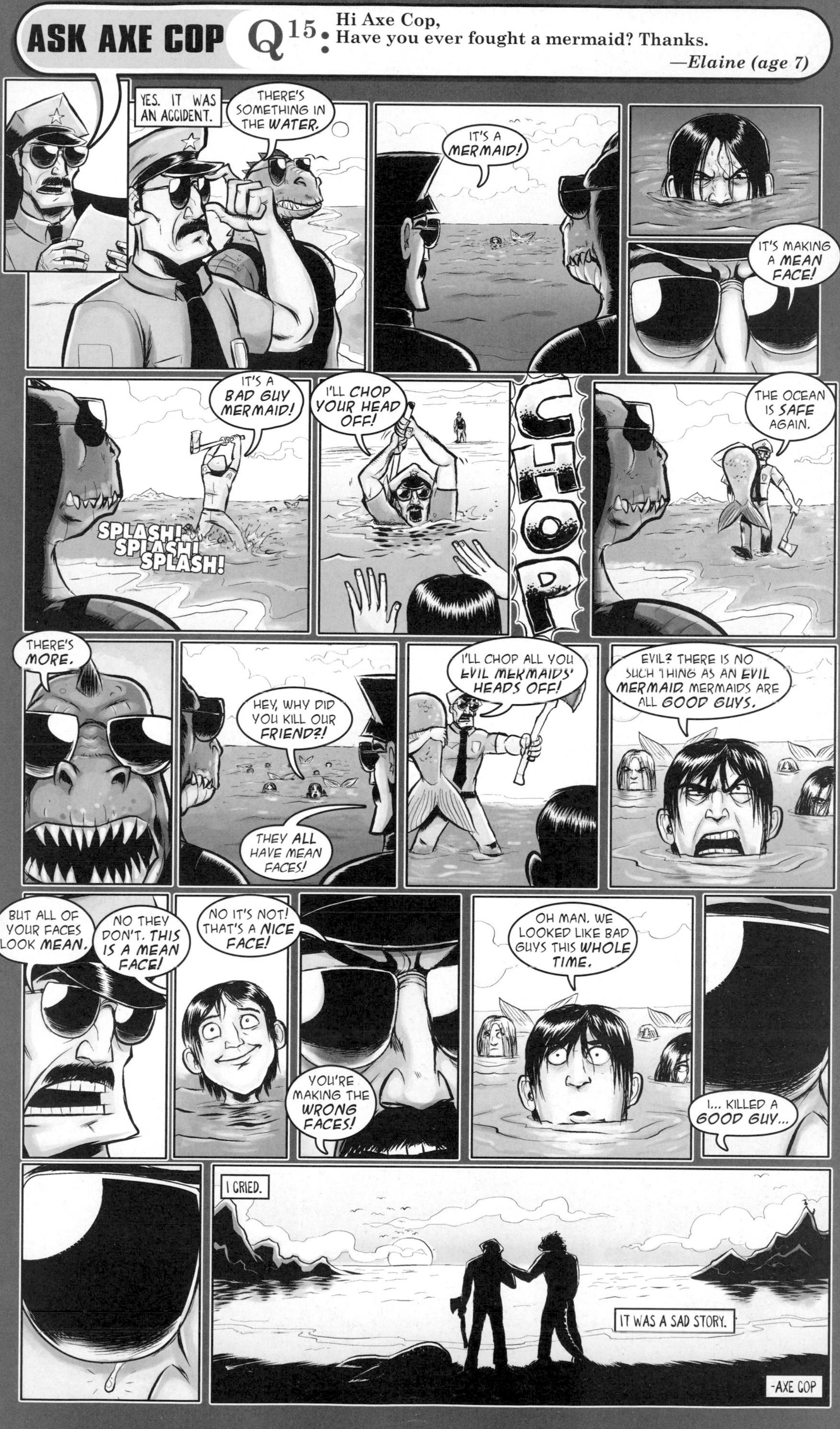
ASK AXE COP
Q15: Hi Axe Cop,
Have you ever fought a mermaid? Thanks.
—Elaine (age 7)
YES. IT WAS AN ACCIDENT.
THERE'S SOMETHING IN THE WATER.
IT'S A MERMAID!
IT'S MAKING A MEAN FACE!
IT'S A BAD GUY MERMAID!
SPLASH! SPLASH! SPLASH!
I'LL CHOP YOUR HEAD OFF!
CHOP
THE OCEAN IS SAFE AGAIN.
THERE'S MORE.
HEY, WHY DID YOU KILL OUR FRIEND?!
THEY ALL HAVE MEAN FACES!
I'LL CHOP ALL YOU EVIL MERMAIDS' HEADS OFF!
EVIL? THERE IS NO SUCH THING AS AN EVIL MERMAID. MERMAIDS ARE ALL GOOD GUYS.
BUT ALL OF YOUR FACES LOOK MEAN.
NO THEY DON'T. THIS IS A MEAN FACE!
NO IT'S NOT! THAT'S A NICE FACE!
YOU'RE MAKING THE WRONG FACES!
OH MAN. WE LOOKED LIKE BAD GUYS THIS WHOLE TIME.
I... KILLED A GOOD GUY...
I CRIED.
IT WAS A SAD STORY.
-AXE COP

ASK AXE COP

Q16: Dear Axe Cop,
Do you think you will ever have kids?

—Anonymous

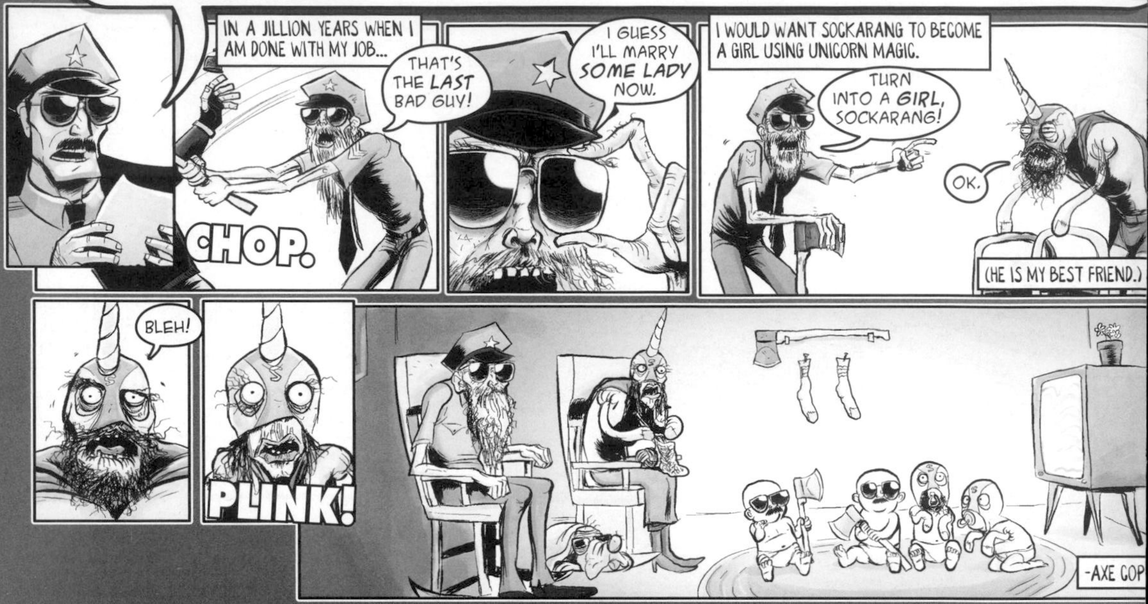
IN A JILLION YEARS WHEN I AM DONE WITH MY JOB...
THAT'S THE LAST BAD GUY!
CHOP.
I GUESS I'LL MARRY SOME LADY NOW.
I WOULD WANT SOCKARANG TO BECOME A GIRL USING UNICORN MAGIC.
TURN INTO A GIRL, SOCKARANG!
OK.
(HE IS MY BEST FRIEND.)
BLEH!
PLINK!
-AXE COP

ASK AXE COP

Q17: Dear Axe Cop,
Do you ever pray?

—Doug

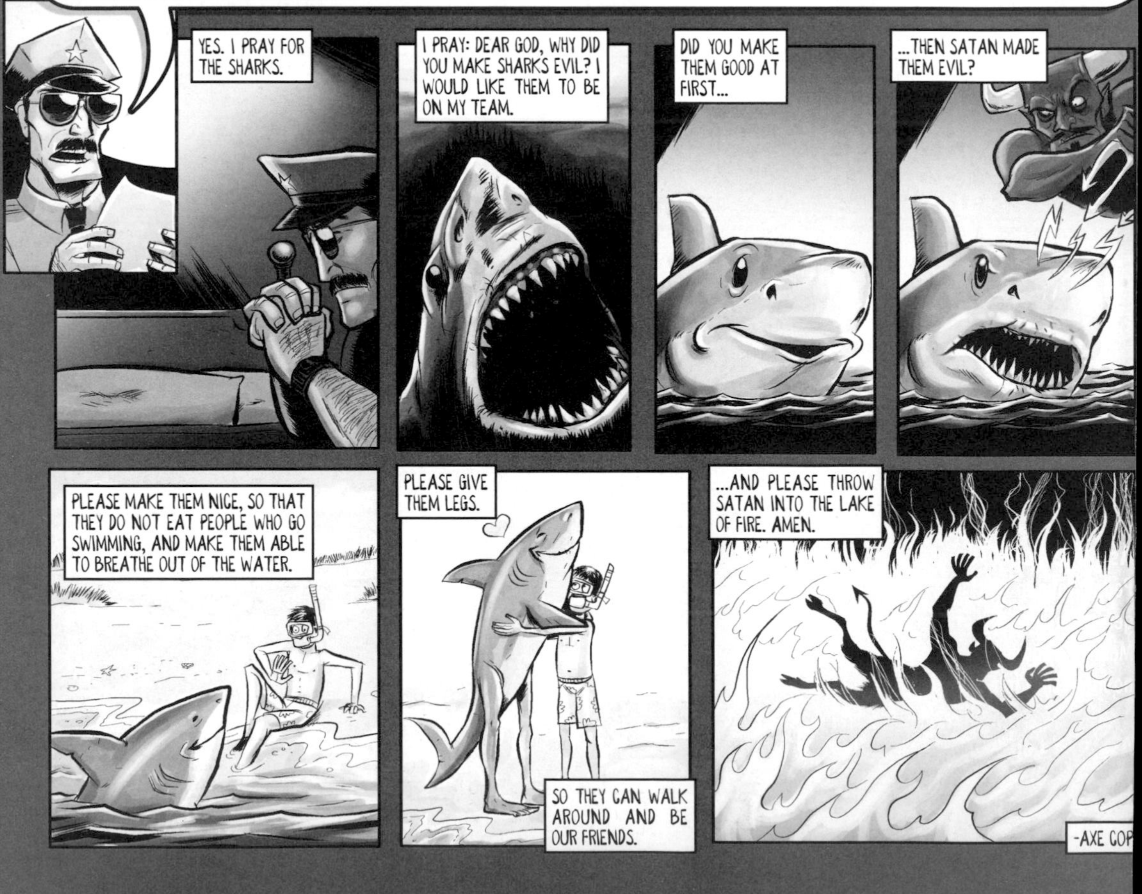
YES. I PRAY FOR THE SHARKS.
I PRAY: DEAR GOD, WHY DID YOU MAKE SHARKS EVIL? I WOULD LIKE THEM TO BE ON MY TEAM.
DID YOU MAKE THEM GOOD AT FIRST...
...THEN SATAN MADE THEM EVIL?
PLEASE MAKE THEM NICE, SO THAT THEY DO NOT EAT PEOPLE WHO GO SWIMMING, AND MAKE THEM ABLE TO BREATHE OUT OF THE WATER.
PLEASE GIVE THEM LEGS.
SO THEY CAN WALK AROUND AND BE OUR FRIENDS.
...AND PLEASE THROW SATAN INTO THE LAKE OF FIRE. AMEN.
-AXE COP

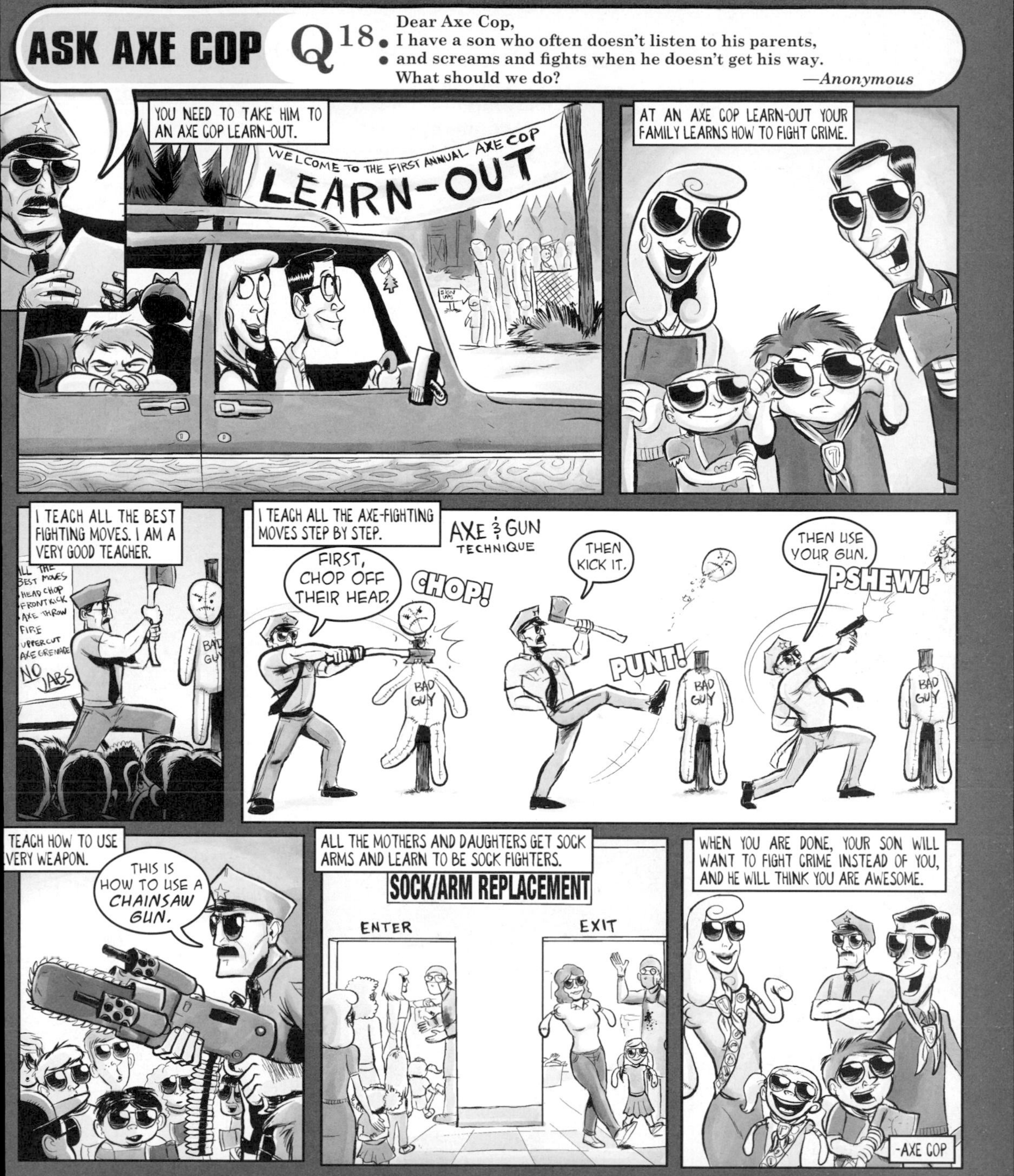
ASK AXE COP
Q18.
Dear Axe Cop,
I have a son who often doesn't listen to his parents, and screams and fights when he doesn't get his way. What should we do?
—Anonymous
YOU NEED TO TAKE HIM TO AN AXE COP LEARN-OUT.
WELCOME TO THE FIRST ANNUAL AXE COP LEARN-OUT
AT AN AXE COP LEARN-OUT YOUR FAMILY LEARNS HOW TO FIGHT CRIME.
I TEACH ALL THE BEST FIGHTING MOVES. I AM A VERY GOOD TEACHER.
ALL THE BEST MOVES
HEAD CHOP
FRONT KICK
AXE THROW
FIRE
UPPERCUT
AXE GRENADE
NO JABS
BAD GUY
I TEACH ALL THE AXE-FIGHTING MOVES STEP BY STEP.
AXE & GUN TECHNIQUE
FIRST, CHOP OFF THEIR HEAD.
CHOP!
BAD GUY
THEN KICK IT.
PUNT!
BAD GUY
THEN USE YOUR GUN.
PSHEW!
BAD GUY
I TEACH HOW TO USE EVERY WEAPON.
THIS IS HOW TO USE A CHAINSAW GUN.
ALL THE MOTHERS AND DAUGHTERS GET SOCK ARMS AND LEARN TO BE SOCK FIGHTERS.
SOCK/ARM REPLACEMENT
ENTER
EXIT
WHEN YOU ARE DONE, YOUR SON WILL WANT TO FIGHT CRIME INSTEAD OF YOU, AND HE WILL THINK YOU ARE AWESOME.
-AXE COP

Ask Axe Cop #16

People love to read into what Malachai comes up with. Whatever you get out of this one, I think it comes down to the simple idea that if Malachai has to spend the rest of his life with someone and he has no interest in females, he would rather spend it with his best friend.

Ask Axe Cop #17

This was actually a prayer Malachai came up with when we were talking about sharks one day, including the last panel. It was actually a pretty serious conversation. I loved it so much I made it into Axe Cop's prayer for the sharks.

Ask Axe Cop #18

I have never heard of a "learn-out" but I assume it is something Malachai has done at school. Whatever it is, ever since making this I have loved the idea of having a real annual "Axe Cop Learn-Out." Sort of like an Axe Cop convention, except I have no idea what anyone would do.

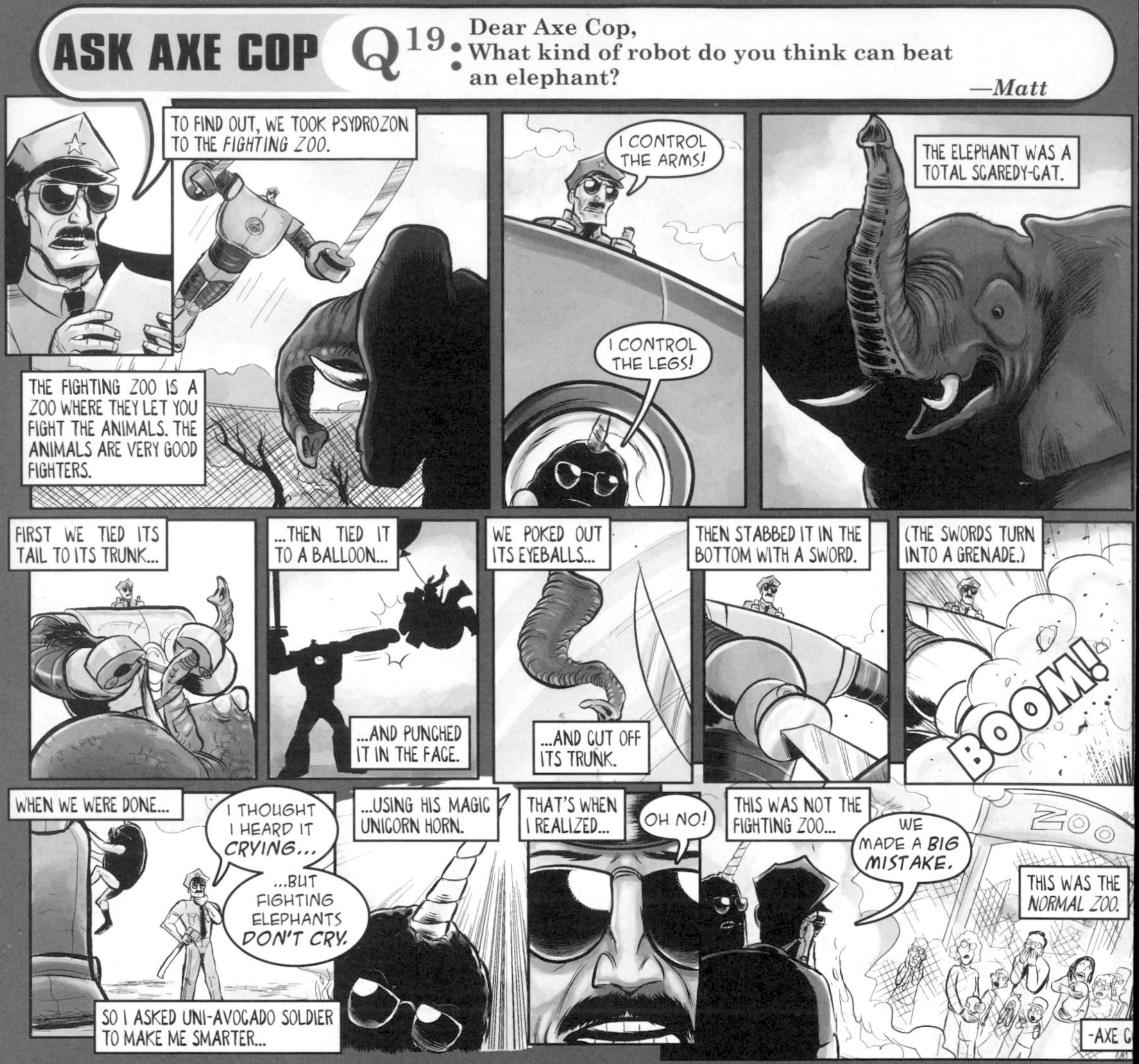
ASK AXE COP
Q19: Dear Axe Cop,
What kind of robot do you think can beat an elephant?
—Matt
TO FIND OUT, WE TOOK PSYDROZON TO THE FIGHTING ZOO.
THE FIGHTING ZOO IS A ZOO WHERE THEY LET YOU FIGHT THE ANIMALS. THE ANIMALS ARE VERY GOOD FIGHTERS.
I CONTROL THE ARMS!
I CONTROL THE LEGS!
THE ELEPHANT WAS A TOTAL SCAREDY-CAT.
FIRST WE TIED ITS TAIL TO ITS TRUNK...
...THEN TIED IT TO A BALLOON...
...AND PUNCHED IT IN THE FACE.
WE POKED OUT ITS EYEBALLS...
...AND CUT OFF ITS TRUNK.
THEN STABBED IT IN THE BOTTOM WITH A SWORD.
(THE SWORDS TURN INTO A GRENADE.)
BOOM!
WHEN WE WERE DONE...
I THOUGHT I HEARD IT CRYING...
...BUT FIGHTING ELEPHANTS DON'T CRY.
SO I ASKED UNI-AVOCADO SOLDIER TO MAKE ME SMARTER...
...USING HIS MAGIC UNICORN HORN.
THAT'S WHEN I REALIZED...
OH NO!
THIS WAS NOT THE FIGHTING ZOO...
WE MADE A BIG MISTAKE.
THIS WAS THE NORMAL ZOO.

Ask Axe Cop #19

This was one of the first questions Malachai answered, but he never gave me a good ending, so I kept putting it off. He basically just came up with all these attacks Axe Cop used on an elephant. Every time we would get on the phone he would ask where the elephant one was. I kept telling him I needed more material for it. Somehow after lots of discussion and in a roundabout way, Malachai came up with this hilarious and tragic ending. In fact, Axe Cop was supposed to cry on this one too but I didn't want to overdo the crying so close to the last strip so I didn't emphasize it. After all that waiting, Malachai finally got his elephant episode and he didn't like it because it was sad.

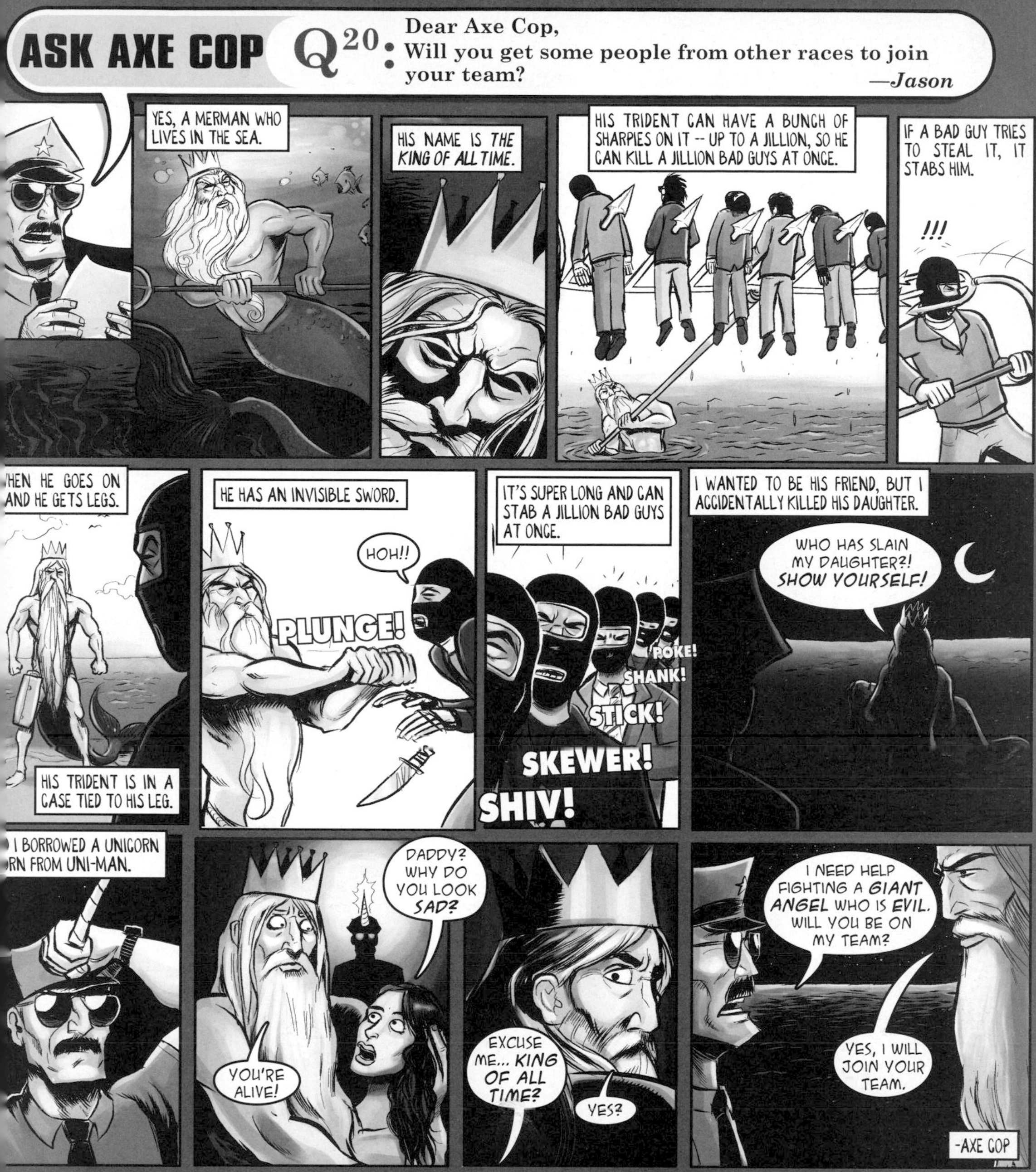
ASK AXE COP
Q20:
Dear Axe Cop,
Will you get some people from other races to join your team?
—Jason
YES, A MERMAN WHO LIVES IN THE SEA.
HIS NAME IS THE KING OF ALL TIME.
HIS TRIDENT CAN HAVE A BUNCH OF SHARPIES ON IT -- UP TO A JILLION, SO HE CAN KILL A JILLION BAD GUYS AT ONCE.
IF A BAD GUY TRIES TO STEAL IT, IT STABS HIM.
!!!
HEN HE GOES ON
AND HE GETS LEGS.
HIS TRIDENT IS IN A CASE TIED TO HIS LEG.
HE HAS AN INVISIBLE SWORD.
HOH!!
PLUNGE!
IT'S SUPER LONG AND CAN STAB A JILLION BAD GUYS AT ONCE.
POKE!
SHANK!
STICK!
SKEWER!
SHIV!
I WANTED TO BE HIS FRIEND, BUT I ACCIDENTALLY KILLED HIS DAUGHTER.
WHO HAS SLAIN MY DAUGHTER?! SHOW YOURSELF!
I BORROWED A UNICORN
RN FROM UNI-MAN.
DADDY? WHY DO YOU LOOK SAD?
YOU'RE ALIVE!
EXCUSE ME... KING OF ALL TIME?
YES?
I NEED HELP FIGHTING A GIANT ANGEL WHO IS EVIL. WILL YOU BE ON MY TEAM?
YES, I WILL JOIN YOUR TEAM.
-AXE COP

Ask Axe Cop #20

A guy asked me if there would be any black characters so that he would have something to dress up as for Halloween. I asked Malachai if he could make a black character and he said, "No, a peach merman named the King of All Time."

Malachai called me the day the mermaid episode went up and told me he didn't want the mermaid to die anymore. I told him he can do whatever he wants; it's his story. He can bring her back to life if he wants. So he told me he wanted Axe Cop to bring her back to life because she was the King of All Time's daughter, and to add him to his team.

ASK AXE COP

Q²¹: Dear Axe Cop,
I was wondering what you did before you were Axe Cop?

—*Alex*

I LIVED IN A HOUSE WITH NO FRIENDS, NO TV, NO COMPUTER, AND I COULDN'T PLAY VIDEO GAMES.

MY HOUSE ONLY HAD A BED, A TABLE, AND FOOD.

I WOULD SLEEP ALL NIGHT...

...AND EAT ALL DAY.

NOMF NOM NUM NARME!

I JUST ATE AND ATE...

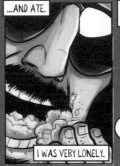

...AND ATE.

I WAS VERY LONELY.

THEN ONE DAY A BAD GUY BROKE INTO MY HOUSE.

GIVE ME ALL YOUR *MONEY.*

I ONLY HAVE *FOOD.*

ALL RIGHT, GIVE ME *FOOD.*

JUST THEN, A MAGIC APPLE CAME OUT OF MY HAND.

IT WAS THE APPLE I JUST ATE!

SO I GAVE IT TO HIM.

THANKSH NOMF NOMSH NUMSH

HE DIED BECAUSE IT WAS POISON.

BLEH!

WHATEVER I ATE CAME OUT OF MY HAND AS POISON TO KILL BAD GUYS.

THAT WAS A *SECRET ATTACK!*

THAT'S WHEN I DECI[...] WANTED TO BE A COP [...] COULD KILL BAD GUYS [...] DAY AND NIGHT.

—AXE[...]

▲ **Ask Axe Cop #21**
Again, we learn that Axe Cop is kind of a psycho and his background is pretty questionable. He apparently had an eating disorder and lived a very lonely life. This also answers the question of where he gets all his poison. He just eats something, then a poisonous version comes out of his hand.

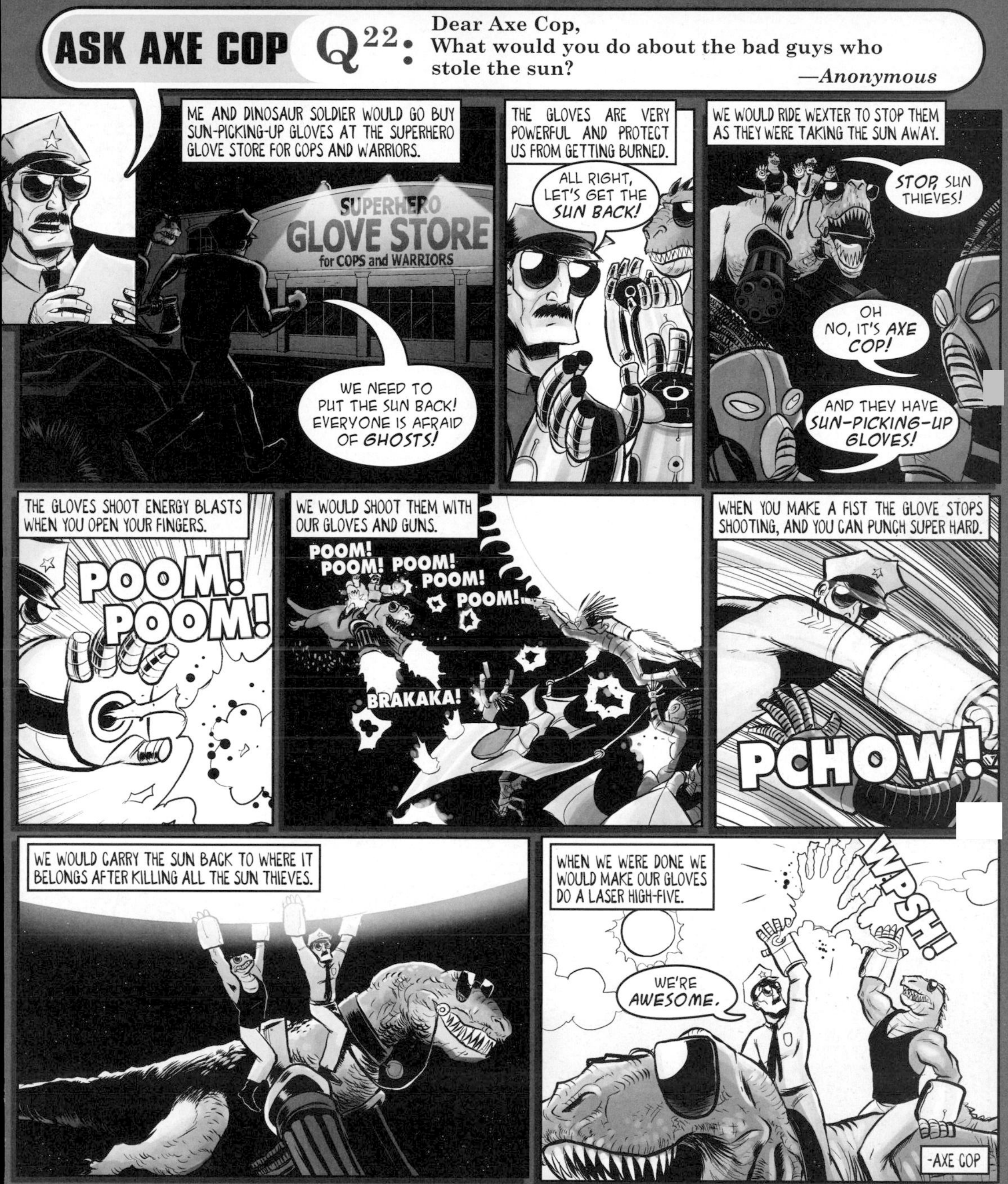
ASK AXE COP
Q22:
Dear Axe Cop,
What would you do about the bad guys who stole the sun?
—Anonymous
ME AND DINOSAUR SOLDIER WOULD GO BUY SUN-PICKING-UP GLOVES AT THE SUPERHERO GLOVE STORE FOR COPS AND WARRIORS.
SUPERHERO GLOVE STORE for COPS and WARRIORS
WE NEED TO PUT THE SUN BACK! EVERYONE IS AFRAID OF GHOSTS!
THE GLOVES ARE VERY POWERFUL AND PROTECT US FROM GETTING BURNED.
ALL RIGHT, LET'S GET THE SUN BACK!
WE WOULD RIDE WEXTER TO STOP THEM AS THEY WERE TAKING THE SUN AWAY.
STOP, SUN THIEVES!
OH NO, IT'S AXE COP!
AND THEY HAVE SUN-PICKING-UP GLOVES!
THE GLOVES SHOOT ENERGY BLASTS WHEN YOU OPEN YOUR FINGERS.
POOM! POOM!
WE WOULD SHOOT THEM WITH OUR GLOVES AND GUNS.
POOM! POOM! POOM! POOM! POOM!
BRAKAKA!
WHEN YOU MAKE A FIST THE GLOVE STOPS SHOOTING, AND YOU CAN PUNCH SUPER HARD.
PCHOW!
WE WOULD CARRY THE SUN BACK TO WHERE IT BELONGS AFTER KILLING ALL THE SUN THIEVES.
WHEN WE WERE DONE WE WOULD MAKE OUR GLOVES DO A LASER HIGH-FIVE.
WPSH!
WE'RE AWESOME.
-AXE COP

Ask Axe Cop #22

Another very fun episode. Malachai didn't give me a description for the sun thieves so I had fun designing them. "Laser High-Five" has become a staple Axe Cop saying among *Axe Cop* fans.

ASK AXE COP
Q23: Dear Axe Cop,
What's the coolest way you've ever killed someone?
Yours truly,
—Rom Maniac
THERE HAVE BEEN TWO WAYS I RANK THE COOLEST.
KNOCK! KNOCK!
AXE COP! ARE YOU HERE TO FIGHT?!
NOPE, I JUST BROUGHT YOU THIS FLOWER.
SMELL IT. IT SMELLS GREAT.
OH OK, THANKS... SNIFF SNIFF
KOFF!! BLECH!! GUH!!
THAT'S CALLED A POISONOUS FLOWER ATTACK.
THE OTHER WAY IS VERY SIMILAR.
KNOCK! KNOCK!
AXE COP! HOW DARE YOU SHOW UP AT MY HOUSE!
I JUST WANTED TO GIVE YOU THIS FLOWER.
GIVE IT A SNIFF.
HMM. OK, THANKS. SNIFF SNIFF
WAIT, WHAT...?
THAT'S CALLED A POISONOUS KID FLOWER ATTACK.
BLEH!!
-AXE C

Ask Axe Cop #23
Any time I asked Malachai for a good way to kill a bad guy, trickery and poison usually came into play. Usually this is a bad guy method, but I think Malachai likes how simple it is. There is no struggle, no danger . . . just hand it to them and they die. "Here you go, have some death." Why turn them into a kid first? I just trust Axe Cop on that one.

Ask Axe Cop #24
I tried to give Malachai a brief history of who Abe Lincoln was before we started this one and he basically ignored it. He also, for some reason, thought Abraham Lincoln was a girl. After I explained he was a man, Malachai said that Axe Cop would think he's a girl and proceeded to give me one of the most insane answers yet. If there is ever an *Axe Cop* video game I would love to be able to summon "Abraham Lincoln: Explosion God" as a special attack.

Q24: Dear Axe Cop,
Did you ever shake hands with Abraham Lincoln?
Anonymous

NOT EXACTLY...

I WISH FOR ABRAHAM LINCOLN TO COME BE MY **WIFE.**

I WAS A LITTLE SHOCKED WHEN HE APPEARED.

...HELLO.

WHAT THE **HECK?** I THOUGHT ABRAHAM LINCOLN WAS A **GIRL!**

WHO AM I KIDDING? I HAVE TOO MANY **BAD GUYS** TO KILL, EVEN IF YOU **WERE** A GIRL. I CAN'T GET **MARRIED!**

HMM... THERE **MAY** STILL BE A WAY.

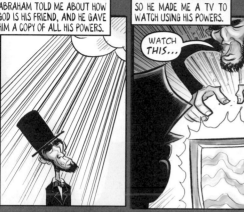

ABRAHAM TOLD ME ABOUT HOW GOD IS HIS FRIEND, AND HE GAVE HIM A COPY OF ALL HIS POWERS.

SO HE MADE ME A TV TO WATCH USING HIS POWERS.

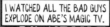

WATCH **THIS...**

THEN, HE TURNED INTO...

ABRAHAM LINCOLN: **EXPLOSION GOD**

I PUT A **BOMB** INSIDE EVERY BAD GUY!

SO EVERY BAD GUY DIDN'T EVEN KNOW IT, BUT THERE WAS A BOMB INSIDE OF THEM FROM ABRAHAM LINCOLN.

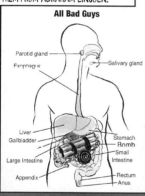

All Bad Guys

Parotid gland
Esophagus
Salivary gland
Liver
Gallbladder
Stomach
Bomb
Small Intestine
Large Intestine
Rectum
Appendix
Anus

I WATCHED ALL THE BAD GUYS EXPLODE ON ABE'S MAGIC TV.

MUNCH MUNCH MUNCH

PSHEW! PFSK

POPCORN

WITH ALL THE BAD GUYS EXPLODED, WE WERE FREE TO MARRY, SO I USED MY MAGIC UNICORN HORN...

I WISH FOR ABRAHAM LINCOLN TO BE A **GIRL.**

THEN WE GOT MARRIED AND LIVED HAPPILY EVER AFTER...

...UNTIL I GOT REALLY BORED.

I MISS FIGHTING **BAD GUYS.**

-AXE COP

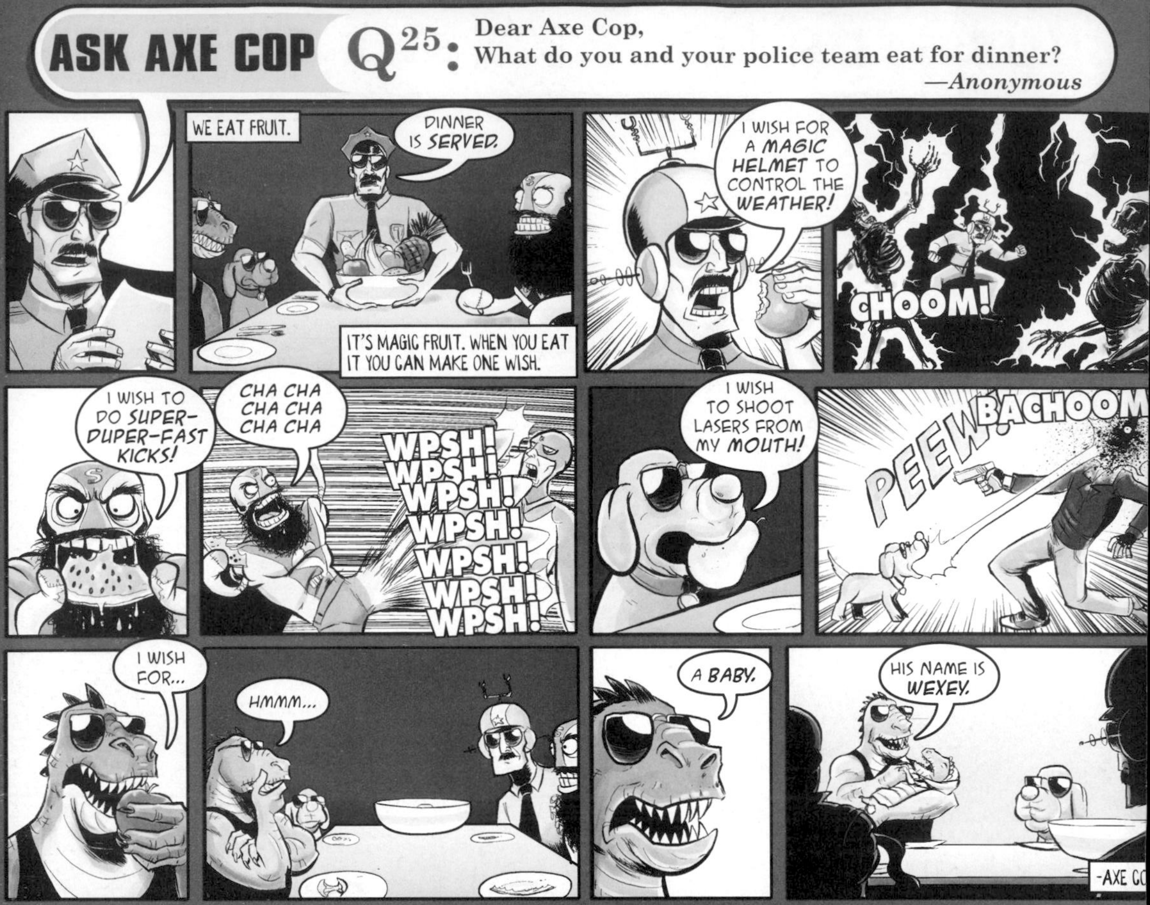
ASK AXE COP
Q25: Dear Axe Cop,
What do you and your police team eat for dinner?
—Anonymous
WE EAT FRUIT.
DINNER IS SERVED.
IT'S MAGIC FRUIT. WHEN YOU EAT IT YOU CAN MAKE ONE WISH.
I WISH FOR A MAGIC HELMET TO CONTROL THE WEATHER!
CHOOM!
I WISH TO DO SUPER-DUPER-FAST KICKS!
CHA CHA CHA CHA CHA CHA
WPSH! WPSH! WPSH! WPSH! WPSH! WPSH! WPSH!
I WISH TO SHOOT LASERS FROM MY MOUTH!
PEEW! BACHOOM
I WISH FOR...
HMMM...
A BABY.
HIS NAME IS WEXEY.
-AXE CO

Ask Axe Cop #25

Many people assume that this is Wexter's origin story. It's not. Dinosaur Soldier wishes for a baby and names it Wexey; that's it. It has no relation to Wexter. It will be interesting to see if Wexey ever shows up again. As for the other wishes . . . I can only assume they wear off after the food is digested.

Malachai loves the concept of food that gives you a wish. He once told me he had a dream he was fishing on a boat and he caught a wishing fish. He couldn't remember what he wished for, but probably not a baby.

Part Five: The Moon Warriors

Episodes 9–22

The Moon Warriors were characters Malachai was talking about all the way back during my Christmas visit. Malachai kept telling me he had made up new characters called the Moon Warriors. They are ninjas who live on the moon. They are awake at night and they go to sleep in the morning.

All significant *Axe Cop* characters come in pairs. This is because usually when we are writing, Malachai is not saying character names. Usually he is saying, "you and me." He has to think in terms of who we are so we can act it out. Usually he refers to me as Axe Cop and to himself as Dinosaur Soldier. In the Moon Warriors, he is Vampire Wolfer and I am Fire Slicer. In a yet-to-be-released story I even did this with bad guys. This worked amazingly. Having Malachai imagine us as bad guys helped him to create some very formidable bad guys, not quite as dumb and easy to kill as a typical *Axe Cop* bad guy.

The first few pages of the Moon Warriors sort of went viral all on their own. It was the first time we did not have Axe Cop in the story for a few pages and it was a whole new introduction to brand-new characters. Malachai would get so excited when he would tell me about the Moon Warriors; I could hear him running around his room in circles and jumping on his bed as he described their awesome moves. He was constantly trying to layer on the awesome, and as he did they quickly became Vampire Ninja Werewolf Wizards . . .
from the Moon.

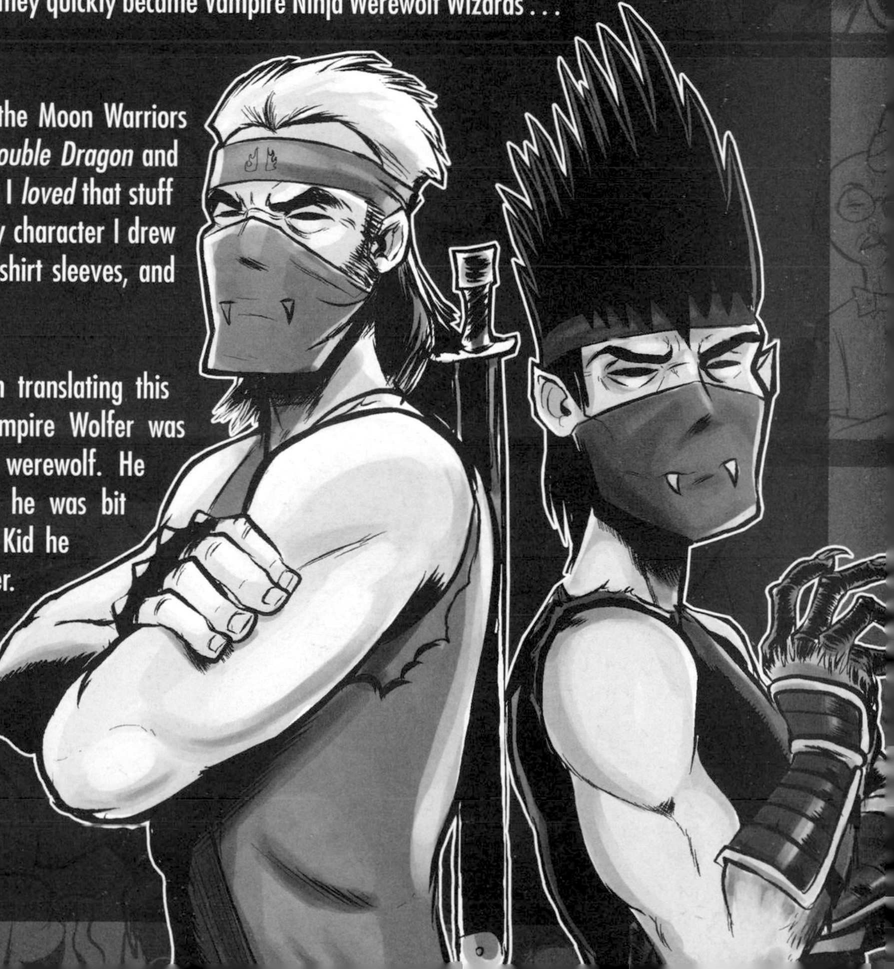

If it isn't obvious enough, the Moon Warriors are my own little nod to *Double Dragon* and old Capcom fighting games. I *loved* that stuff when I was a kid, and every character I drew had fingerless gloves, torn shirt sleeves, and often a mullet.

I did make one mistake in translating this story, and that is that Vampire Wolfer was always a vampire and a werewolf. He was born that way. When he was bit by the Vampire Man Baby Kid he got *double* vampire power. Malachai informed me of this mistake after the page went up online.

—Ethan

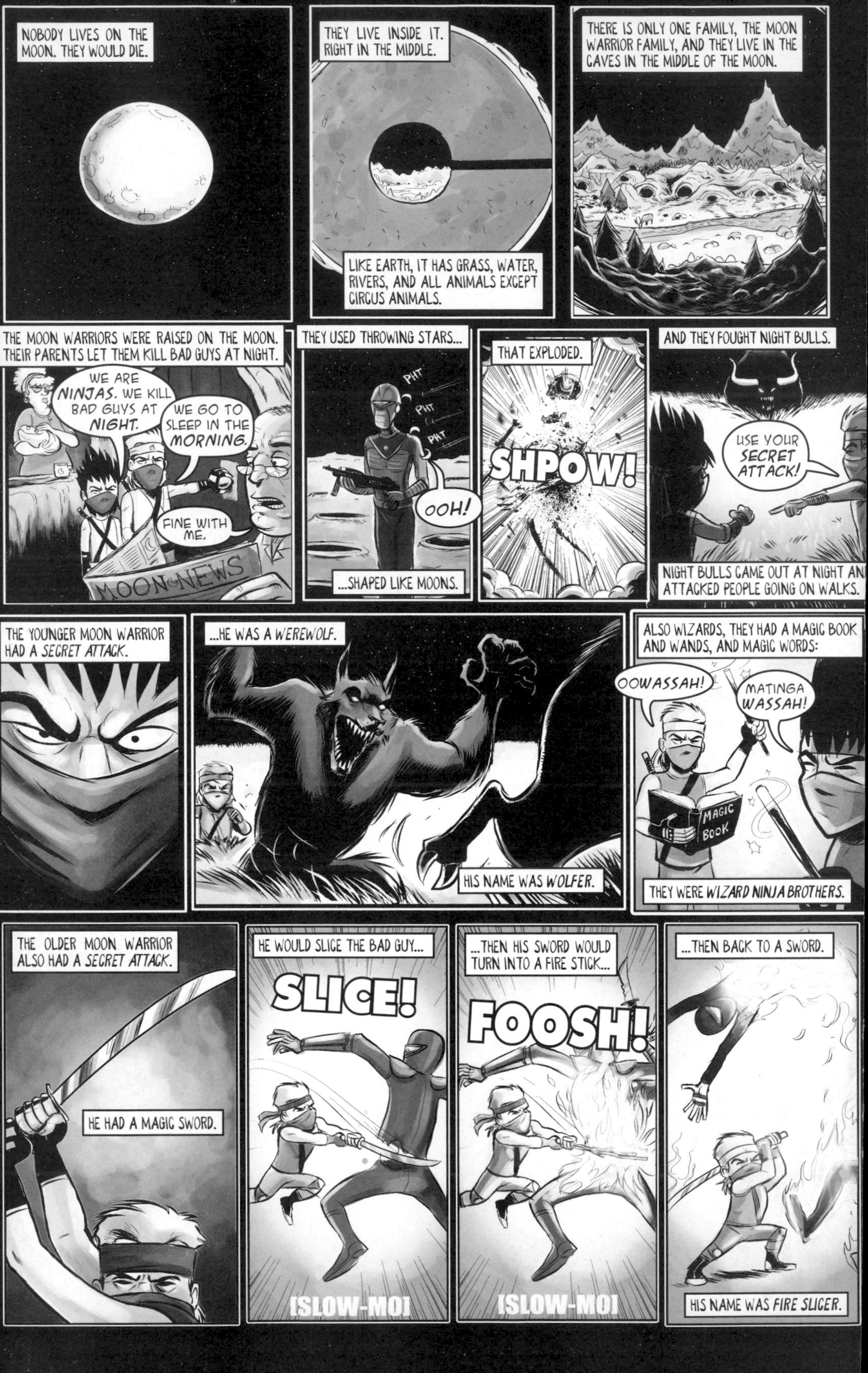
NOBODY LIVES ON THE MOON. THEY WOULD DIE.
THEY LIVE INSIDE IT. RIGHT IN THE MIDDLE.
LIKE EARTH, IT HAS GRASS, WATER, RIVERS, AND ALL ANIMALS EXCEPT CIRCUS ANIMALS.
THERE IS ONLY ONE FAMILY, THE MOON WARRIOR FAMILY, AND THEY LIVE IN THE CAVES IN THE MIDDLE OF THE MOON.
THE MOON WARRIORS WERE RAISED ON THE MOON. THEIR PARENTS LET THEM KILL BAD GUYS AT NIGHT.
WE ARE NINJAS. WE KILL BAD GUYS AT NIGHT.
WE GO TO SLEEP IN THE MORNING.
FINE WITH ME.
MOON NEWS
THEY USED THROWING STARS...
PHT
PHT
PHT
OOH!
...SHAPED LIKE MOONS.
THAT EXPLODED.
SHPOW!
AND THEY FOUGHT NIGHT BULLS.
USE YOUR SECRET ATTACK!
NIGHT BULLS CAME OUT AT NIGHT AN ATTACKED PEOPLE GOING ON WALKS.
THE YOUNGER MOON WARRIOR HAD A SECRET ATTACK.
...HE WAS A WEREWOLF.
HIS NAME WAS WOLFER.
ALSO WIZARDS, THEY HAD A MAGIC BOOK AND WANDS, AND MAGIC WORDS:
OOWASSAH!
MATINGA WASSAH!
MAGIC BOOK
THEY WERE WIZARD NINJA BROTHERS.
THE OLDER MOON WARRIOR ALSO HAD A SECRET ATTACK.
HE HAD A MAGIC SWORD.
HE WOULD SLICE THE BAD GUY...
SLICE!
[SLOW-MO]
...THEN HIS SWORD WOULD TURN INTO A FIRE STICK...
FOOSH!
[SLOW-MO]
...THEN BACK TO A SWORD.
HIS NAME WAS FIRE SLICER.

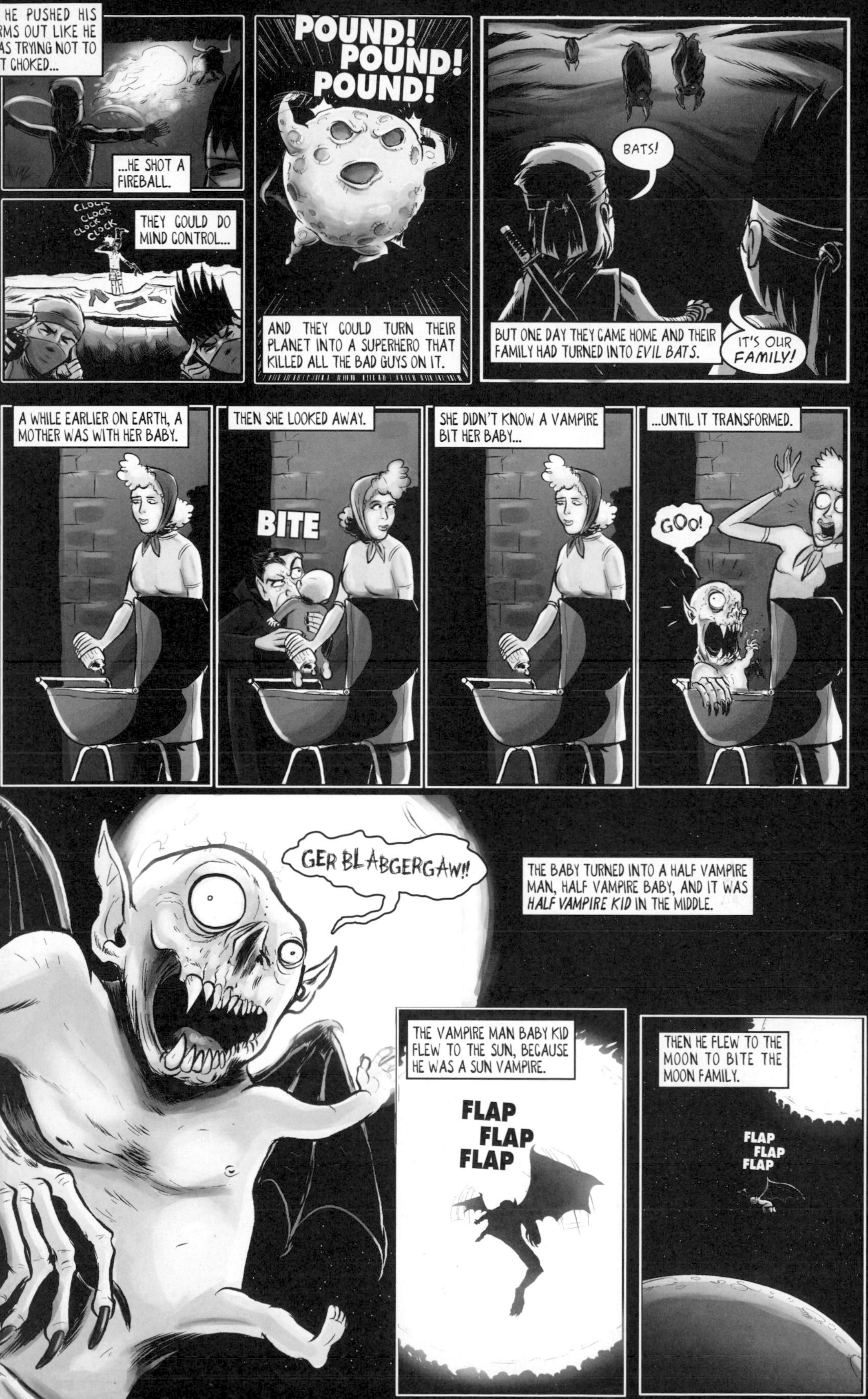

HE PUSHED HIS
RMS OUT LIKE HE
AS TRYING NOT TO
T CHOKED...
...HE SHOT A FIREBALL.
CLOCK CLOCK CLOCK CLOCK
THEY COULD DO MIND CONTROL...
POUND! POUND! POUND!
AND THEY COULD TURN THEIR PLANET INTO A SUPERHERO THAT KILLED ALL THE BAD GUYS ON IT.
BATS!
BUT ONE DAY THEY CAME HOME AND THEIR FAMILY HAD TURNED INTO EVIL BATS.
IT'S OUR FAMILY!
A WHILE EARLIER ON EARTH, A MOTHER WAS WITH HER BABY.
THEN SHE LOOKED AWAY.
BITE
SHE DIDN'T KNOW A VAMPIRE BIT HER BABY...
...UNTIL IT TRANSFORMED.
GOO!
GER BLABGERGAW!!
THE BABY TURNED INTO A HALF VAMPIRE MAN, HALF VAMPIRE BABY, AND IT WAS HALF VAMPIRE KID IN THE MIDDLE.
THE VAMPIRE MAN BABY KID FLEW TO THE SUN, BECAUSE HE WAS A SUN VAMPIRE.
FLAP FLAP FLAP
THEN HE FLEW TO THE MOON TO BITE THE MOON FAMILY.
FLAP FLAP FLAP

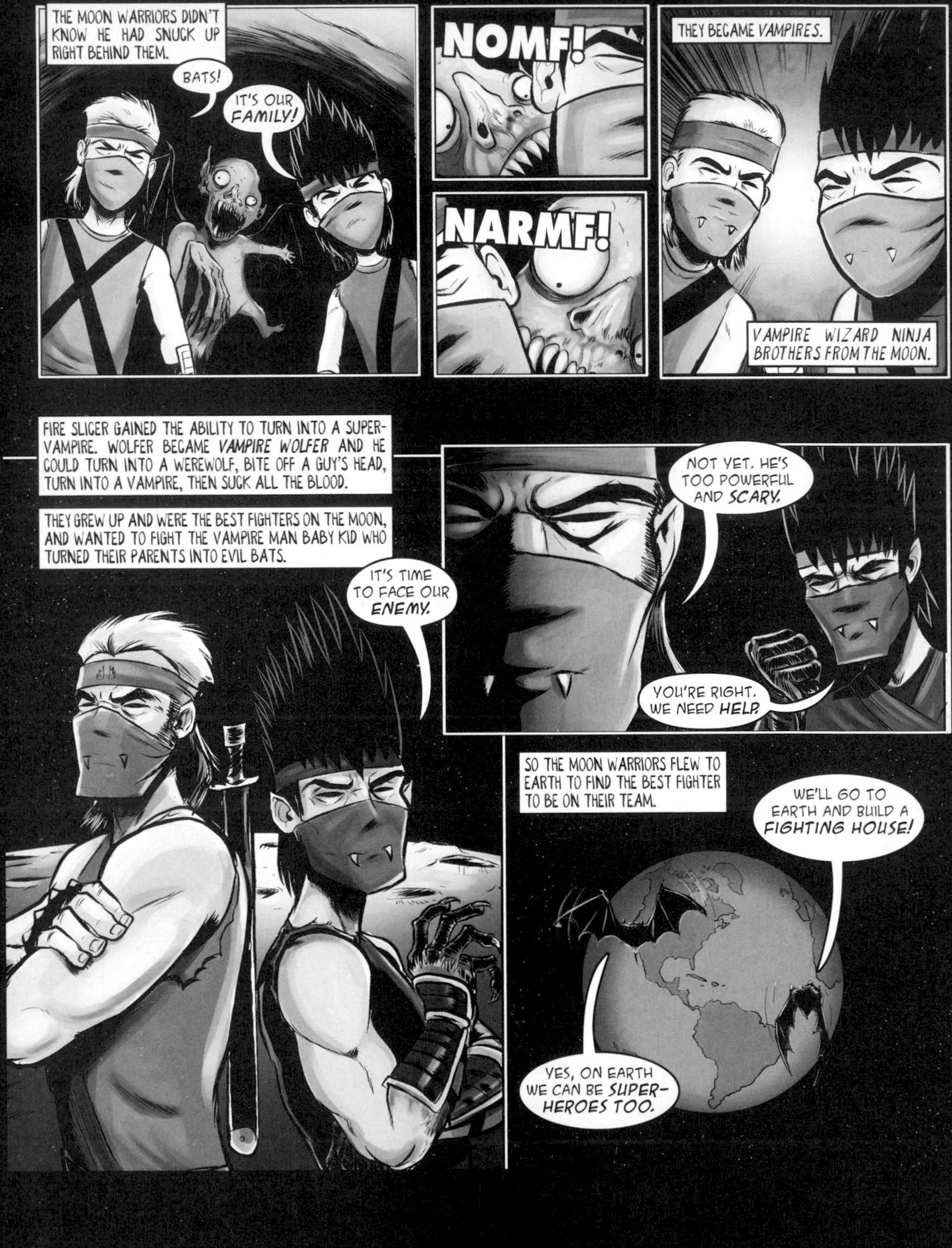
THE MOON WARRIORS DIDN'T KNOW HE HAD SNUCK UP RIGHT BEHIND THEM.
BATS!
IT'S OUR FAMILY!
NOMF!
NARMF!
THEY BECAME VAMPIRES.
VAMPIRE WIZARD NINJA BROTHERS FROM THE MOON.
FIRE SLICER GAINED THE ABILITY TO TURN INTO A SUPER-VAMPIRE. WOLFER BECAME VAMPIRE WOLFER AND HE COULD TURN INTO A WEREWOLF, BITE OFF A GUY'S HEAD, TURN INTO A VAMPIRE, THEN SUCK ALL THE BLOOD.
THEY GREW UP AND WERE THE BEST FIGHTERS ON THE MOON, AND WANTED TO FIGHT THE VAMPIRE MAN BABY KID WHO TURNED THEIR PARENTS INTO EVIL BATS.
IT'S TIME TO FACE OUR ENEMY.
NOT YET. HE'S TOO POWERFUL AND SCARY.
YOU'RE RIGHT. WE NEED HELP.
SO THE MOON WARRIORS FLEW TO EARTH TO FIND THE BEST FIGHTER TO BE ON THEIR TEAM.
WE'LL GO TO EARTH AND BUILD A FIGHTING HOUSE!
YES, ON EARTH WE CAN BE SUPER-HEROES TOO.

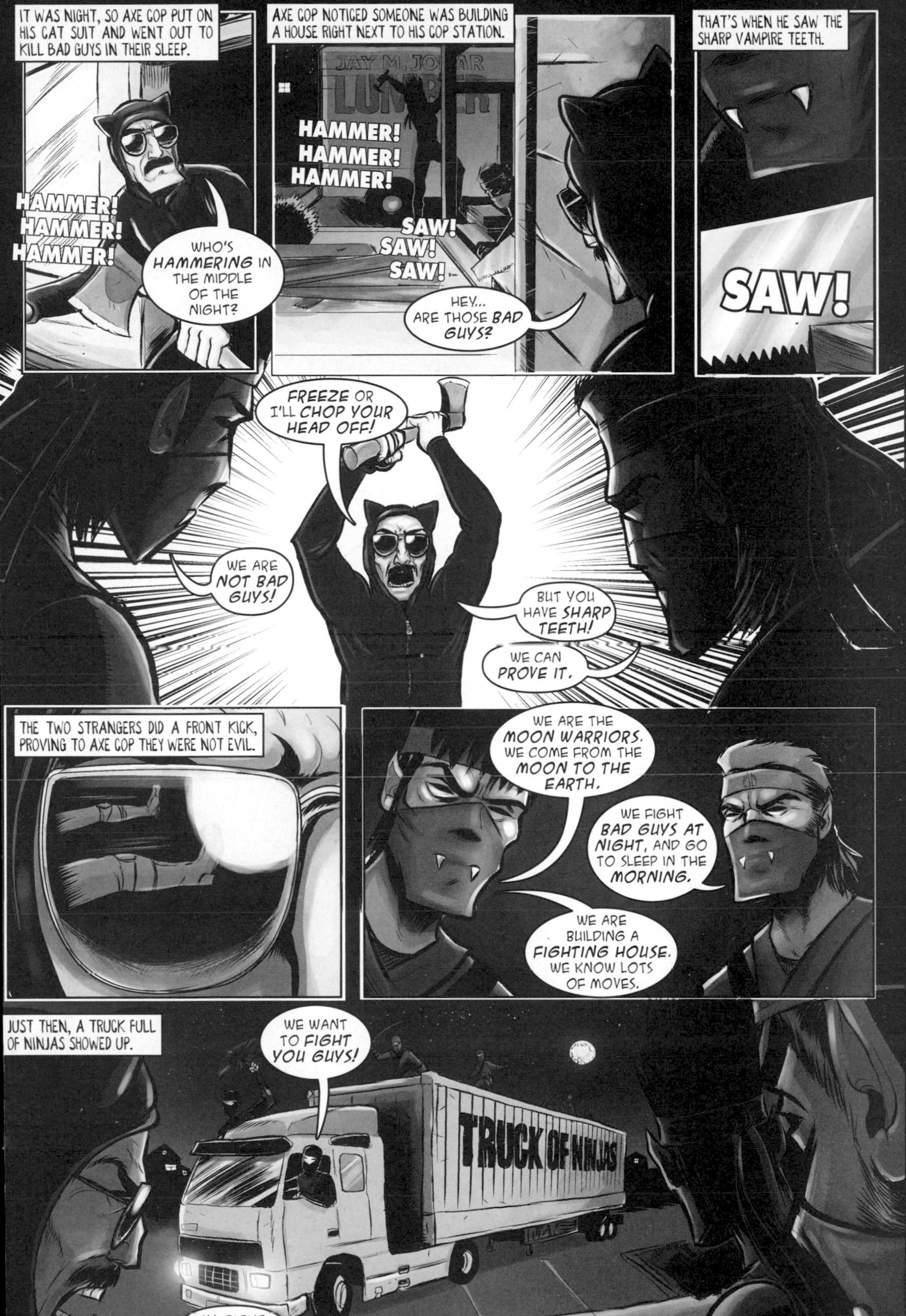
IT WAS NIGHT, SO AXE COP PUT ON HIS CAT SUIT AND WENT OUT TO KILL BAD GUYS IN THEIR SLEEP.
HAMMER! HAMMER! HAMMER!
WHO'S HAMMERING IN THE MIDDLE OF THE NIGHT?
AXE COP NOTICED SOMEONE WAS BUILDING A HOUSE RIGHT NEXT TO HIS COP STATION.
JAY M. JOHAR LUMBER
HAMMER! HAMMER! HAMMER!
SAW! SAW! SAW!
HEY... ARE THOSE BAD GUYS?
THAT'S WHEN HE SAW THE SHARP VAMPIRE TEETH.
SAW!
FREEZE OR I'LL CHOP YOUR HEAD OFF!
WE ARE NOT BAD GUYS!
BUT YOU HAVE SHARP TEETH!
WE CAN PROVE IT.
THE TWO STRANGERS DID A FRONT KICK, PROVING TO AXE COP THEY WERE NOT EVIL.
WE ARE THE MOON WARRIORS. WE COME FROM THE MOON TO THE EARTH.
WE FIGHT BAD GUYS AT NIGHT, AND GO TO SLEEP IN THE MORNING.
WE ARE BUILDING A FIGHTING HOUSE. WE KNOW LOTS OF MOVES.
JUST THEN, A TRUCK FULL OF NINJAS SHOWED UP.
WE WANT TO FIGHT YOU GUYS!
TRUCK OF NINJAS
ALL RIGHT, GUYS, SHOW ME ALL YOUR MOVES.

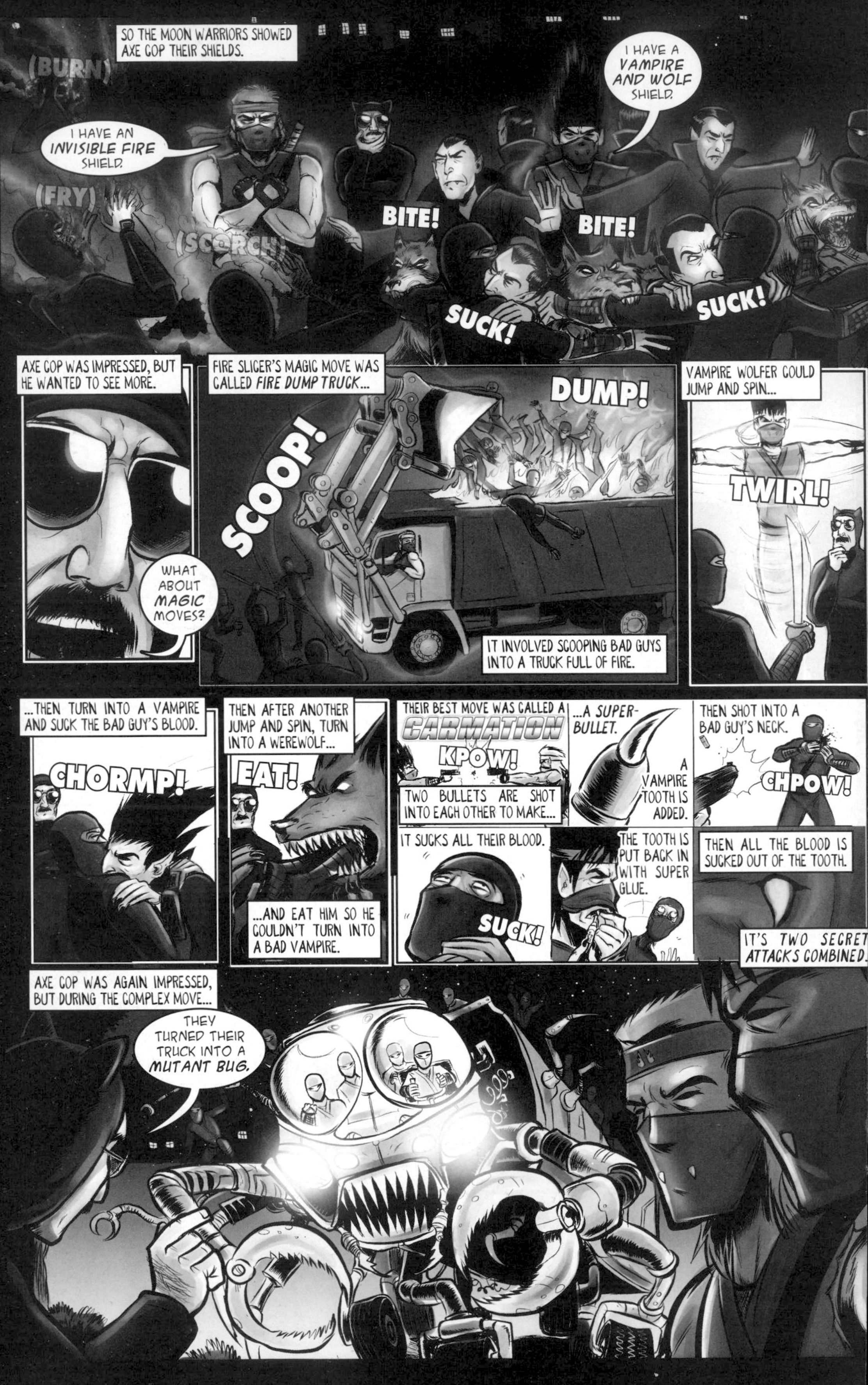

SO THE MOON WARRIORS SHOWED AXE COP THEIR SHIELDS.
(BURN)
I HAVE AN INVISIBLE FIRE SHIELD.
(FRY)
(SCORCH)
I HAVE A VAMPIRE AND WOLF SHIELD.
BITE!
BITE!
SUCK!
SUCK!
AXE COP WAS IMPRESSED, BUT HE WANTED TO SEE MORE.
WHAT ABOUT MAGIC MOVES?
FIRE SLICER'S MAGIC MOVE WAS CALLED FIRE DUMP TRUCK...
SCOOP!
DUMP!
IT INVOLVED SCOOPING BAD GUYS INTO A TRUCK FULL OF FIRE.
VAMPIRE WOLFER COULD JUMP AND SPIN...
TWIRL!
...THEN TURN INTO A VAMPIRE AND SUCK THE BAD GUY'S BLOOD.
CHORMP!
THEN AFTER ANOTHER JUMP AND SPIN, TURN INTO A WEREWOLF...
EAT!
...AND EAT HIM SO HE COULDN'T TURN INTO A BAD VAMPIRE.
THEIR BEST MOVE WAS CALLED A
CARMATION
KPOW!
TWO BULLETS ARE SHOT INTO EACH OTHER TO MAKE...
...A SUPER-BULLET.
A VAMPIRE TOOTH IS ADDED.
THEN SHOT INTO A BAD GUY'S NECK.
CHPOW!
IT SUCKS ALL THEIR BLOOD.
SUCK!
THE TOOTH IS PUT BACK IN WITH SUPER GLUE.
THEN ALL THE BLOOD IS SUCKED OUT OF THE TOOTH.
IT'S TWO SECRET ATTACKS COMBINED.
AXE COP WAS AGAIN IMPRESSED, BUT DURING THE COMPLEX MOVE...
THEY TURNED THEIR TRUCK INTO A MUTANT BUG.

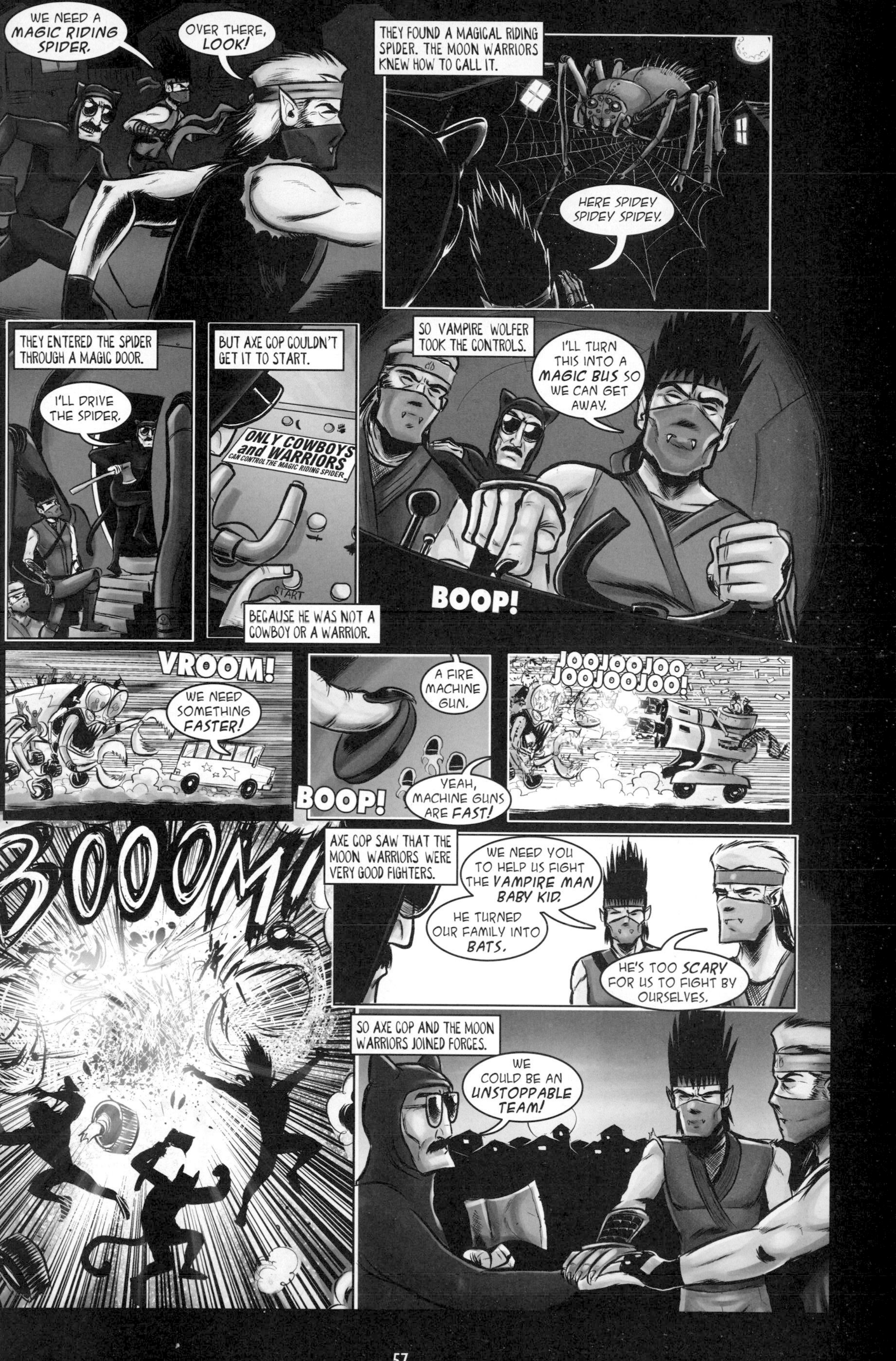
WE NEED A MAGIC RIDING SPIDER.
OVER THERE, LOOK!
THEY FOUND A MAGICAL RIDING SPIDER. THE MOON WARRIORS KNEW HOW TO CALL IT.
HERE SPIDEY SPIDEY SPIDEY.
THEY ENTERED THE SPIDER THROUGH A MAGIC DOOR.
I'LL DRIVE THE SPIDER.
BUT AXE COP COULDN'T GET IT TO START.
ONLY COWBOYS and WARRIORS CAN CONTROL THE MAGIC RIDING SPIDER.
START
BECAUSE HE WAS NOT A COWBOY OR A WARRIOR.
SO VAMPIRE WOLFER TOOK THE CONTROLS.
I'LL TURN THIS INTO A MAGIC BUS SO WE CAN GET AWAY.
BOOP!
VROOM!
WE NEED SOMETHING FASTER!
A FIRE MACHINE GUN.
BOOP!
YEAH, MACHINE GUNS ARE FAST!
JOOJOOJOO JOOJOOJOO!
BOOOM!
AXE COP SAW THAT THE MOON WARRIORS WERE VERY GOOD FIGHTERS.
WE NEED YOU TO HELP US FIGHT THE VAMPIRE MAN BABY KID.
HE TURNED OUR FAMILY INTO BATS.
HE'S TOO SCARY FOR US TO FIGHT BY OURSELVES.
SO AXE COP AND THE MOON WARRIORS JOINED FORCES.
WE COULD BE AN UNSTOPPABLE TEAM!

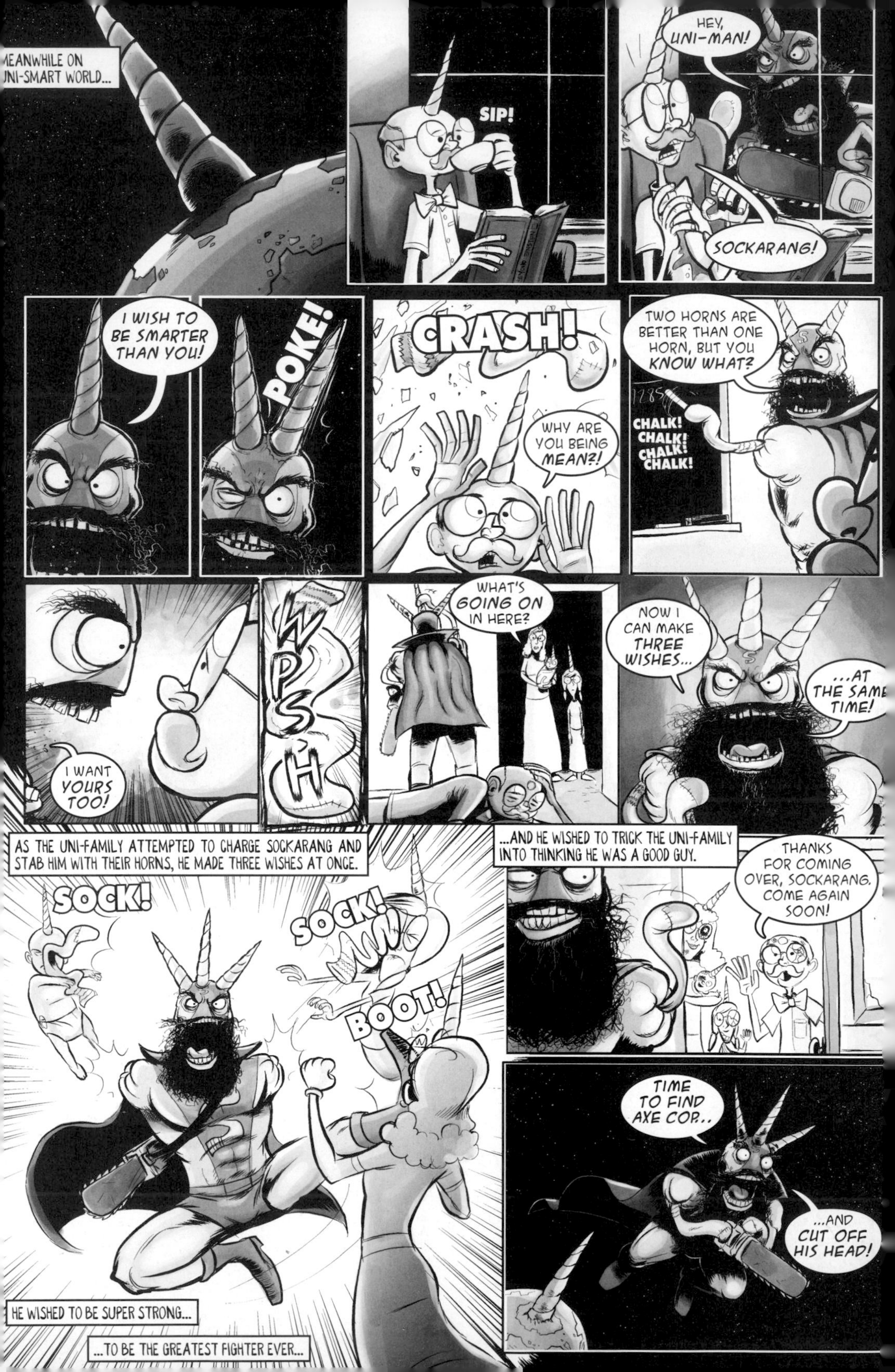
MEANWHILE ON
UNI-SMART WORLD...
SIP!
HEY, UNI-MAN!
SOCKARANG!
I WISH TO BE SMARTER THAN YOU!
POKE!
CRASH!
WHY ARE YOU BEING MEAN?!
TWO HORNS ARE BETTER THAN ONE HORN, BUT YOU KNOW WHAT?
CHALK! CHALK! CHALK! CHALK!
I WANT YOURS TOO!
WPSH
WHAT'S GOING ON IN HERE?
NOW I CAN MAKE THREE WISHES...
...AT THE SAME TIME!
AS THE UNI-FAMILY ATTEMPTED TO CHARGE SOCKARANG AND STAB HIM WITH THEIR HORNS, HE MADE THREE WISHES AT ONCE.
SOCK!
SOCK!
BOOT!
HE WISHED TO BE SUPER STRONG...
...TO BE THE GREATEST FIGHTER EVER...
...AND HE WISHED TO TRICK THE UNI-FAMILY INTO THINKING HE WAS A GOOD GUY.
THANKS FOR COMING OVER, SOCKARANG. COME AGAIN SOON!
TIME TO FIND AXE COP...
...AND CUT OFF HIS HEAD!

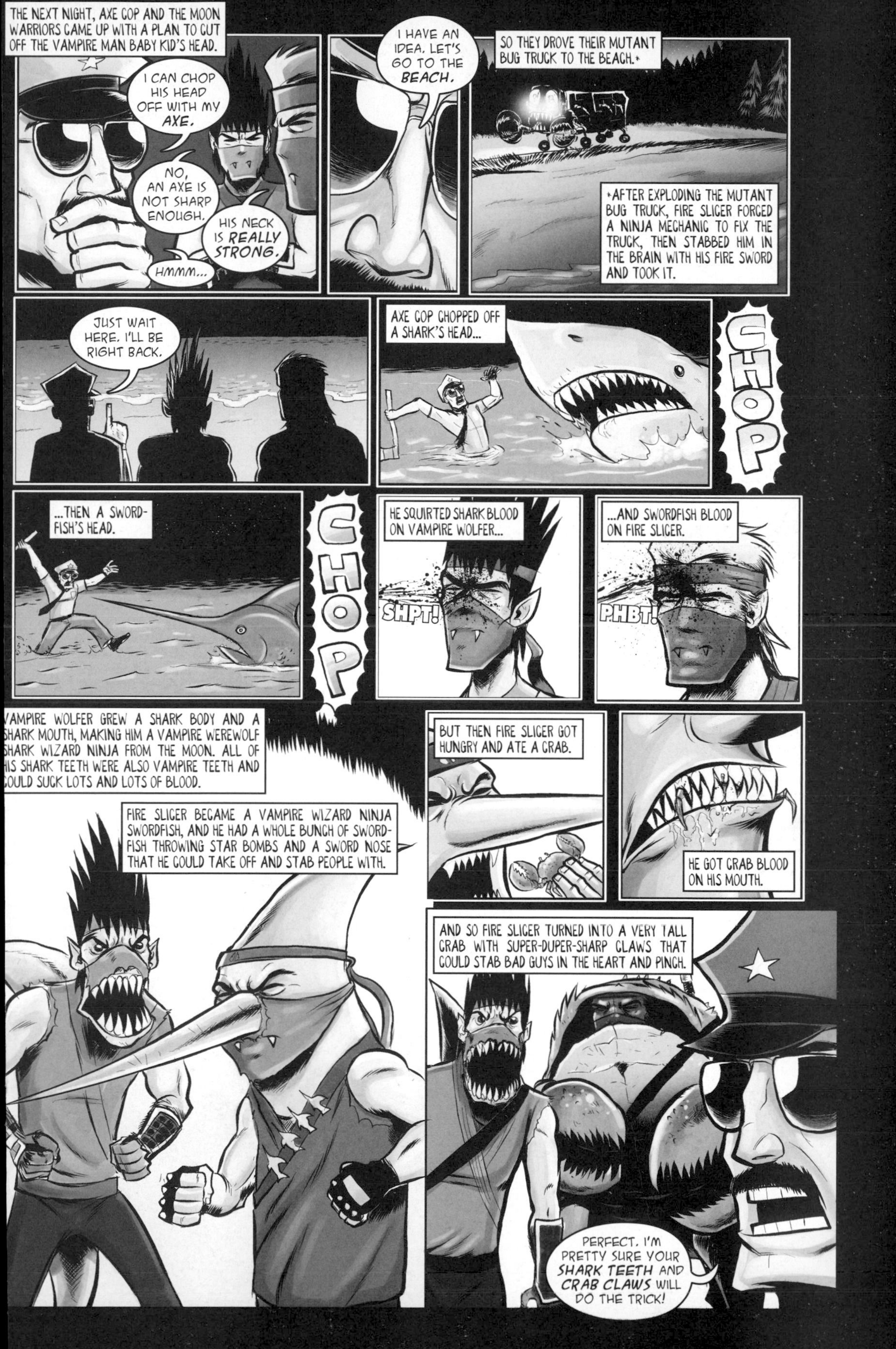
THE NEXT NIGHT, AXE COP AND THE MOON WARRIORS CAME UP WITH A PLAN TO CUT OFF THE VAMPIRE MAN BABY KID'S HEAD.
I CAN CHOP HIS HEAD OFF WITH MY AXE.
NO, AN AXE IS NOT SHARP ENOUGH.
HIS NECK IS REALLY STRONG.
HMMM...
I HAVE AN IDEA. LET'S GO TO THE BEACH.
SO THEY DROVE THEIR MUTANT BUG TRUCK TO THE BEACH.*
*AFTER EXPLODING THE MUTANT BUG TRUCK, FIRE SLICER FORCED A NINJA MECHANIC TO FIX THE TRUCK, THEN STABBED HIM IN THE BRAIN WITH HIS FIRE SWORD AND TOOK IT.
JUST WAIT HERE. I'LL BE RIGHT BACK.
AXE COP CHOPPED OFF A SHARK'S HEAD...
CHOP
...THEN A SWORD-FISH'S HEAD.
CHOP
HE SQUIRTED SHARK BLOOD ON VAMPIRE WOLFER...
SHPT!
...AND SWORDFISH BLOOD ON FIRE SLICER.
PHBT!
VAMPIRE WOLFER GREW A SHARK BODY AND A SHARK MOUTH, MAKING HIM A VAMPIRE WEREWOLF SHARK WIZARD NINJA FROM THE MOON. ALL OF HIS SHARK TEETH WERE ALSO VAMPIRE TEETH AND COULD SUCK LOTS AND LOTS OF BLOOD.
FIRE SLICER BECAME A VAMPIRE WIZARD NINJA SWORDFISH, AND HE HAD A WHOLE BUNCH OF SWORD-FISH THROWING STAR BOMBS AND A SWORD NOSE THAT HE COULD TAKE OFF AND STAB PEOPLE WITH.
BUT THEN FIRE SLICER GOT HUNGRY AND ATE A CRAB.
HE GOT CRAB BLOOD ON HIS MOUTH.
AND SO FIRE SLICER TURNED INTO A VERY TALL CRAB WITH SUPER-DUPER-SHARP CLAWS THAT COULD STAB BAD GUYS IN THE HEART AND PINCH.
PERFECT. I'M PRETTY SURE YOUR SHARK TEETH AND CRAB CLAWS WILL DO THE TRICK!

MEANWHILE, INSIDE A NEARBY SWORDFISH...

GRRAH...

THE VAMPIRE MAN BABY KID HAD BEEN WAITING TO STRIKE!

BGERBGAH!!

HE IS REALLY SCARY!

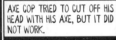

AXE COP TRIED TO CUT OFF HIS HEAD WITH HIS AXE, BUT IT DID NOT WORK.

THUD

VAMPIRE WOLFER'S NEW SHARK TEETH COULD NOT BITE IT OFF EITHER.

GRR!! RRRAH!! GRRAH!!! RRH!!

GNAW GNAW

AND EVEN FIRE SLICER'S SUPER-POWERFUL CRAB CLAWS COULD NOT PINCH HIS HEAD OFF.

CLAMP

CLAMP CLAMP

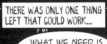

THERE WAS ONLY ONE THING LEFT THAT COULD WORK...

WHAT WE NEED IS A *CHAINSAW!* MY FRIEND *SOCKARANG* HAS ONE!

SO AXE COP BLEW HIS WHISTLE TO SUMMON HIS FRIEND.

TWEET!

HEY, *AXE COP!* I'M GONNA *SAW* YOUR HEAD OFF!

WHAT?!

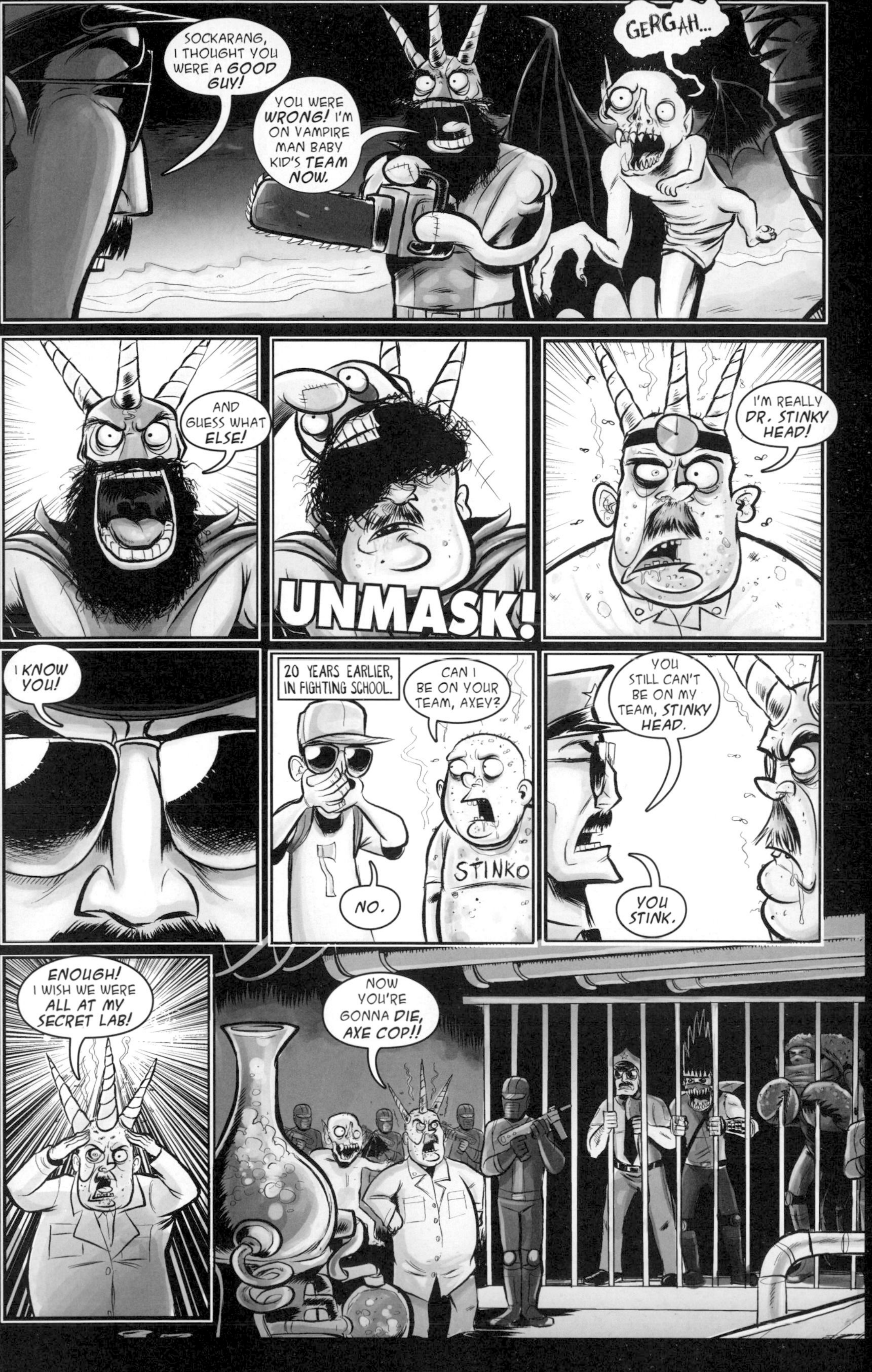
SOCKARANG, I THOUGHT YOU WERE A GOOD GUY!
YOU WERE WRONG! I'M ON VAMPIRE MAN BABY KID'S TEAM NOW.
GERGAH...
AND GUESS WHAT ELSE!
UNMASK!
I'M REALLY DR. STINKY HEAD!
I KNOW YOU!
20 YEARS EARLIER, IN FIGHTING SCHOOL.
CAN I BE ON YOUR TEAM, AXEY?
NO.
STINKO
YOU STILL CAN'T BE ON MY TEAM, STINKY HEAD.
YOU STINK.
ENOUGH! I WISH WE WERE ALL AT MY SECRET LAB!
NOW YOU'RE GONNA DIE, AXE COP!!

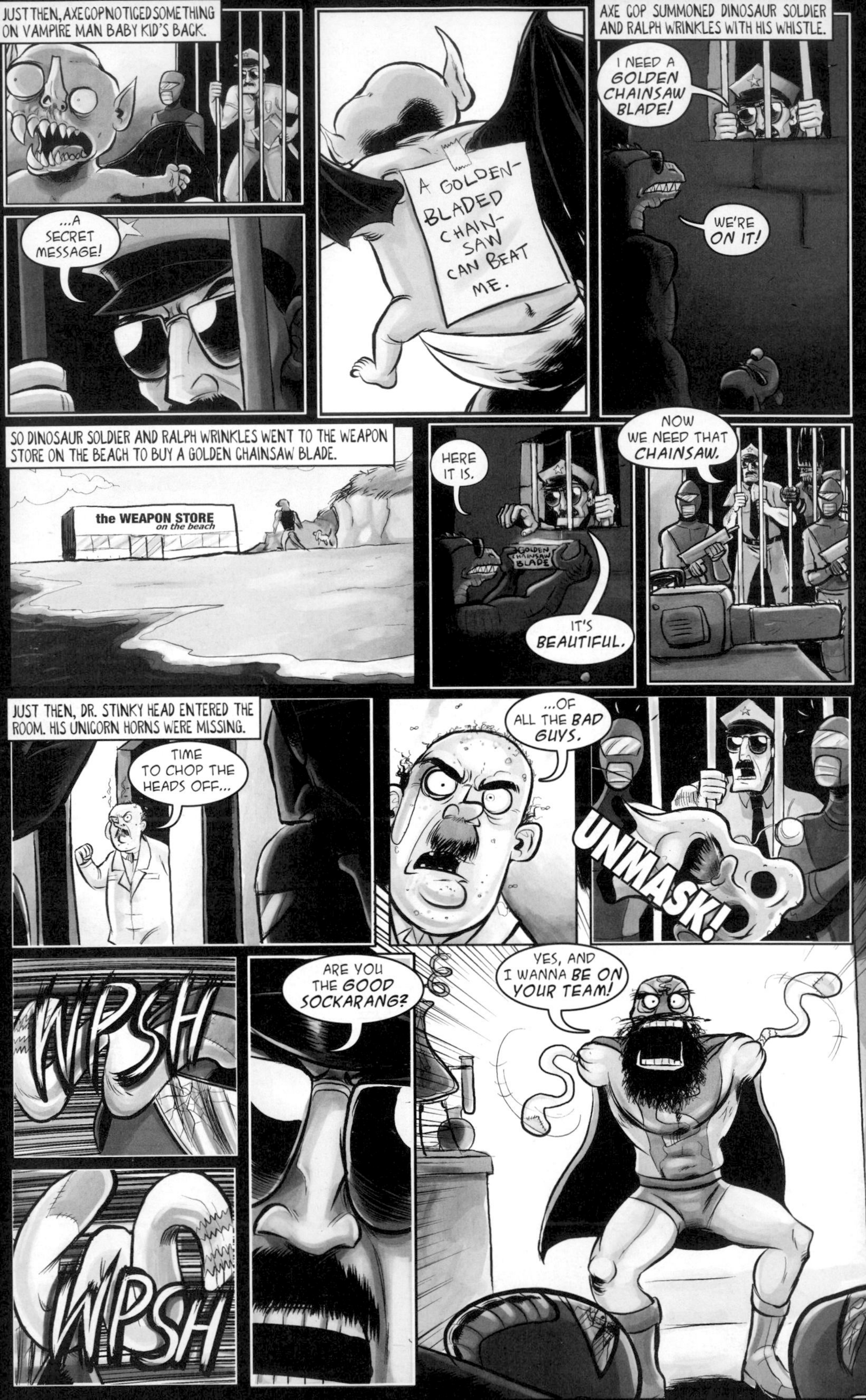
JUST THEN, AXE COP NOTICED SOMETHING ON VAMPIRE MAN BABY KID'S BACK.
...A SECRET MESSAGE!
A GOLDEN-BLADED CHAIN-SAW CAN BEAT ME.
AXE COP SUMMONED DINOSAUR SOLDIER AND RALPH WRINKLES WITH HIS WHISTLE.
I NEED A GOLDEN CHAINSAW BLADE!
WE'RE ON IT!
SO DINOSAUR SOLDIER AND RALPH WRINKLES WENT TO THE WEAPON STORE ON THE BEACH TO BUY A GOLDEN CHAINSAW BLADE.
the WEAPON STORE on the beach
HERE IT IS.
GOLDEN CHAINSAW BLADE
IT'S BEAUTIFUL.
NOW WE NEED THAT CHAINSAW.
JUST THEN, DR. STINKY HEAD ENTERED THE ROOM. HIS UNICORN HORNS WERE MISSING.
TIME TO CHOP THE HEADS OFF...
...OF ALL THE BAD GUYS.
UNMASK!
WPSH
WPSH
ARE YOU THE GOOD SOCKARANG?
YES, AND I WANNA BE ON YOUR TEAM!

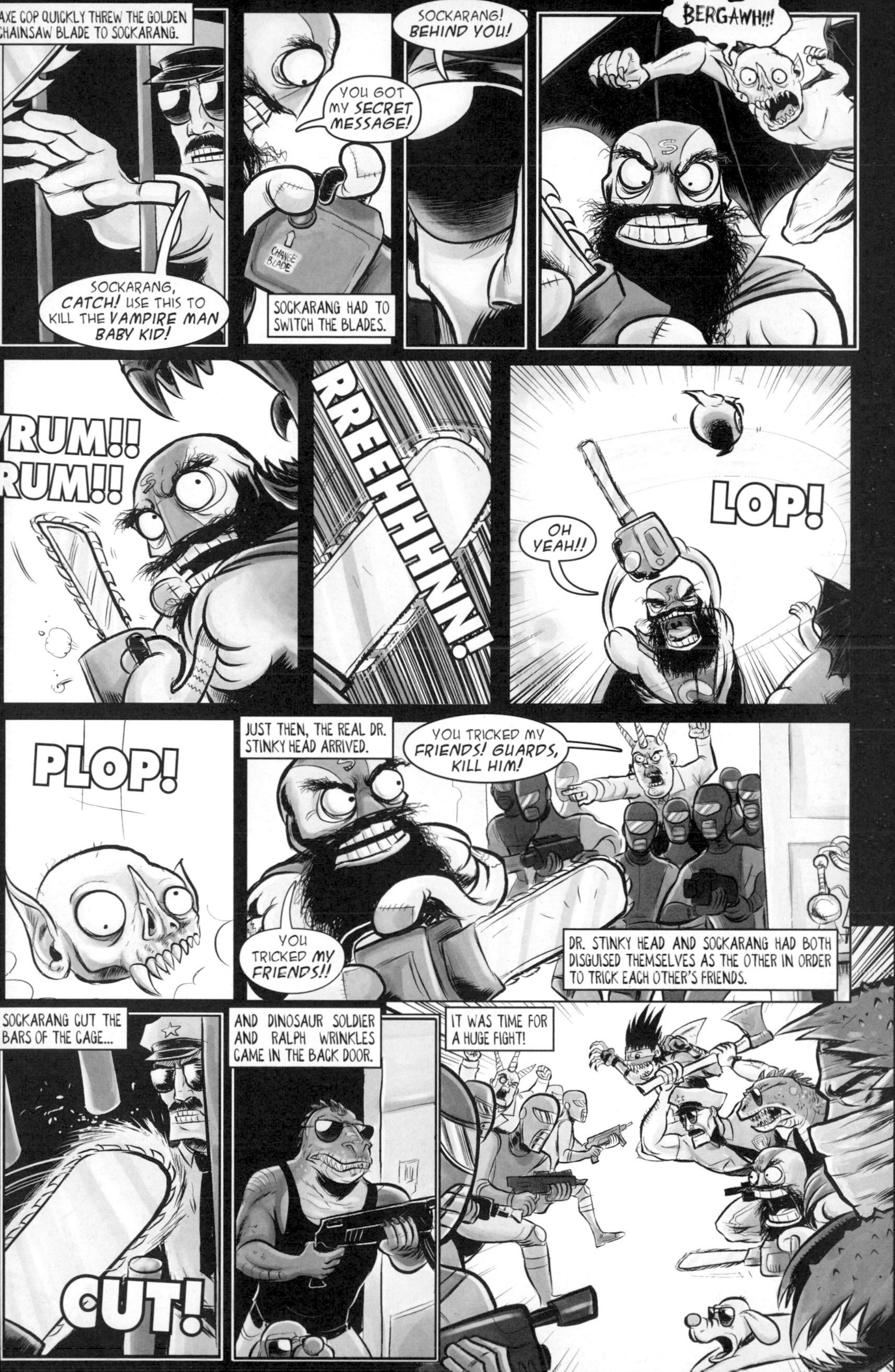
AXE COP QUICKLY THREW THE GOLDEN CHAINSAW BLADE TO SOCKARANG.
SOCKARANG, CATCH! USE THIS TO KILL THE VAMPIRE MAN BABY KID!
YOU GOT MY SECRET MESSAGE!
CHANGE BLADE
SOCKARANG HAD TO SWITCH THE BLADES.
SOCKARANG! BEHIND YOU!
BERGAWH!!!
VRUM!! RUM!!
RREEHHHHNN!
OH YEAH!!
LOP!
PLOP!
JUST THEN, THE REAL DR. STINKY HEAD ARRIVED.
YOU TRICKED MY FRIENDS! GUARDS, KILL HIM!
YOU TRICKED MY FRIENDS!!
DR. STINKY HEAD AND SOCKARANG HAD BOTH DISGUISED THEMSELVES AS THE OTHER IN ORDER TO TRICK EACH OTHER'S FRIENDS.
SOCKARANG CUT THE BARS OF THE CAGE...
CUT!
AND DINOSAUR SOLDIER AND RALPH WRINKLES CAME IN THE BACK DOOR.
IT WAS TIME FOR A HUGE FIGHT!

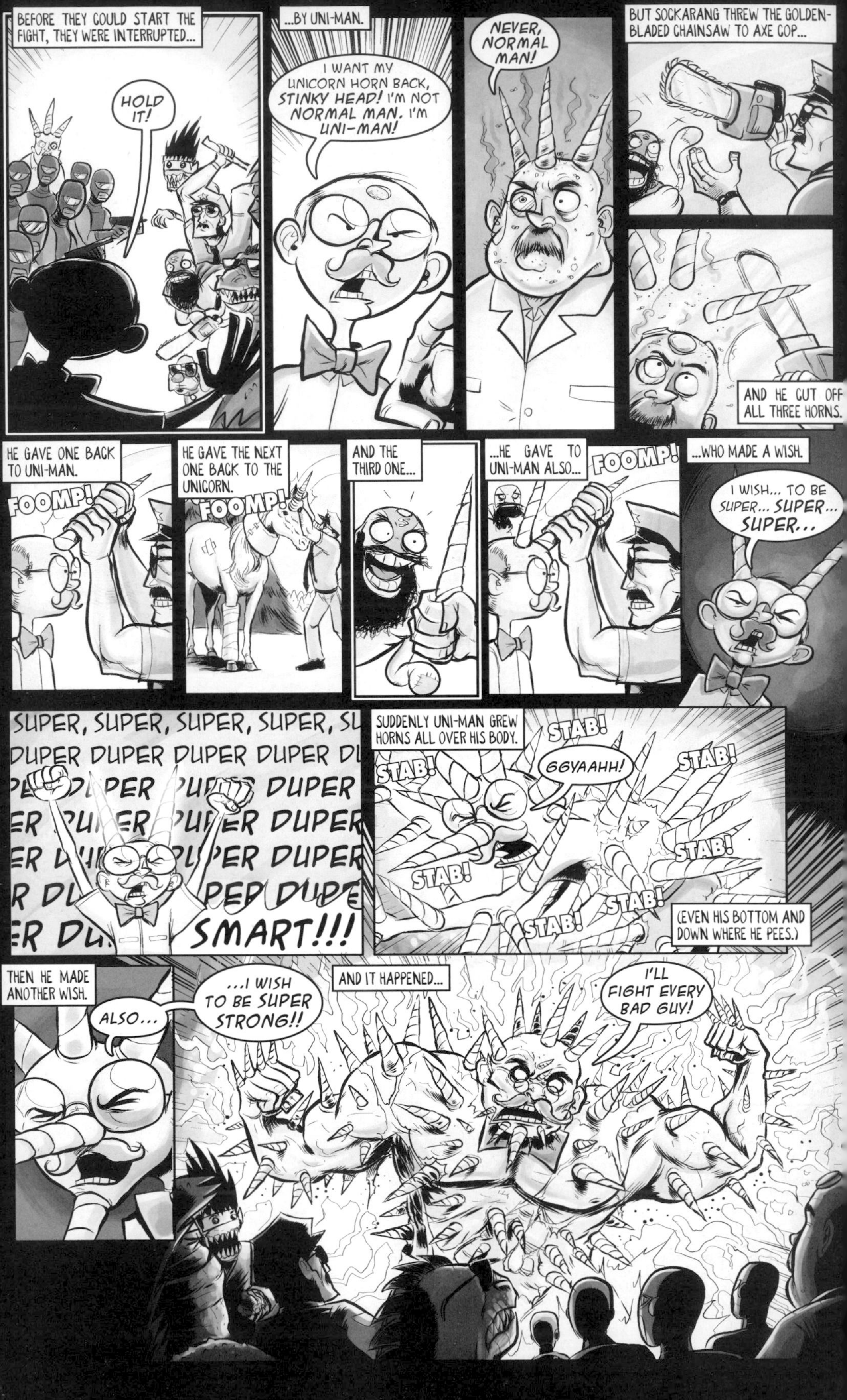
BEFORE THEY COULD START THE FIGHT, THEY WERE INTERRUPTED...
HOLD IT!
...BY UNI-MAN.
I WANT MY UNICORN HORN BACK, STINKY HEAD! I'M NOT NORMAL MAN. I'M UNI-MAN!
NEVER, NORMAL MAN!
BUT SOCKARANG THREW THE GOLDEN-BLADED CHAINSAW TO AXE COP...
AND HE CUT OFF ALL THREE HORNS.
HE GAVE ONE BACK TO UNI-MAN.
FOOMP!
HE GAVE THE NEXT ONE BACK TO THE UNICORN.
FOOMP!
AND THE THIRD ONE...
...HE GAVE TO UNI-MAN ALSO...
FOOMP!
...WHO MADE A WISH.
I WISH... TO BE SUPER... SUPER... SUPER...
SUPER, SUPER, SUPER, SUPER,
DUPER DUPER DUPER DUPER
DUPER DUPER
DUPER
DUPER
SMART!!!
SUDDENLY UNI-MAN GREW HORNS ALL OVER HIS BODY.
STAB!
GGYAAHH!
STAB!
STAB!
STAB!
STAB!
STAB!
STAB!
(EVEN HIS BOTTOM AND DOWN WHERE HE PEES.)
THEN HE MADE ANOTHER WISH.
ALSO...
...I WISH TO BE SUPER STRONG!!
AND IT HAPPENED...
I'LL FIGHT EVERY BAD GUY!

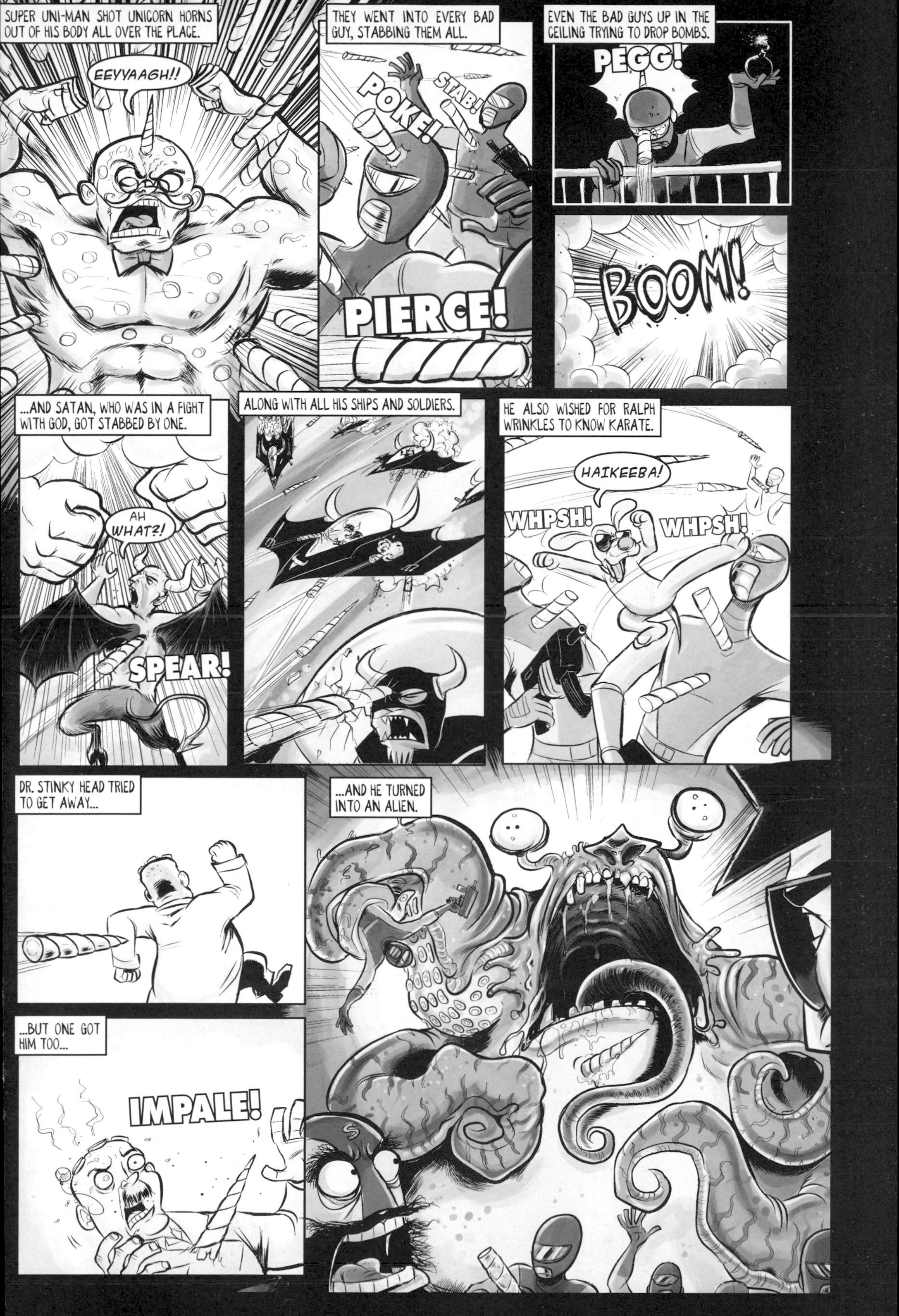
SUPER UNI-MAN SHOT UNICORN HORNS OUT OF HIS BODY ALL OVER THE PLACE.
EEYYAAGH!!
THEY WENT INTO EVERY BAD GUY, STABBING THEM ALL.
POKE!
STAB!
PIERCE!
EVEN THE BAD GUYS UP IN THE CEILING TRYING TO DROP BOMBS.
PEGG!
BOOM!
...AND SATAN, WHO WAS IN A FIGHT WITH GOD, GOT STABBED BY ONE.
AH WHAT?!
SPEAR!
ALONG WITH ALL HIS SHIPS AND SOLDIERS.
HE ALSO WISHED FOR RALPH WRINKLES TO KNOW KARATE.
HAIKEEBA!
WHPSH!
WHPSH!
DR. STINKY HEAD TRIED TO GET AWAY...
...BUT ONE GOT HIM TOO...
IMPALE!
...AND HE TURNED INTO AN ALIEN.

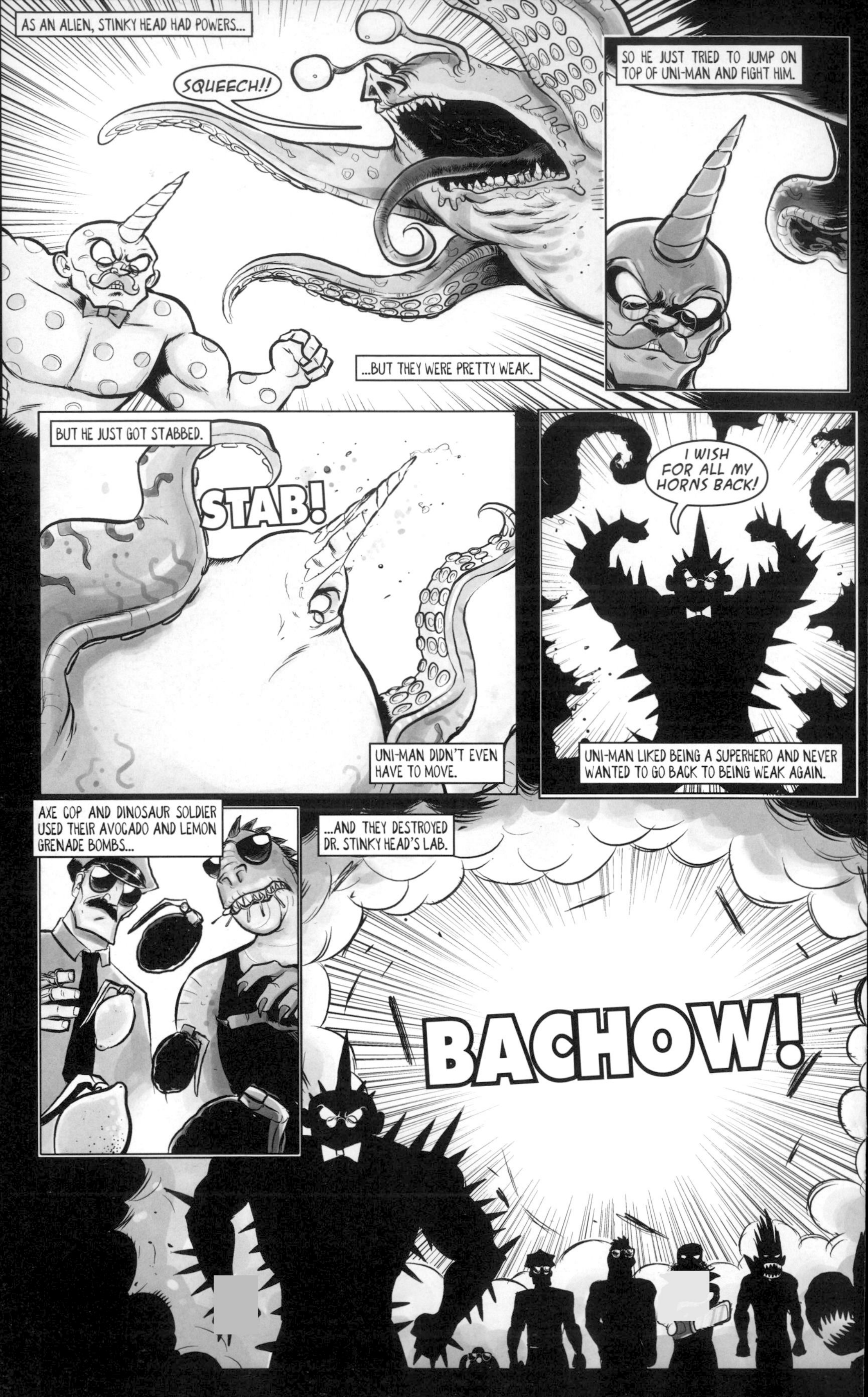
AS AN ALIEN, STINKY HEAD HAD POWERS...
SQUEECH!!
...BUT THEY WERE PRETTY WEAK.
SO HE JUST TRIED TO JUMP ON TOP OF UNI-MAN AND FIGHT HIM.
BUT HE JUST GOT STABBED.
STAB!
UNI-MAN DIDN'T EVEN HAVE TO MOVE.
I WISH FOR ALL MY HORNS BACK!
UNI-MAN LIKED BEING A SUPERHERO AND NEVER WANTED TO GO BACK TO BEING WEAK AGAIN.
AXE COP AND DINOSAUR SOLDIER USED THEIR AVOCADO AND LEMON GRENADE BOMBS...
...AND THEY DESTROYED DR. STINKY HEAD'S LAB.
BACHOW!

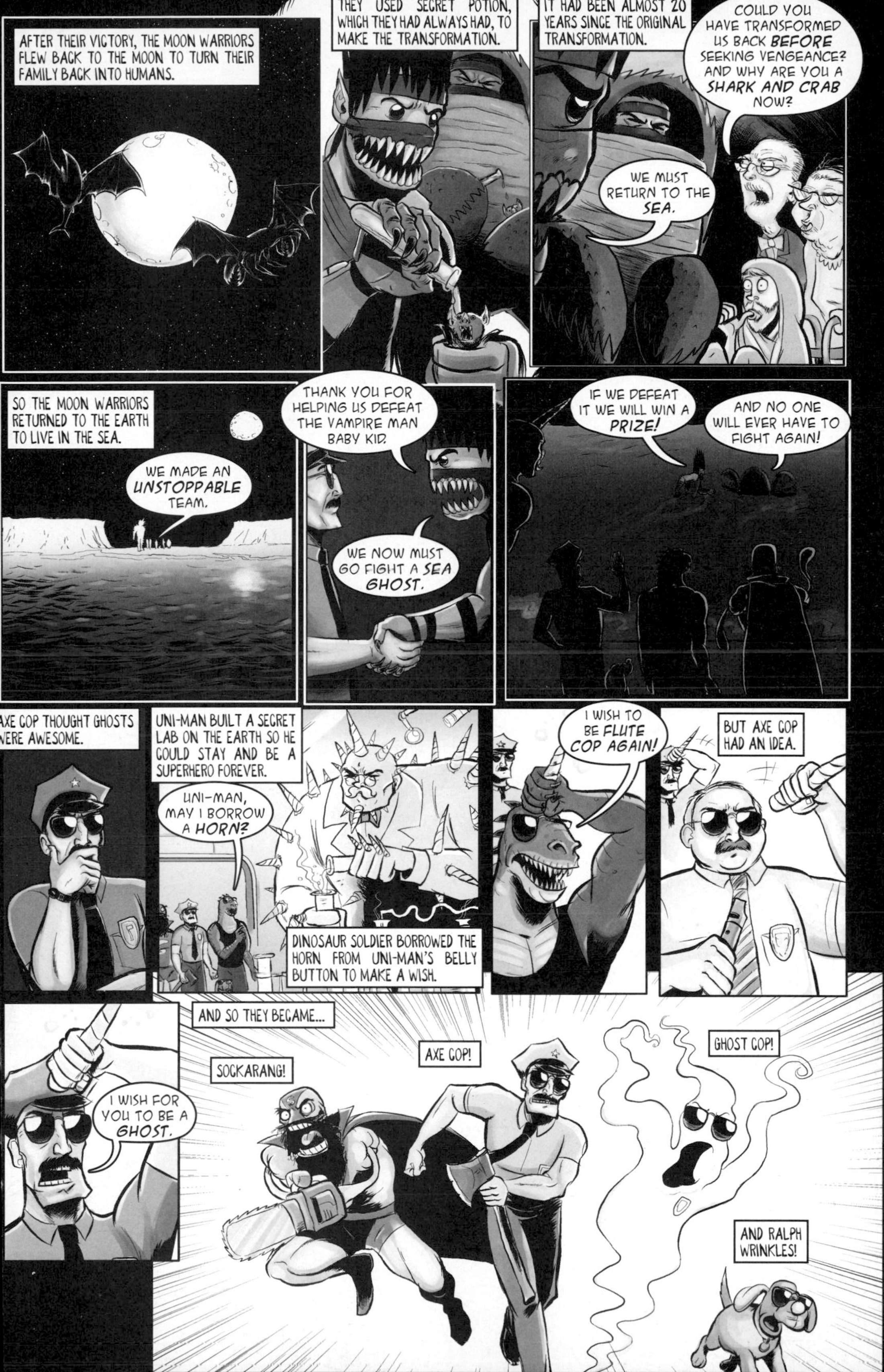
AFTER THEIR VICTORY, THE MOON WARRIORS FLEW BACK TO THE MOON TO TURN THEIR FAMILY BACK INTO HUMANS.
THEY USED SECRET POTION, WHICH THEY HAD ALWAYS HAD, TO MAKE THE TRANSFORMATION.
IT HAD BEEN ALMOST 20 YEARS SINCE THE ORIGINAL TRANSFORMATION.
COULD YOU HAVE TRANSFORMED US BACK BEFORE SEEKING VENGEANCE? AND WHY ARE YOU A SHARK AND CRAB NOW?
WE MUST RETURN TO THE SEA.
SO THE MOON WARRIORS RETURNED TO THE EARTH TO LIVE IN THE SEA.
WE MADE AN UNSTOPPABLE TEAM.
THANK YOU FOR HELPING US DEFEAT THE VAMPIRE MAN BABY KID.
WE NOW MUST GO FIGHT A SEA GHOST.
IF WE DEFEAT IT WE WILL WIN A PRIZE!
AND NO ONE WILL EVER HAVE TO FIGHT AGAIN!
AXE COP THOUGHT GHOSTS WERE AWESOME.
UNI-MAN BUILT A SECRET LAB ON THE EARTH SO HE COULD STAY AND BE A SUPERHERO FOREVER.
UNI-MAN, MAY I BORROW A HORN?
DINOSAUR SOLDIER BORROWED THE HORN FROM UNI-MAN'S BELLY BUTTON TO MAKE A WISH.
I WISH TO BE FLUTE COP AGAIN!
BUT AXE COP HAD AN IDEA.
I WISH FOR YOU TO BE A GHOST.
AND SO THEY BECAME...
SOCKARANG!
AXE COP!
GHOST COP!
AND RALPH WRINKLES!

Best Big Brother Ever?

Ask Axe Cop Questions 26–42

Ever since *Axe Cop* went viral I have had two common responses to me as a brother. Most commonly, people say that I am the best big brother in the world. There are others who say that I am exploiting my little brother and liken me to a beauty-pageant mom (translation: I am the worst big brother in the world). It became very quickly apparent that there is a fine line between the two, and it is a boundary line I have to be conscious of at all times.

When *Axe Cop* became popular, it really caught me off guard. If someone had said, "Hey, do you want to make a webcomic with your five-year-old brother and publish it online to be read by millions of people?" I would have been able to think everything over and strategize about how to do this right. Foolishly, I simply had not even considered this comic going "big" an option. I just didn't think that would ever happen in a million years.

So I decided to try to walk that fine line and continue creating with Malachai. My little brother became something of an Internet celebrity, but he doesn't even really know what that means. So far it seems that he thinks that if you have a brother who draws comics, then this is all very normal. People joke with me about child labor, but the truth is that unless we are playing, you get no *Axe Cop*. If Malachai isn't having fun, he's not going to write. He can't force himself to work on a story even if he is not in the mood like most writers have to, and neither can I. I have to work on his schedule, wait for him to want to do more, and it has to always be fun. I do inspire him to be thinking of stories by bribing him now and then with a new video game. He had wanted a Nintendo DS for a long time and he was able to get one using his *Axe Cop* pay.

I figure I've been given a very unique position with this project, and I don't know that it has ever been done before. It all happened sort of by accident, and it is as if it were handed to us like a gift or a chore, or a bit of both. I always say that as long as Malachai is having fun and I'm having fun and the readers are having fun, we'll keep it up. The moment we lose one of those, we'll know it's time to move on.

—Ethan

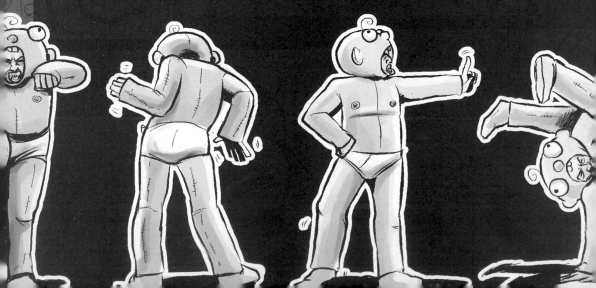

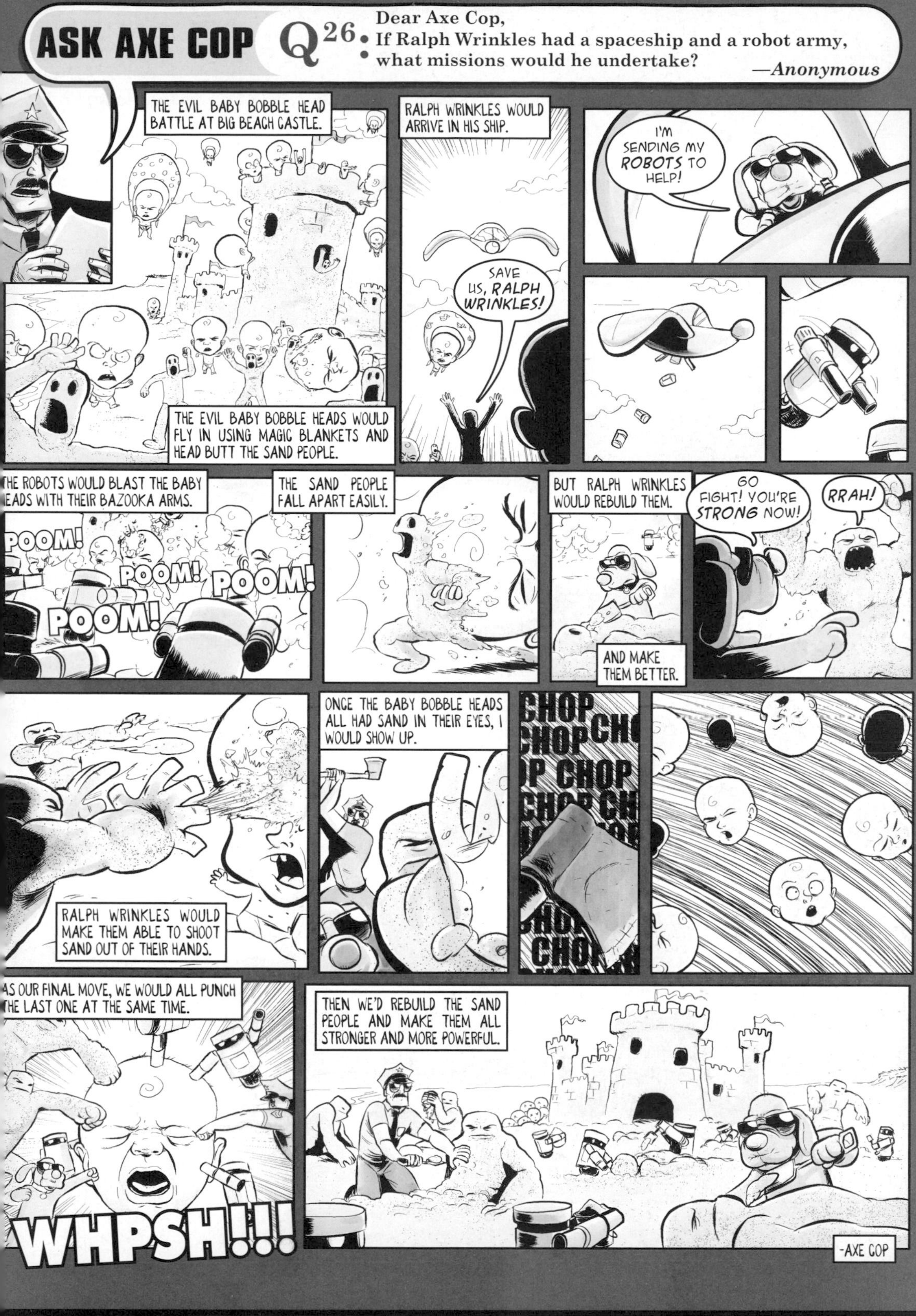
ASK AXE COP
Q26: Dear Axe Cop,
If Ralph Wrinkles had a spaceship and a robot army, what missions would he undertake?
—Anonymous
THE EVIL BABY BOBBLE HEAD BATTLE AT BIG BEACH CASTLE.
THE EVIL BABY BOBBLE HEADS WOULD FLY IN USING MAGIC BLANKETS AND HEAD BUTT THE SAND PEOPLE.
RALPH WRINKLES WOULD ARRIVE IN HIS SHIP.
SAVE US, RALPH WRINKLES!
I'M SENDING MY ROBOTS TO HELP!
THE ROBOTS WOULD BLAST THE BABY HEADS WITH THEIR BAZOOKA ARMS.
POOM!
POOM!
POOM!
POOM!
THE SAND PEOPLE FALL APART EASILY.
BUT RALPH WRINKLES WOULD REBUILD THEM.
AND MAKE THEM BETTER.
GO FIGHT! YOU'RE STRONG NOW!
RRAH!
RALPH WRINKLES WOULD MAKE THEM ABLE TO SHOOT SAND OUT OF THEIR HANDS.
ONCE THE BABY BOBBLE HEADS ALL HAD SAND IN THEIR EYES, I WOULD SHOW UP.
CHOP CHOP CHOP CHOP
AS OUR FINAL MOVE, WE WOULD ALL PUNCH THE LAST ONE AT THE SAME TIME.
WHPSH!!!
THEN WE'D REBUILD THE SAND PEOPLE AND MAKE THEM ALL STRONGER AND MORE POWERFUL.
-AXE COP

Ask Axe Cop #26

There is just so much to love about this episode I don't know if I even need to say anything. All *Axe Cop* comics are representative of a kid's imagination unleashed, but I think this does that particularly well. It has all the terror of tyranny and war, but the innocence of baby bobble heads and sandcastles. It's basically a day at the beach with Malachai.

ASK AXE COP Q27:

Dear Axe Cop,
I was wondering what you thought about the effectiveness of using a green banana as a crime-fighting tool.
—Mutoman

THE GREEN-BANANA GUN IS ONE OF THE MOST EFFECTIVE CRIME-FIGHTING TOOLS OUT THERE.

IT IS MADE BY THE FATHER OF THE TEN BEN-MATANGA.

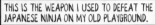

TO GET AMMO FOR IT, YOU HAVE TO SNEAK INTO THE JUNGLE AT NIGHT AND STEAL THE GREEN BANANAS FROM THE MONKEYS WHILE THEY SLEEP.

THEN YOU HAVE TO CUT THE END OFF OF EACH BANANA SO THAT IT CAN SHOOT OUT OF THE SKIN.

CHOP!

THIS IS THE WEAPON I USED TO DEFEAT THE JAPANESE NINJA ON MY OLD PLAYGROUND.

COME ON OUT, MR. MUTANI ESU!

YOU CAN NOT BEAT ME, *FOOL!* ONLY *ONE* WEAPON CAN KILL ME...

IS IT A GREEN-BANANA GUN?

HWAH?!!

JOO
JOO
JOO
JOO
JOO
JOO
JOO

-AXE CO

Ask Axe Cop #27
This is a good example of a Frankenstein episode of Ask Axe Cop. I didn't have a lot of new material from Malachai but I wanted to put something out, so I went through a bunch of old notes from our conversations and pieced this together. The general rule of *Axe Cop* is that all of the content comes from Malachai; I just have to make sense out of it.

Ask Axe Cop #28 and #29 (next pages)
I don't know how many times I get to call an episode of Ask Axe Cop my favorite, but these two are up there. This was the first two-part Ask Axe Cop because Malachai gave me so much information I decided to split it in two. It's another glimpse into the everyday life of Axe Cop, which I love. I promise you, the Axe Cop motivational posters he hangs in his kitchen were copied verbatim from Malachai's mouth.

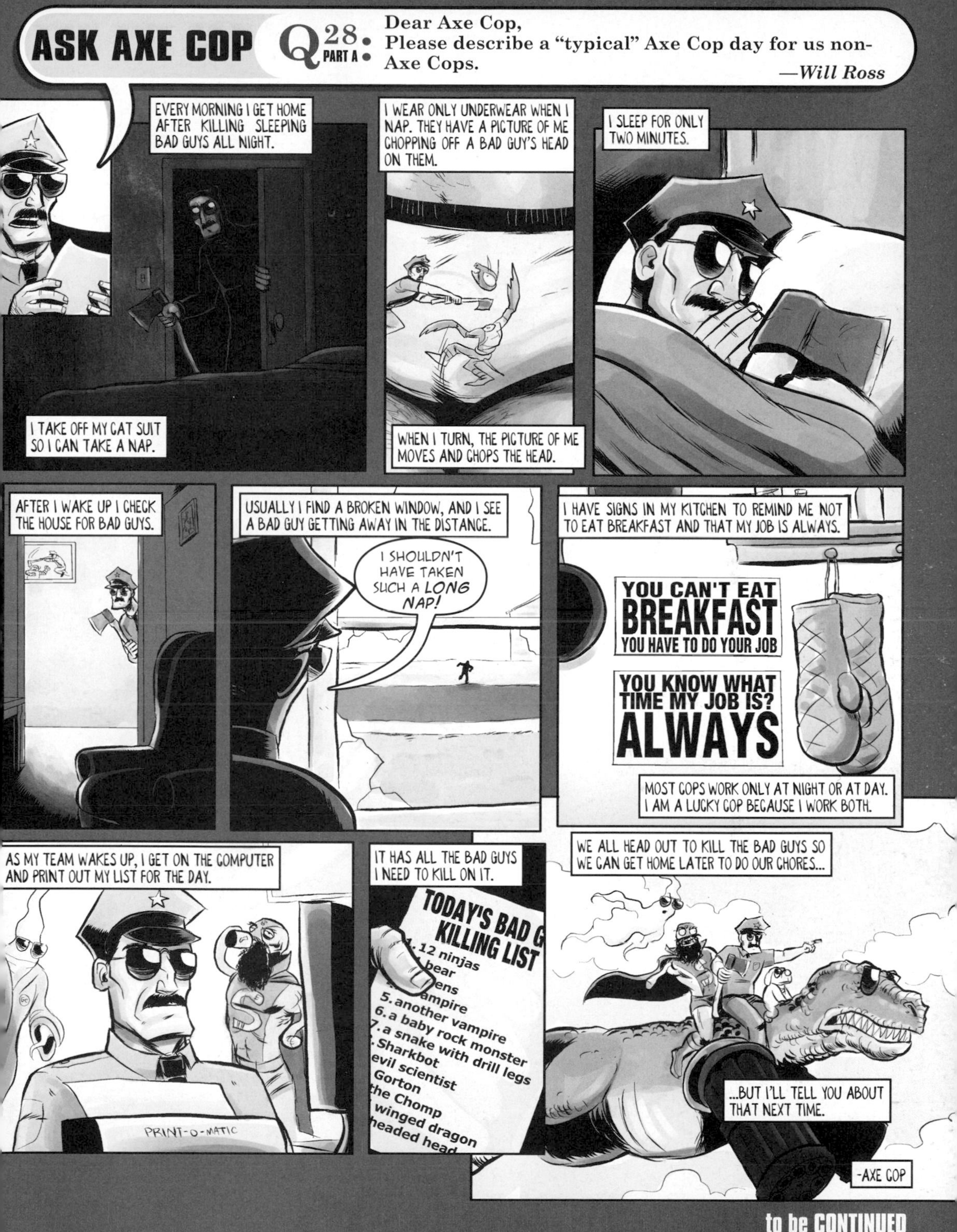

ASK AXE COP
Q28. PART A:
Dear Axe Cop,
Please describe a "typical" Axe Cop day for us non-Axe Cops.
—Will Ross
EVERY MORNING I GET HOME AFTER KILLING SLEEPING BAD GUYS ALL NIGHT.
I TAKE OFF MY CAT SUIT SO I CAN TAKE A NAP.
I WEAR ONLY UNDERWEAR WHEN I NAP. THEY HAVE A PICTURE OF ME CHOPPING OFF A BAD GUY'S HEAD ON THEM.
WHEN I TURN, THE PICTURE OF ME MOVES AND CHOPS THE HEAD.
I SLEEP FOR ONLY TWO MINUTES.
AFTER I WAKE UP I CHECK THE HOUSE FOR BAD GUYS.
USUALLY I FIND A BROKEN WINDOW, AND I SEE A BAD GUY GETTING AWAY IN THE DISTANCE.
I SHOULDN'T HAVE TAKEN SUCH A LONG NAP!
I HAVE SIGNS IN MY KITCHEN TO REMIND ME NOT TO EAT BREAKFAST AND THAT MY JOB IS ALWAYS.
YOU CAN'T EAT BREAKFAST YOU HAVE TO DO YOUR JOB
YOU KNOW WHAT TIME MY JOB IS? ALWAYS
MOST COPS WORK ONLY AT NIGHT OR AT DAY. I AM A LUCKY COP BECAUSE I WORK BOTH.
AS MY TEAM WAKES UP, I GET ON THE COMPUTER AND PRINT OUT MY LIST FOR THE DAY.
PRINT-O-MATIC
IT HAS ALL THE BAD GUYS I NEED TO KILL ON IT.
TODAY'S BAD G
KILLING LIST
1. 12 ninjas
bear
ens
ampire
5. another vampire
6. a baby rock monster
7. a snake with drill legs
. Sharkbot
evil scientist
Gorton
the Chomp
winged dragon
headed head
WE ALL HEAD OUT TO KILL THE BAD GUYS SO WE CAN GET HOME LATER TO DO OUR CHORES...
...BUT I'LL TELL YOU ABOUT THAT NEXT TIME.
-AXE COP

to be CONTINUED

ASK AXE COP
Q29. PART B:
Dear Axe Cop,
Please describe a "typical" Axe Cop day for us non-Axe Cops.
—Will Ross
ONCE I GET HOME FROM CRIME FIGHTING I USUALLY HAVE TO FIX THE WINDOWS.
OTHER CHORES INCLUDE WORKING ON TWO INVISIBLE DOORS. ONE FOR WEXTER, AND ONE FOR ME. THIS IS SO THE BAD GUYS DON'T KNOW HOW TO GET IN.
AND WE ALSO WORK ON OUR GIANT WALL SURROUNDING THE HOUSE. MY GOAL IS TO MAKE IT SO TALL IT REACHES THE MOON PLANET.
THEN I FEED MY PETS. I GIVE RALPH WRINKLES SUPERPOWER FOOD.
ENERGY METER
I FEED HIM UNTIL HIS ENERGY STATUS IS ALL THE WAY UP AND HE IS SUPER STRONG.
RALPH WRINKLES
USUALLY WEXTER JUST FINDS BAD GUYS TO EAT WHO ARE TRYING TO GET IN OUR HOUSE.
AFTER THAT WE ALL PLAY "LEGO STAR WARS" ON NINTENDO DS AGAINST EACH OTHER. I ALWAYS GET THE TOP SCORE BECAUSE I HAVE EVERY WEAPON.
ONCE NIGHT FALLS, I TAKE MY PETS OUT TO KILL SLEEPING BAD GUYS. WE ALL WEAR CAT SUITS.
WEXTER WEARS A FULL CAT COSTUME. RALPH WRINKLES JUST WEARS CAT EARS.
TOMORROW WE DO IT ALL AGAIN, BECAUSE MY JOB IS NOT DAY SHIFT OR NIGHT SHIFT. IT'S ALWAYS SHIFT.
-AXE COP

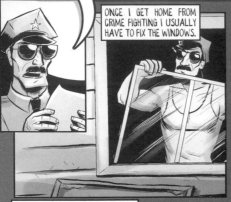

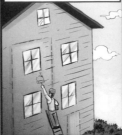

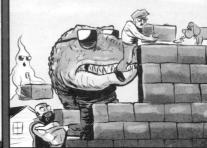

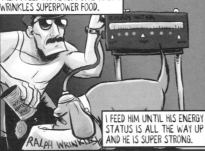

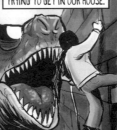

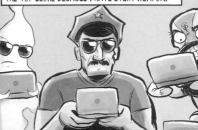

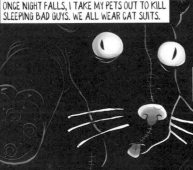

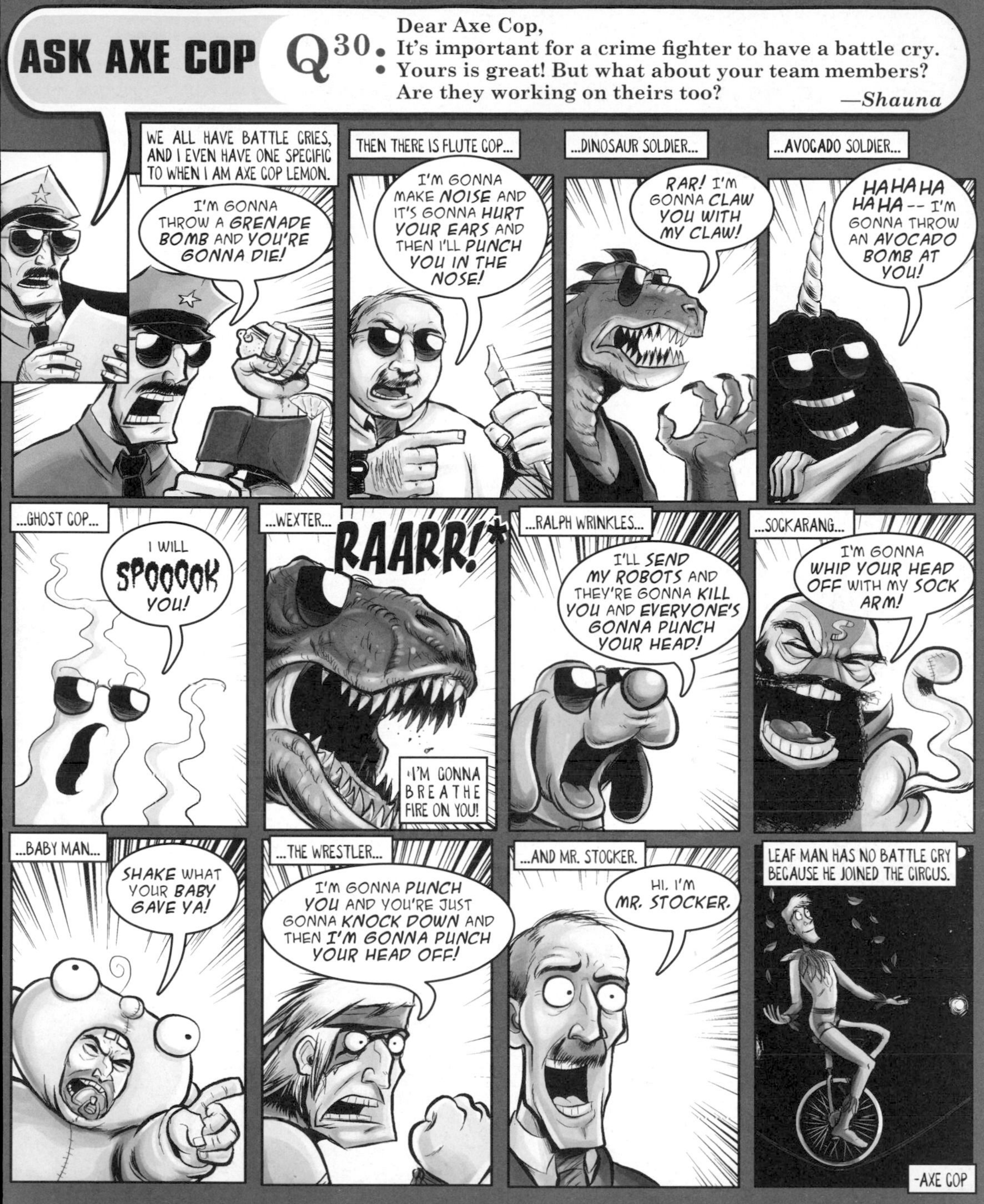
ASK AXE COP
Q30.
Dear Axe Cop,
It's important for a crime fighter to have a battle cry. Yours is great! But what about your team members? Are they working on theirs too?
—Shauna
WE ALL HAVE BATTLE CRIES, AND I EVEN HAVE ONE SPECIFIC TO WHEN I AM AXE COP LEMON.
I'M GONNA THROW A GRENADE BOMB AND YOU'RE GONNA DIE!
THEN THERE IS FLUTE COP...
I'M GONNA MAKE NOISE AND IT'S GONNA HURT YOUR EARS AND THEN I'LL PUNCH YOU IN THE NOSE!
...DINOSAUR SOLDIER...
RAR! I'M GONNA CLAW YOU WITH MY CLAW!
...AVOCADO SOLDIER...
HAHAHA HAHA -- I'M GONNA THROW AN AVOCADO BOMB AT YOU!
...GHOST COP...
I WILL SPOOOOK YOU!
...WEXTER...
RAARR!*
*I'M GONNA BREATHE FIRE ON YOU!
...RALPH WRINKLES...
I'LL SEND MY ROBOTS AND THEY'RE GONNA KILL YOU AND EVERYONE'S GONNA PUNCH YOUR HEAD!
...SOCKARANG...
I'M GONNA WHIP YOUR HEAD OFF WITH MY SOCK ARM!
...BABY MAN...
SHAKE WHAT YOUR BABY GAVE YA!
...THE WRESTLER...
I'M GONNA PUNCH YOU AND YOU'RE JUST GONNA KNOCK DOWN AND THEN I'M GONNA PUNCH YOUR HEAD OFF!
...AND MR. STOCKER.
HI. I'M MR. STOCKER.
LEAF MAN HAS NO BATTLE CRY BECAUSE HE JOINED THE CIRCUS.
-AXE COP

Ask Axe Cop #30

This episode answers the mystery of how Flute Cop fights. He actually is not a good flute player; he is a very bad flute player. He plays his flute so bad that he hurts your ears and stuns you so he can punch you in the nose. He could just as well be Trombone Cop . . . but Flute Cop has a better ring to it.

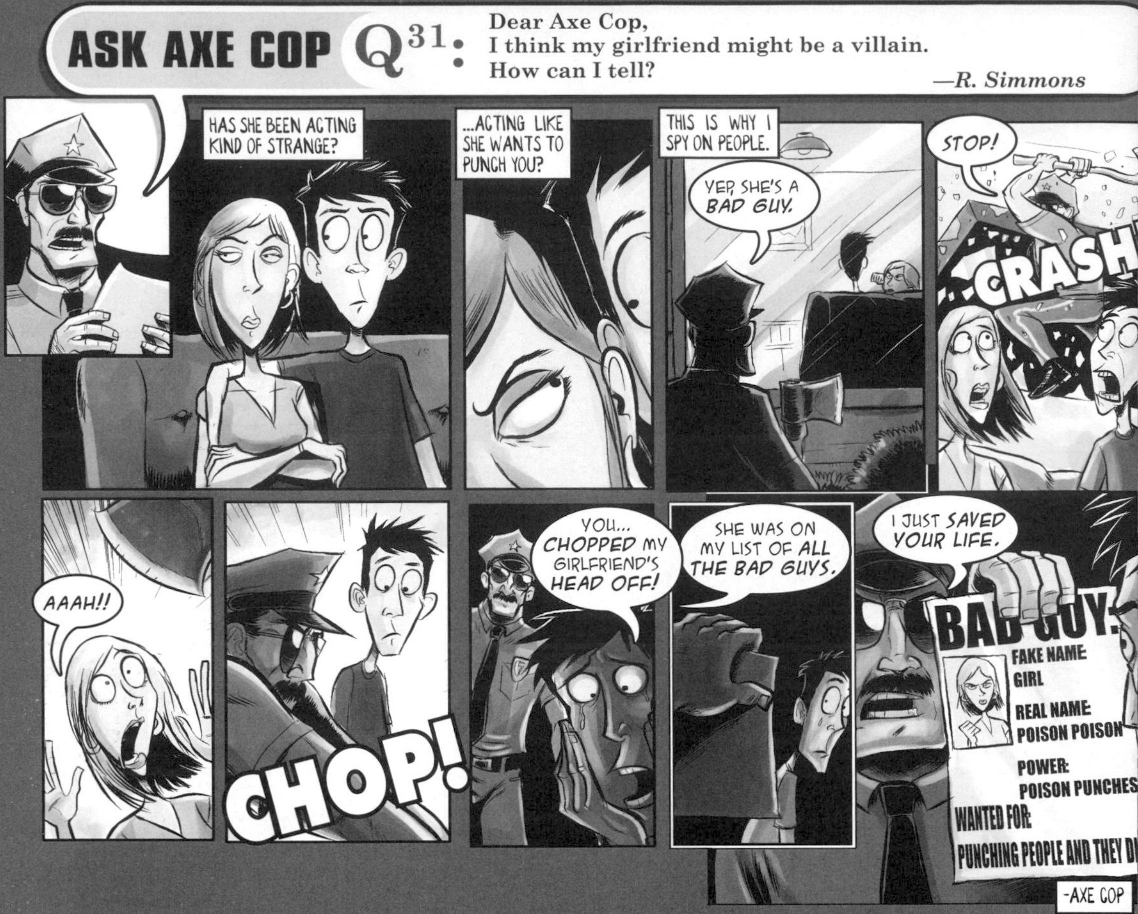
ASK AXE COP
Q31:
Dear Axe Cop,
I think my girlfriend might be a villain.
How can I tell?
—R. Simmons
HAS SHE BEEN ACTING KIND OF STRANGE?
...ACTING LIKE SHE WANTS TO PUNCH YOU?
THIS IS WHY I SPY ON PEOPLE.
YEP, SHE'S A BAD GUY.
STOP!
CRASH
AAAH!!
CHOP!
YOU... CHOPPED MY GIRLFRIEND'S HEAD OFF!
SHE WAS ON MY LIST OF ALL THE BAD GUYS.
I JUST SAVED YOUR LIFE.
BAD GUY
FAKE NAME: GIRL
REAL NAME: POISON POISON
POWER: POISON PUNCHES
WANTED FOR: PUNCHING PEOPLE AND THEY
-AXE COP

Ask Axe Cop #31
More evidence that Axe Cop is kind of a psycho. He hides in the bushes with an axe and spies on couples who are about to make out. He also has no problem with beheading a woman if he is pretty sure she is a bad guy.

Ask Axe Cop #32
This is one of the most common questions we get asked, and I resisted asking Malachai for a long time, but I'm glad I finally did. I saw a forum online debating who would win in a fight between Axe Cop and Samurai Jack. Everyone was saying Jack, until someone posted a link to this episode and then a bunch of them switched to Axe Cop. He has a robot in his face!

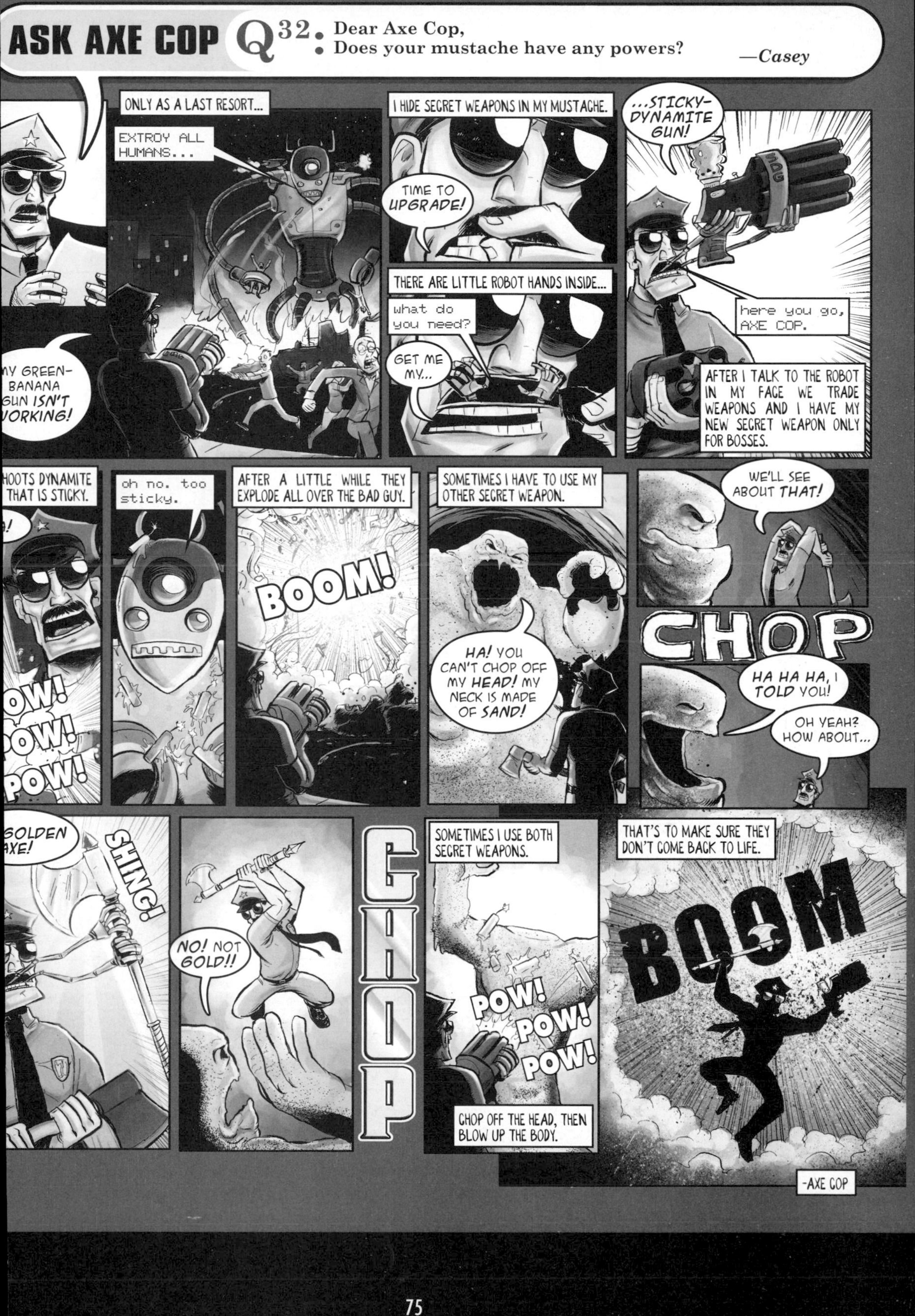
ASK AXE COP
Q32: Dear Axe Cop,
Does your mustache have any powers?
—Casey
ONLY AS A LAST RESORT...
EXTROY ALL HUMANS...
MY GREEN-BANANA GUN ISN'T WORKING!
I HIDE SECRET WEAPONS IN MY MUSTACHE.
TIME TO UPGRADE!
THERE ARE LITTLE ROBOT HANDS INSIDE...
what do you need?
GET ME MY...
...STICKY-DYNAMITE GUN!
SDG
here you go, AXE COP.
AFTER I TALK TO THE ROBOT IN MY FACE WE TRADE WEAPONS AND I HAVE MY NEW SECRET WEAPON ONLY FOR BOSSES.
HOOTS DYNAMITE THAT IS STICKY.
OW! OW! POW!
oh no. too sticky.
AFTER A LITTLE WHILE THEY EXPLODE ALL OVER THE BAD GUY.
BOOM!
SOMETIMES I HAVE TO USE MY OTHER SECRET WEAPON.
HA! YOU CAN'T CHOP OFF MY HEAD! MY NECK IS MADE OF SAND!
WE'LL SEE ABOUT THAT!
CHOP
HA HA HA, I TOLD YOU!
OH YEAH? HOW ABOUT...
GOLDEN AXE!
SHING!
NO! NOT GOLD!!
CHOP
SOMETIMES I USE BOTH SECRET WEAPONS.
POW! POW! POW!
CHOP OFF THE HEAD, THEN BLOW UP THE BODY.
THAT'S TO MAKE SURE THEY DON'T COME BACK TO LIFE.
BOOM
-AXE COP

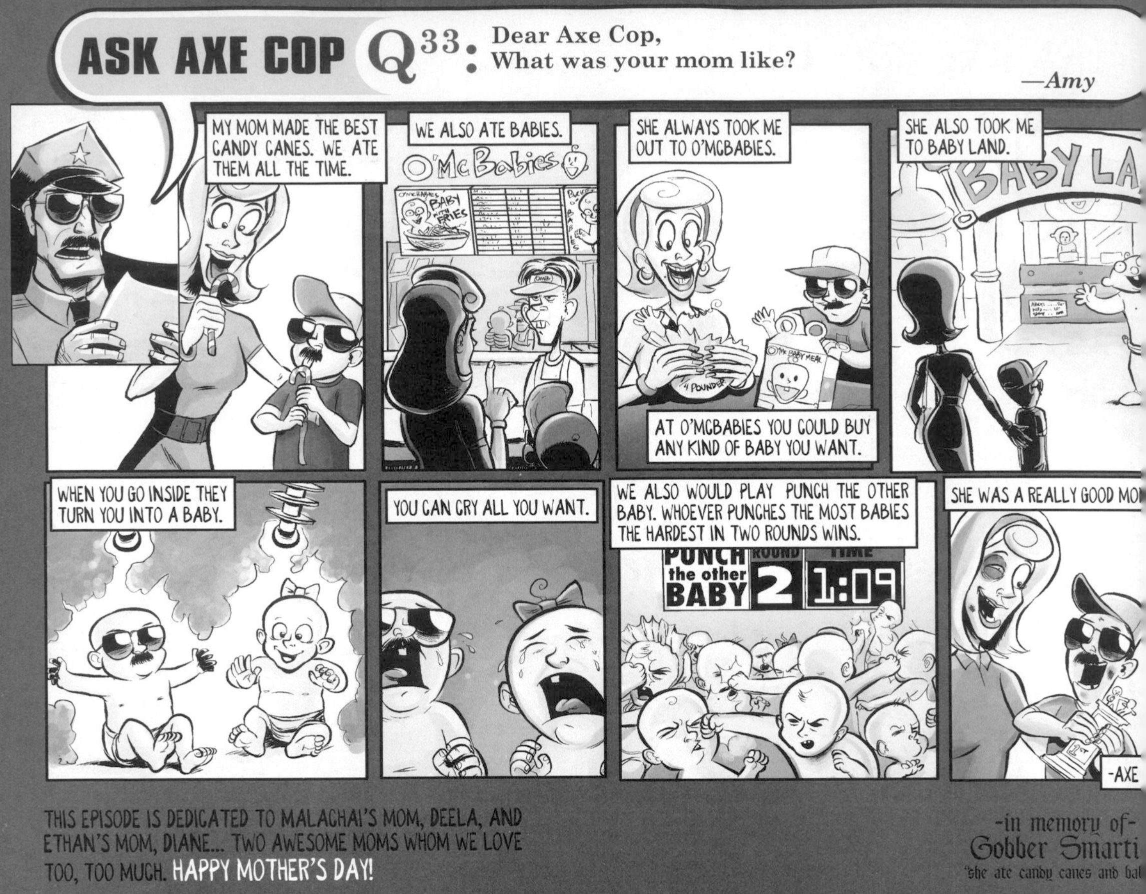
ASK AXE COP
Q33: Dear Axe Cop,
What was your mom like?
—Amy
MY MOM MADE THE BEST CANDY CANES. WE ATE THEM ALL THE TIME.
WE ALSO ATE BABIES.
O'McBabies
BABY FRIES
SHE ALWAYS TOOK ME OUT TO O'MCBABIES.
AT O'MCBABIES YOU COULD BUY ANY KIND OF BABY YOU WANT.
SHE ALSO TOOK ME TO BABY LAND.
WHEN YOU GO INSIDE THEY TURN YOU INTO A BABY.
YOU CAN CRY ALL YOU WANT.
WE ALSO WOULD PLAY PUNCH THE OTHER BABY. WHOEVER PUNCHES THE MOST BABIES THE HARDEST IN TWO ROUNDS WINS.
PUNCH the other BABY
2
1:09
SHE WAS A REALLY GOOD MO
-AXE
THIS EPISODE IS DEDICATED TO MALACHAI'S MOM, DEELA, AND ETHAN'S MOM, DIANE... TWO AWESOME MOMS WHOM WE LOVE TOO, TOO MUCH. HAPPY MOTHER'S DAY!
-in memory of-
Gobber Smarti

Ask Axe Cop #33
Mother's Day was close so we decided to do a Mother's Day episode, which ended up involving eating babies. Fortunately both my mom and Malachai's mom don't stay caught up on the comic very well, so they probably won't even see this until it is in print.

Ask Axe Cop #34
Malachai seems to have a real fascination with Spanish. He is always making up Spanish-sounding words. Also, the third dog from the left in the graduation picture is based on a real chihuahua named Lucy, owned by my friends Anthony and Amy, who helped create the *Axe Cop* website and ran the Axe Shop for its first few months.

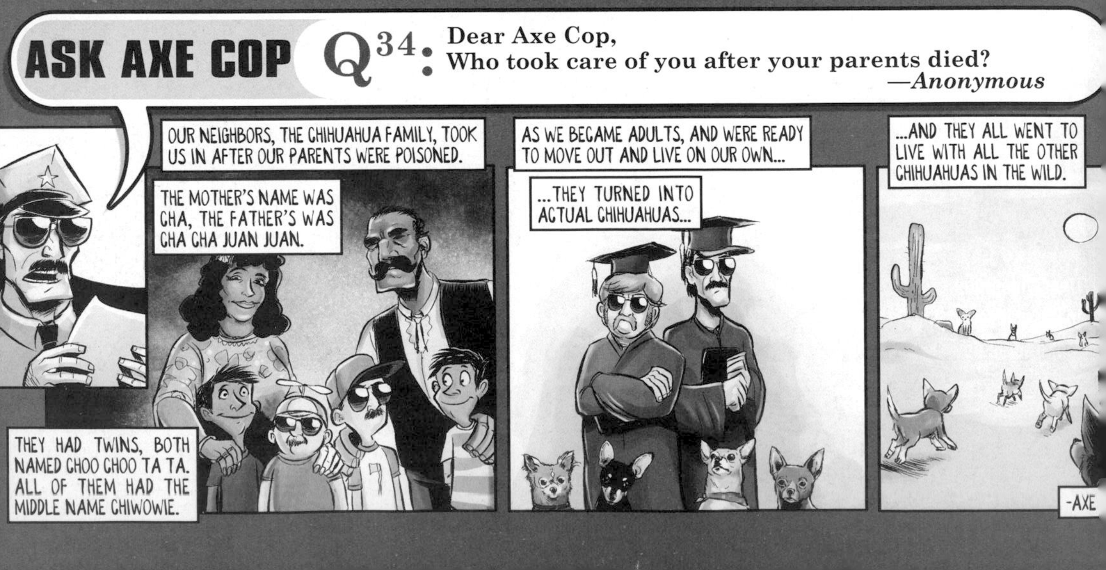
ASK AXE COP
Q34: Dear Axe Cop,
Who took care of you after your parents died?
—Anonymous
OUR NEIGHBORS, THE CHIHUAHUA FAMILY, TOOK US IN AFTER OUR PARENTS WERE POISONED.
THE MOTHER'S NAME WAS CHA, THE FATHER'S WAS CHA CHA JUAN JUAN.
THEY HAD TWINS, BOTH NAMED CHOO CHOO TA TA. ALL OF THEM HAD THE MIDDLE NAME CHIWOWIE.
AS WE BECAME ADULTS, AND WERE READY TO MOVE OUT AND LIVE ON OUR OWN...
...THEY TURNED INTO ACTUAL CHIHUAHUAS...
...AND THEY ALL WENT TO LIVE WITH ALL THE OTHER CHIHUAHUAS IN THE WILD.
-AXE

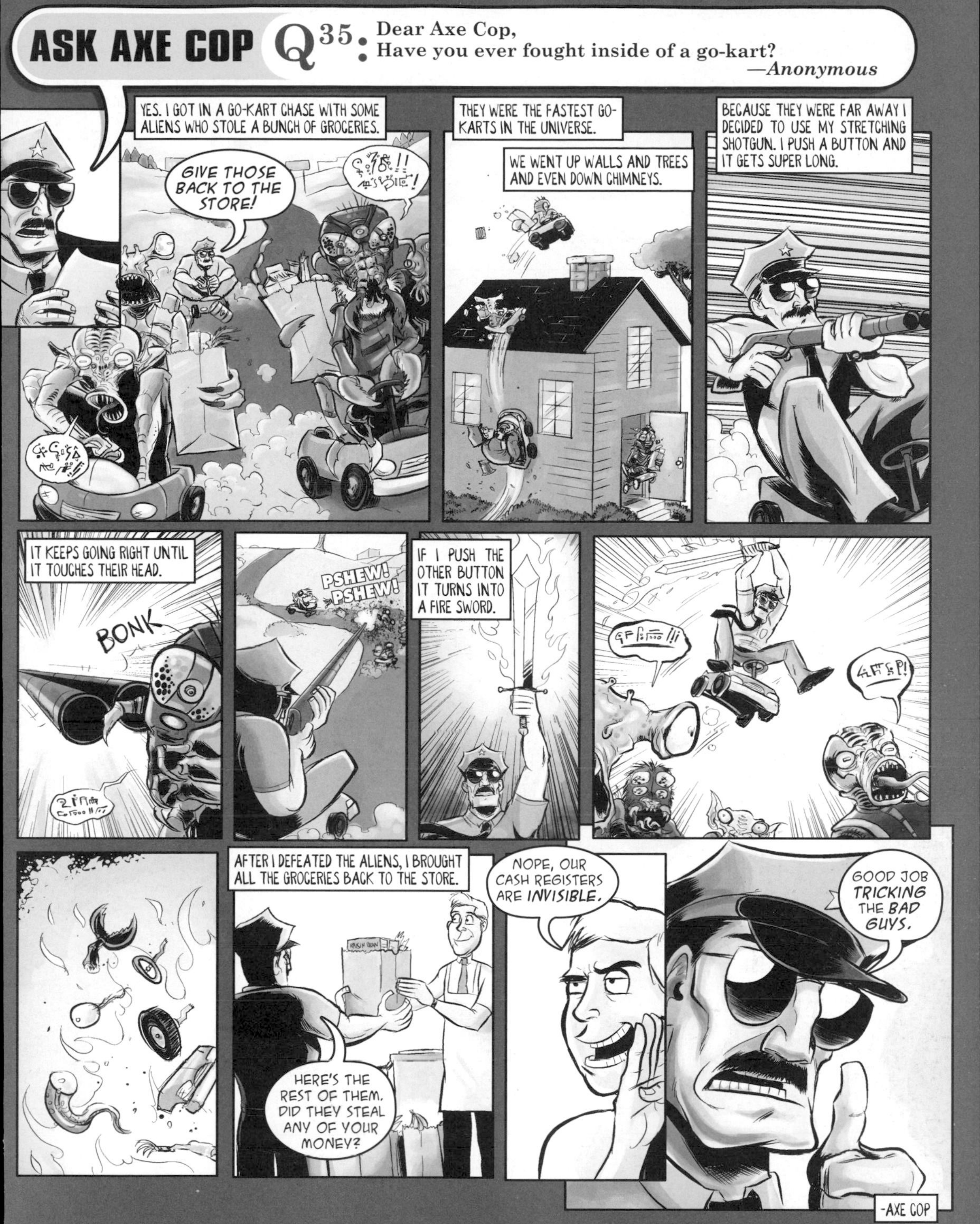
ASK AXE COP
Q35: Dear Axe Cop,
Have you ever fought inside of a go-kart?
—Anonymous
YES. I GOT IN A GO-KART CHASE WITH SOME ALIENS WHO STOLE A BUNCH OF GROCERIES.
GIVE THOSE BACK TO THE STORE!
THEY WERE THE FASTEST GO-KARTS IN THE UNIVERSE.
WE WENT UP WALLS AND TREES AND EVEN DOWN CHIMNEYS.
BECAUSE THEY WERE FAR AWAY I DECIDED TO USE MY STRETCHING SHOTGUN. I PUSH A BUTTON AND IT GETS SUPER LONG.
IT KEEPS GOING RIGHT UNTIL IT TOUCHES THEIR HEAD.
BONK
PSHEW! PSHEW!
IF I PUSH THE OTHER BUTTON IT TURNS INTO A FIRE SWORD.
AFTER I DEFEATED THE ALIENS, I BROUGHT ALL THE GROCERIES BACK TO THE STORE.
HERE'S THE REST OF THEM. DID THEY STEAL ANY OF YOUR MONEY?
NOPE, OUR CASH REGISTERS ARE INVISIBLE.
GOOD JOB TRICKING THE BAD GUYS.
-AXE COP

Ask Axe Cop #35
Dear video-game companies: I want this to be a level in the *Axe Cop* game you make some day.

Ask Axe Cop #36 (next page)
This episode was written with the help of our sister Megan. She would give Malachai pop-song ideas and he would make Axe Cop versions of them. *Ring of Fire* is one of Malachai's favorite songs.

Ask Axe Cop #37 (next facing page)
Sometimes Malachai makes up ideas that are so dumb that we put them on the "dumb list." Stupid Rhino Head is a character from the dumb list. He is really, really dumb. Also, seeing Axe Cop get owned by a flower is hilarious to me.

ASK AXE COP Q[36]: Hey Axe Cop,
Have you ever been in a band? What was its name and what kind of music did you play?
—*Rob*

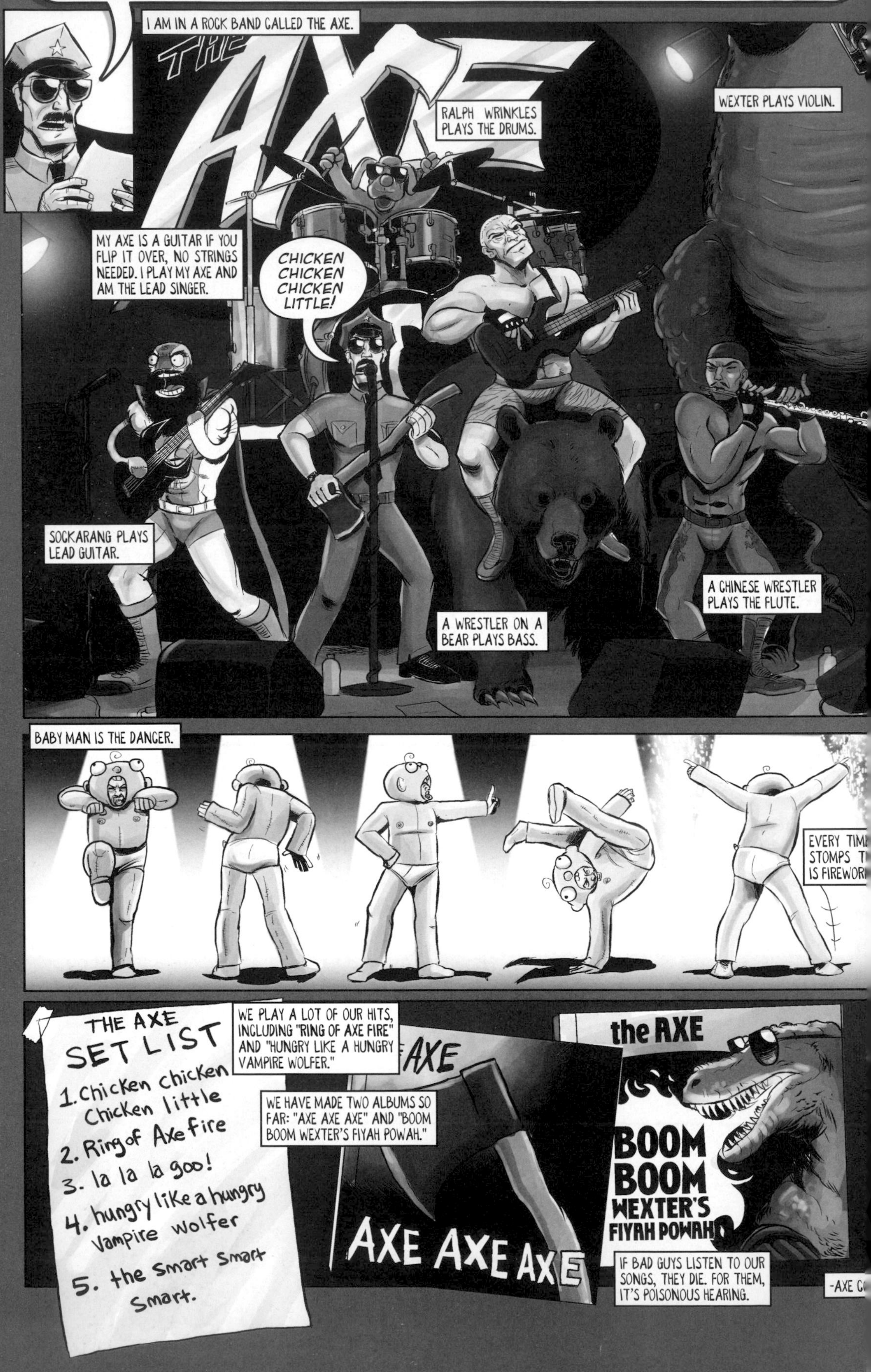

I AM IN A ROCK BAND CALLED THE AXE.
THE AXE
RALPH WRINKLES PLAYS THE DRUMS.
WEXTER PLAYS VIOLIN.
MY AXE IS A GUITAR IF YOU FLIP IT OVER, NO STRINGS NEEDED. I PLAY MY AXE AND AM THE LEAD SINGER.
CHICKEN CHICKEN CHICKEN LITTLE!
SOCKARANG PLAYS LEAD GUITAR.
A WRESTLER ON A BEAR PLAYS BASS.
A CHINESE WRESTLER PLAYS THE FLUTE.
BABY MAN IS THE DANCER.
EVERY TIM STOMPS T IS FIREWOR
THE AXE SET LIST
1. Chicken chicken Chicken little
2. Ring of Axe fire
3. la la la goo!
4. hungry like a hungry Vampire wolfer
5. the Smart Smart Smart.
WE PLAY A LOT OF OUR HITS, INCLUDING "RING OF AXE FIRE" AND "HUNGRY LIKE A HUNGRY VAMPIRE WOLFER."
WE HAVE MADE TWO ALBUMS SO FAR: "AXE AXE AXE" AND "BOOM BOOM WEXTER'S FIYAH POWAH."
AXE AXE AXE
the AXE
BOOM BOOM WEXTER'S FIYAH POWAH
IF BAD GUYS LISTEN TO OUR SONGS, THEY DIE. FOR THEM, IT'S POISONOUS HEARING.
-AXE C

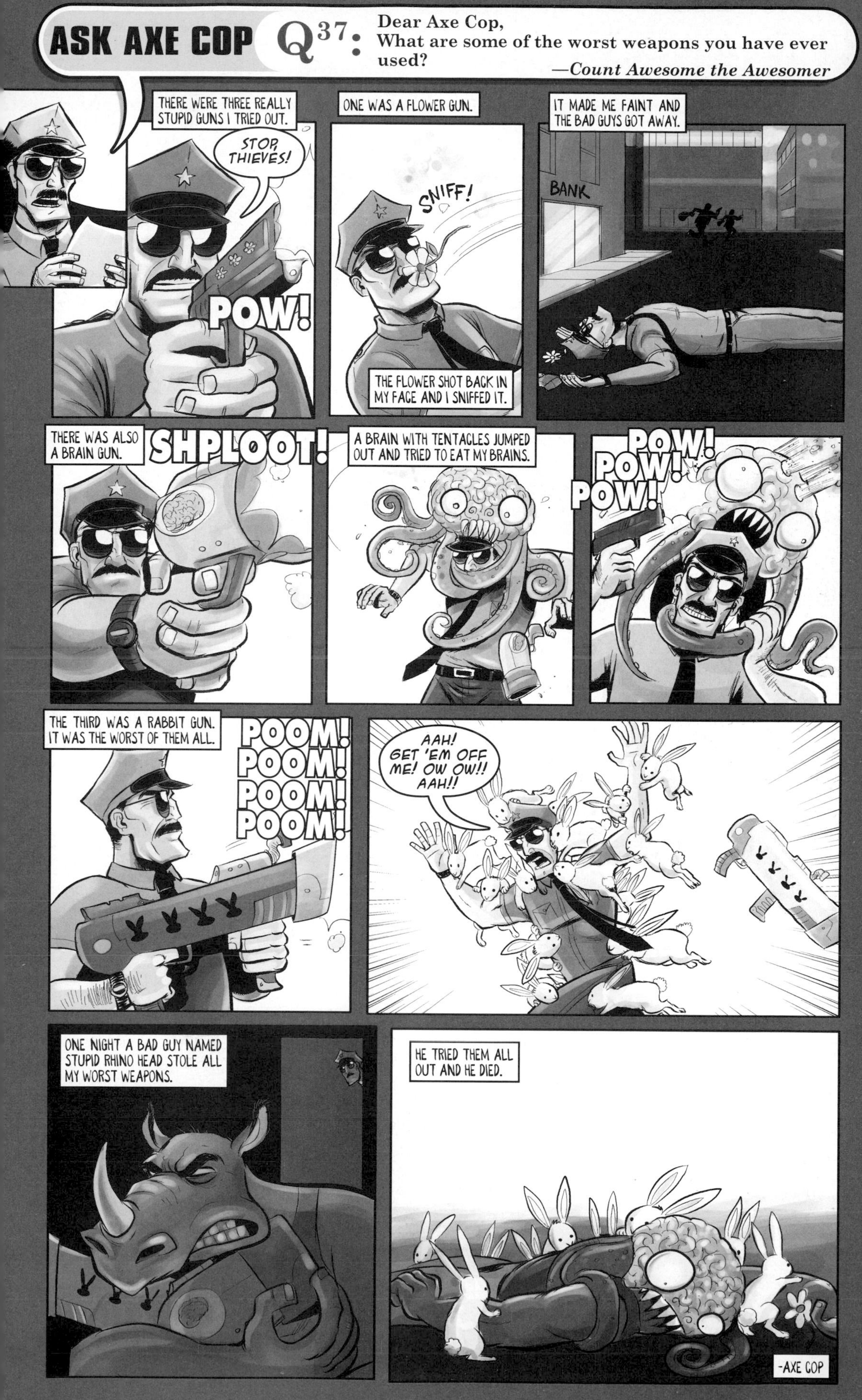
ASK AXE COP
Q37:
Dear Axe Cop,
What are some of the worst weapons you have ever used?
—Count Awesome the Awesomer
THERE WERE THREE REALLY STUPID GUNS I TRIED OUT.
STOP, THIEVES!
POW!
ONE WAS A FLOWER GUN.
SNIFF!
THE FLOWER SHOT BACK IN MY FACE AND I SNIFFED IT.
IT MADE ME FAINT AND THE BAD GUYS GOT AWAY.
BANK
THERE WAS ALSO A BRAIN GUN.
SHPLOOT!
A BRAIN WITH TENTACLES JUMPED OUT AND TRIED TO EAT MY BRAINS.
POW! POW! POW!
THE THIRD WAS A RABBIT GUN. IT WAS THE WORST OF THEM ALL.
POOM! POOM! POOM! POOM!
AAH! GET 'EM OFF ME! OW OW!! AAH!!
ONE NIGHT A BAD GUY NAMED STUPID RHINO HEAD STOLE ALL MY WORST WEAPONS.
HE TRIED THEM ALL OUT AND HE DIED.
-AXE COP

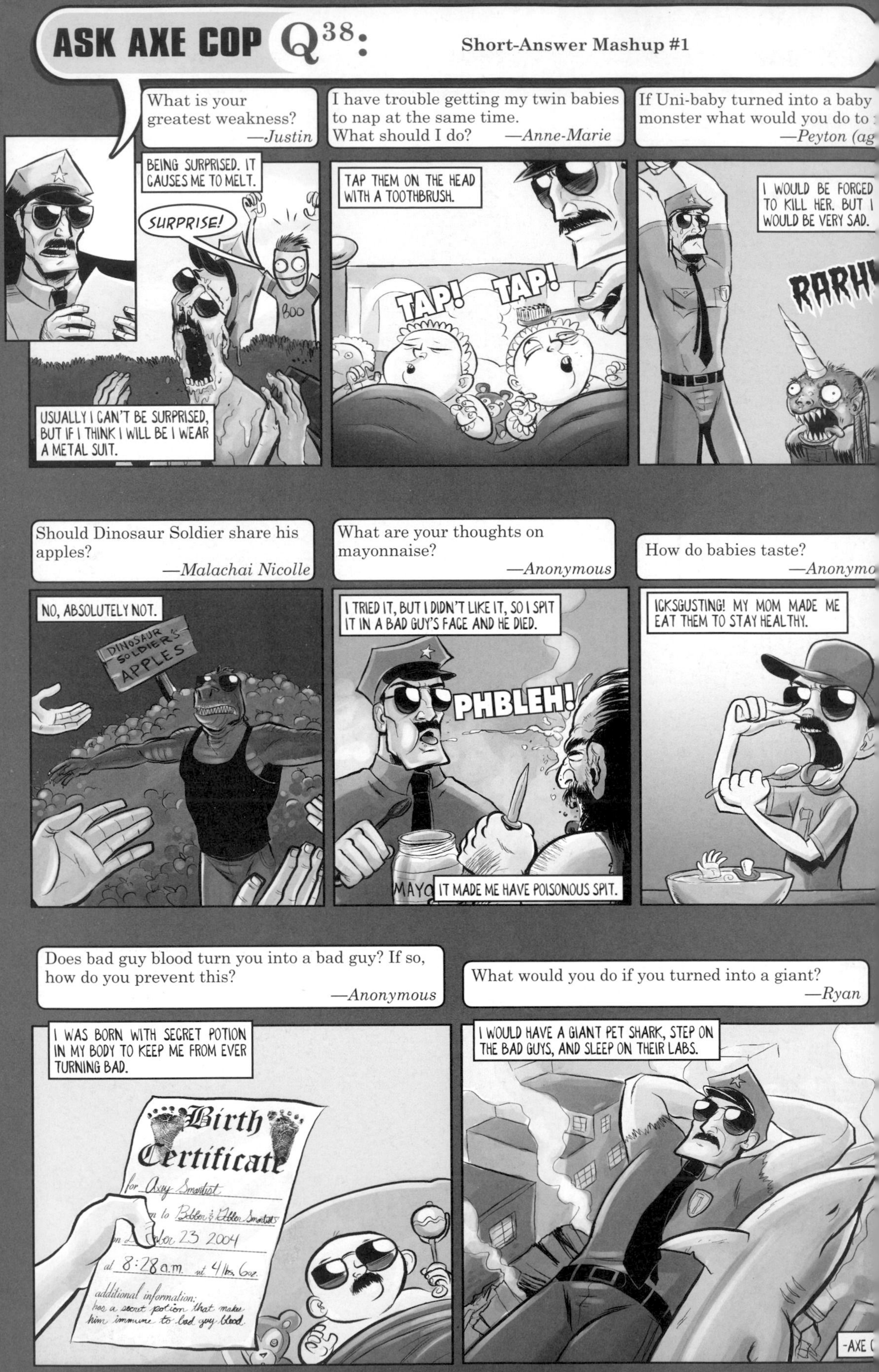

ASK AXE COP Q38:
Short-Answer Mashup #1
What is your greatest weakness? —Justin
BEING SURPRISED. IT CAUSES ME TO MELT.
SURPRISE!
BOO
USUALLY I CAN'T BE SURPRISED, BUT IF I THINK I WILL BE I WEAR A METAL SUIT.
I have trouble getting my twin babies to nap at the same time. What should I do? —Anne-Marie
TAP THEM ON THE HEAD WITH A TOOTHBRUSH.
TAP! TAP!
If Uni-baby turned into a baby monster what would you do to
—Peyton (ag
I WOULD BE FORCED TO KILL HER. BUT I WOULD BE VERY SAD.
RARH
Should Dinosaur Soldier share his apples? —Malachai Nicolle
NO, ABSOLUTELY NOT.
DINOSAUR SOLDIER'S APPLES
What are your thoughts on mayonnaise? —Anonymous
I TRIED IT, BUT I DIDN'T LIKE IT, SO I SPIT IT IN A BAD GUY'S FACE AND HE DIED.
PHBLEH!
MAYO
IT MADE ME HAVE POISONOUS SPIT.
How do babies taste? —Anonymo
ICKSGUSTING! MY MOM MADE ME EAT THEM TO STAY HEALTHY.
Does bad guy blood turn you into a bad guy? If so, how do you prevent this? —Anonymous
I WAS BORN WITH SECRET POTION IN MY BODY TO KEEP ME FROM EVER TURNING BAD.
Birth Certificate
at 8:28 a.m.
additional information: has a secret potion that makes him immune to bad guy blood.
What would you do if you turned into a giant? —Ryan
I WOULD HAVE A GIANT PET SHARK, STEP ON THE BAD GUYS, AND SLEEP ON THEIR LABS.
-AXE

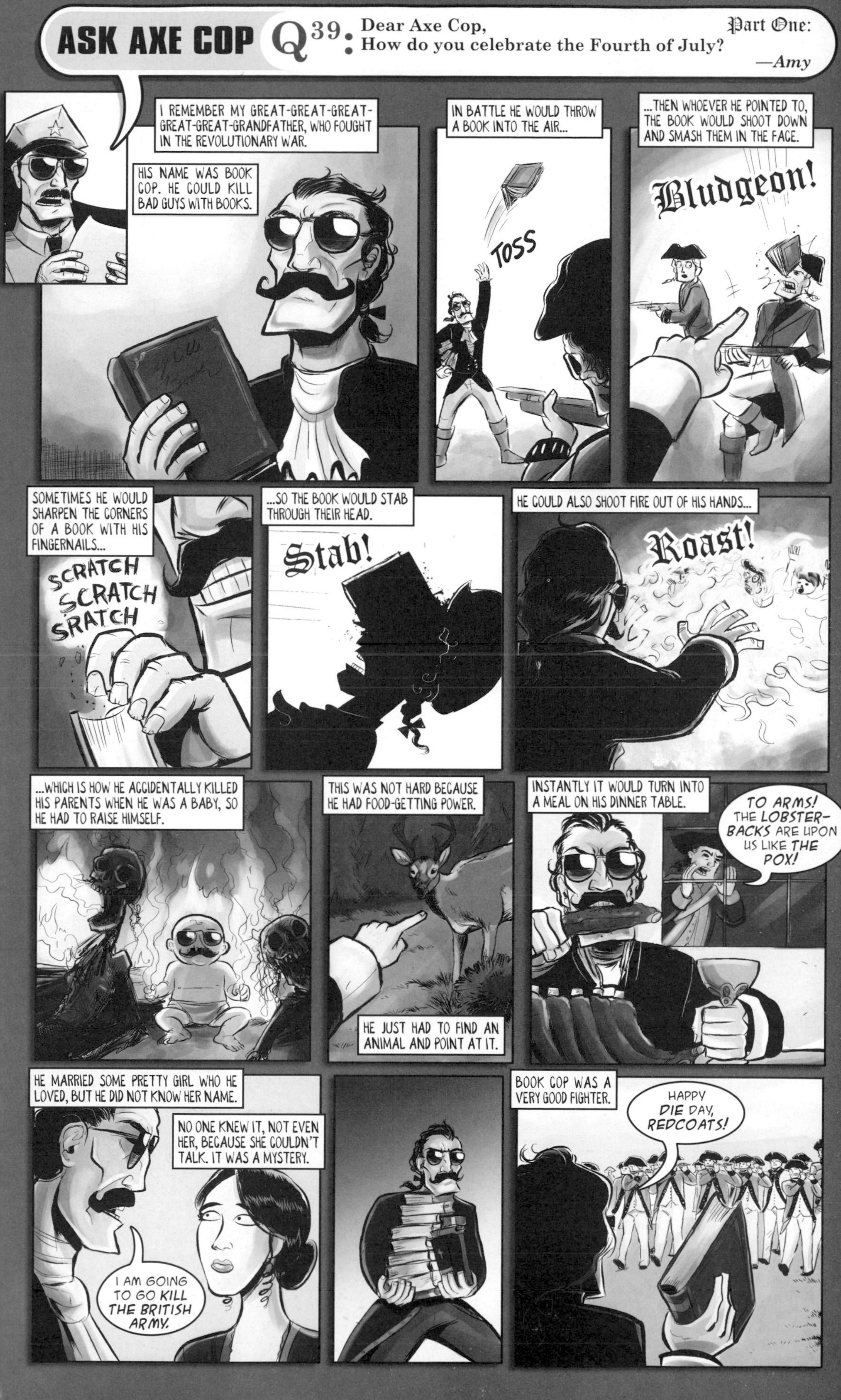
ASK AXE COP
Q39: Dear Axe Cop,
How do you celebrate the Fourth of July?
Part One:
—Amy
I REMEMBER MY GREAT-GREAT-GREAT-GREAT-GREAT-GRANDFATHER, WHO FOUGHT IN THE REVOLUTIONARY WAR.
HIS NAME WAS BOOK COP. HE COULD KILL BAD GUYS WITH BOOKS.
IN BATTLE HE WOULD THROW A BOOK INTO THE AIR...
TOSS
...THEN WHOEVER HE POINTED TO, THE BOOK WOULD SHOOT DOWN AND SMASH THEM IN THE FACE.
Bludgeon!
SOMETIMES HE WOULD SHARPEN THE CORNERS OF A BOOK WITH HIS FINGERNAILS...
SCRATCH SCRATCH SRATCH
...SO THE BOOK WOULD STAB THROUGH THEIR HEAD.
Stab!
HE COULD ALSO SHOOT FIRE OUT OF HIS HANDS...
Roast!
...WHICH IS HOW HE ACCIDENTALLY KILLED HIS PARENTS WHEN HE WAS A BABY, SO HE HAD TO RAISE HIMSELF.
THIS WAS NOT HARD BECAUSE HE HAD FOOD-GETTING POWER.
HE JUST HAD TO FIND AN ANIMAL AND POINT AT IT.
INSTANTLY IT WOULD TURN INTO A MEAL ON HIS DINNER TABLE.
TO ARMS! THE LOBSTER-BACKS ARE UPON US LIKE THE POX!
HE MARRIED SOME PRETTY GIRL WHO HE LOVED, BUT HE DID NOT KNOW HER NAME.
NO ONE KNEW IT, NOT EVEN HER, BECAUSE SHE COULDN'T TALK. IT WAS A MYSTERY.
I AM GOING TO GO KILL THE BRITISH ARMY.
BOOK COP WAS A VERY GOOD FIGHTER.
HAPPY DIE DAY, REDCOATS!

ASK AXE COP Q[40]: Dear Axe Cop,
How do you celebrate the Fourth of July?

Part Two:

—Amy

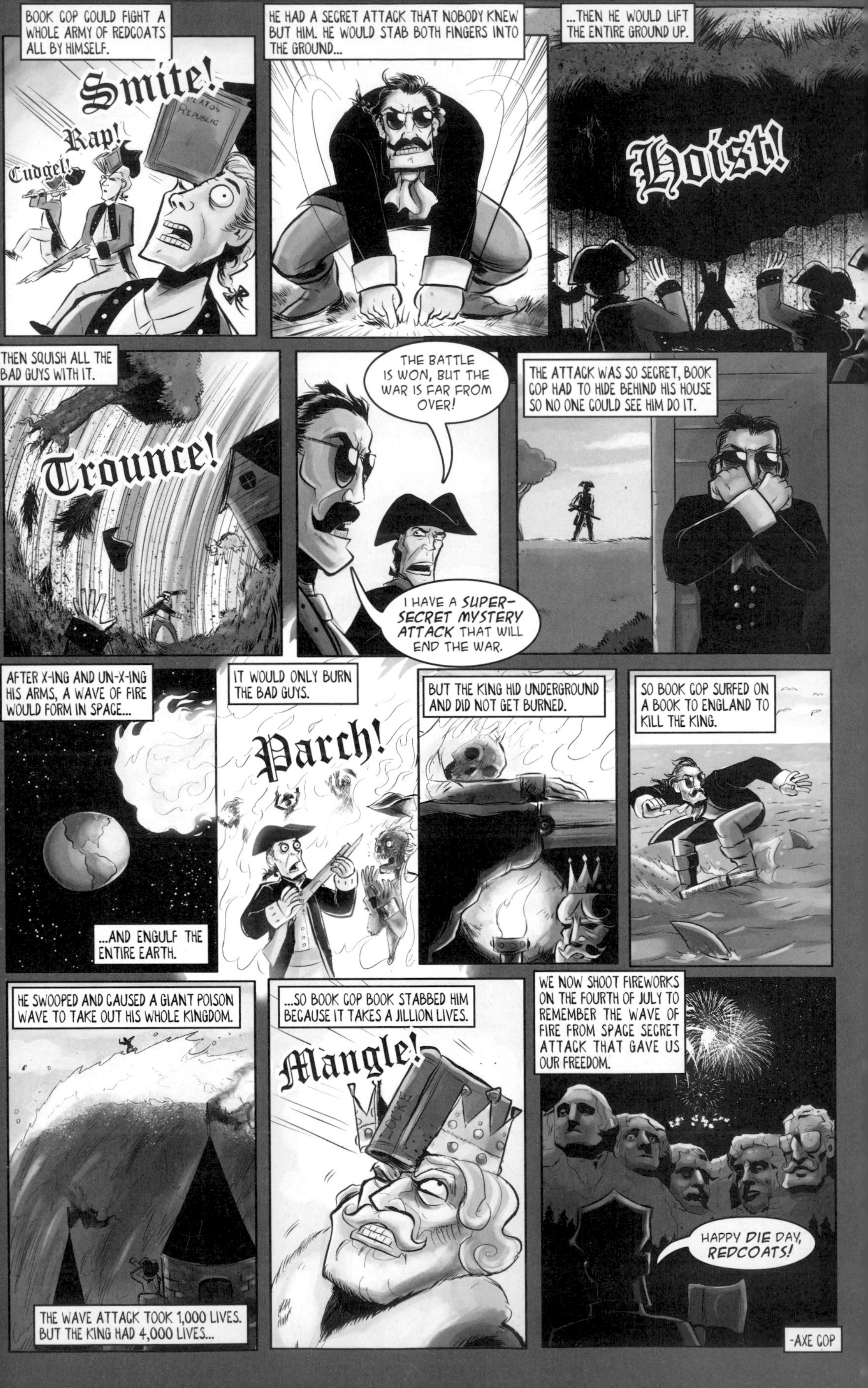

BOOK COP COULD FIGHT A WHOLE ARMY OF REDCOATS ALL BY HIMSELF.
Smite!
PLATO'S REPUBLIC
Rap!
Cudgel!
HE HAD A SECRET ATTACK THAT NOBODY KNEW BUT HIM. HE WOULD STAB BOTH FINGERS INTO THE GROUND...
...THEN HE WOULD LIFT THE ENTIRE GROUND UP.
Hoist!
THEN SQUISH ALL THE BAD GUYS WITH IT.
Trounce!
THE BATTLE IS WON, BUT THE WAR IS FAR FROM OVER!
I HAVE A SUPER-SECRET MYSTERY ATTACK THAT WILL END THE WAR.
THE ATTACK WAS SO SECRET, BOOK COP HAD TO HIDE BEHIND HIS HOUSE SO NO ONE COULD SEE HIM DO IT.
AFTER X-ING AND UN-X-ING HIS ARMS, A WAVE OF FIRE WOULD FORM IN SPACE...
...AND ENGULF THE ENTIRE EARTH.
IT WOULD ONLY BURN THE BAD GUYS.
Parch!
BUT THE KING HID UNDERGROUND AND DID NOT GET BURNED.
SO BOOK COP SURFED ON A BOOK TO ENGLAND TO KILL THE KING.
HE SWOOPED AND CAUSED A GIANT POISON WAVE TO TAKE OUT HIS WHOLE KINGDOM.
THE WAVE ATTACK TOOK 1,000 LIVES. BUT THE KING HAD 4,000 LIVES...
...SO BOOK COP BOOK STABBED HIM BECAUSE IT TAKES A JILLION LIVES.
Mangle!
LOCKE
WE NOW SHOOT FIREWORKS ON THE FOURTH OF JULY TO REMEMBER THE WAVE OF FIRE FROM SPACE SECRET ATTACK THAT GAVE US OUR FREEDOM.
HAPPY DIE DAY, REDCOATS!
-AXE COP

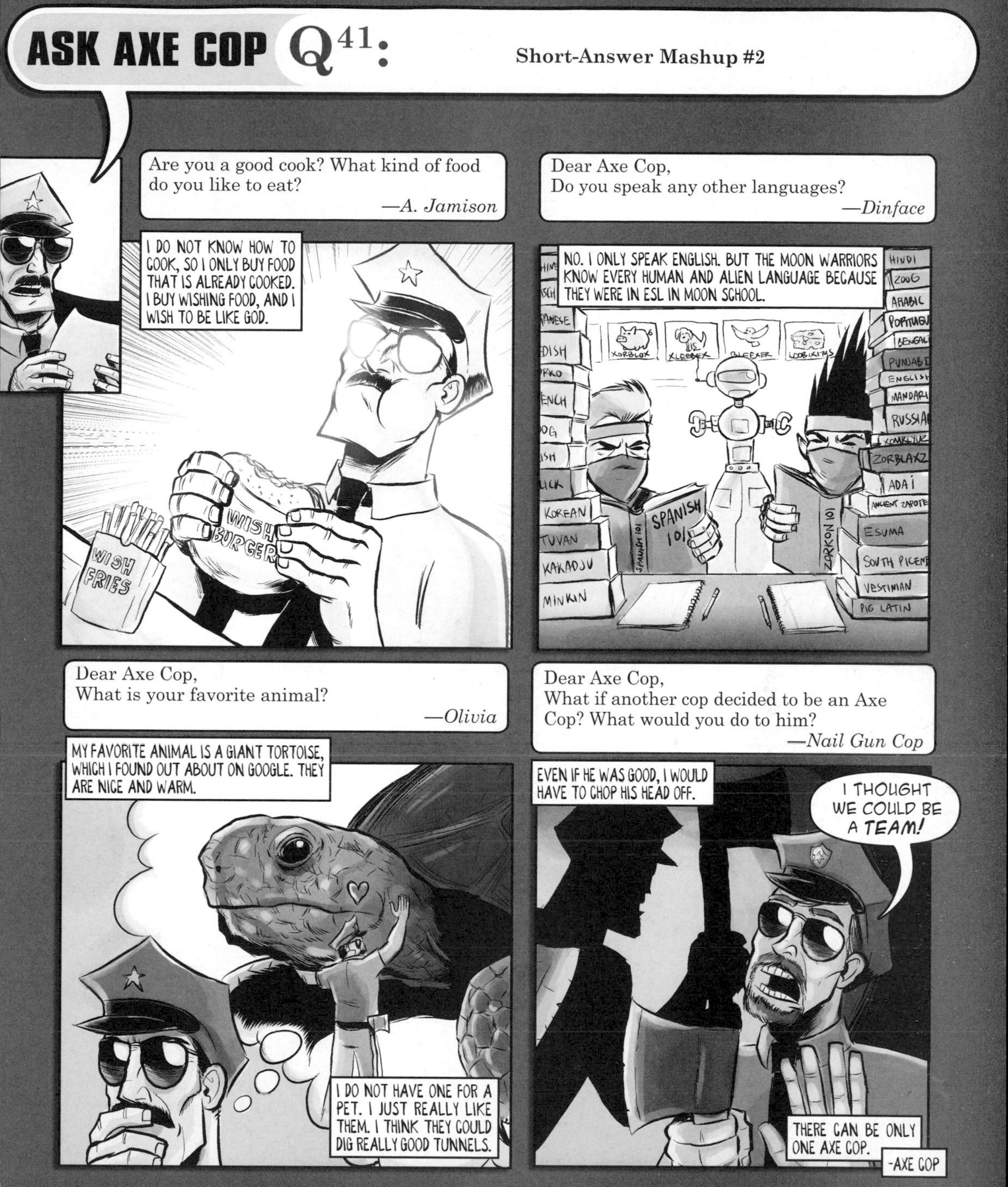
ASK AXE COP Q41:
Short-Answer Mashup #2
Are you a good cook? What kind of food do you like to eat?
—A. Jamison
I DO NOT KNOW HOW TO COOK, SO I ONLY BUY FOOD THAT IS ALREADY COOKED. I BUY WISHING FOOD, AND I WISH TO BE LIKE GOD.
WISH BURGER
WISH FRIES
Dear Axe Cop,
Do you speak any other languages?
—Dinface
NO. I ONLY SPEAK ENGLISH. BUT THE MOON WARRIORS KNOW EVERY HUMAN AND ALIEN LANGUAGE BECAUSE THEY WERE IN ESL IN MOON SCHOOL.
SPANISH 101
ZORKON 101
Dear Axe Cop,
What is your favorite animal?
—Olivia
MY FAVORITE ANIMAL IS A GIANT TORTOISE, WHICH I FOUND OUT ABOUT ON GOOGLE. THEY ARE NICE AND WARM.
I DO NOT HAVE ONE FOR A PET. I JUST REALLY LIKE THEM. I THINK THEY COULD DIG REALLY GOOD TUNNELS.
Dear Axe Cop,
What if another cop decided to be an Axe Cop? What would you do to him?
—Nail Gun Cop
EVEN IF HE WAS GOOD, I WOULD HAVE TO CHOP HIS HEAD OFF.
I THOUGHT WE COULD BE A TEAM!
THERE CAN BE ONLY ONE AXE COP.
-AXE COP

Ask Axe Cop #39 and #40
Another double episode of Ask Axe Cop. I really loved this one. I had a lot of fun looking in the thesaurus for sound effects. I tried to give Malachai a very basic/horrible history of the American Revolution and this is what we made of it.

Ask Axe Cop #38 and #41
I have a massive document of Axe Cop questions and answers from Malachai. Often he gives an answer that is too short for a full strip, so I save it for later. He was so worn out from giving me tons of material for the Fourth of July episode that I decided to clear out all my short answers and give him a break.

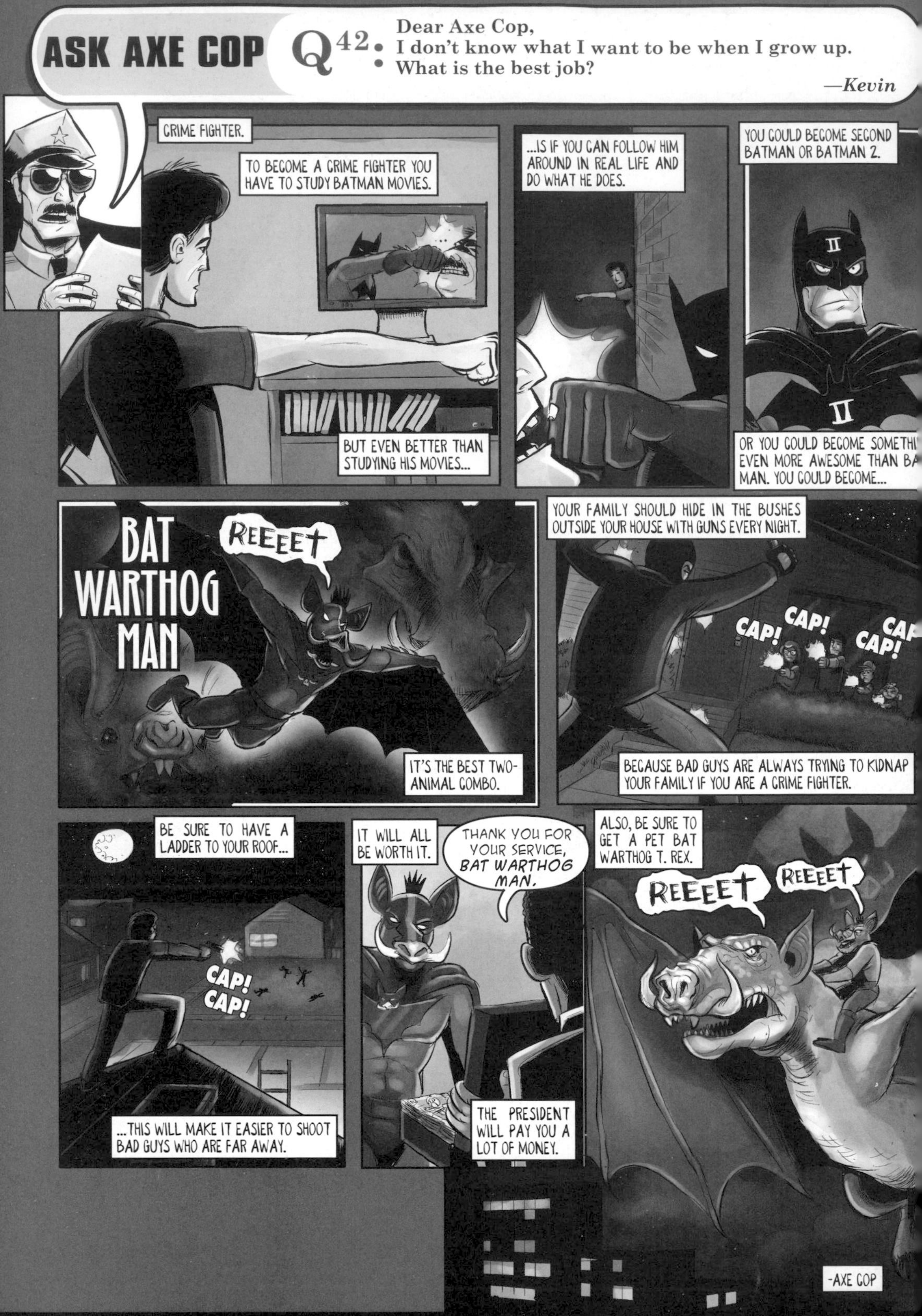
ASK AXE COP
Q42: Dear Axe Cop,
I don't know what I want to be when I grow up.
What is the best job?
—Kevin
CRIME FIGHTER.
TO BECOME A CRIME FIGHTER YOU HAVE TO STUDY BATMAN MOVIES.
BUT EVEN BETTER THAN STUDYING HIS MOVIES...
...IS IF YOU CAN FOLLOW HIM AROUND IN REAL LIFE AND DO WHAT HE DOES.
YOU COULD BECOME SECOND BATMAN OR BATMAN 2.
OR YOU COULD BECOME SOMETHI EVEN MORE AWESOME THAN BA MAN. YOU COULD BECOME...
BAT WARTHOG MAN
REEEET
IT'S THE BEST TWO-ANIMAL COMBO.
YOUR FAMILY SHOULD HIDE IN THE BUSHES OUTSIDE YOUR HOUSE WITH GUNS EVERY NIGHT.
CAP! CAP! CAP! CA
BECAUSE BAD GUYS ARE ALWAYS TRYING TO KIDNAP YOUR FAMILY IF YOU ARE A CRIME FIGHTER.
BE SURE TO HAVE A LADDER TO YOUR ROOF...
CAP! CAP!
...THIS WILL MAKE IT EASIER TO SHOOT BAD GUYS WHO ARE FAR AWAY.
IT WILL ALL BE WORTH IT.
THANK YOU FOR YOUR SERVICE, BAT WARTHOG MAN.
THE PRESIDENT WILL PAY YOU A LOT OF MONEY.
ALSO, BE SURE TO GET A PET BAT WARTHOG T. REX.
REEEET
REEEET
-AXE COP

Ask Axe Cop #42
Last time I visited Malachai I brought some books of animals and asked him to pick out some cool animal combinations. He discovered the warthog (he pronounces it "war hog") and the bat, and closed the books, declaring he had found the best two-animal combo and had no need to look any further. Later, when looking into improving Batman, he knew exactly what was missing. He needed to be part warthog.

Part Seven:
The Ultimate Battle

Episodes 23–70

After finishing "The Moon Warriors," I asked Malachai what he wanted to title our next story. He said, "The Ultimate Battle," without skipping a beat. After that he started talking about a zombie dog woman named Hasta Mia. There was no ultimate battle in sight, and I didn't even know if we would actually get to one. What's amazing about this story is there actually is one, and it almost looks like we planned it all along.

This story was new ground in many ways. It was by far the longest episode, spanning over forty-five pages. It also was our first story to have a subplot: the Baby Man story.

A lot of people loved Baby Man, including me. I wanted to see more of him. During one of Malachai's dry spells I thought maybe to fill space on the site I would do a comic where Baby Man chases a duck, and when I can't get an update from Malachai, for filler I would have him chase a duck and make it epic. Well, the day I started to draw it, Malachai called and gave me a bunch of material. So I asked him if he wanted to do a story about Baby Man chasing a duck. He laughed really hard and took it from there. We wrote most of the Baby Man story right there. It was a simple story of a series of chases. A cat-and-mouse story. Of course my vision for it was *Die Hard* in a baby suit. But to really make it a chase I couldn't have narration skipping over all the good parts, so I tried doing a story with no narration, which was a first in the *Axe Cop* universe. Some people didn't like it. Others, including me, loved it. I think that it will read much better in this book because it will move fast like it is supposed to. No long waits between pages like online.

I rearranged the order of the pages in this story so that it would read a little smoother. Online, the two subplots switched off every day. I clumped scenes together more naturally for the book.

This story ended up being twice as long as planned. I estimated it to be a twenty-two pager and it surpassed forty-five. Malachai would add so much great stuff every time I called him, and the Baby Man story took up so many pages, that it ended up becoming quite the epic tale. It was a lot of fun to draw, and it was good practice for the next project Malachai and I are working on, which is a three-part miniseries that will be at least sixty-six pages.

—Ethan

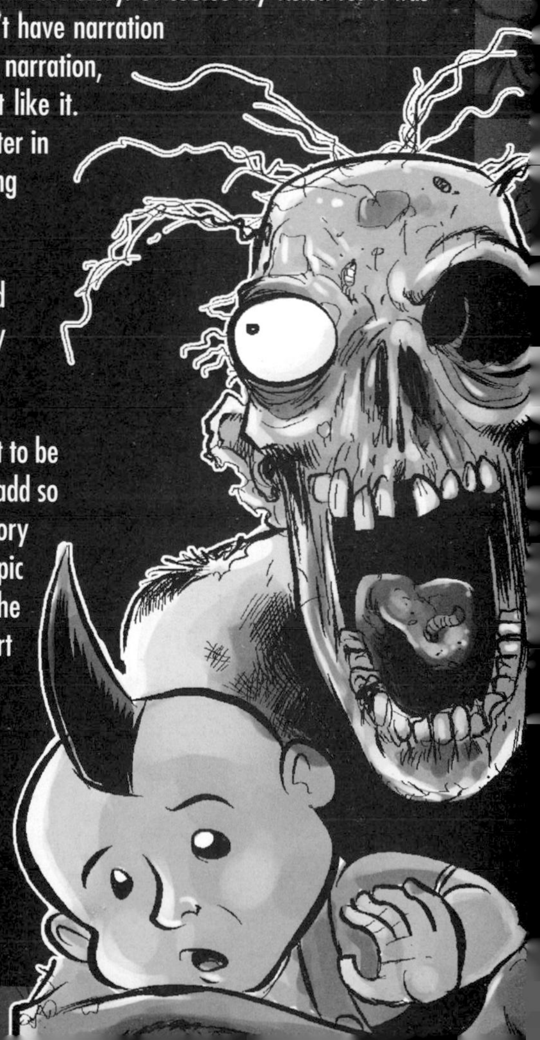

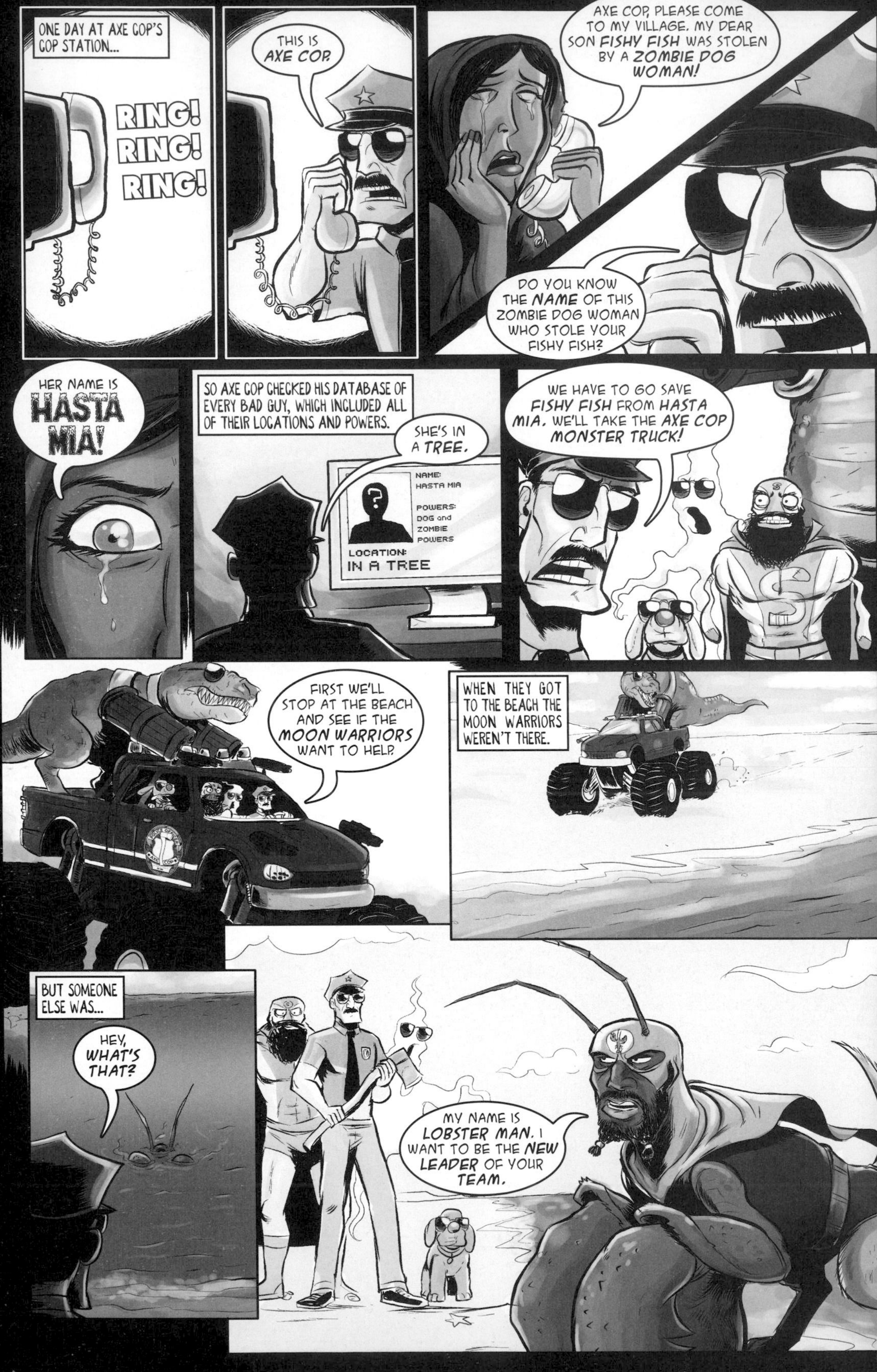

ONE DAY AT AXE COP'S COP STATION...
RING! RING! RING!
THIS IS AXE COP.
AXE COP, PLEASE COME TO MY VILLAGE. MY DEAR SON FISHY FISH WAS STOLEN BY A ZOMBIE DOG WOMAN!
DO YOU KNOW THE NAME OF THIS ZOMBIE DOG WOMAN WHO STOLE YOUR FISHY FISH?
HER NAME IS HASTA MIA!
SO AXE COP CHECKED HIS DATABASE OF EVERY BAD GUY, WHICH INCLUDED ALL OF THEIR LOCATIONS AND POWERS.
SHE'S IN A TREE.
NAME: HASTA MIA
POWERS: DOG and ZOMBIE POWERS
LOCATION: IN A TREE
WE HAVE TO GO SAVE FISHY FISH FROM HASTA MIA. WE'LL TAKE THE AXE COP MONSTER TRUCK!
FIRST WE'LL STOP AT THE BEACH AND SEE IF THE MOON WARRIORS WANT TO HELP.
WHEN THEY GOT TO THE BEACH THE MOON WARRIORS WEREN'T THERE.
BUT SOMEONE ELSE WAS...
HEY, WHAT'S THAT?
MY NAME IS LOBSTER MAN. I WANT TO BE THE NEW LEADER OF YOUR TEAM.

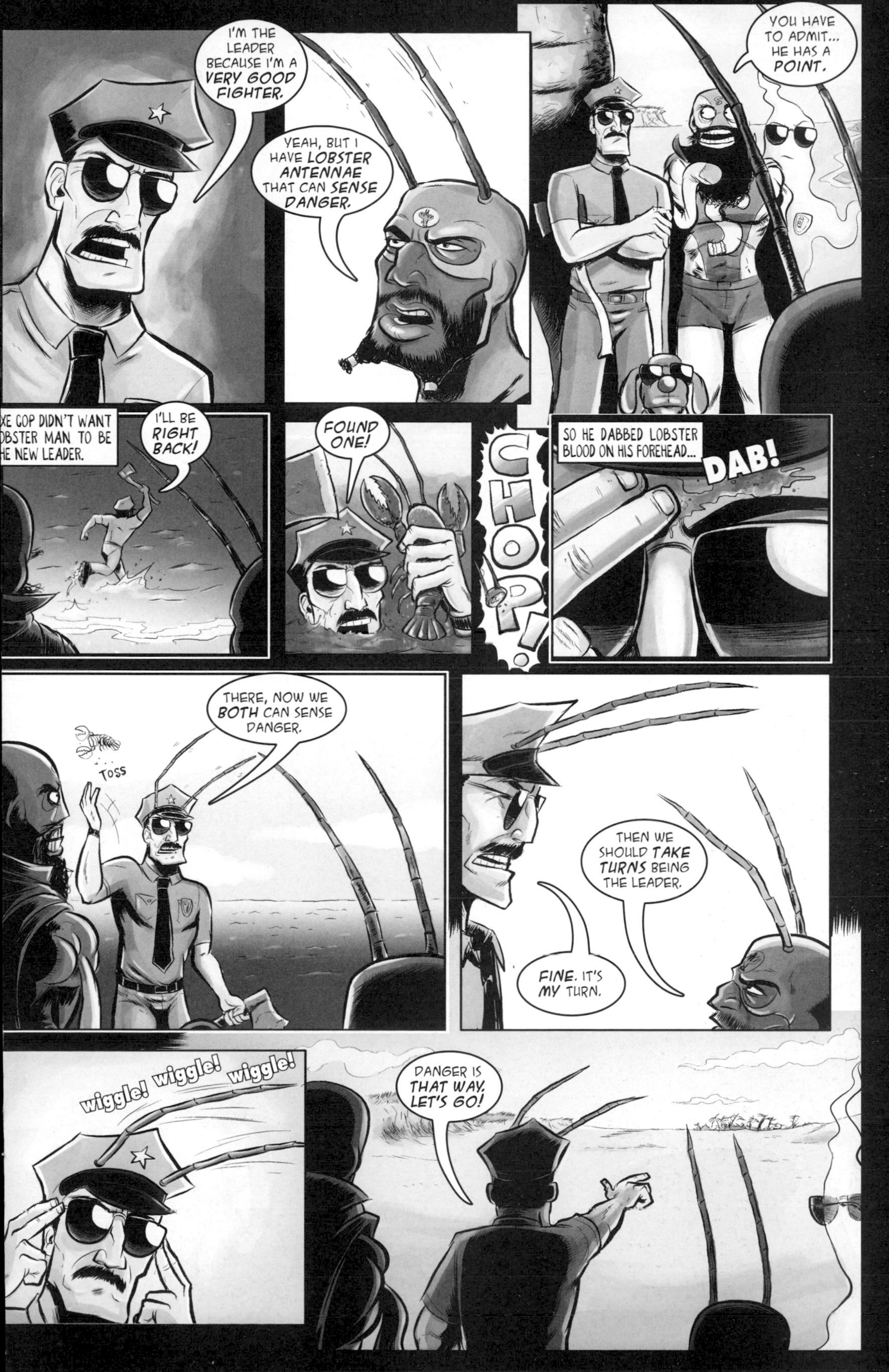
I'M THE LEADER BECAUSE I'M A VERY GOOD FIGHTER.
YEAH, BUT I HAVE LOBSTER ANTENNAE THAT CAN SENSE DANGER.
YOU HAVE TO ADMIT... HE HAS A POINT.
XE COP DIDN'T WANT OBSTER MAN TO BE HE NEW LEADER.
I'LL BE RIGHT BACK!
FOUND ONE!
CHOP!
SO HE DABBED LOBSTER BLOOD ON HIS FOREHEAD...
DAB!
THERE, NOW WE BOTH CAN SENSE DANGER.
TOSS
THEN WE SHOULD TAKE TURNS BEING THE LEADER.
FINE. IT'S MY TURN.
wiggle! wiggle! wiggle!
DANGER IS THAT WAY. LET'S GO!

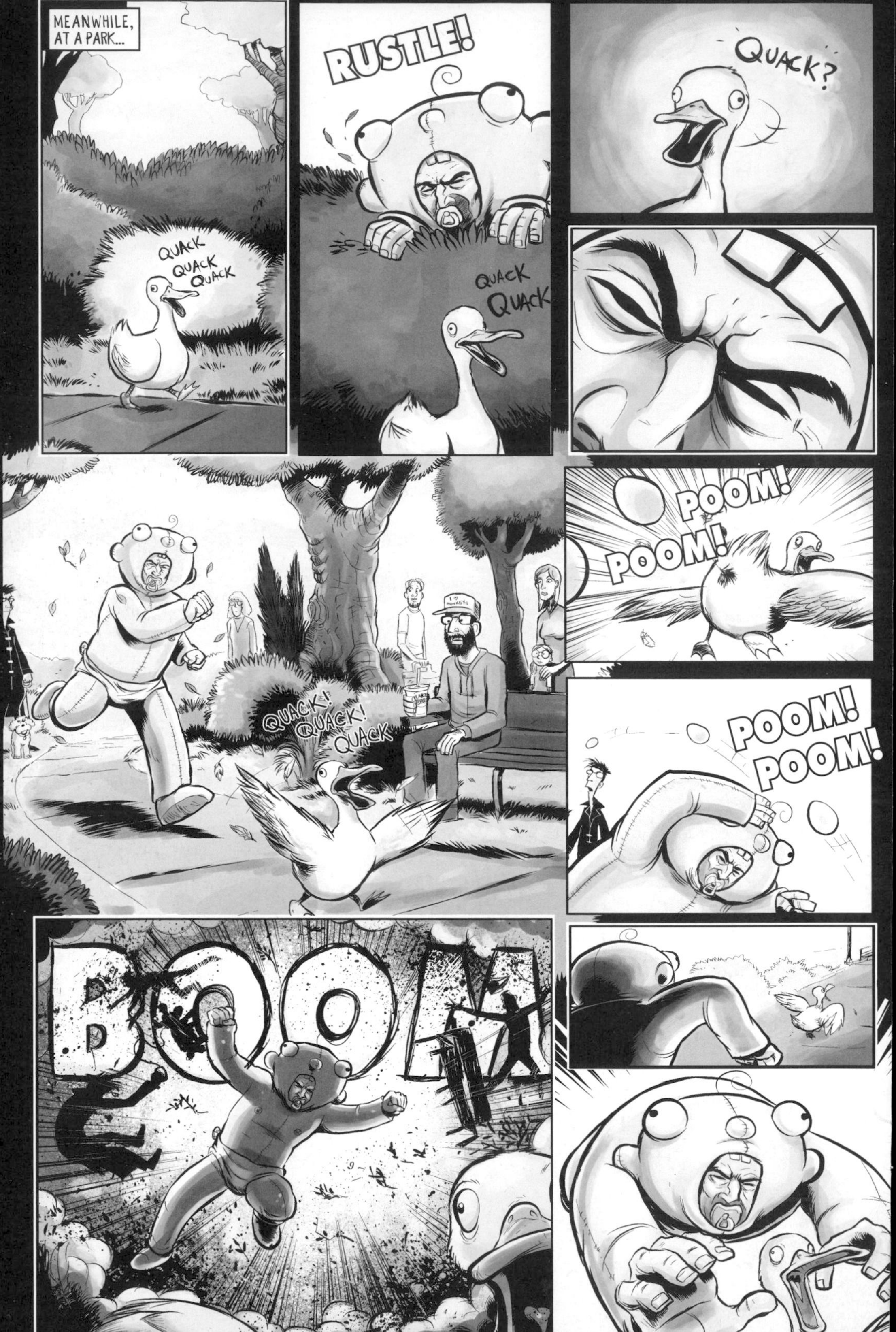
MEANWHILE, AT A PARK...
QUACK QUACK QUACK
RUSTLE!
QUACK QUACK
QUACK?
POOM! POOM!
QUACK! QUACK! QUACK
POOM! POOM!
BOOM

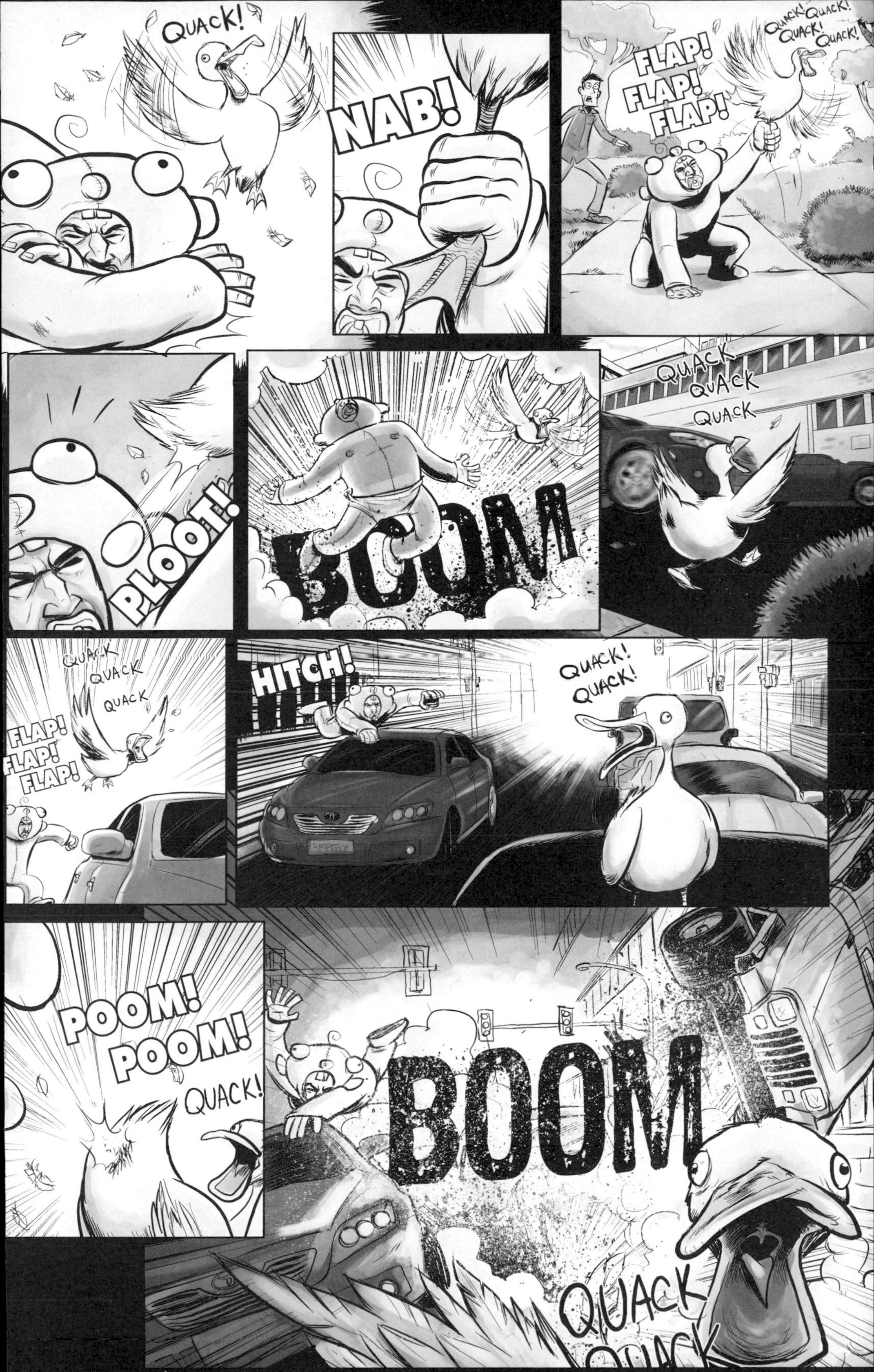
QUACK!
NAB!
FLAP! FLAP! FLAP!
QUACK! QUACK! QUACK! QUACK!
PLOOT!
BOOM
QUACK QUACK QUACK
QUACK QUACK QUACK
FLAP! FLAP! FLAP!
HITCH!
QUACK! QUACK!
POOM! POOM!
QUACK!
BOOM
QUACK

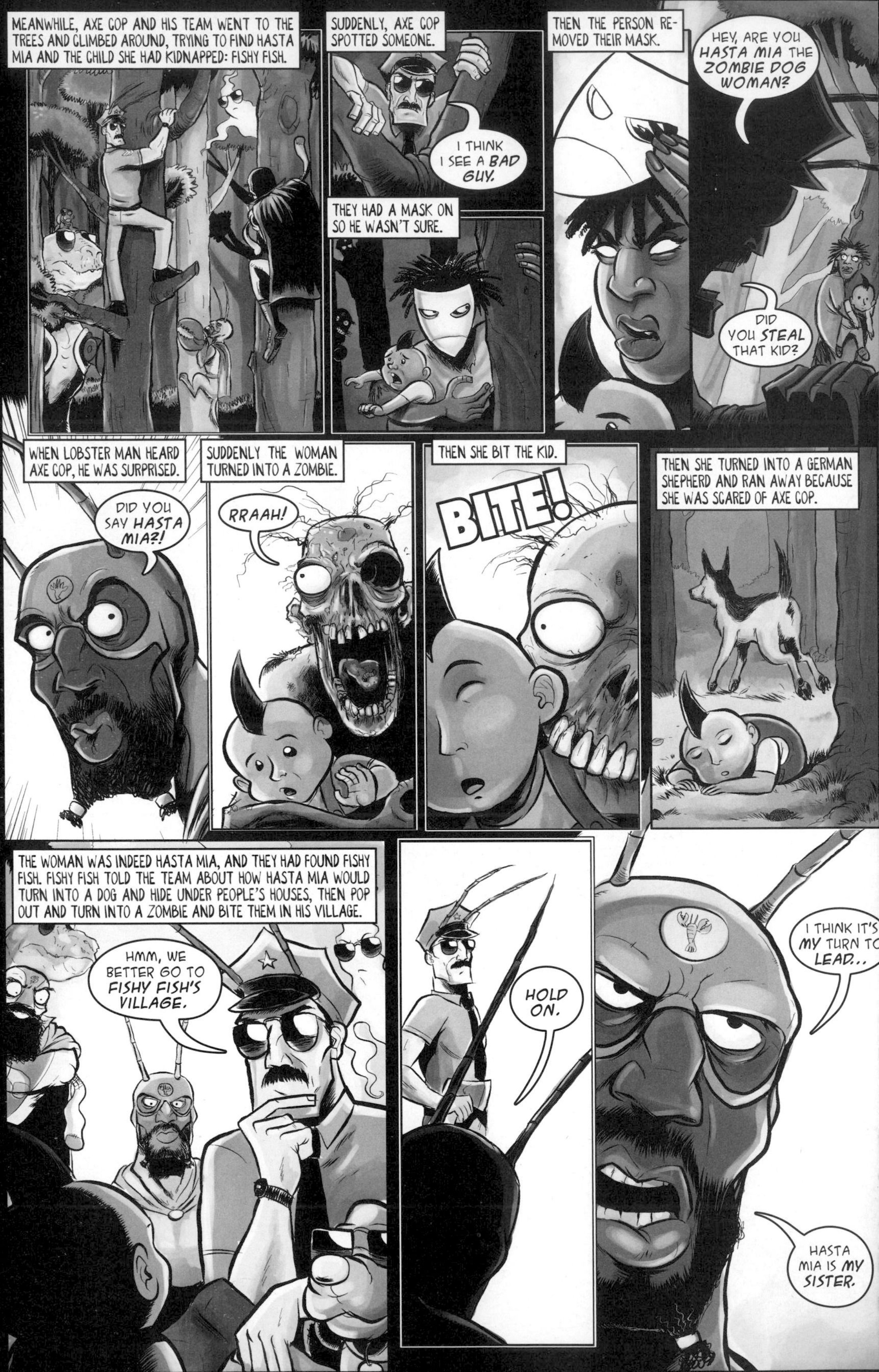

MEANWHILE, AXE COP AND HIS TEAM WENT TO THE TREES AND CLIMBED AROUND, TRYING TO FIND HASTA MIA AND THE CHILD SHE HAD KIDNAPPED: FISHY FISH.
SUDDENLY, AXE COP SPOTTED SOMEONE.
I THINK I SEE A BAD GUY.
THEY HAD A MASK ON SO HE WASN'T SURE.
THEN THE PERSON REMOVED THEIR MASK.
HEY, ARE YOU HASTA MIA THE ZOMBIE DOG WOMAN?
DID YOU STEAL THAT KID?
WHEN LOBSTER MAN HEARD AXE COP, HE WAS SURPRISED.
DID YOU SAY HASTA MIA?!
SUDDENLY THE WOMAN TURNED INTO A ZOMBIE.
RRAAH!
THEN SHE BIT THE KID.
BITE!
THEN SHE TURNED INTO A GERMAN SHEPHERD AND RAN AWAY BECAUSE SHE WAS SCARED OF AXE COP.
THE WOMAN WAS INDEED HASTA MIA, AND THEY HAD FOUND FISHY FISH. FISHY FISH TOLD THE TEAM ABOUT HOW HASTA MIA WOULD TURN INTO A DOG AND HIDE UNDER PEOPLE'S HOUSES, THEN POP OUT AND TURN INTO A ZOMBIE AND BITE THEM IN HIS VILLAGE.
HMM, WE BETTER GO TO FISHY FISH'S VILLAGE.
HOLD ON.
I THINK IT'S MY TURN TO LEAD...
HASTA MIA IS MY SISTER.

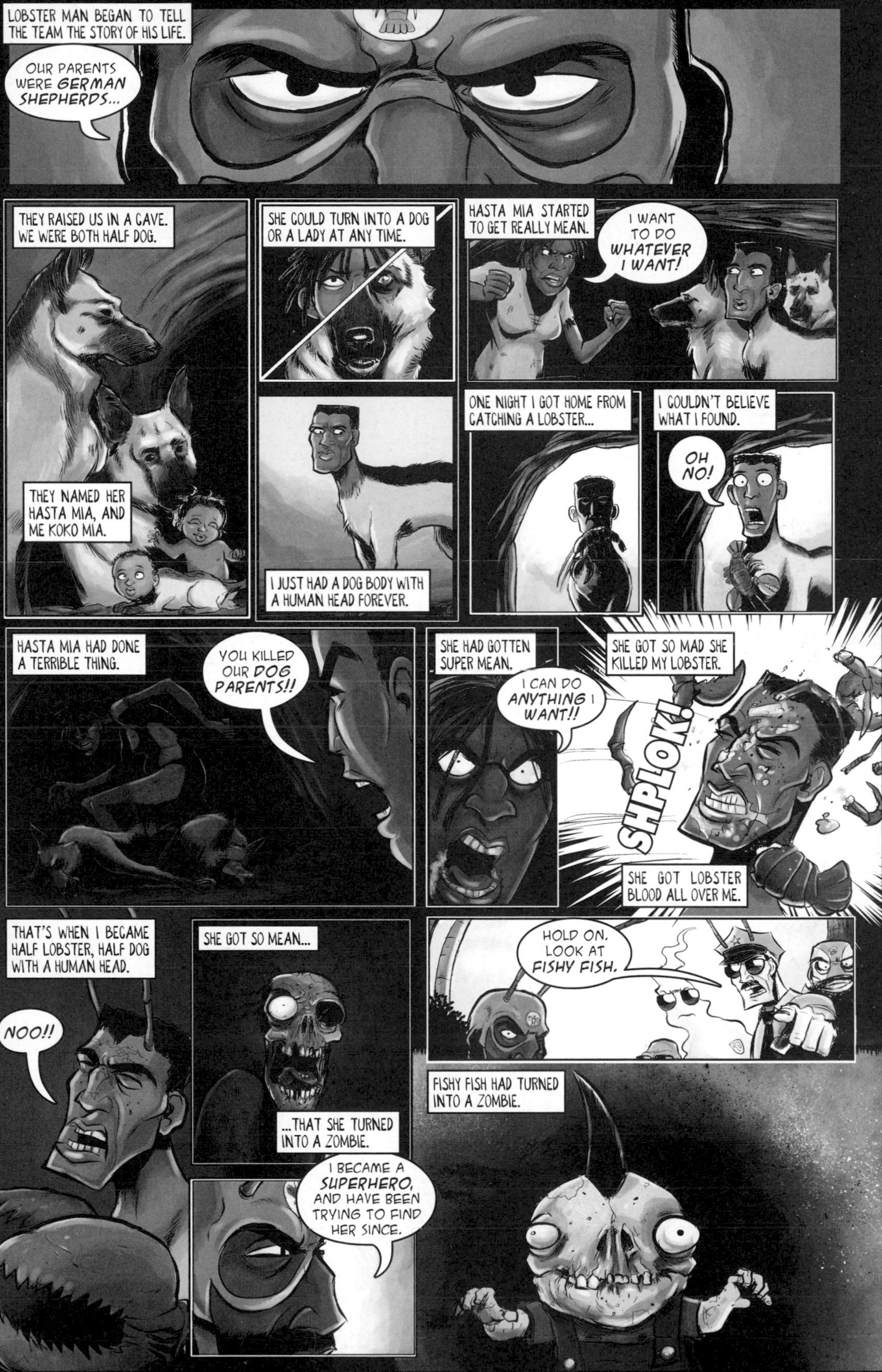

LOBSTER MAN BEGAN TO TELL THE TEAM THE STORY OF HIS LIFE.
OUR PARENTS WERE GERMAN SHEPHERDS...
THEY RAISED US IN A CAVE. WE WERE BOTH HALF DOG.
THEY NAMED HER HASTA MIA, AND ME KOKO MIA.
SHE COULD TURN INTO A DOG OR A LADY AT ANY TIME.
I JUST HAD A DOG BODY WITH A HUMAN HEAD FOREVER.
HASTA MIA STARTED TO GET REALLY MEAN.
I WANT TO DO WHATEVER I WANT!
ONE NIGHT I GOT HOME FROM CATCHING A LOBSTER...
I COULDN'T BELIEVE WHAT I FOUND.
OH NO!
HASTA MIA HAD DONE A TERRIBLE THING.
YOU KILLED OUR DOG PARENTS!!
SHE HAD GOTTEN SUPER MEAN.
I CAN DO ANYTHING I WANT!!
SHE GOT SO MAD SHE KILLED MY LOBSTER.
SHPLOK!
SHE GOT LOBSTER BLOOD ALL OVER ME.
THAT'S WHEN I BECAME HALF LOBSTER, HALF DOG WITH A HUMAN HEAD.
NOO!!
SHE GOT SO MEAN...
...THAT SHE TURNED INTO A ZOMBIE.
I BECAME A SUPERHERO, AND HAVE BEEN TRYING TO FIND HER SINCE.
HOLD ON. LOOK AT FISHY FISH.
FISHY FISH HAD TURNED INTO A ZOMBIE.

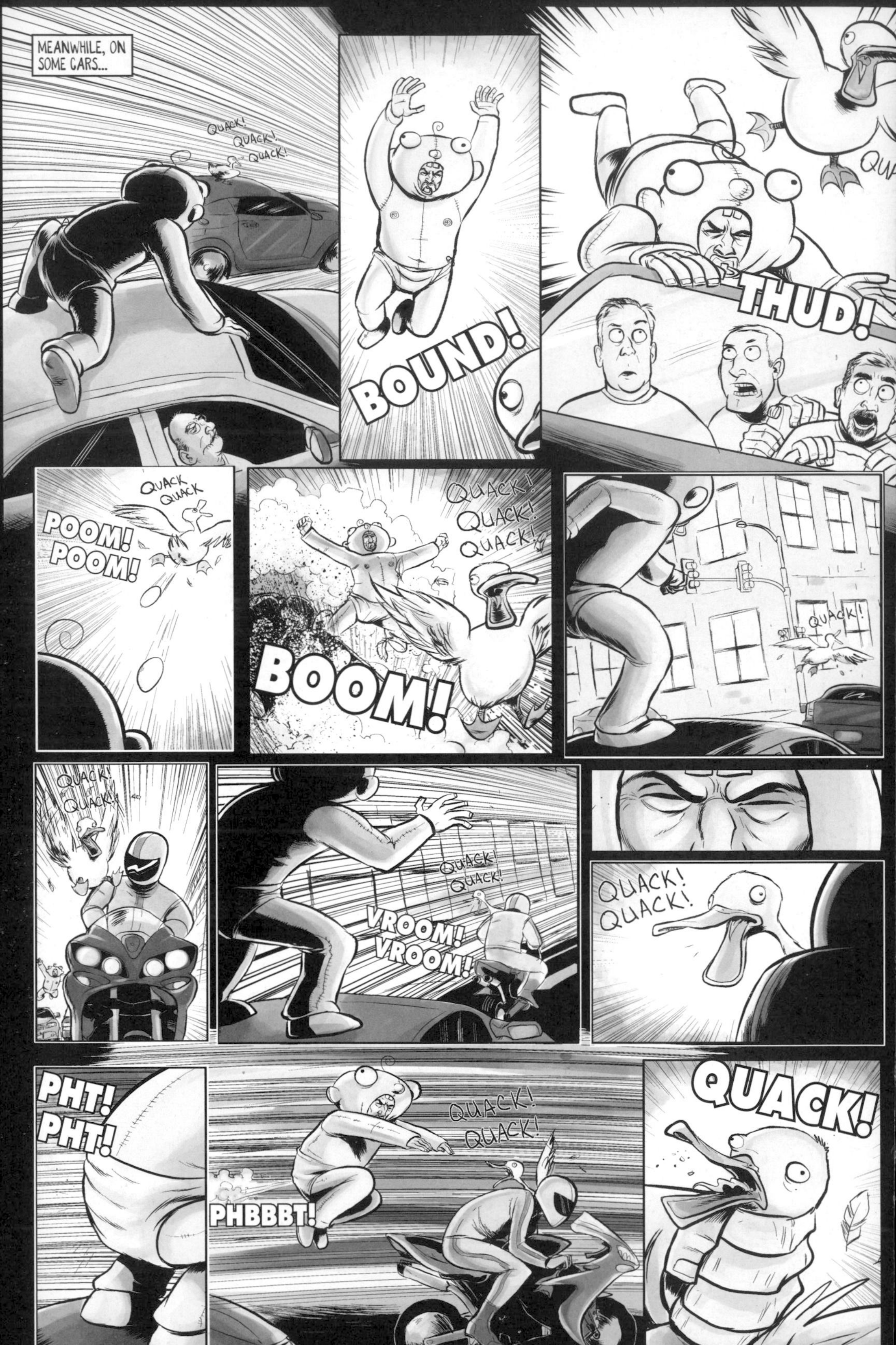

MEANWHILE, ON SOME CARS...
QUACK! QUACK! QUACK!
BOUND!
THUD!
QUACK QUACK
POOM! POOM!
QUACK! QUACK! QUACK!
BOOM!
QUACK!
QUACK! QUACK!
QUACK! QUACK!
VROOM! VROOM!
QUACK! QUACK!
PHT! PHT!
QUACK! QUACK!
PHBBBT!
QUACK!

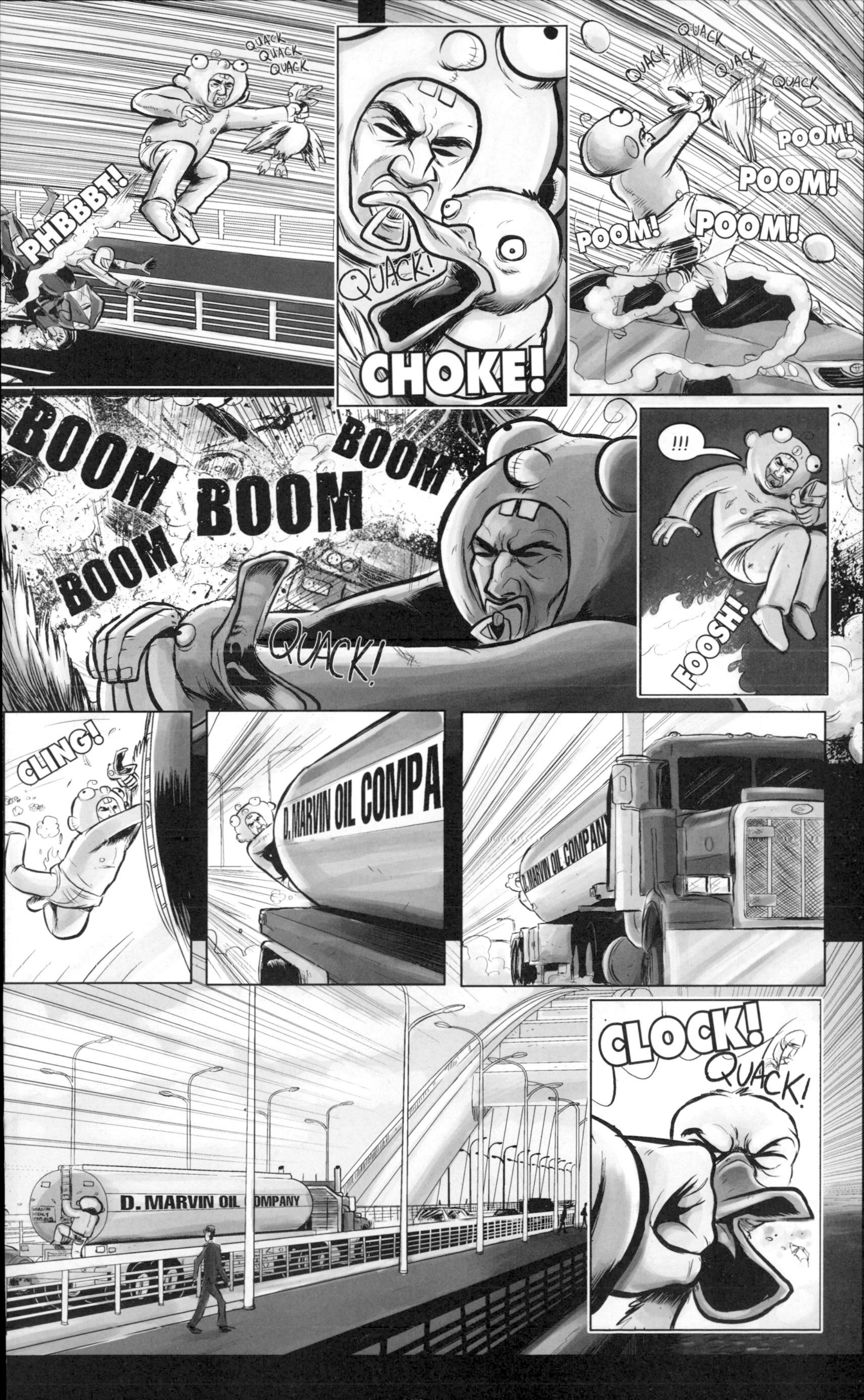
QUACK
QUACK
QUACK
PHBBBT!
QUACK!
CHOKE!
QUACK
QUACK
QUACK
QUACK
POOM!
POOM!
POOM!
POOM!
BOOM
BOOM
BOOM
BOOM
QUACK!
!!!
FOOSH!
CLING!
D. MARVIN OIL COMPA
D. MARVIN OIL COMPANY
D. MARVIN OIL COMPANY
CLOCK!
QUACK!

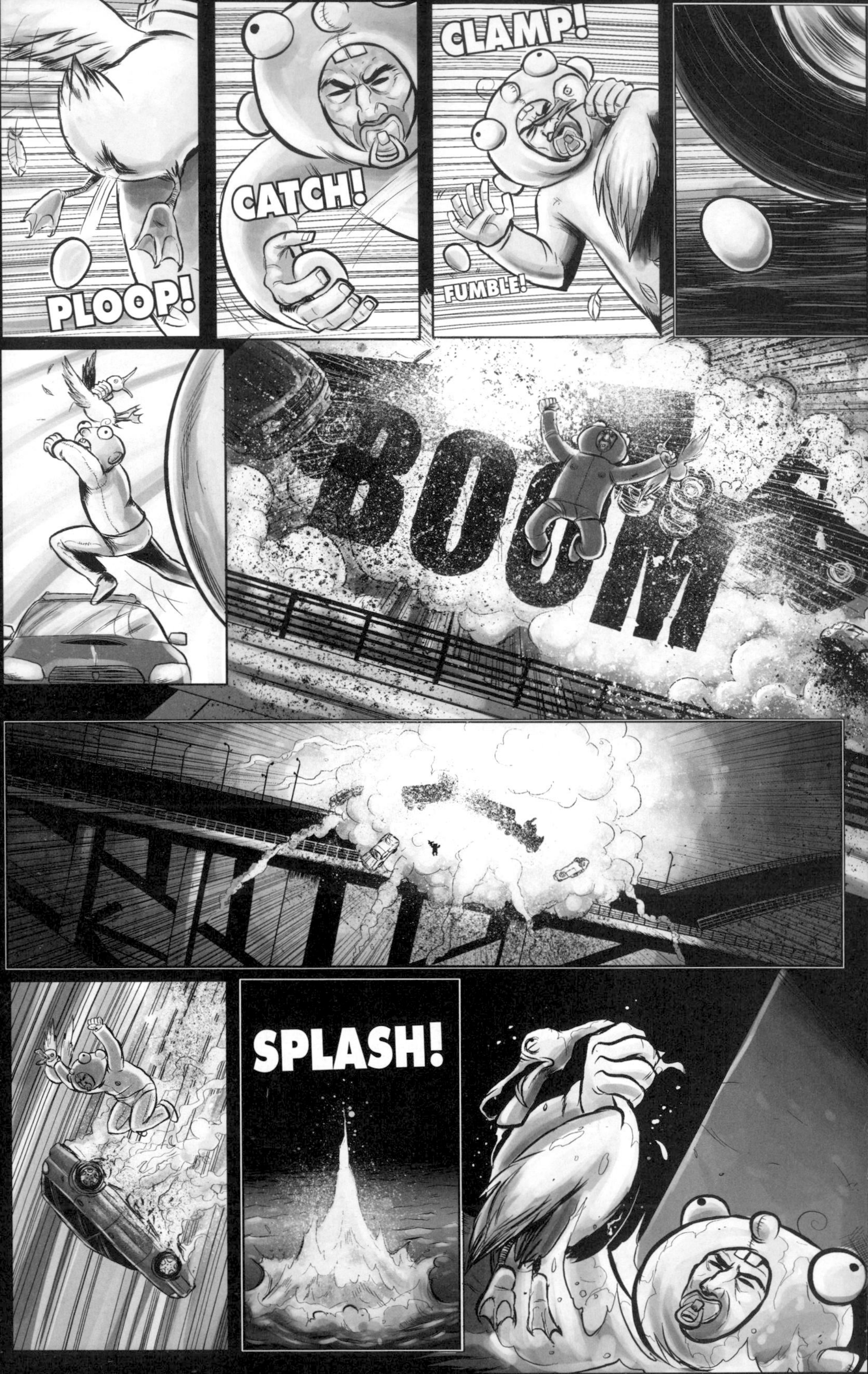
PLOOP!
CATCH!
CLAMP!
FUMBLE!
BOOM
SPLASH!

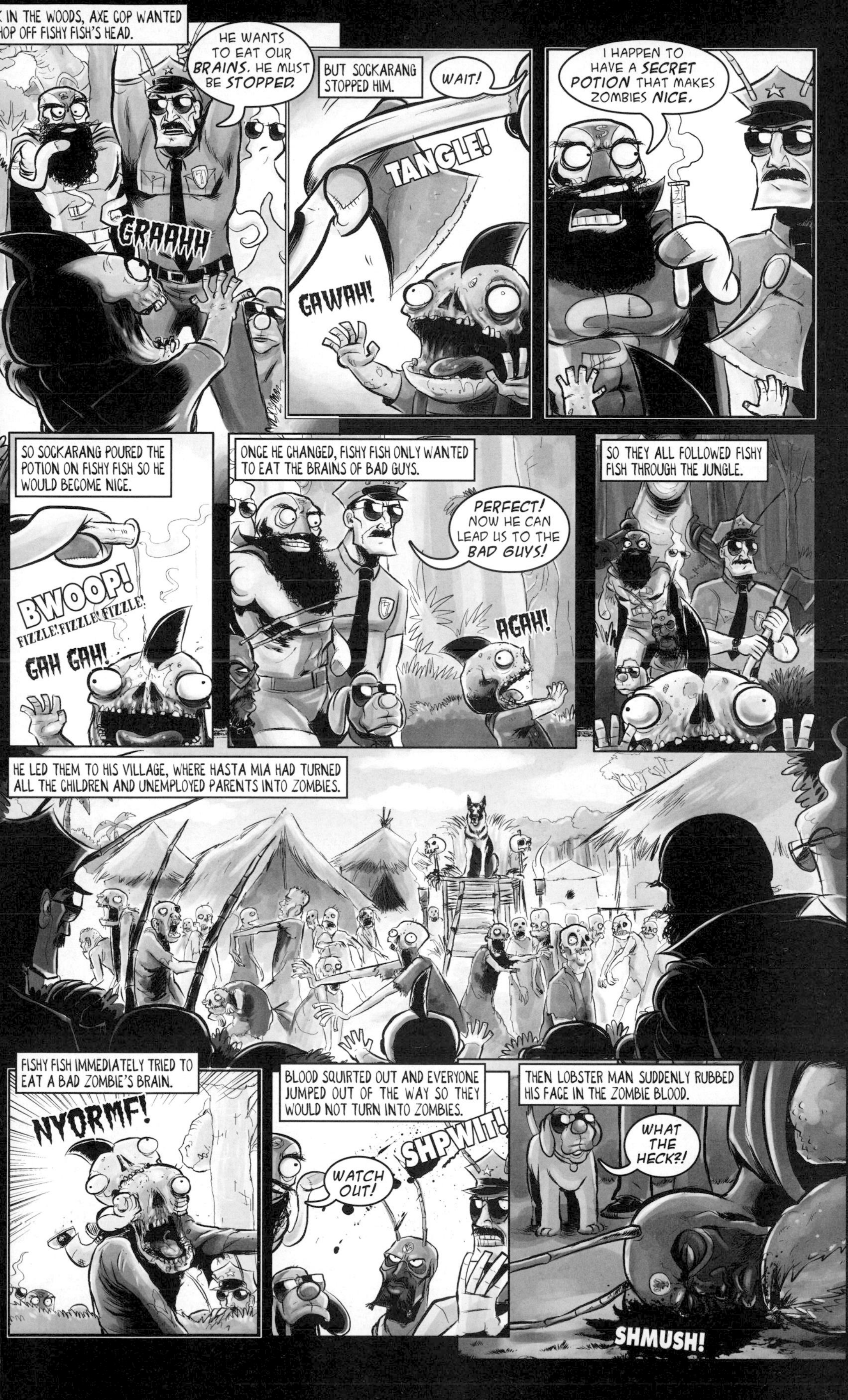

K IN THE WOODS, AXE COP WANTED
HOP OFF FISHY FISH'S HEAD.
HE WANTS TO EAT OUR BRAINS. HE MUST BE STOPPED.
GRAAHH
BUT SOCKARANG STOPPED HIM.
WAIT!
TANGLE!
GAWAH!
I HAPPEN TO HAVE A SECRET POTION THAT MAKES ZOMBIES NICE.
SO SOCKARANG POURED THE POTION ON FISHY FISH SO HE WOULD BECOME NICE.
BWOOP!
FIZZLE! FIZZLE! FIZZLE!
GAH GAH!
ONCE HE CHANGED, FISHY FISH ONLY WANTED TO EAT THE BRAINS OF BAD GUYS.
PERFECT! NOW HE CAN LEAD US TO THE BAD GUYS!
AGAH!
SO THEY ALL FOLLOWED FISHY FISH THROUGH THE JUNGLE.
HE LED THEM TO HIS VILLAGE, WHERE HASTA MIA HAD TURNED ALL THE CHILDREN AND UNEMPLOYED PARENTS INTO ZOMBIES.
FISHY FISH IMMEDIATELY TRIED TO EAT A BAD ZOMBIE'S BRAIN.
NYORMF!
BLOOD SQUIRTED OUT AND EVERYONE JUMPED OUT OF THE WAY SO THEY WOULD NOT TURN INTO ZOMBIES.
SHPWIT!
WATCH OUT!
THEN LOBSTER MAN SUDDENLY RUBBED HIS FACE IN THE ZOMBIE BLOOD.
WHAT THE HECK?!
SHMUSH!

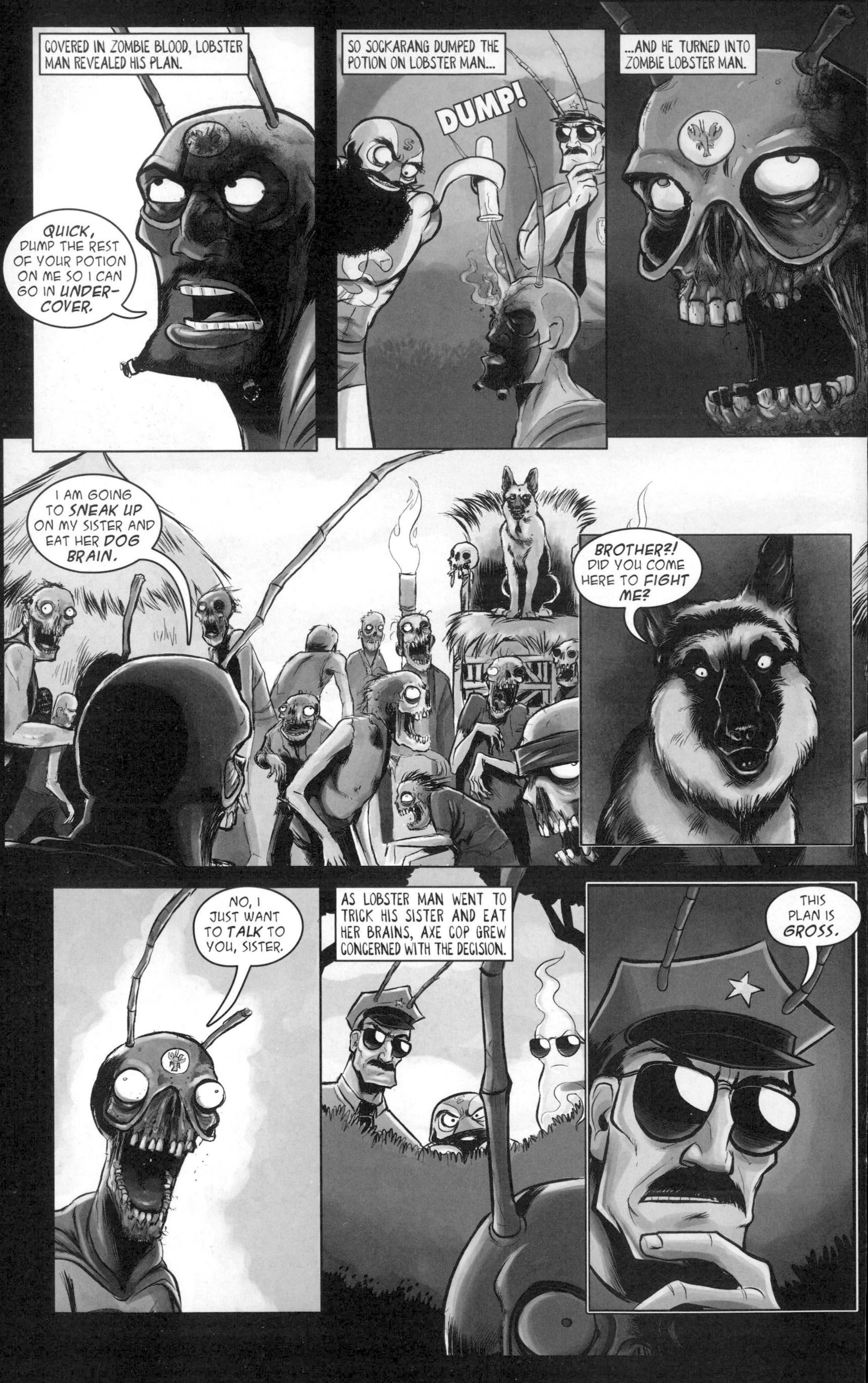
COVERED IN ZOMBIE BLOOD, LOBSTER MAN REVEALED HIS PLAN.
QUICK, DUMP THE REST OF YOUR POTION ON ME SO I CAN GO IN UNDER-COVER.
SO SOCKARANG DUMPED THE POTION ON LOBSTER MAN...
DUMP!
...AND HE TURNED INTO ZOMBIE LOBSTER MAN.
I AM GOING TO SNEAK UP ON MY SISTER AND EAT HER DOG BRAIN.
BROTHER?! DID YOU COME HERE TO FIGHT ME?
NO, I JUST WANT TO TALK TO YOU, SISTER.
AS LOBSTER MAN WENT TO TRICK HIS SISTER AND EAT HER BRAINS, AXE COP GREW CONCERNED WITH THE DECISION.
THIS PLAN IS GROSS.

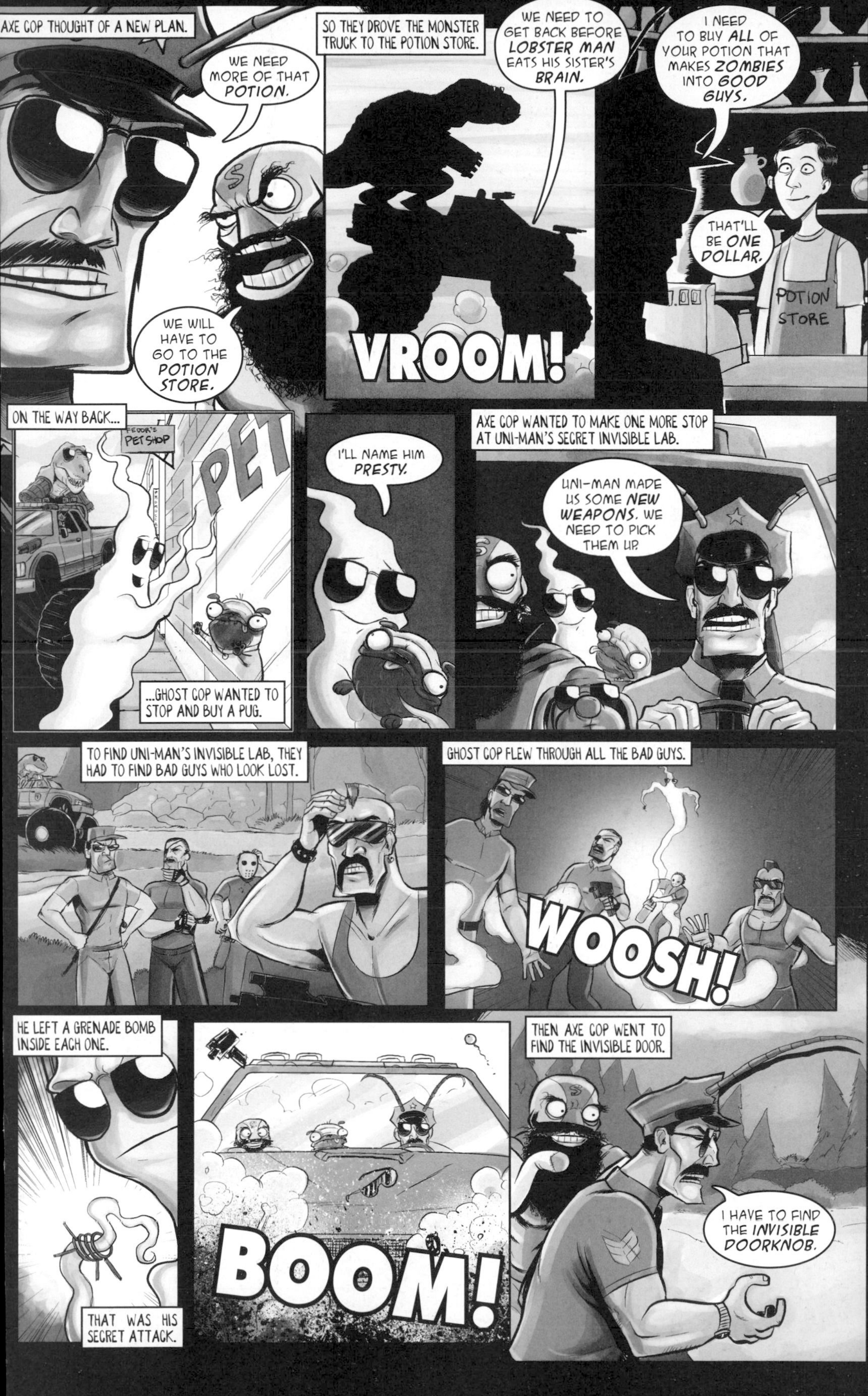

AXE COP THOUGHT OF A NEW PLAN.
WE NEED MORE OF THAT POTION.
WE WILL HAVE TO GO TO THE POTION STORE.
SO THEY DROVE THE MONSTER TRUCK TO THE POTION STORE.
WE NEED TO GET BACK BEFORE LOBSTER MAN EATS HIS SISTER'S BRAIN.
VROOM!
I NEED TO BUY ALL OF YOUR POTION THAT MAKES ZOMBIES INTO GOOD GUYS.
THAT'LL BE ONE DOLLAR.
POTION STORE
ON THE WAY BACK...
PET SHOP
PET
...GHOST COP WANTED TO STOP AND BUY A PUG.
I'LL NAME HIM PRESTY.
AXE COP WANTED TO MAKE ONE MORE STOP AT UNI-MAN'S SECRET INVISIBLE LAB.
UNI-MAN MADE US SOME NEW WEAPONS. WE NEED TO PICK THEM UP.
TO FIND UNI-MAN'S INVISIBLE LAB, THEY HAD TO FIND BAD GUYS WHO LOOK LOST.
GHOST COP FLEW THROUGH ALL THE BAD GUYS.
WOOSH!
HE LEFT A GRENADE BOMB INSIDE EACH ONE.
THAT WAS HIS SECRET ATTACK.
BOOM!
THEN AXE COP WENT TO FIND THE INVISIBLE DOOR.
I HAVE TO FIND THE INVISIBLE DOORKNOB.

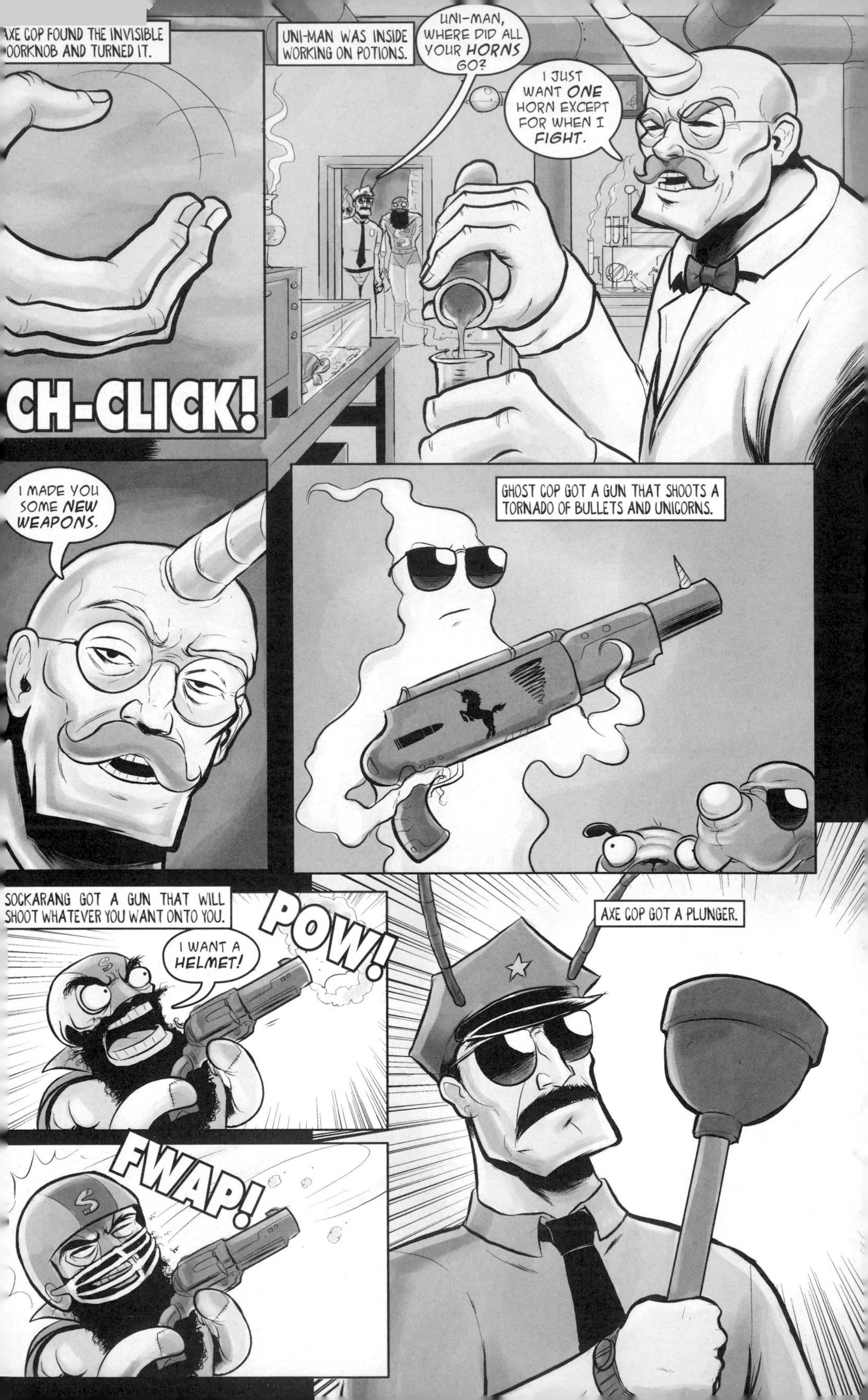
AXE COP FOUND THE INVISIBLE
DOORKNOB AND TURNED IT.
CH-CLICK!
UNI-MAN WAS INSIDE
WORKING ON POTIONS.
UNI-MAN, WHERE DID ALL YOUR HORNS GO?
I JUST WANT ONE HORN EXCEPT FOR WHEN I FIGHT.
I MADE YOU SOME NEW WEAPONS.
GHOST COP GOT A GUN THAT SHOOTS A
TORNADO OF BULLETS AND UNICORNS.
SOCKARANG GOT A GUN THAT WILL
SHOOT WHATEVER YOU WANT ONTO YOU.
POW!
I WANT A HELMET!
FWAP!
AXE COP GOT A PLUNGER.

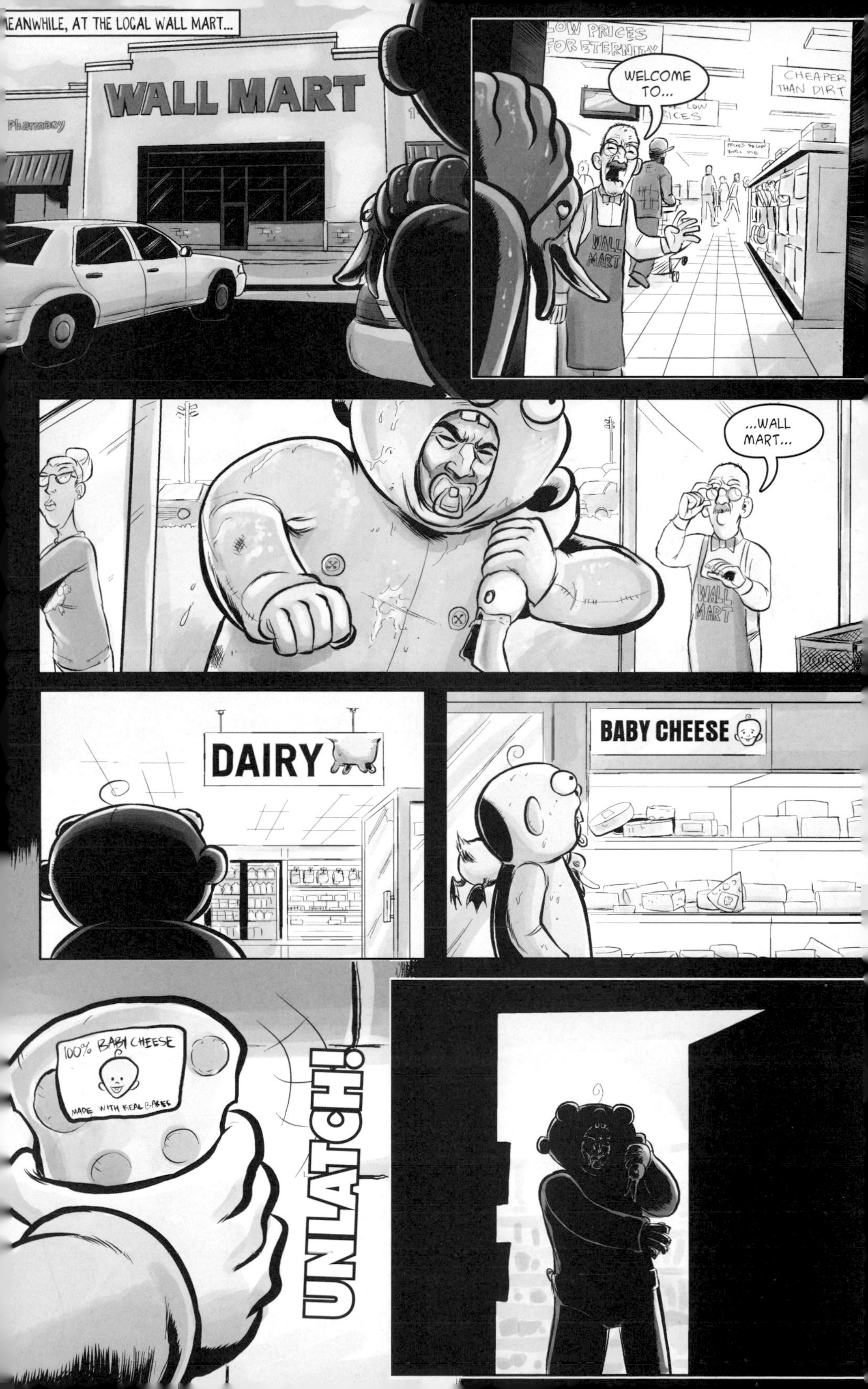
MEANWHILE, AT THE LOCAL WALL MART...
WALL MART
Pharmacy
LOW PRICES FOR ETERNITY
WELCOME TO...
CHEAPER THAN DIRT
WALL MART
...WALL MART...
WALL MART
DAIRY
BABY CHEESE
100% BABI CHEESE
MADE WITH REAL BABIES
UNLATCH!

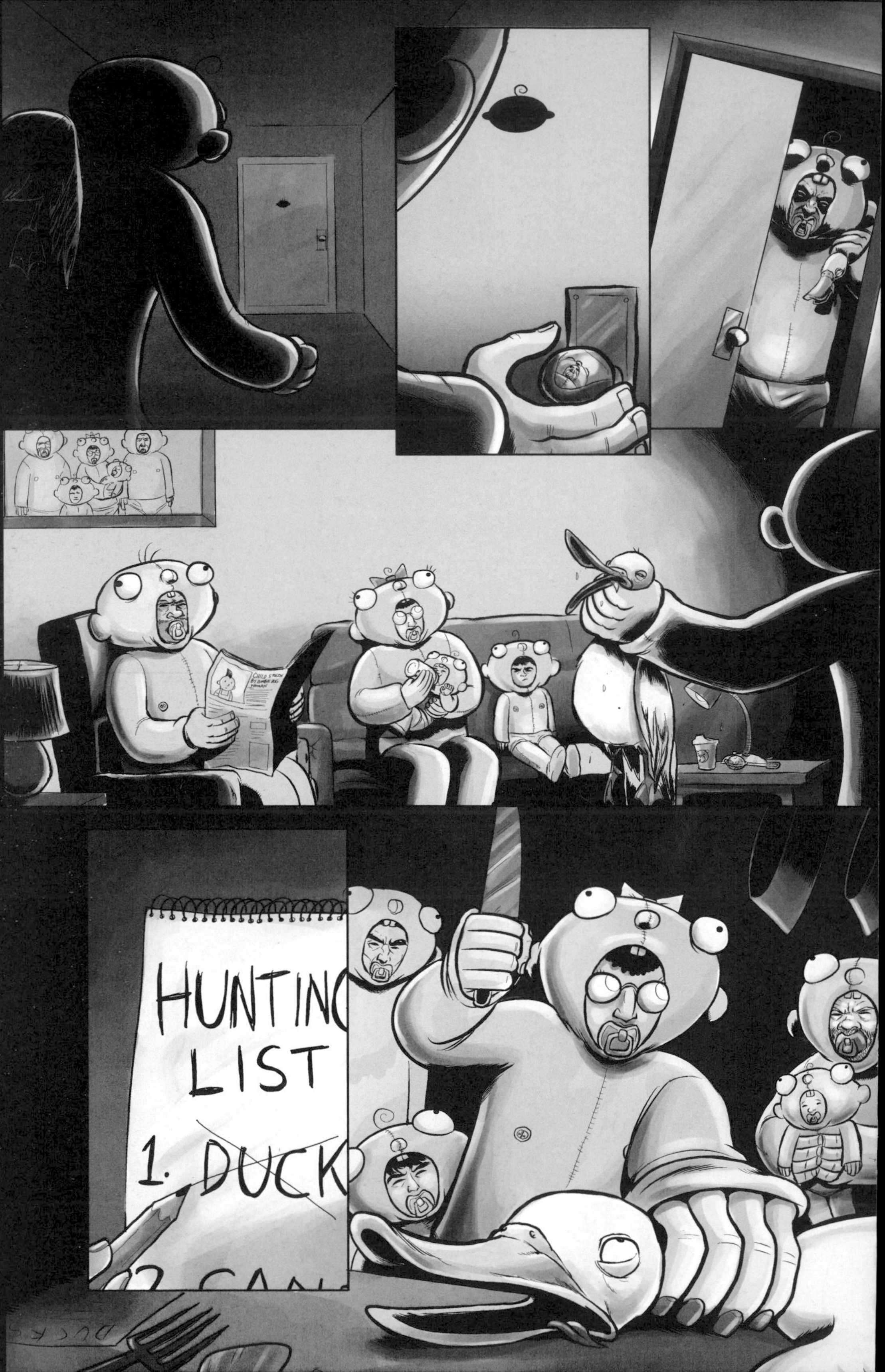
HUNTIN
LIST
1. DUCK
2 CAN

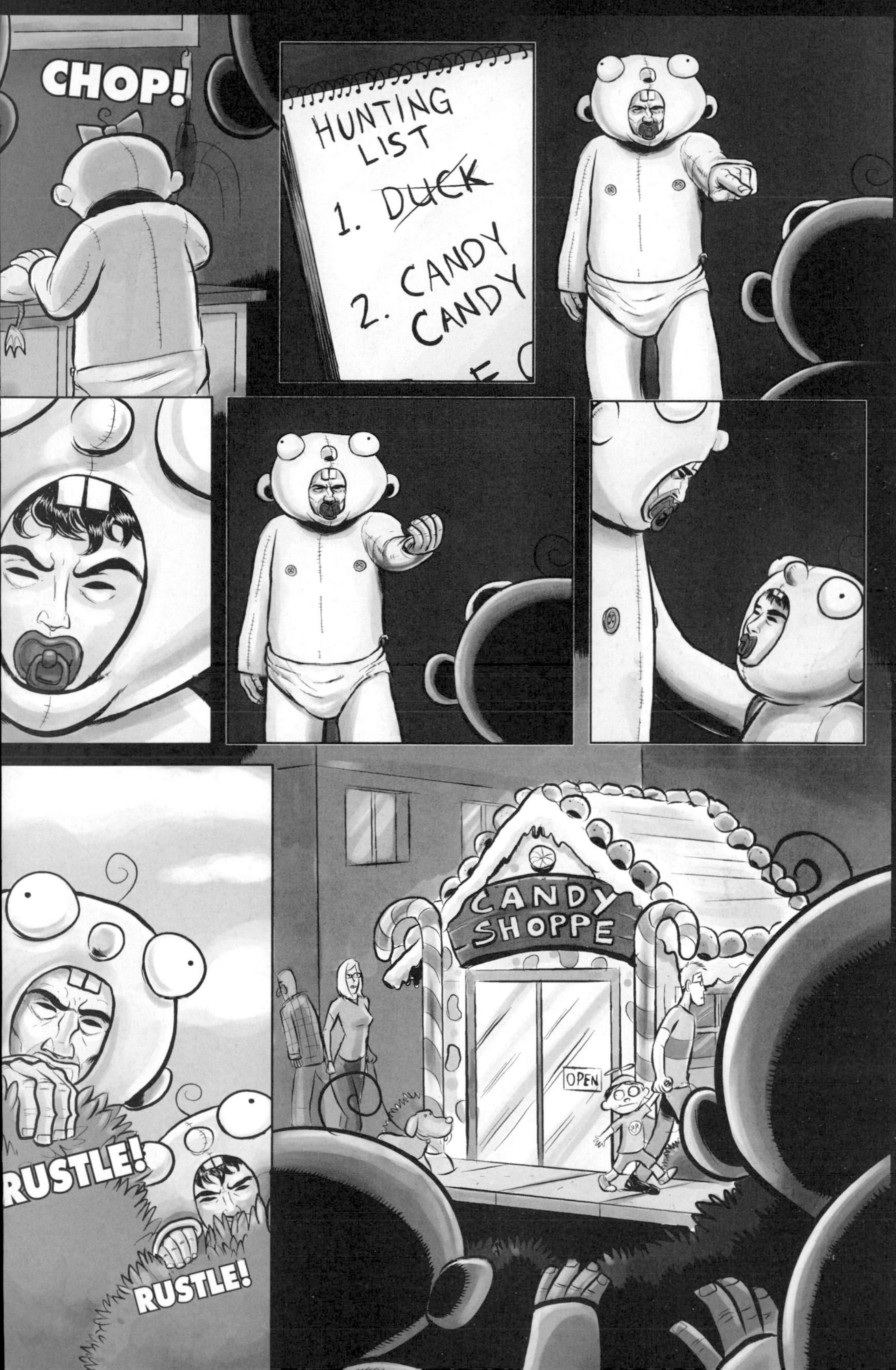
CHOP!
HUNTING
LIST
1. DUCK
2. CANDY
CANDY
CANDY
SHOPPE
OPEN
RUSTLE!
RUSTLE!

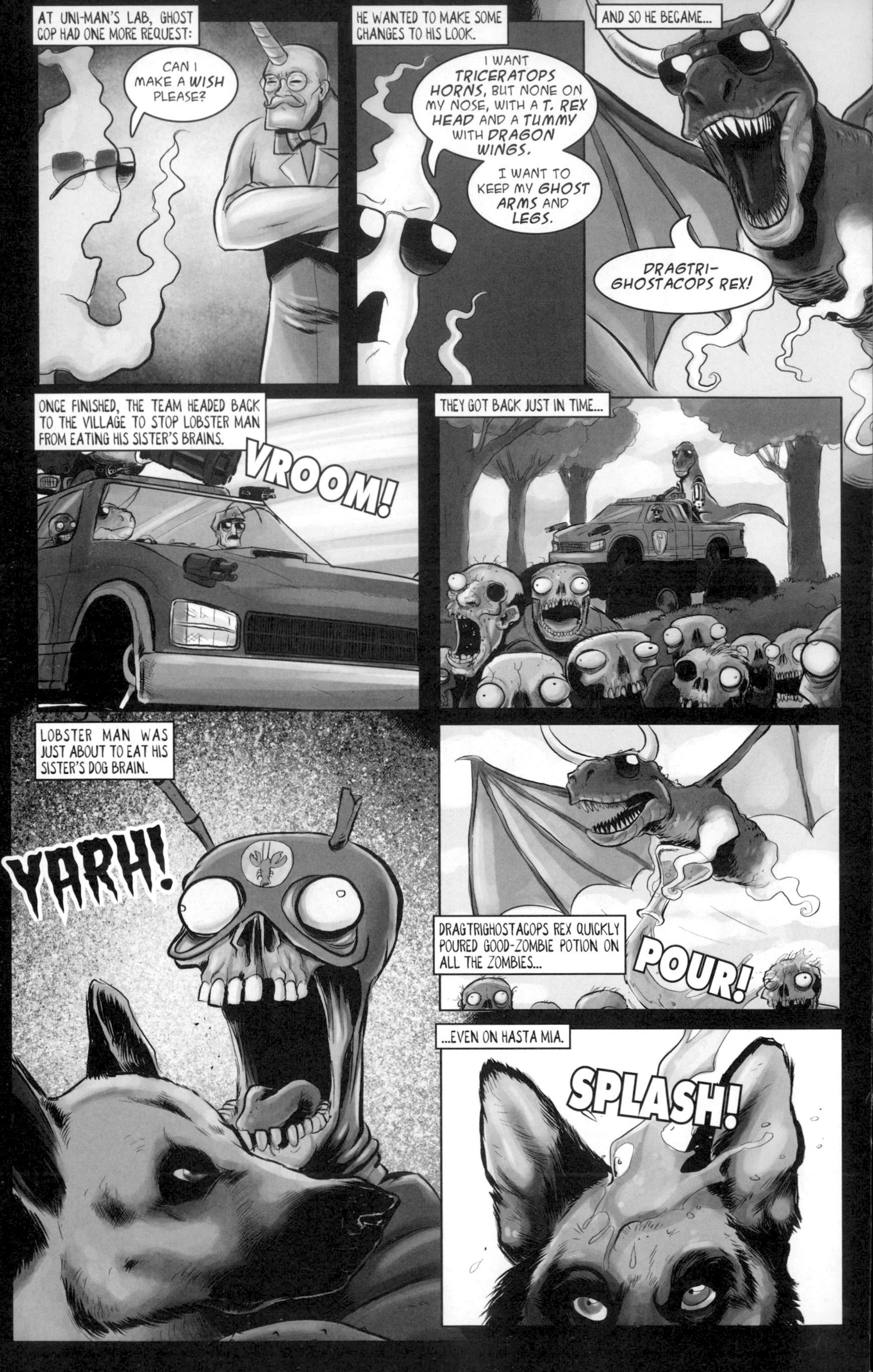

AT UNI-MAN'S LAB, GHOST COP HAD ONE MORE REQUEST:
CAN I MAKE A WISH PLEASE?
HE WANTED TO MAKE SOME CHANGES TO HIS LOOK.
I WANT TRICERATOPS HORNS, BUT NONE ON MY NOSE, WITH A T. REX HEAD AND A TUMMY WITH DRAGON WINGS.
I WANT TO KEEP MY GHOST ARMS AND LEGS.
AND SO HE BECAME...
DRAGTRI-GHOSTACOPS REX!
ONCE FINISHED, THE TEAM HEADED BACK TO THE VILLAGE TO STOP LOBSTER MAN FROM EATING HIS SISTER'S BRAINS.
VROOM!
THEY GOT BACK JUST IN TIME...
LOBSTER MAN WAS JUST ABOUT TO EAT HIS SISTER'S DOG BRAIN.
YARH!
DRAGTRIGHOSTACOPS REX QUICKLY POURED GOOD-ZOMBIE POTION ON ALL THE ZOMBIES...
POUR!
...EVEN ON HASTA MIA.
SPLASH!

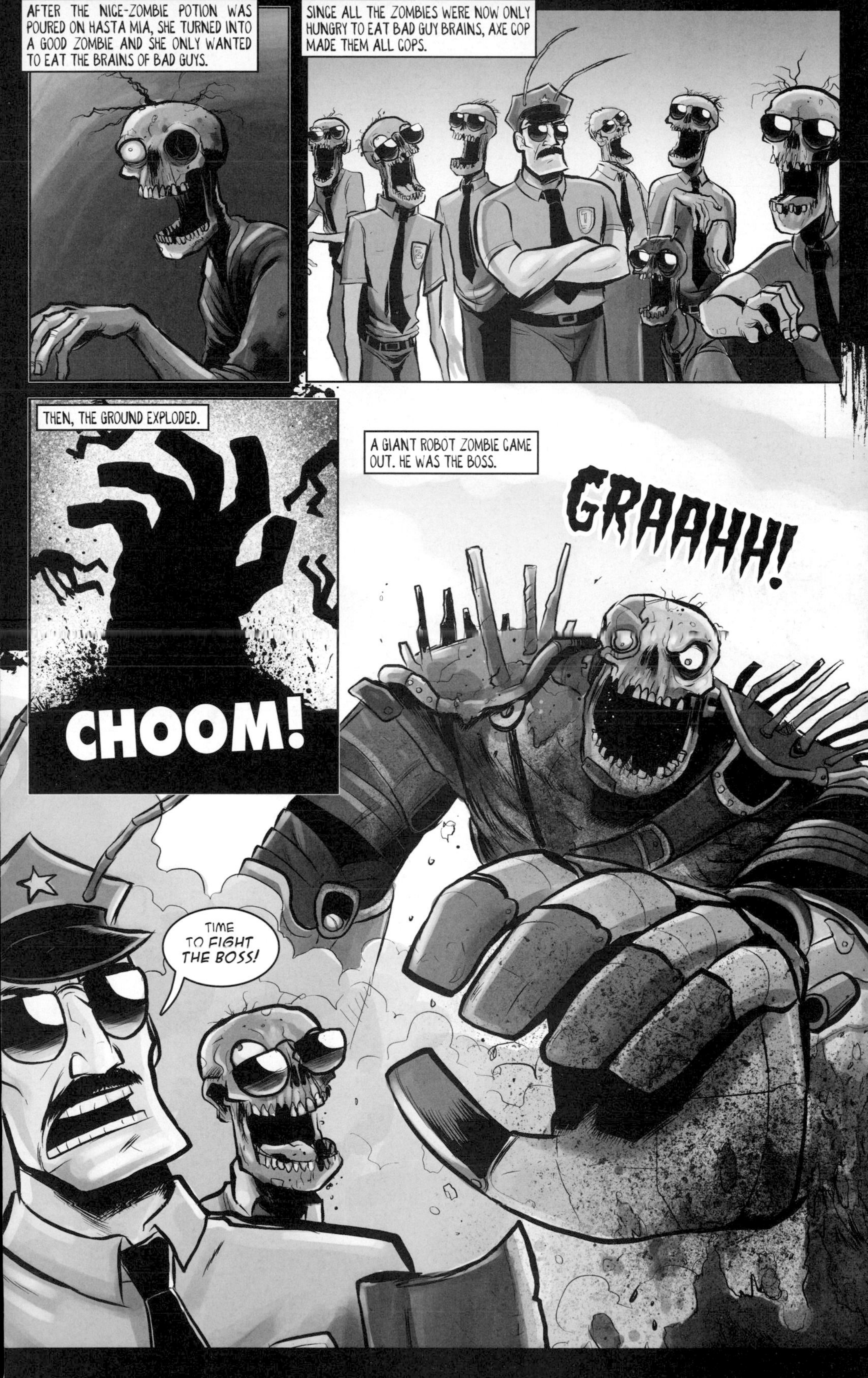
AFTER THE NICE-ZOMBIE POTION WAS POURED ON HASTA MIA, SHE TURNED INTO A GOOD ZOMBIE AND SHE ONLY WANTED TO EAT THE BRAINS OF BAD GUYS.
SINCE ALL THE ZOMBIES WERE NOW ONLY HUNGRY TO EAT BAD GUY BRAINS, AXE COP MADE THEM ALL COPS.
THEN, THE GROUND EXPLODED.
CHOOM!
A GIANT ROBOT ZOMBIE CAME OUT. HE WAS THE BOSS.
GRAAHH!
TIME TO FIGHT THE BOSS!

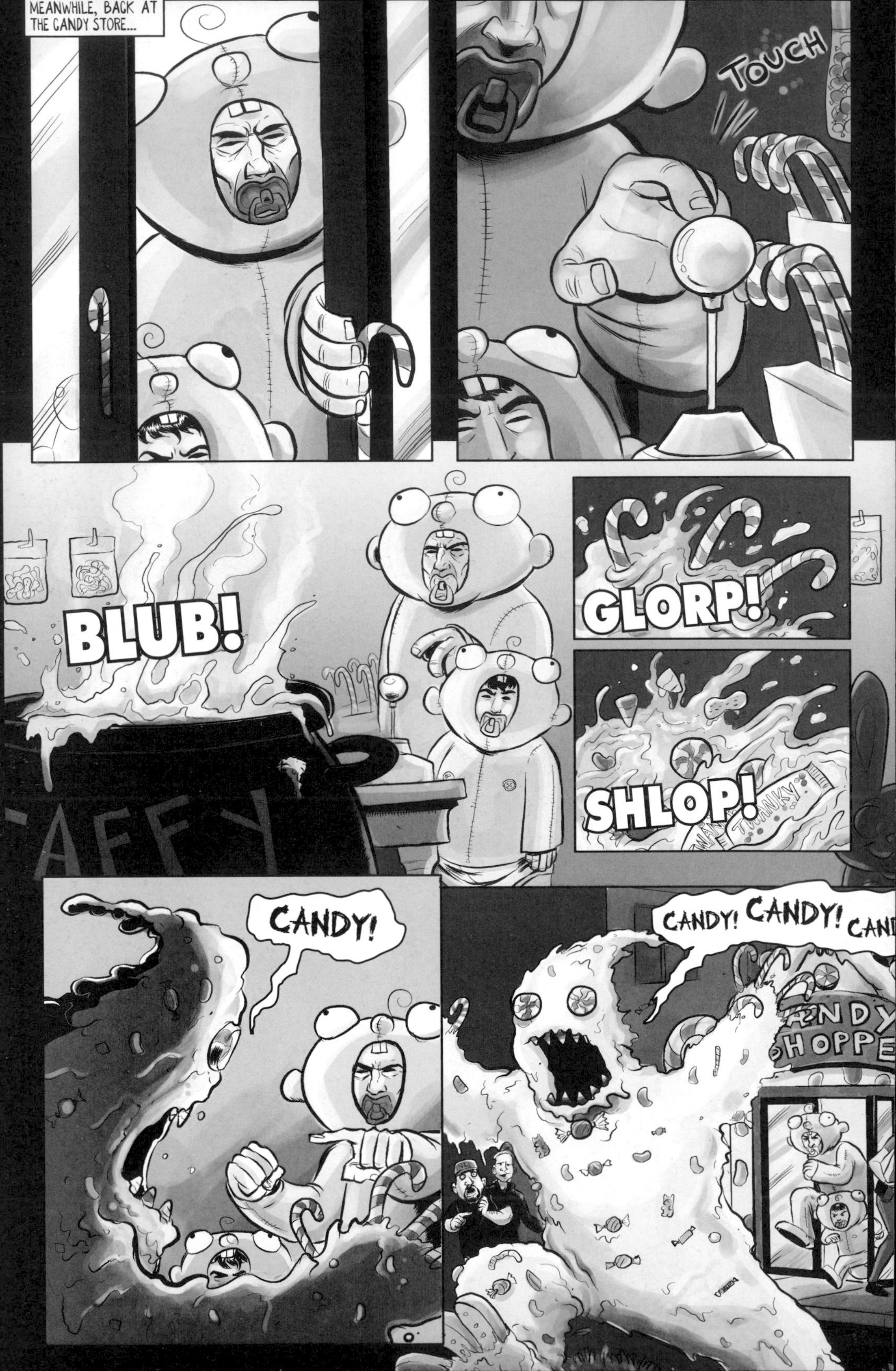
MEANWHILE, BACK AT THE CANDY STORE...
TOUCH
BLUB!
GLORP!
SHLOP!
CANDY!
CANDY! CANDY! CAND

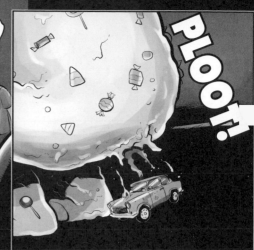

CANDY! CANDY!

PLOOT!

THAT CANDY MONSTER JUST LAID A **TOY CAR**!

CANDY!

GROW!

DUDE, A **FREE** CAR!

DIBS!

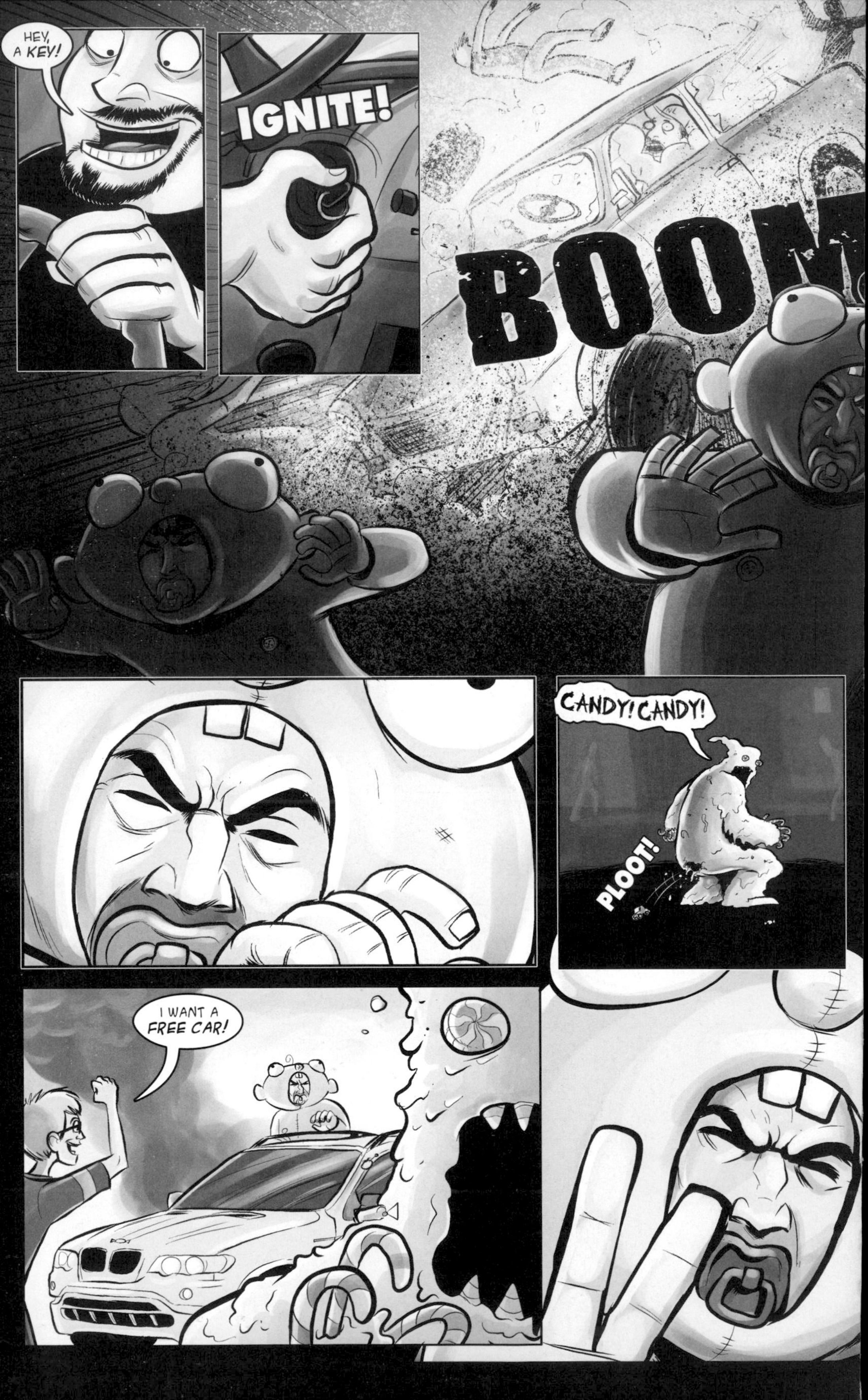
HEY, A KEY!
IGNITE!
BOOM
CANDY! CANDY!
PLOOT!
I WANT A FREE CAR!

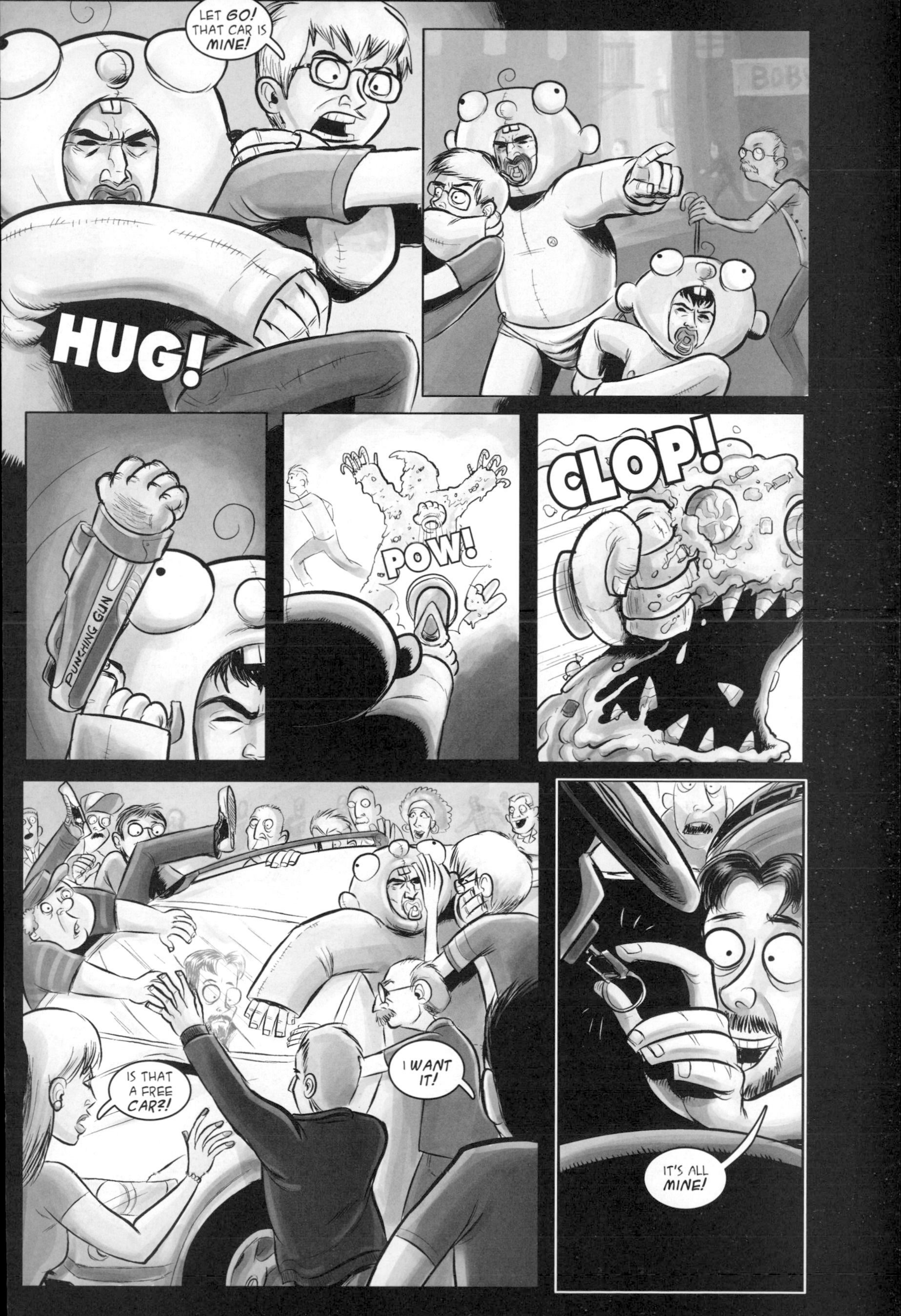
LET GO! THAT CAR IS MINE!
HUG!
BOBY
PUNCHING GUN
POW!
CLOP!
IS THAT A FREE CAR?!
I WANT IT!
IT'S ALL MINE!

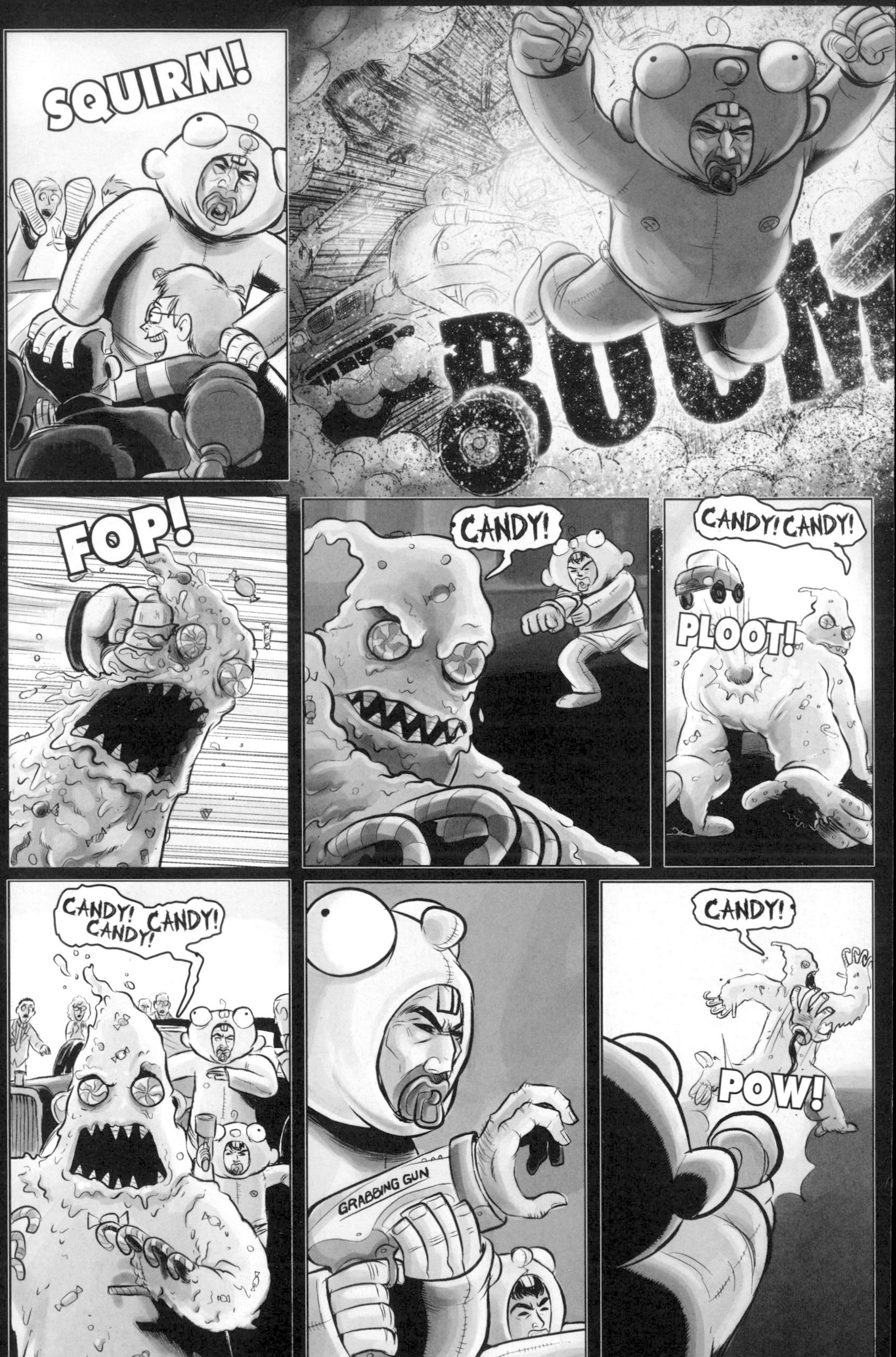
SQUIRM!
BOOM
FOP!
CANDY!
CANDY! CANDY!
PLOOT!
CANDY! CANDY! CANDY!
GRABBING GUN
CANDY!
POW!

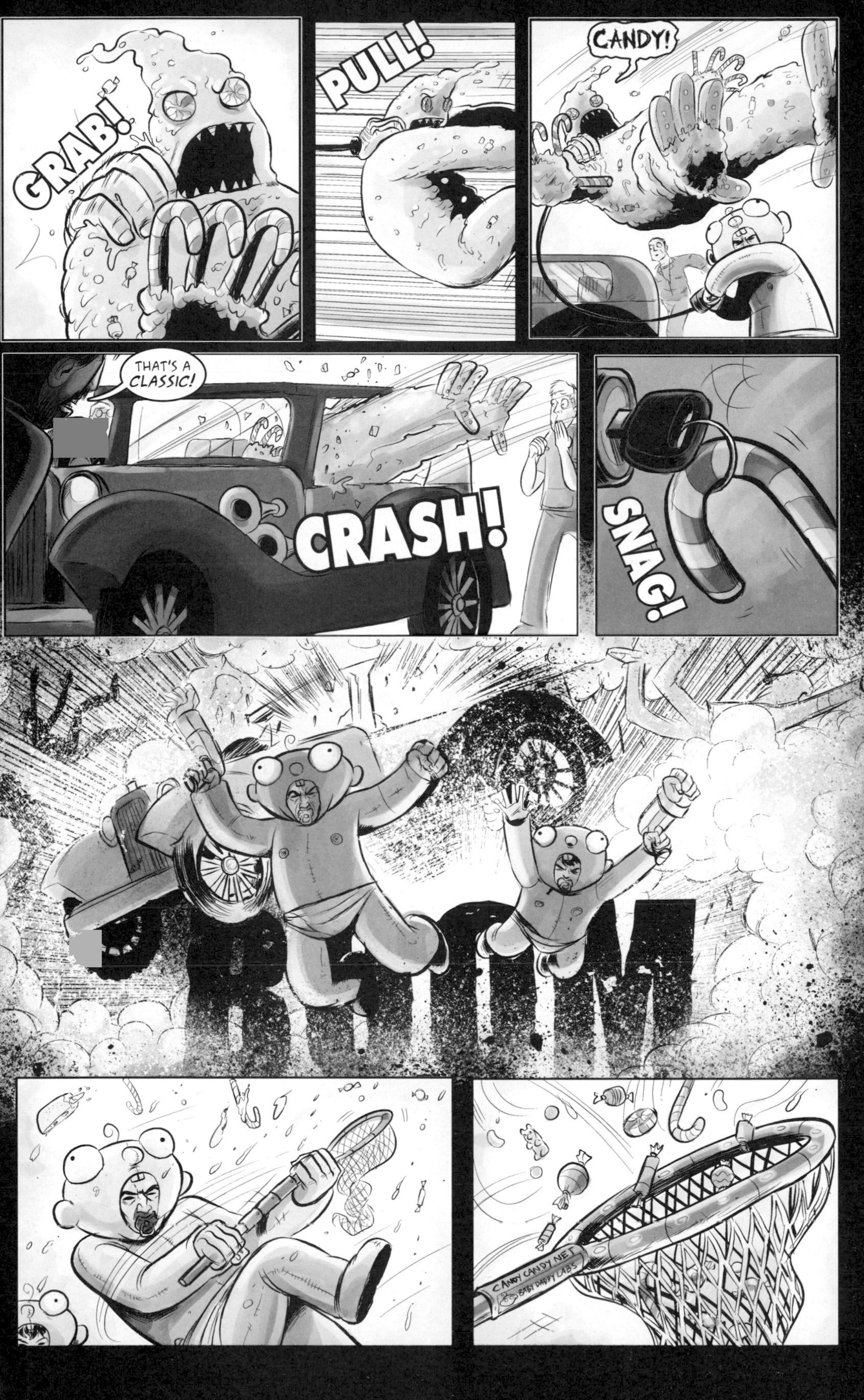
GRAB!
PULL!
CANDY!
THAT'S A CLASSIC!
CRASH!
SNAG!
CANDY CANDY NET
BABY DADDY LABS

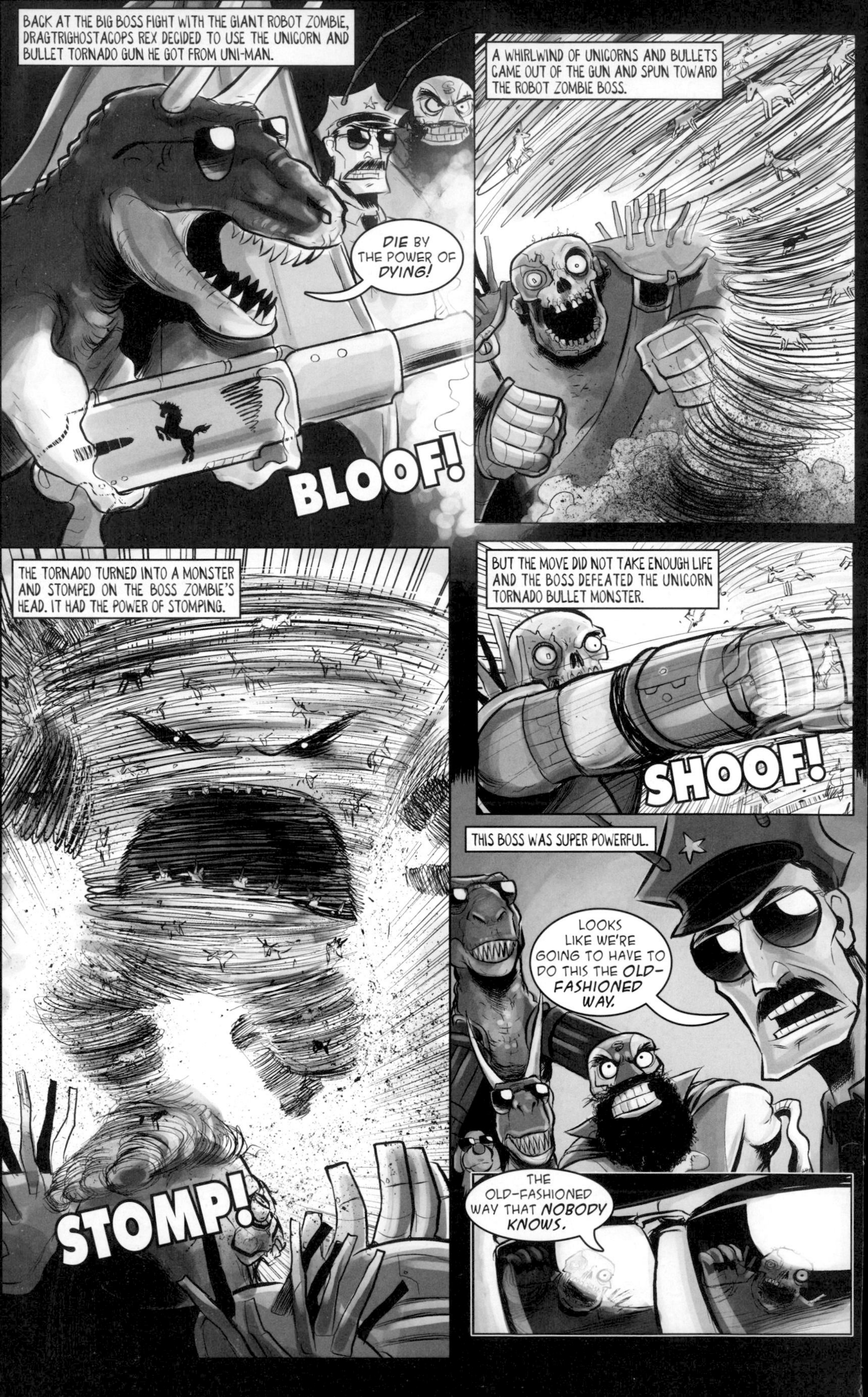

BACK AT THE BIG BOSS FIGHT WITH THE GIANT ROBOT ZOMBIE, DRAGTRIGHOSTACOPS REX DECIDED TO USE THE UNICORN AND BULLET TORNADO GUN HE GOT FROM UNI-MAN.
DIE BY THE POWER OF DYING!
BLOOF!
A WHIRLWIND OF UNICORNS AND BULLETS CAME OUT OF THE GUN AND SPUN TOWARD THE ROBOT ZOMBIE BOSS.
THE TORNADO TURNED INTO A MONSTER AND STOMPED ON THE BOSS ZOMBIE'S HEAD. IT HAD THE POWER OF STOMPING.
STOMP!
BUT THE MOVE DID NOT TAKE ENOUGH LIFE AND THE BOSS DEFEATED THE UNICORN TORNADO BULLET MONSTER.
SHOOF!
THIS BOSS WAS SUPER POWERFUL.
LOOKS LIKE WE'RE GOING TO HAVE TO DO THIS THE OLD-FASHIONED WAY.
THE OLD-FASHIONED WAY THAT NOBODY KNOWS.

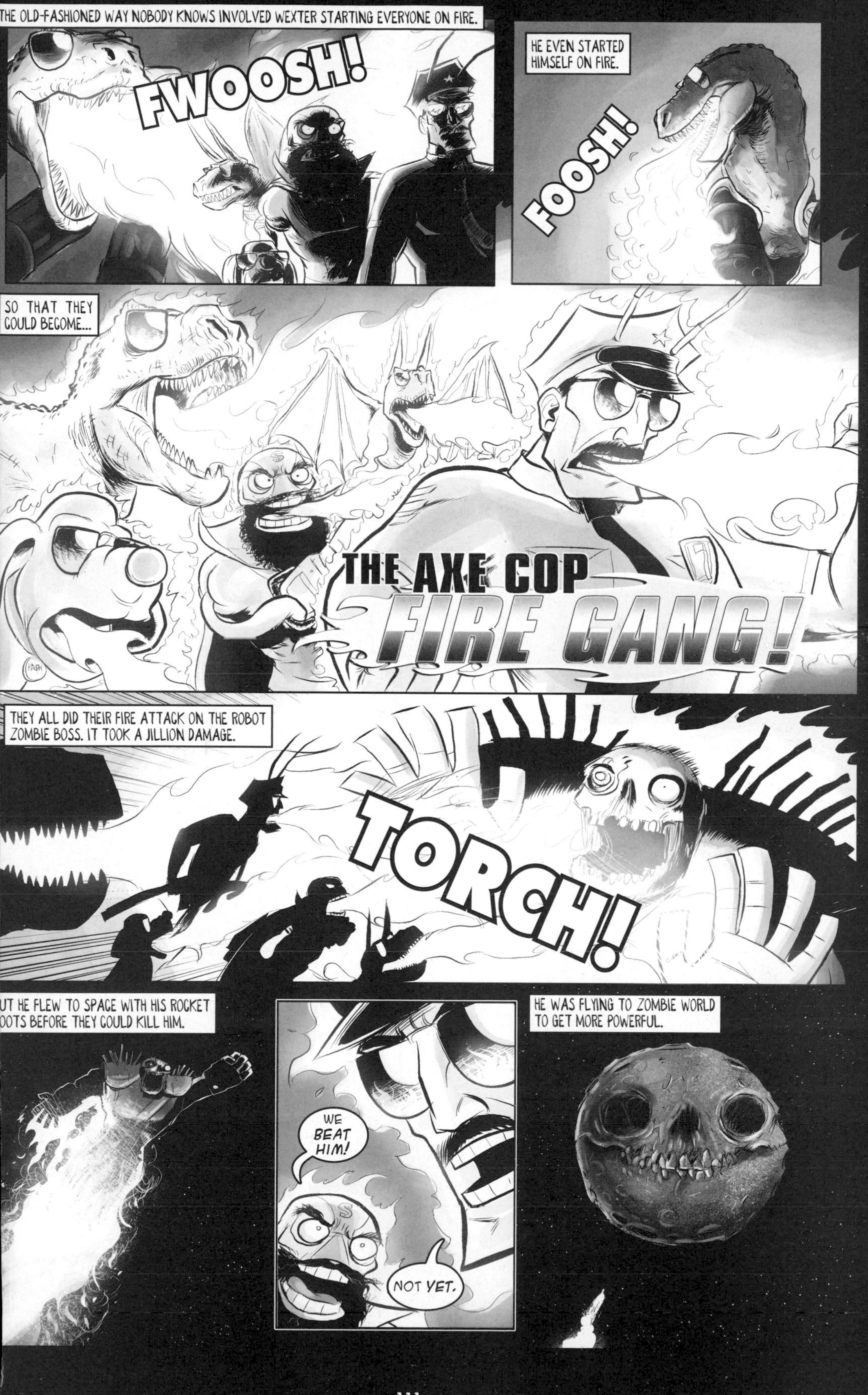
THE OLD-FASHIONED WAY NOBODY KNOWS INVOLVED WEXTER STARTING EVERYONE ON FIRE.
FWOOSH!
HE EVEN STARTED HIMSELF ON FIRE.
FOOSH!
SO THAT THEY COULD BECOME...
THE AXE COP
FIRE GANG!
THEY ALL DID THEIR FIRE ATTACK ON THE ROBOT ZOMBIE BOSS. IT TOOK A JILLION DAMAGE.
TORCH!
UT HE FLEW TO SPACE WITH HIS ROCKET
OOTS BEFORE THEY COULD KILL HIM.
WE BEAT HIM!
NOT YET.
HE WAS FLYING TO ZOMBIE WORLD TO GET MORE POWERFUL.

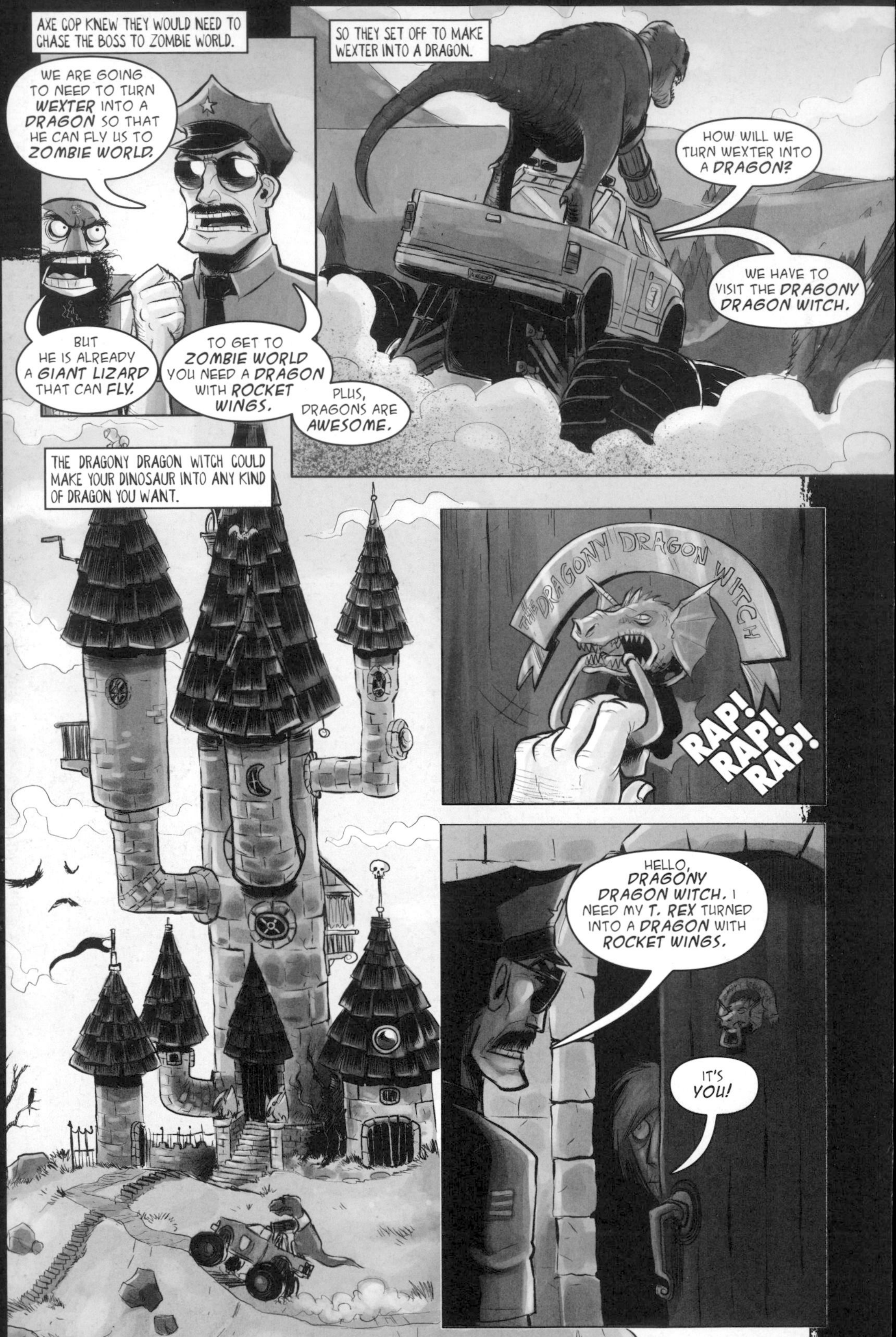
AXE COP KNEW THEY WOULD NEED TO CHASE THE BOSS TO ZOMBIE WORLD.
WE ARE GOING TO NEED TO TURN WEXTER INTO A DRAGON SO THAT HE CAN FLY US TO ZOMBIE WORLD.
BUT HE IS ALREADY A GIANT LIZARD THAT CAN FLY.
TO GET TO ZOMBIE WORLD YOU NEED A DRAGON WITH ROCKET WINGS.
PLUS, DRAGONS ARE AWESOME.
SO THEY SET OFF TO MAKE WEXTER INTO A DRAGON.
HOW WILL WE TURN WEXTER INTO A DRAGON?
WE HAVE TO VISIT THE DRAGONY DRAGON WITCH.
THE DRAGONY DRAGON WITCH COULD MAKE YOUR DINOSAUR INTO ANY KIND OF DRAGON YOU WANT.
THE DRAGONY DRAGON WITCH
RAP! RAP! RAP!
HELLO, DRAGONY DRAGON WITCH. I NEED MY T. REX TURNED INTO A DRAGON WITH ROCKET WINGS.
IT'S YOU!

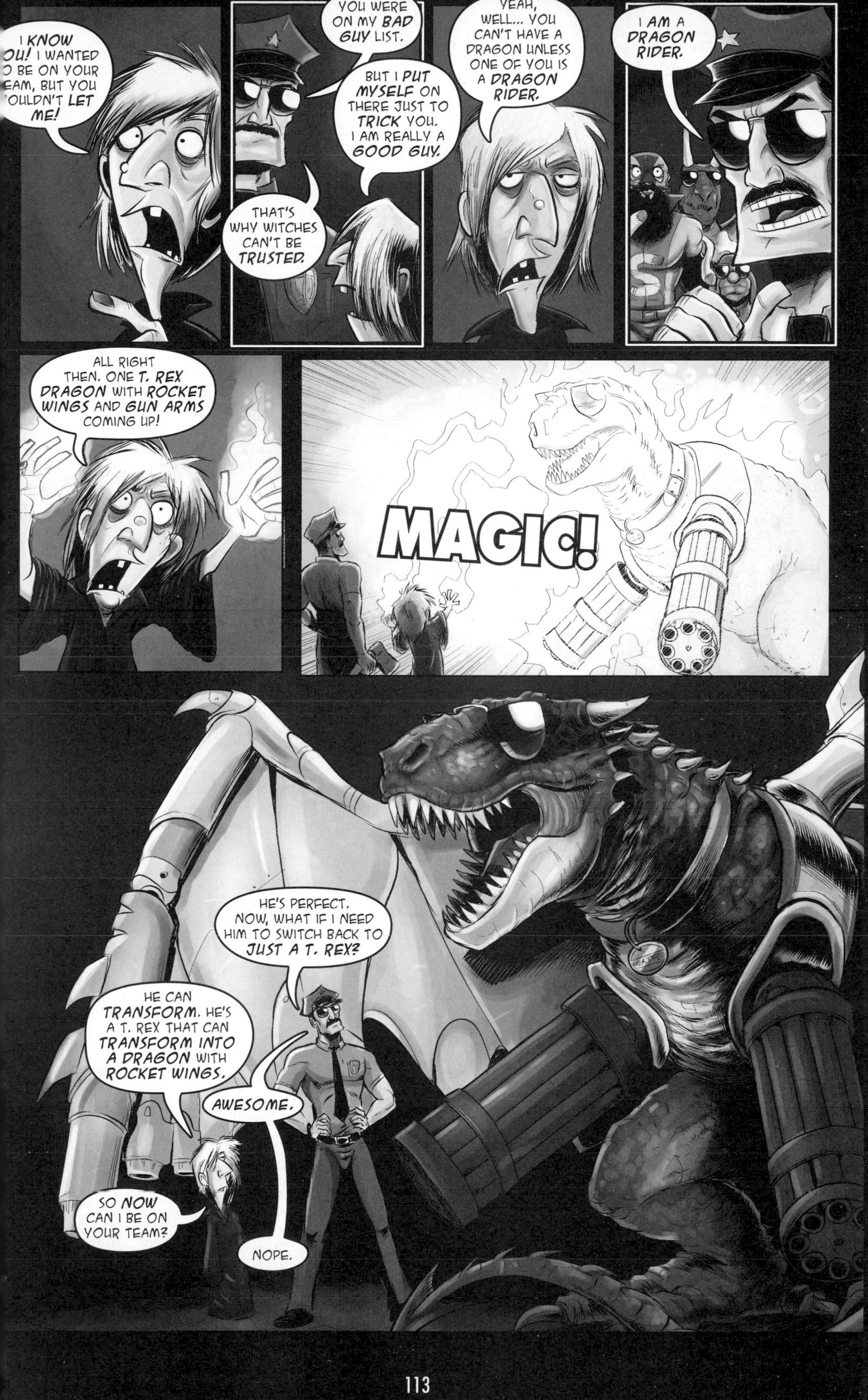

I KNOW OU! I WANTED O BE ON YOUR EAM, BUT YOU OULDN'T LET ME!
YOU WERE ON MY BAD GUY LIST.
BUT I PUT MYSELF ON THERE JUST TO TRICK YOU. I AM REALLY A GOOD GUY.
THAT'S WHY WITCHES CAN'T BE TRUSTED.
YEAH, WELL... YOU CAN'T HAVE A DRAGON UNLESS ONE OF YOU IS A DRAGON RIDER.
I AM A DRAGON RIDER.
ALL RIGHT THEN. ONE T. REX DRAGON WITH ROCKET WINGS AND GUN ARMS COMING UP!
MAGIC!
HE'S PERFECT. NOW, WHAT IF I NEED HIM TO SWITCH BACK TO JUST A T. REX?
HE CAN TRANSFORM. HE'S A T. REX THAT CAN TRANSFORM INTO A DRAGON WITH ROCKET WINGS.
AWESOME.
SO NOW CAN I BE ON YOUR TEAM?
NOPE.

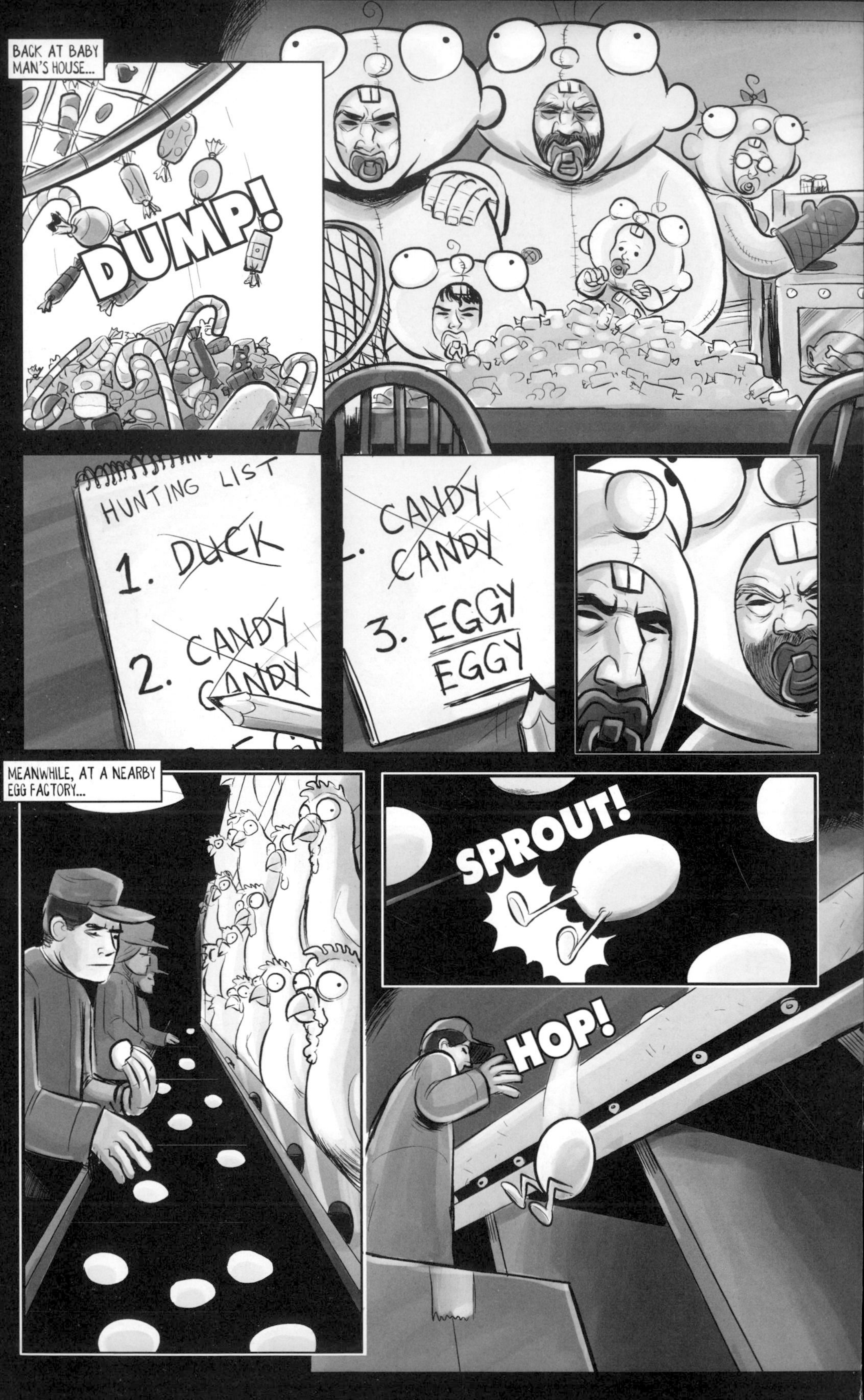

BACK AT BABY MAN'S HOUSE...
DUMP!
HUNTING LIST
1. DUCK
2. CANDY CANDY
2. CANDY CANDY
3. EGGY EGGY
MEANWHILE, AT A NEARBY EGG FACTORY...
SPROUT!
HOP!

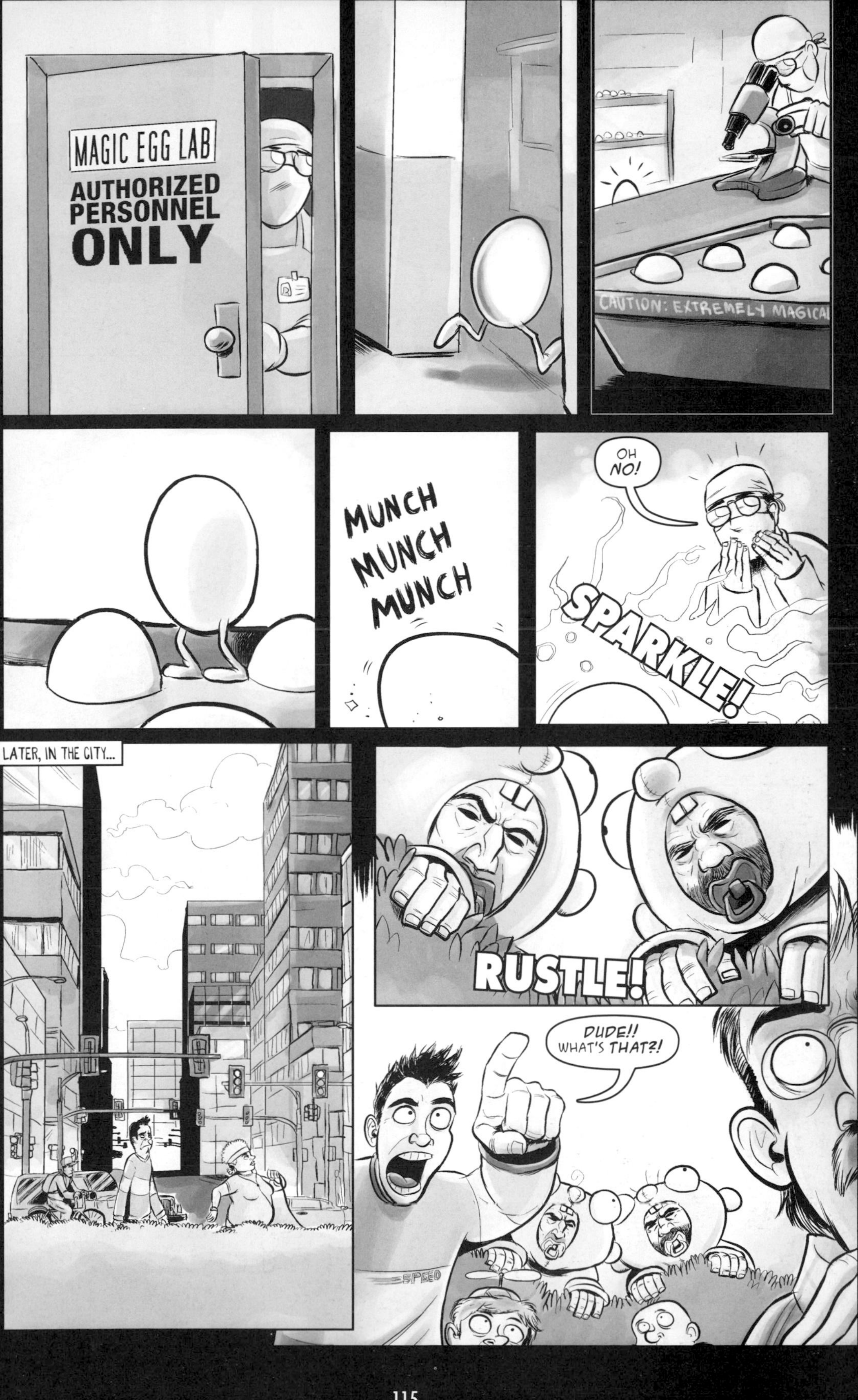
MAGIC EGG LAB
AUTHORIZED PERSONNEL ONLY
CAUTION: EXTREMELY MAGICAL
MUNCH MUNCH MUNCH
OH NO!
SPARKLE!
LATER, IN THE CITY...
RUSTLE!
DUDE!! WHAT'S THAT?!
SPEED

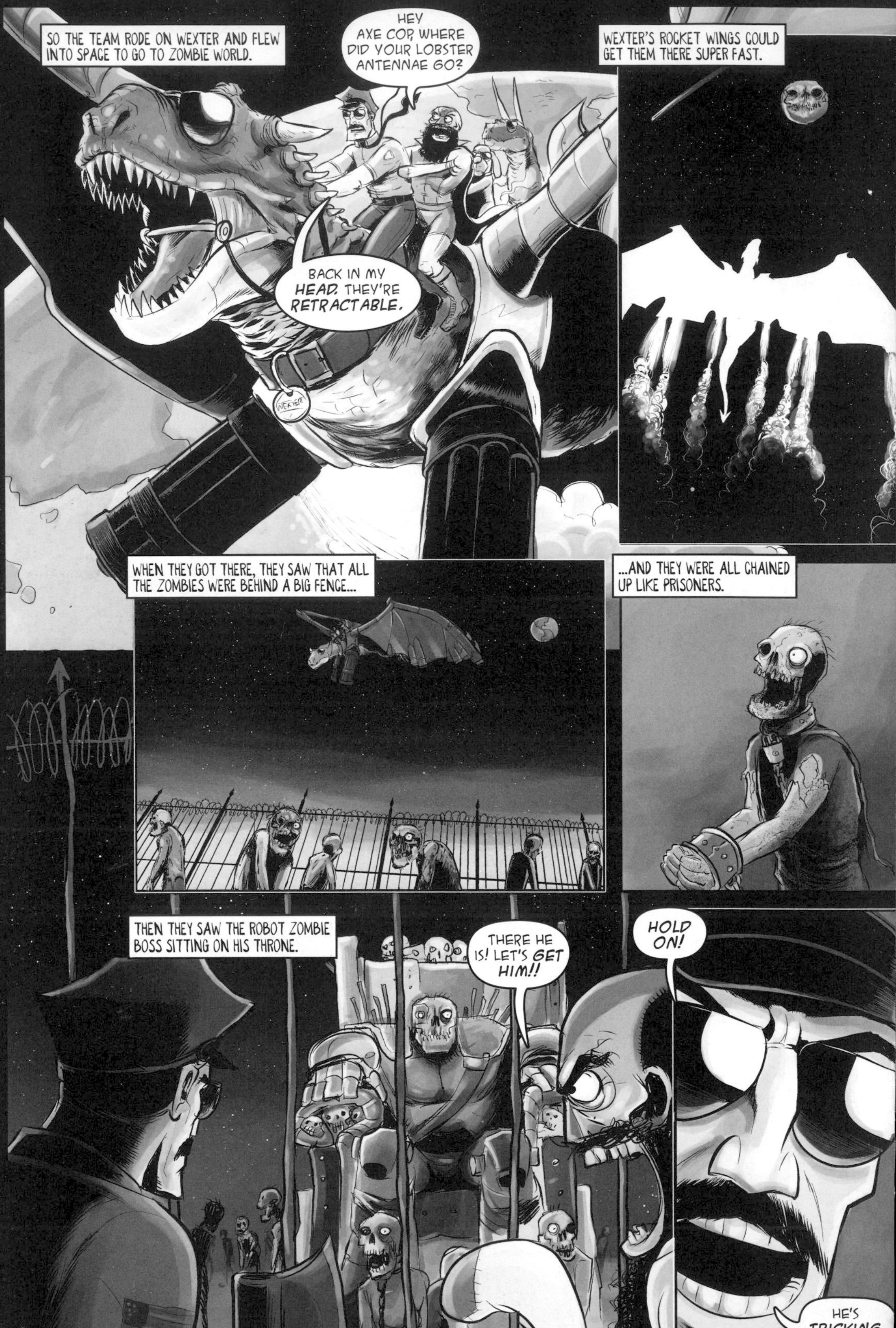
SO THE TEAM RODE ON WEXTER AND FLEW INTO SPACE TO GO TO ZOMBIE WORLD.
HEY AXE COP, WHERE DID YOUR LOBSTER ANTENNAE GO?
BACK IN MY HEAD. THEY'RE RETRACTABLE.
WEXTER
WEXTER'S ROCKET WINGS COULD GET THEM THERE SUPER FAST.
WHEN THEY GOT THERE, THEY SAW THAT ALL THE ZOMBIES WERE BEHIND A BIG FENCE...
...AND THEY WERE ALL CHAINED UP LIKE PRISONERS.
THEN THEY SAW THE ROBOT ZOMBIE BOSS SITTING ON HIS THRONE.
THERE HE IS! LET'S GET HIM!!
HOLD ON!
HE'S TRICKING US.

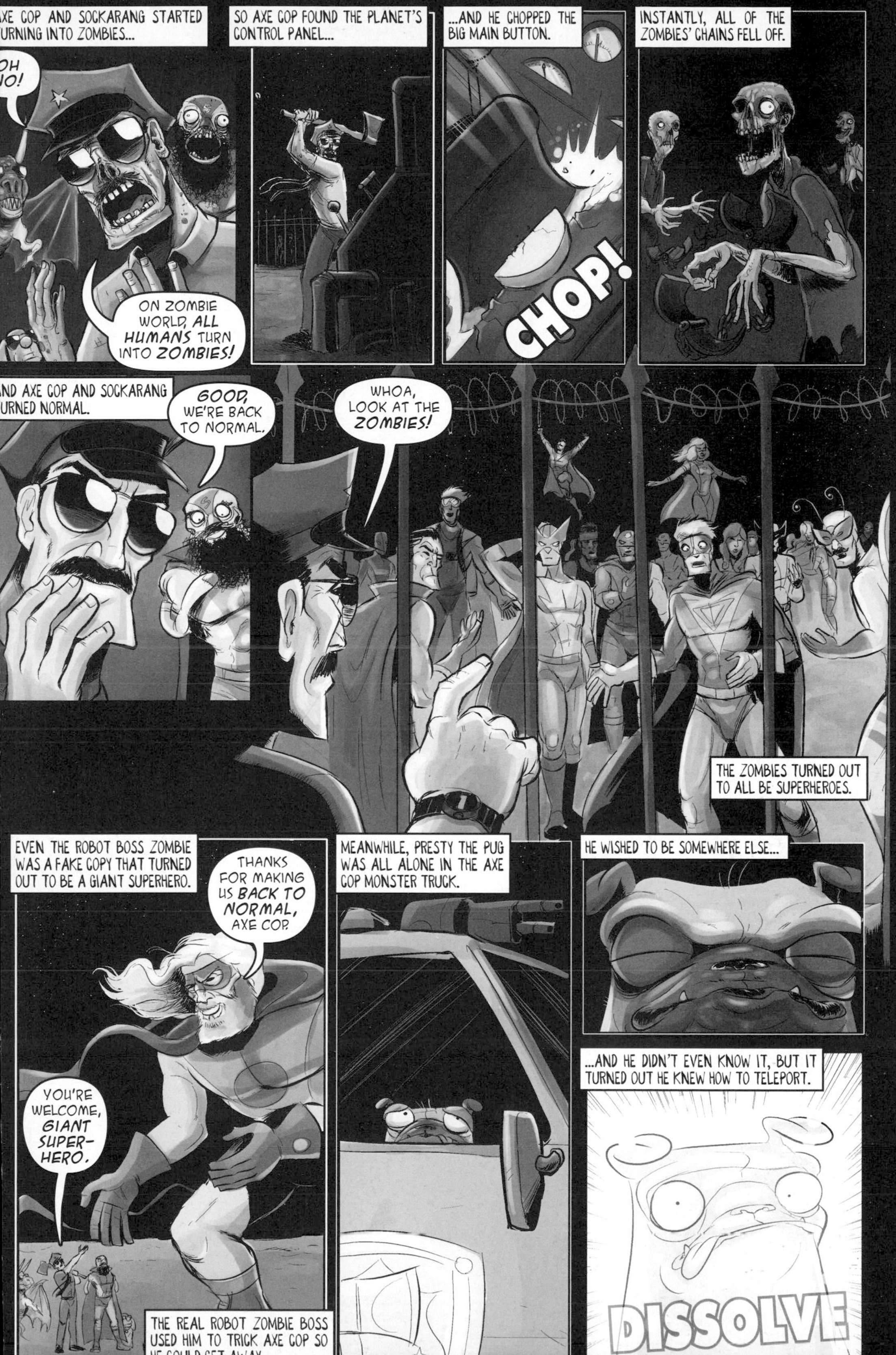
AXE COP AND SOCKARANG STARTED TURNING INTO ZOMBIES...
OH NO!
ON ZOMBIE WORLD, ALL HUMANS TURN INTO ZOMBIES!
SO AXE COP FOUND THE PLANET'S CONTROL PANEL...
...AND HE CHOPPED THE BIG MAIN BUTTON.
CHOP!
INSTANTLY, ALL OF THE ZOMBIES' CHAINS FELL OFF.
AND AXE COP AND SOCKARANG TURNED NORMAL.
GOOD, WE'RE BACK TO NORMAL.
WHOA, LOOK AT THE ZOMBIES!
THE ZOMBIES TURNED OUT TO ALL BE SUPERHEROES.
EVEN THE ROBOT BOSS ZOMBIE WAS A FAKE COPY THAT TURNED OUT TO BE A GIANT SUPERHERO.
THANKS FOR MAKING US BACK TO NORMAL, AXE COP.
YOU'RE WELCOME, GIANT SUPER-HERO.
THE REAL ROBOT ZOMBIE BOSS USED HIM TO TRICK AXE COP SO HE COULD GET AWAY.
MEANWHILE, PRESTY THE PUG WAS ALL ALONE IN THE AXE COP MONSTER TRUCK.
HE WISHED TO BE SOMEWHERE ELSE...
...AND HE DIDN'T EVEN KNOW IT, BUT IT TURNED OUT HE KNEW HOW TO TELEPORT.
DISSOLVE

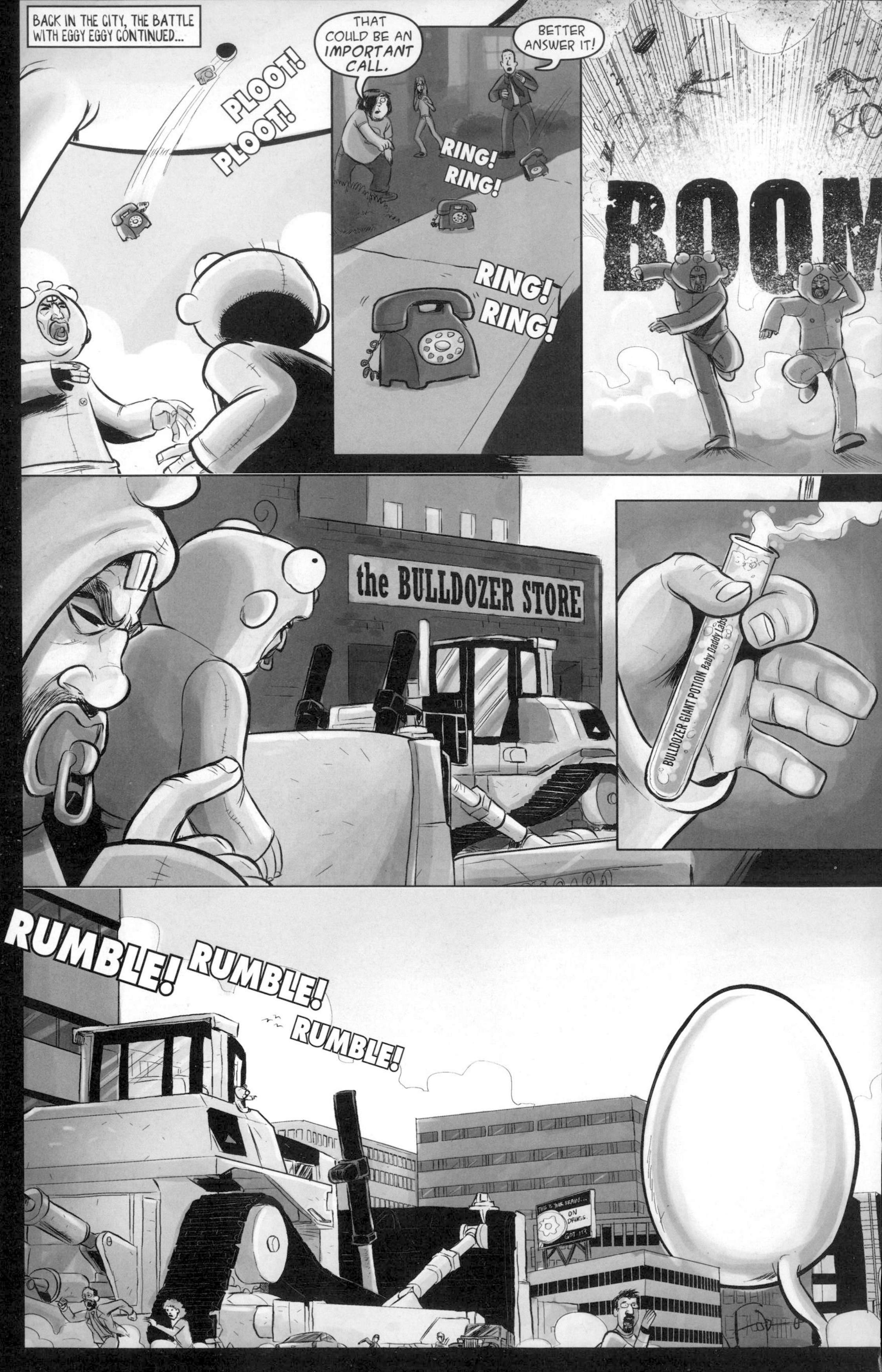

BACK IN THE CITY, THE BATTLE WITH EGGY EGGY CONTINUED...
PLOOT! PLOOT!
THAT COULD BE AN IMPORTANT CALL.
BETTER ANSWER IT!
RING! RING!
RING! RING!
BOOM
the BULLDOZER STORE
BULLDOZER GIANT POTION Baby Daddy Labs
RUMBLE! RUMBLE! RUMBLE!
THIS IS YOUR BRAIN... ON DRUGS. GOT IT?

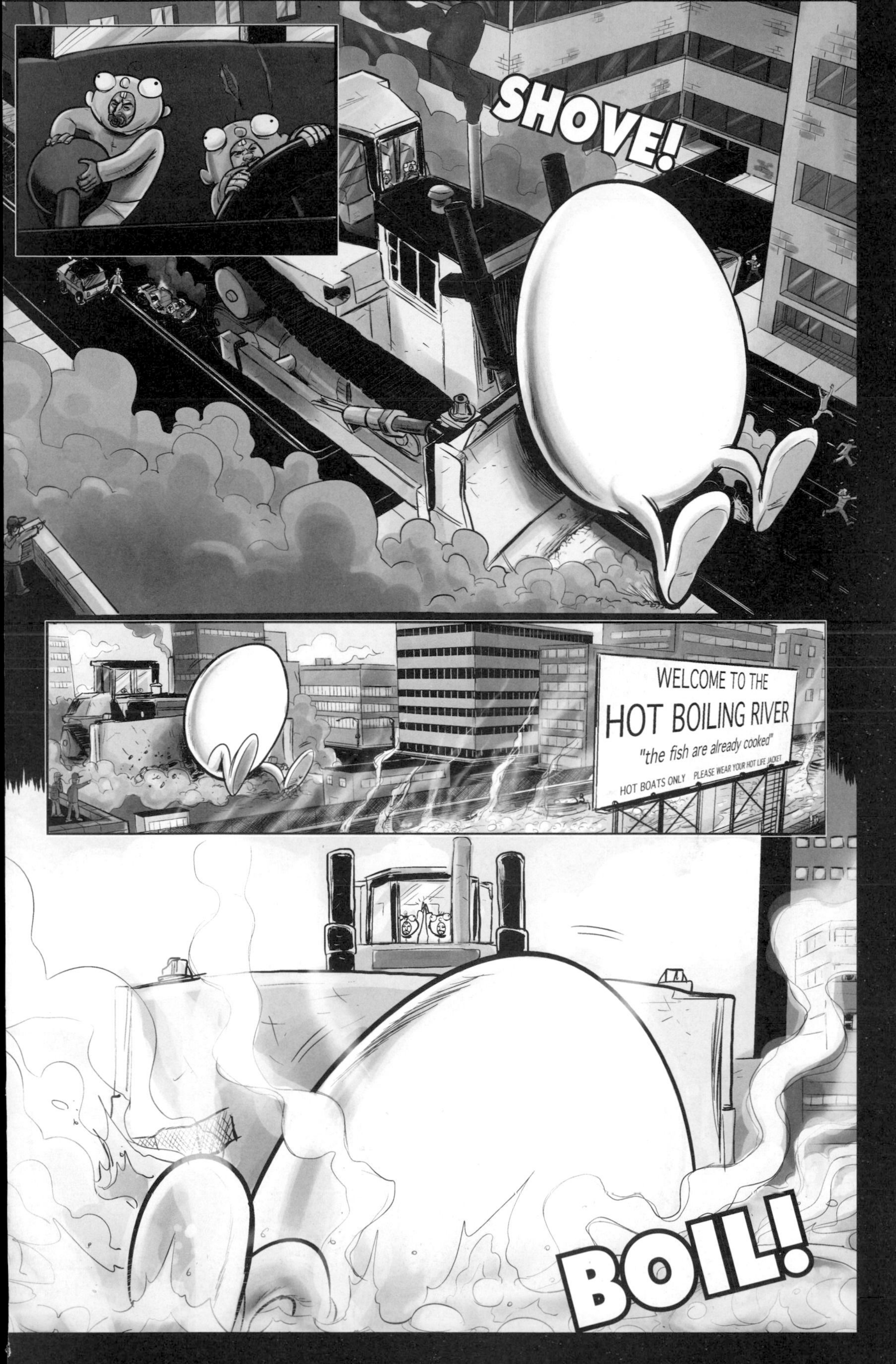
SHOVE!
WELCOME TO THE
HOT BOILING RIVER
"the fish are already cooked"
HOT BOATS ONLY PLEASE WEAR YOUR HOT LIFE JACKET
BOIL!

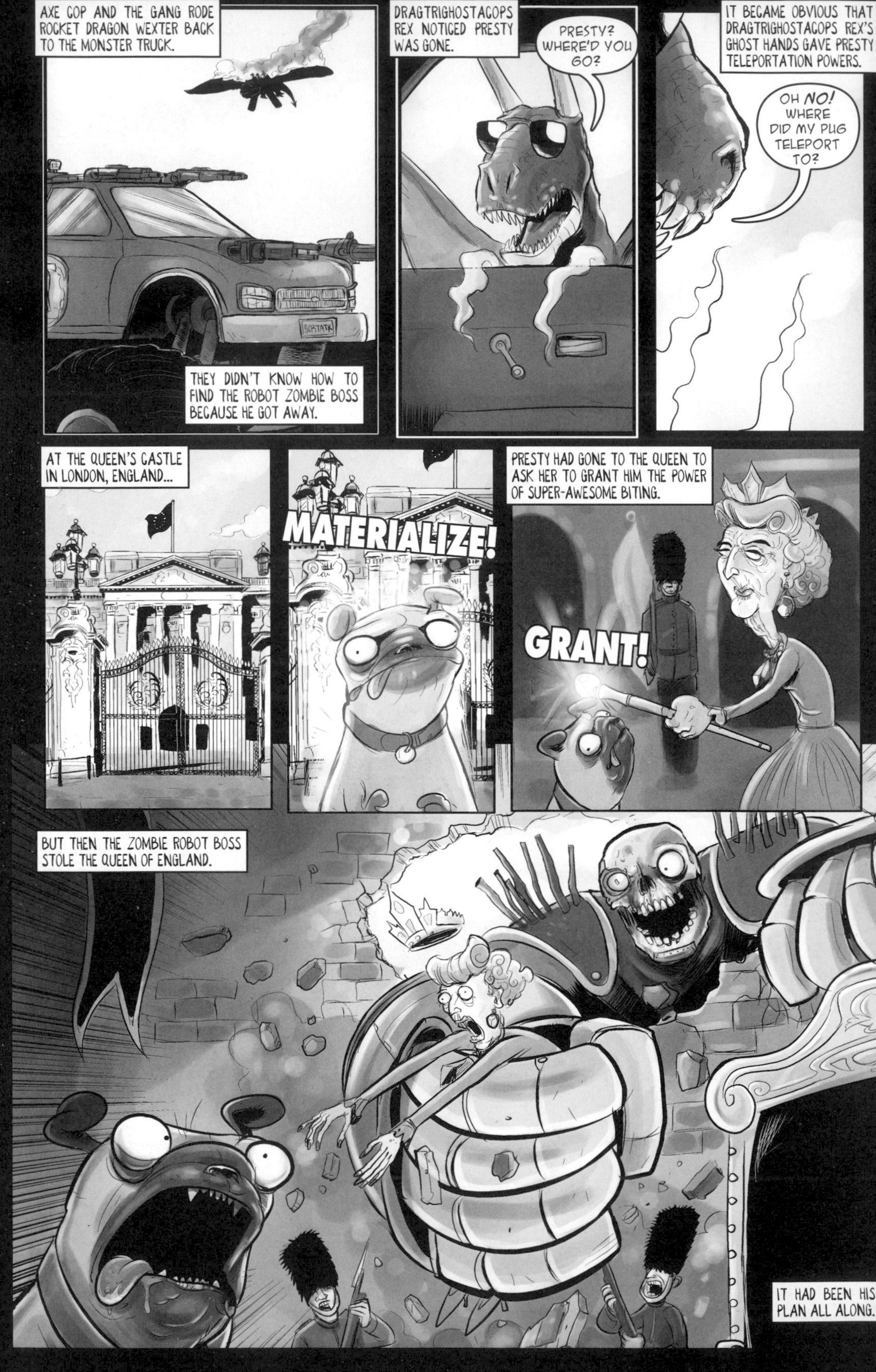
AXE COP AND THE GANG RODE ROCKET DRAGON WEXTER BACK TO THE MONSTER TRUCK.
THEY DIDN'T KNOW HOW TO FIND THE ROBOT ZOMBIE BOSS BECAUSE HE GOT AWAY.
DRAGTRIGHOSTACOPS REX NOTICED PRESTY WAS GONE.
PRESTY? WHERE'D YOU GO?
IT BECAME OBVIOUS THAT DRAGTRIGHOSTACOPS REX'S GHOST HANDS GAVE PRESTY TELEPORTATION POWERS.
OH NO! WHERE DID MY PUG TELEPORT TO?
AT THE QUEEN'S CASTLE IN LONDON, ENGLAND...
MATERIALIZE!
PRESTY HAD GONE TO THE QUEEN TO ASK HER TO GRANT HIM THE POWER OF SUPER-AWESOME BITING.
GRANT!
BUT THEN THE ZOMBIE ROBOT BOSS STOLE THE QUEEN OF ENGLAND.
IT HAD BEEN HIS PLAN ALL ALONG.

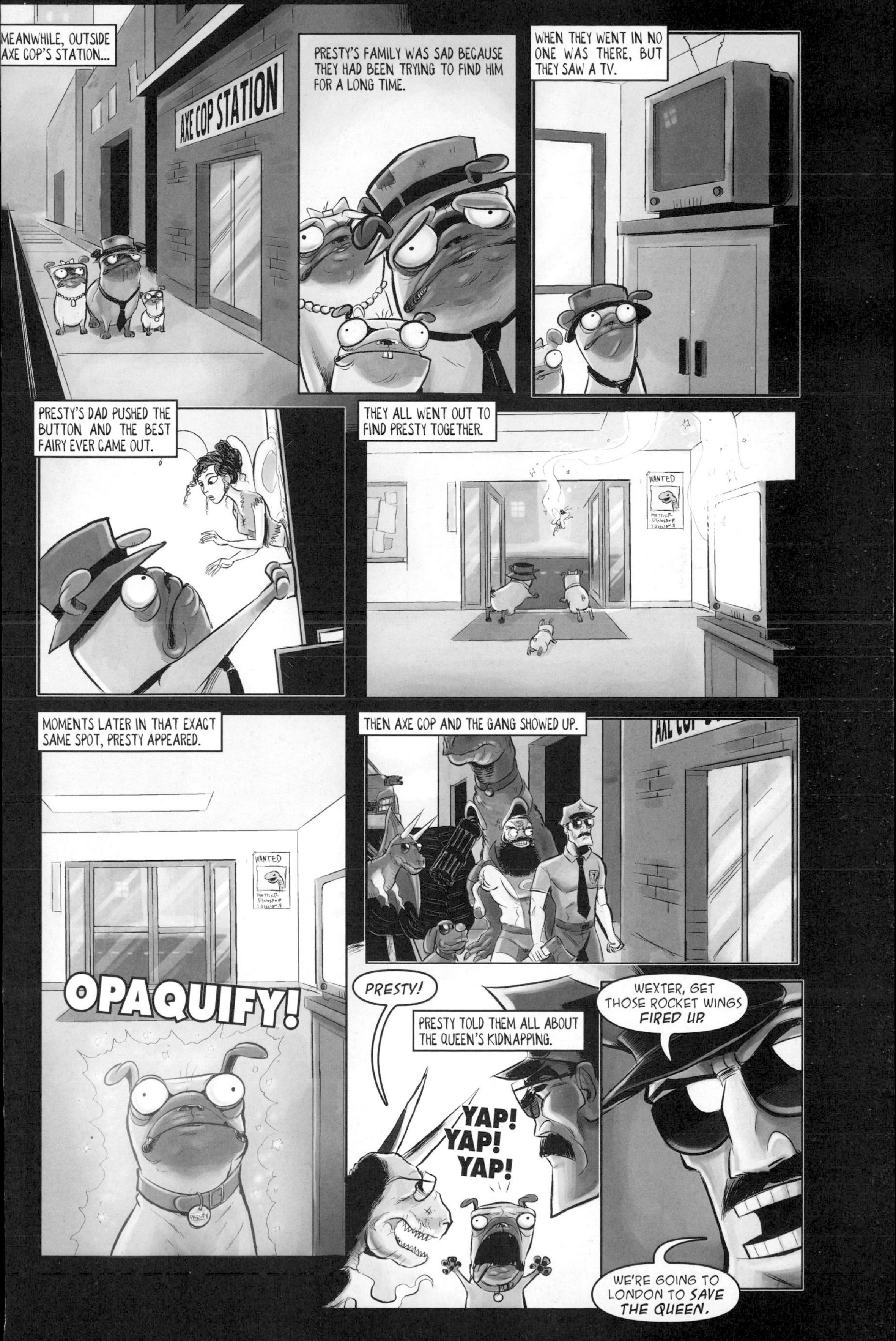
MEANWHILE, OUTSIDE AXE COP'S STATION...
AXE COP STATION
PRESTY'S FAMILY WAS SAD BECAUSE THEY HAD BEEN TRYING TO FIND HIM FOR A LONG TIME.
WHEN THEY WENT IN NO ONE WAS THERE, BUT THEY SAW A TV.
PRESTY'S DAD PUSHED THE BUTTON AND THE BEST FAIRY EVER CAME OUT.
THEY ALL WENT OUT TO FIND PRESTY TOGETHER.
WANTED
MOMENTS LATER IN THAT EXACT SAME SPOT, PRESTY APPEARED.
WANTED
OPAQUIFY!
THEN AXE COP AND THE GANG SHOWED UP.
PRESTY!
PRESTY TOLD THEM ALL ABOUT THE QUEEN'S KIDNAPPING.
YAP! YAP! YAP!
WEXTER, GET THOSE ROCKET WINGS FIRED UP.
WE'RE GOING TO LONDON TO SAVE THE QUEEN.

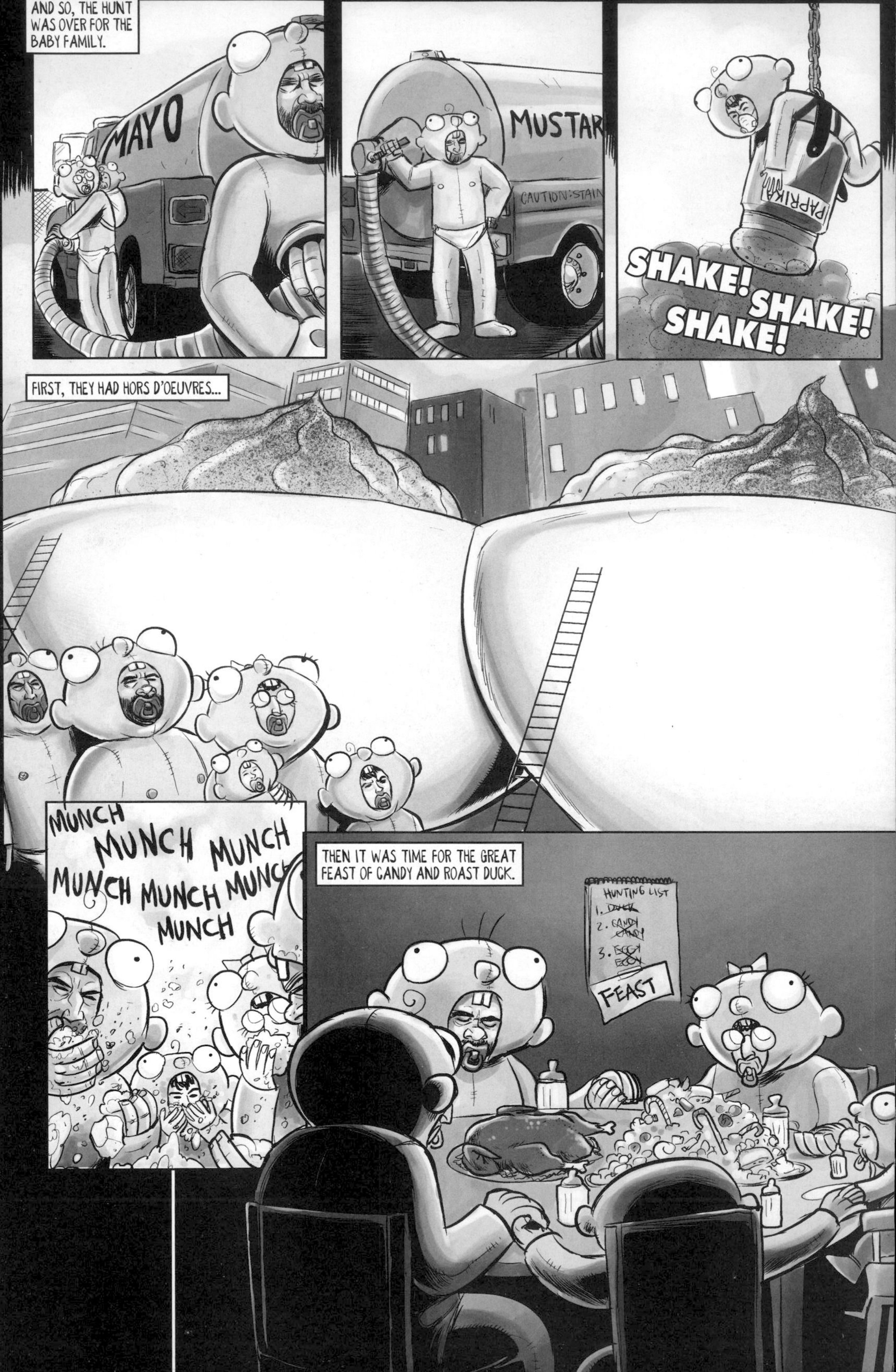
AND SO, THE HUNT WAS OVER FOR THE BABY FAMILY.
MAYO
MUSTAR
CAUTION: STAIN
PAPRIKA
SHAKE! SHAKE! SHAKE!
FIRST, THEY HAD HORS D'OEUVRES...
MUNCH MUNCH MUNCH MUNCH MUNCH MUNCH MUNCH
THEN IT WAS TIME FOR THE GREAT FEAST OF CANDY AND ROAST DUCK.
HUNTING LIST
FEAST

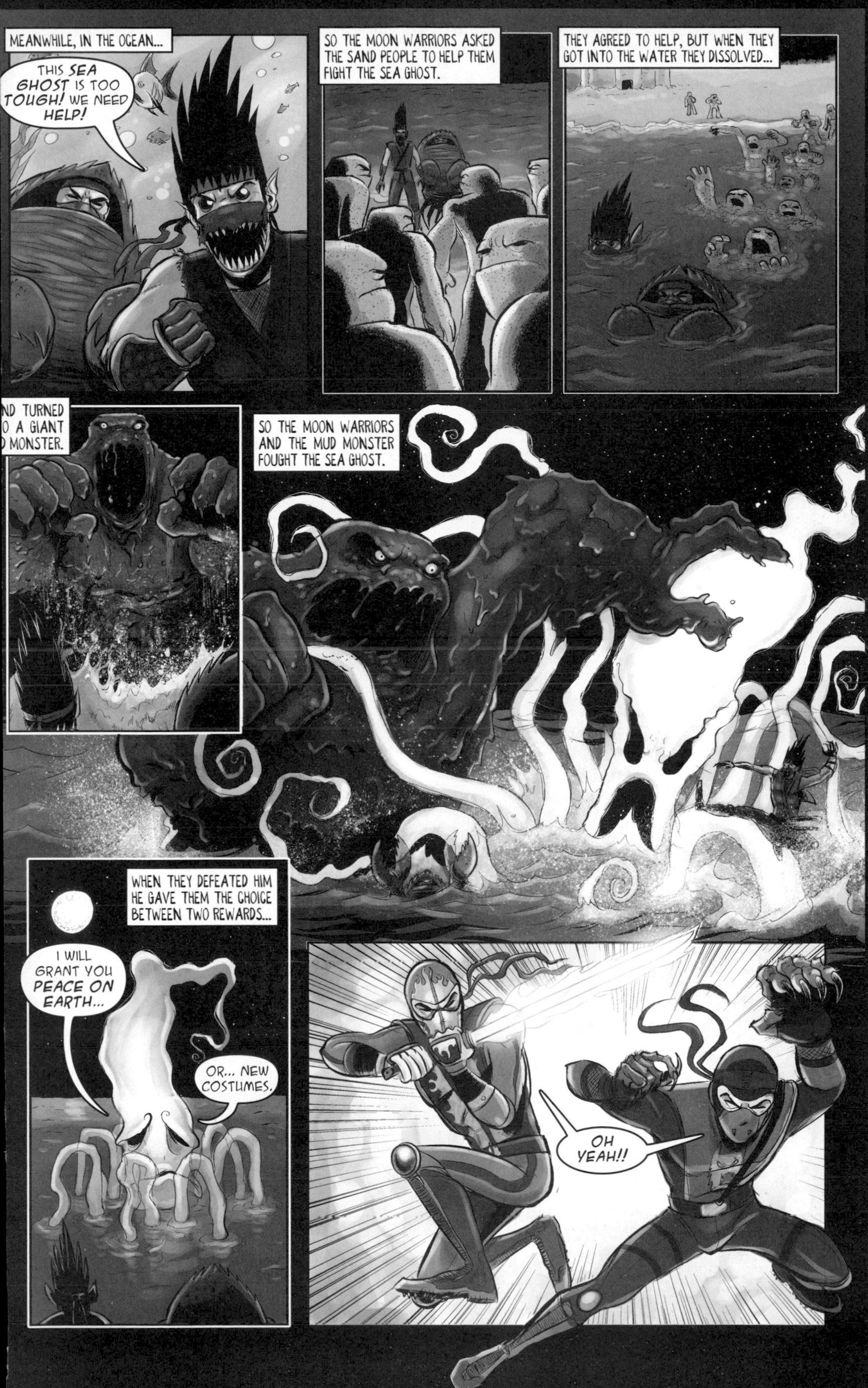
MEANWHILE, IN THE OCEAN...
THIS SEA GHOST IS TOO TOUGH! WE NEED HELP!
SO THE MOON WARRIORS ASKED THE SAND PEOPLE TO HELP THEM FIGHT THE SEA GHOST.
THEY AGREED TO HELP, BUT WHEN THEY GOT INTO THE WATER THEY DISSOLVED...
ND TURNED O A GIANT D MONSTER.
SO THE MOON WARRIORS AND THE MUD MONSTER FOUGHT THE SEA GHOST.
WHEN THEY DEFEATED HIM HE GAVE THEM THE CHOICE BETWEEN TWO REWARDS...
I WILL GRANT YOU PEACE ON EARTH...
OR... NEW COSTUMES.
OH YEAH!!

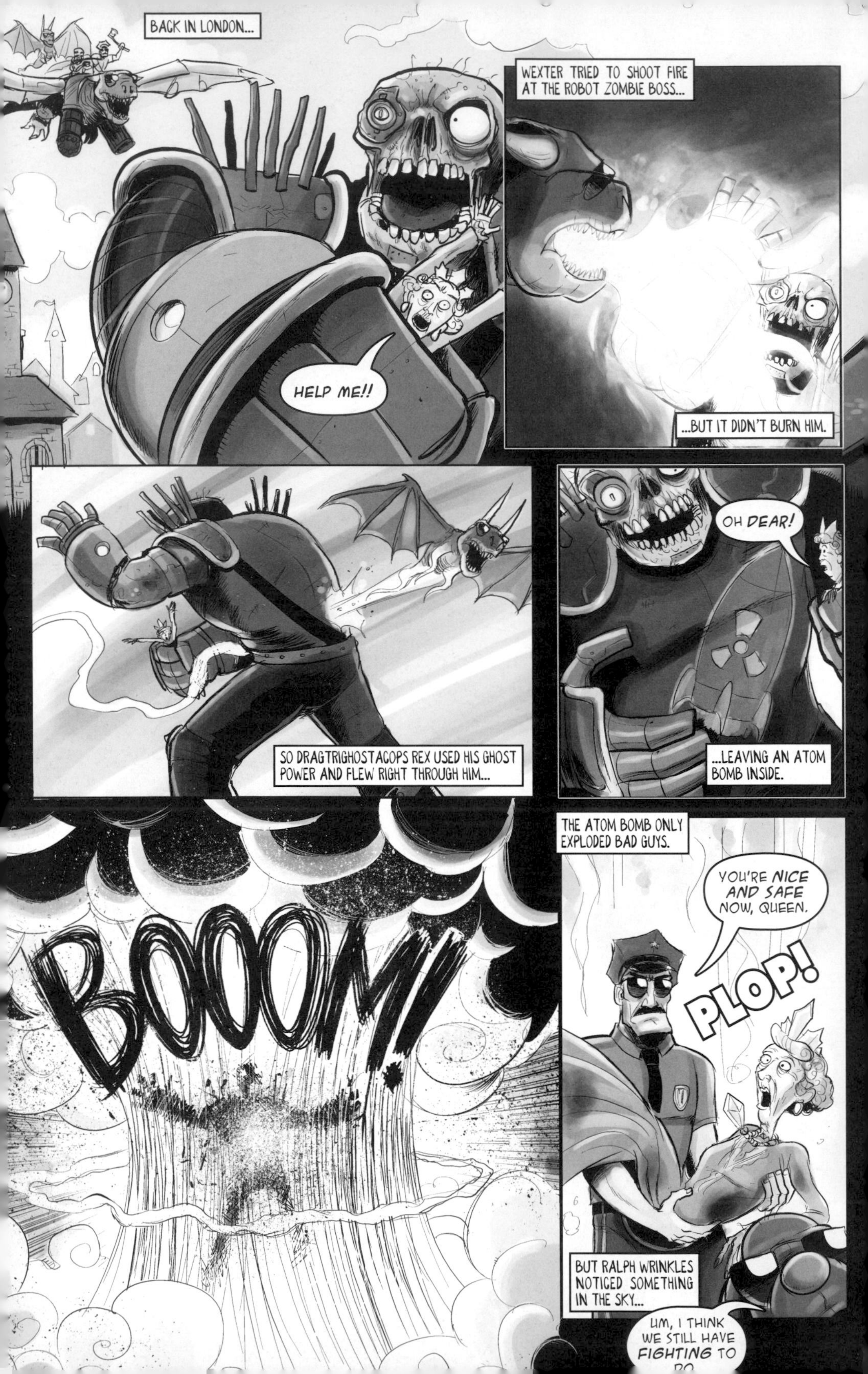

BACK IN LONDON...
HELP ME!!
WEXTER TRIED TO SHOOT FIRE AT THE ROBOT ZOMBIE BOSS...
...BUT IT DIDN'T BURN HIM.
SO DRAGTRIGHOSTACOPS REX USED HIS GHOST POWER AND FLEW RIGHT THROUGH HIM...
OH DEAR!
...LEAVING AN ATOM BOMB INSIDE.
BOOOM!
THE ATOM BOMB ONLY EXPLODED BAD GUYS.
YOU'RE NICE AND SAFE NOW, QUEEN.
PLOP!
BUT RALPH WRINKLES NOTICED SOMETHING IN THE SKY...
UM, I THINK WE STILL HAVE FIGHTING TO

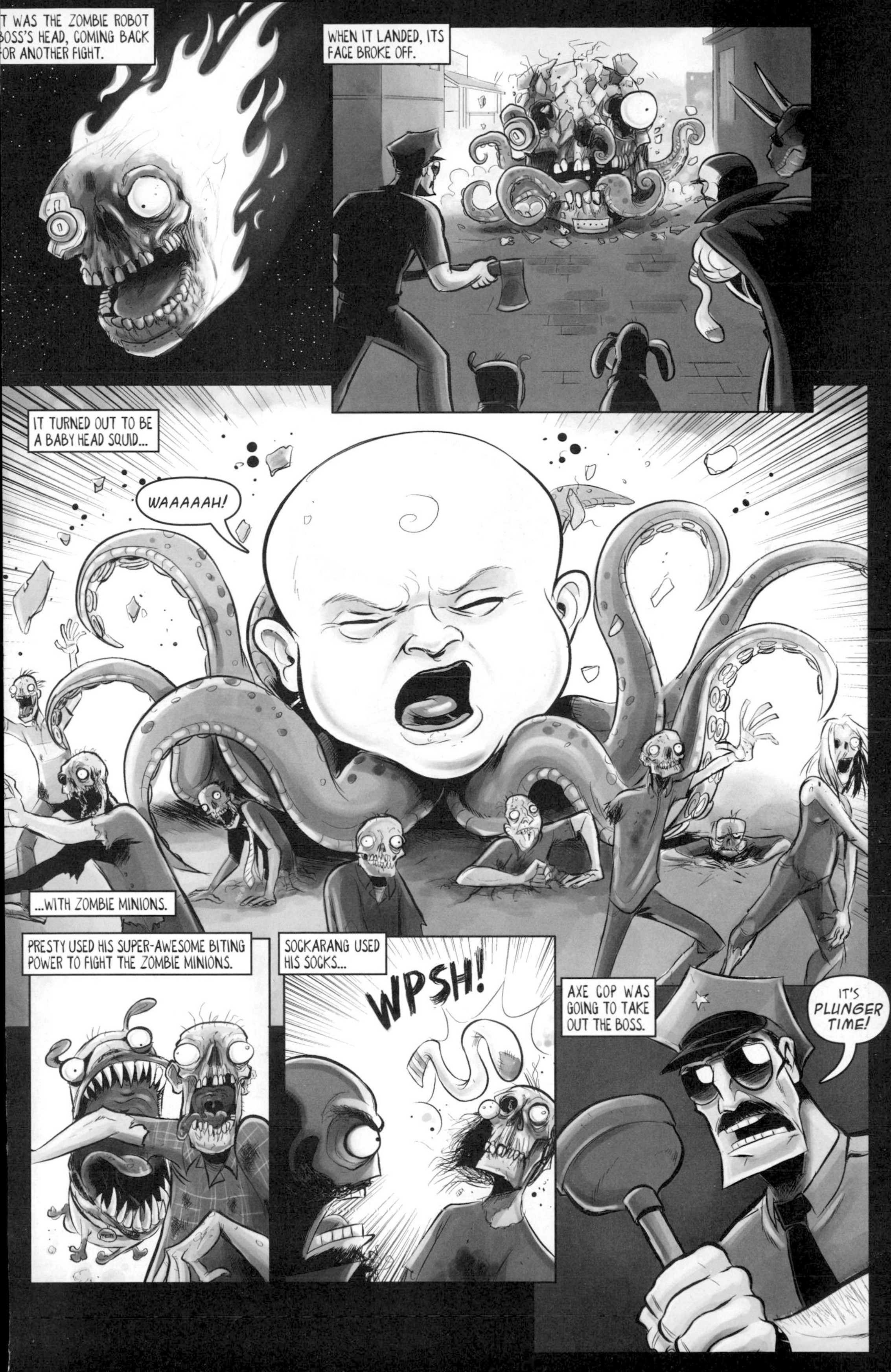

IT WAS THE ZOMBIE ROBOT BOSS'S HEAD, COMING BACK FOR ANOTHER FIGHT.
WHEN IT LANDED, ITS FACE BROKE OFF.
IT TURNED OUT TO BE A BABY HEAD SQUID...
WAAAAAH!
...WITH ZOMBIE MINIONS.
PRESTY USED HIS SUPER-AWESOME BITING POWER TO FIGHT THE ZOMBIE MINIONS.
SOCKARANG USED HIS SOCKS...
WPSH!
AXE COP WAS GOING TO TAKE OUT THE BOSS.
IT'S PLUNGER TIME!

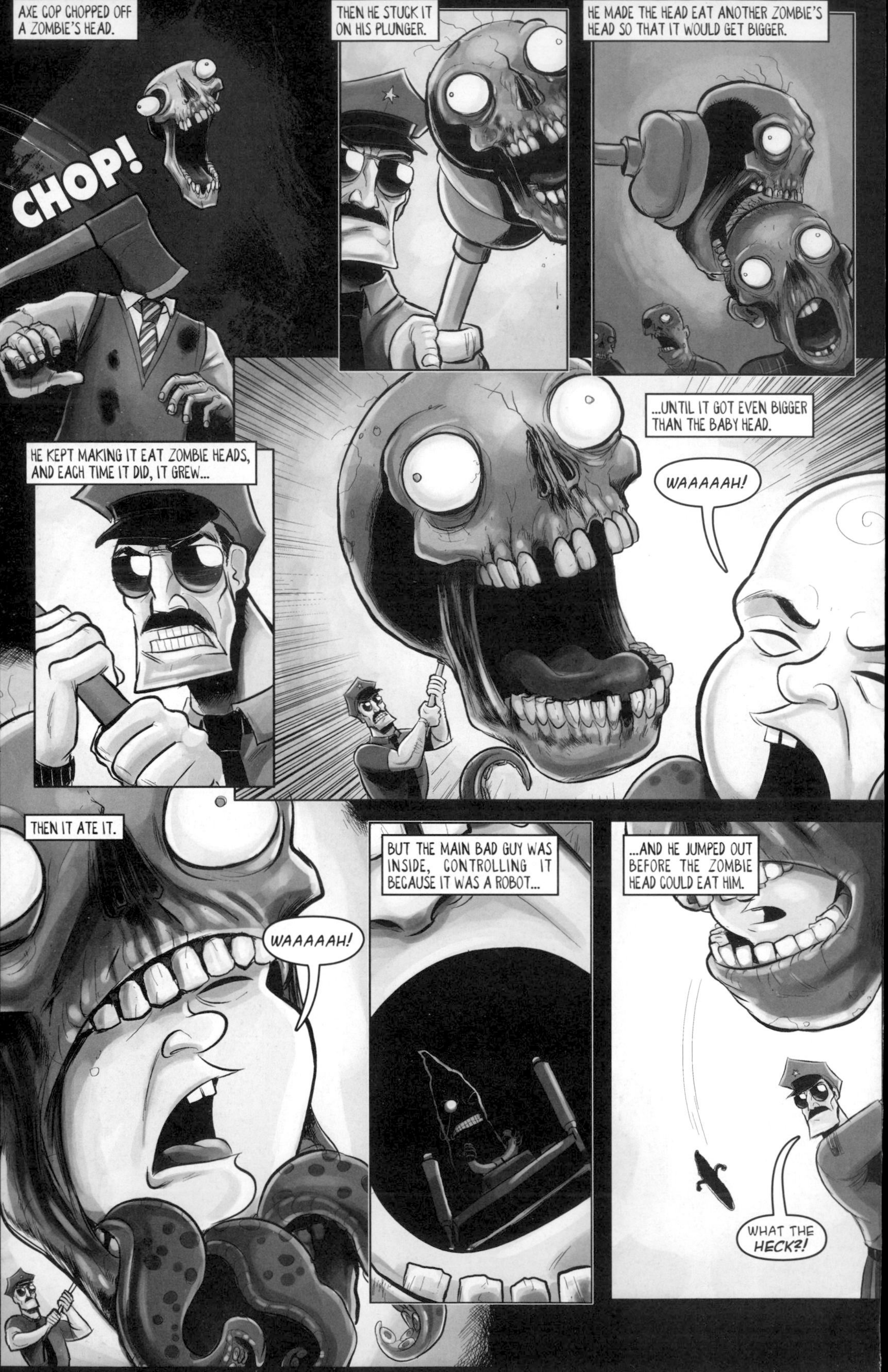
AXE COP CHOPPED OFF A ZOMBIE'S HEAD.
CHOP!
THEN HE STUCK IT ON HIS PLUNGER.
HE MADE THE HEAD EAT ANOTHER ZOMBIE'S HEAD SO THAT IT WOULD GET BIGGER.
HE KEPT MAKING IT EAT ZOMBIE HEADS, AND EACH TIME IT DID, IT GREW...
...UNTIL IT GOT EVEN BIGGER THAN THE BABY HEAD.
WAAAAAH!
THEN IT ATE IT.
WAAAAAH!
BUT THE MAIN BAD GUY WAS INSIDE, CONTROLLING IT BECAUSE IT WAS A ROBOT...
...AND HE JUMPED OUT BEFORE THE ZOMBIE HEAD COULD EAT HIM.
WHAT THE HECK?!

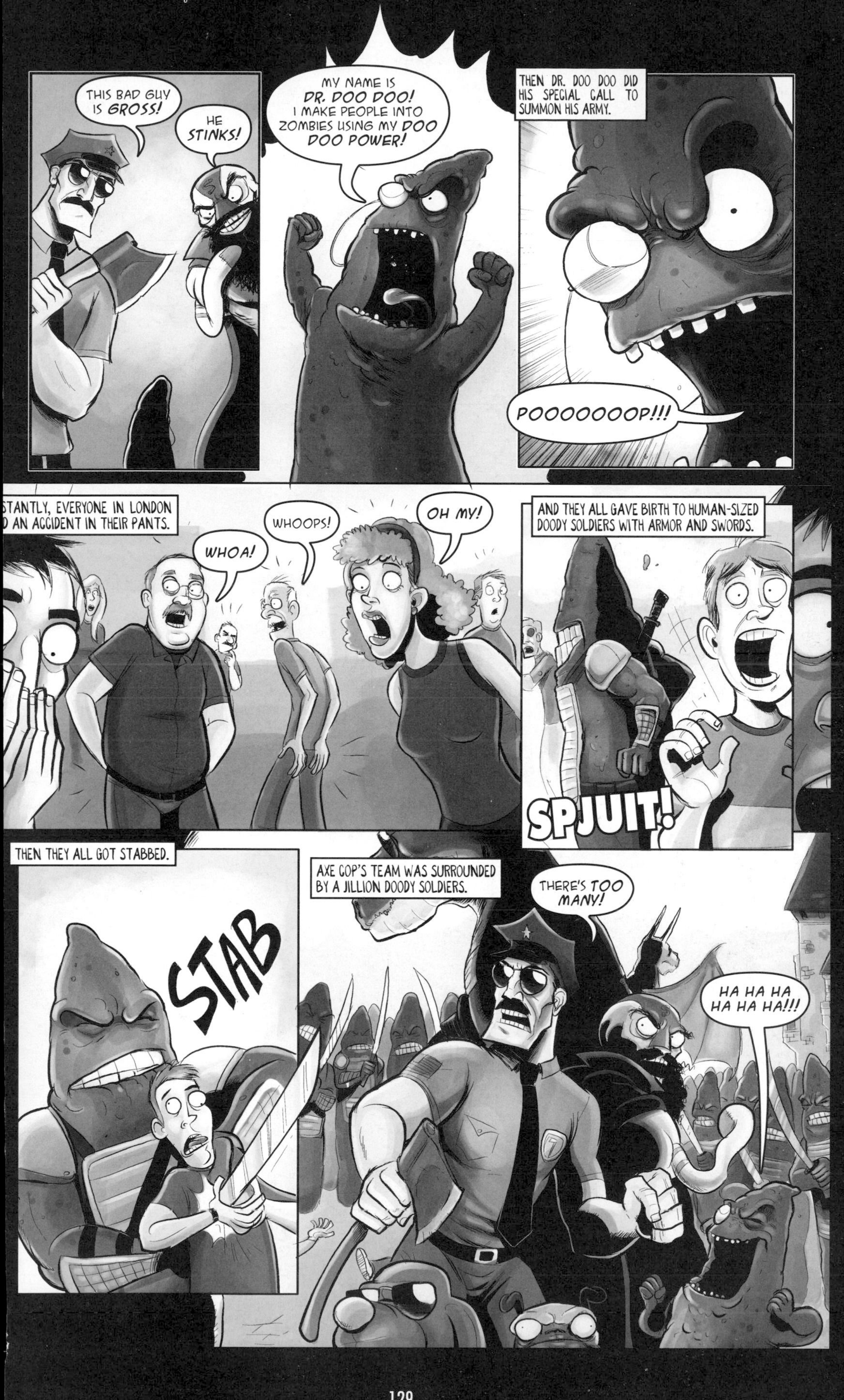
THIS BAD GUY IS GROSS!
HE STINKS!
MY NAME IS DR. DOO DOO! I MAKE PEOPLE INTO ZOMBIES USING MY DOO DOO POWER!
THEN DR. DOO DOO DID HIS SPECIAL CALL TO SUMMON HIS ARMY.
POOOOOOOP!!!
STANTLY, EVERYONE IN LONDON
D AN ACCIDENT IN THEIR PANTS.
WHOA!
WHOOPS!
OH MY!
AND THEY ALL GAVE BIRTH TO HUMAN-SIZED DOODY SOLDIERS WITH ARMOR AND SWORDS.
SPJUIT!
THEN THEY ALL GOT STABBED.
STAB
AXE COP'S TEAM WAS SURROUNDED BY A JILLION DOODY SOLDIERS.
THERE'S TOO MANY!
HA HA HA HA HA HA!!!

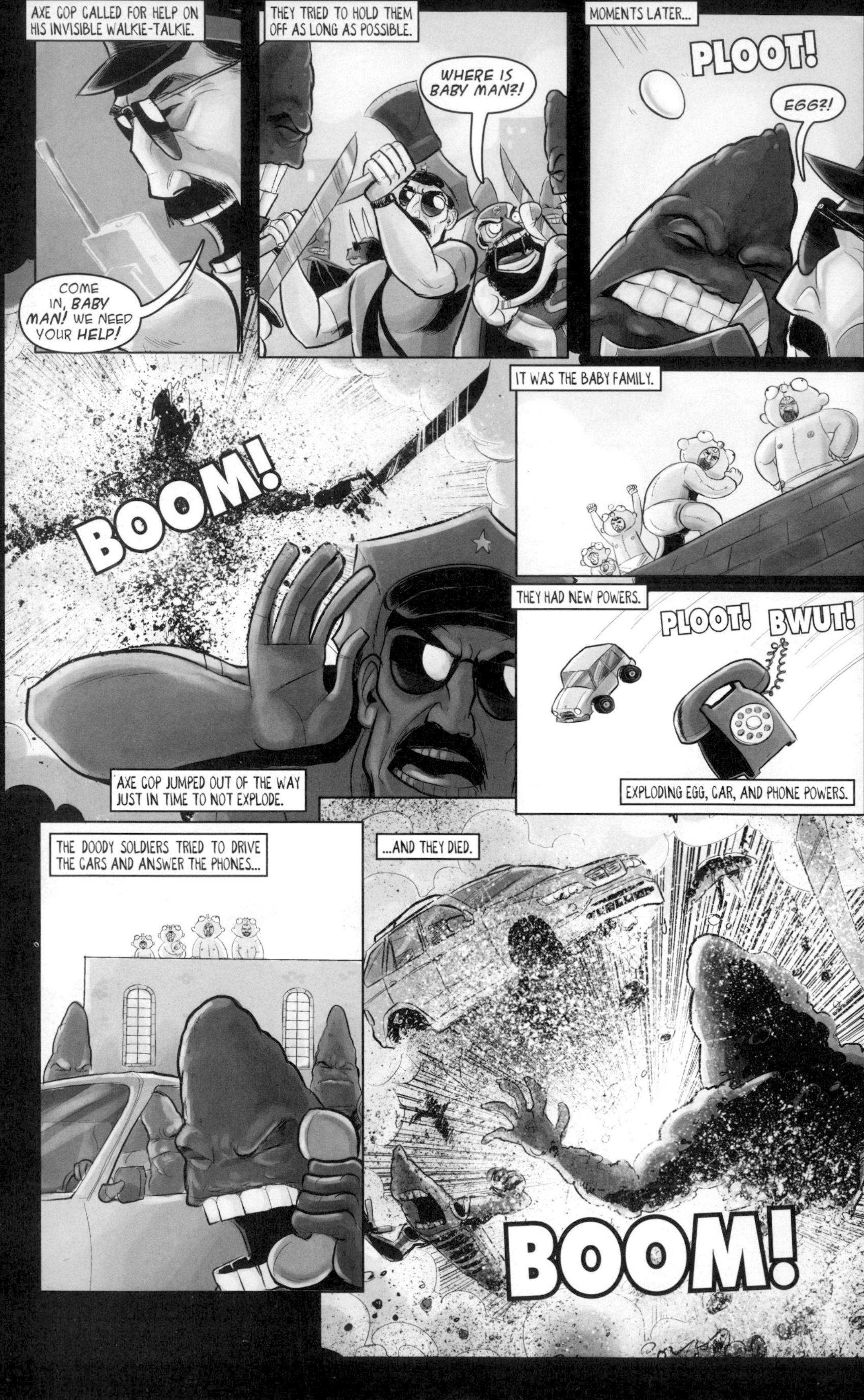
AXE COP CALLED FOR HELP ON HIS INVISIBLE WALKIE-TALKIE.
COME IN, BABY MAN! WE NEED YOUR HELP!
THEY TRIED TO HOLD THEM OFF AS LONG AS POSSIBLE.
WHERE IS BABY MAN?!
MOMENTS LATER...
PLOOT!
EGG?!
BOOM!
AXE COP JUMPED OUT OF THE WAY JUST IN TIME TO NOT EXPLODE.
IT WAS THE BABY FAMILY.
THEY HAD NEW POWERS.
PLOOT! BWUT!
EXPLODING EGG, CAR, AND PHONE POWERS.
THE DOODY SOLDIERS TRIED TO DRIVE THE CARS AND ANSWER THE PHONES...
...AND THEY DIED.
BOOM!

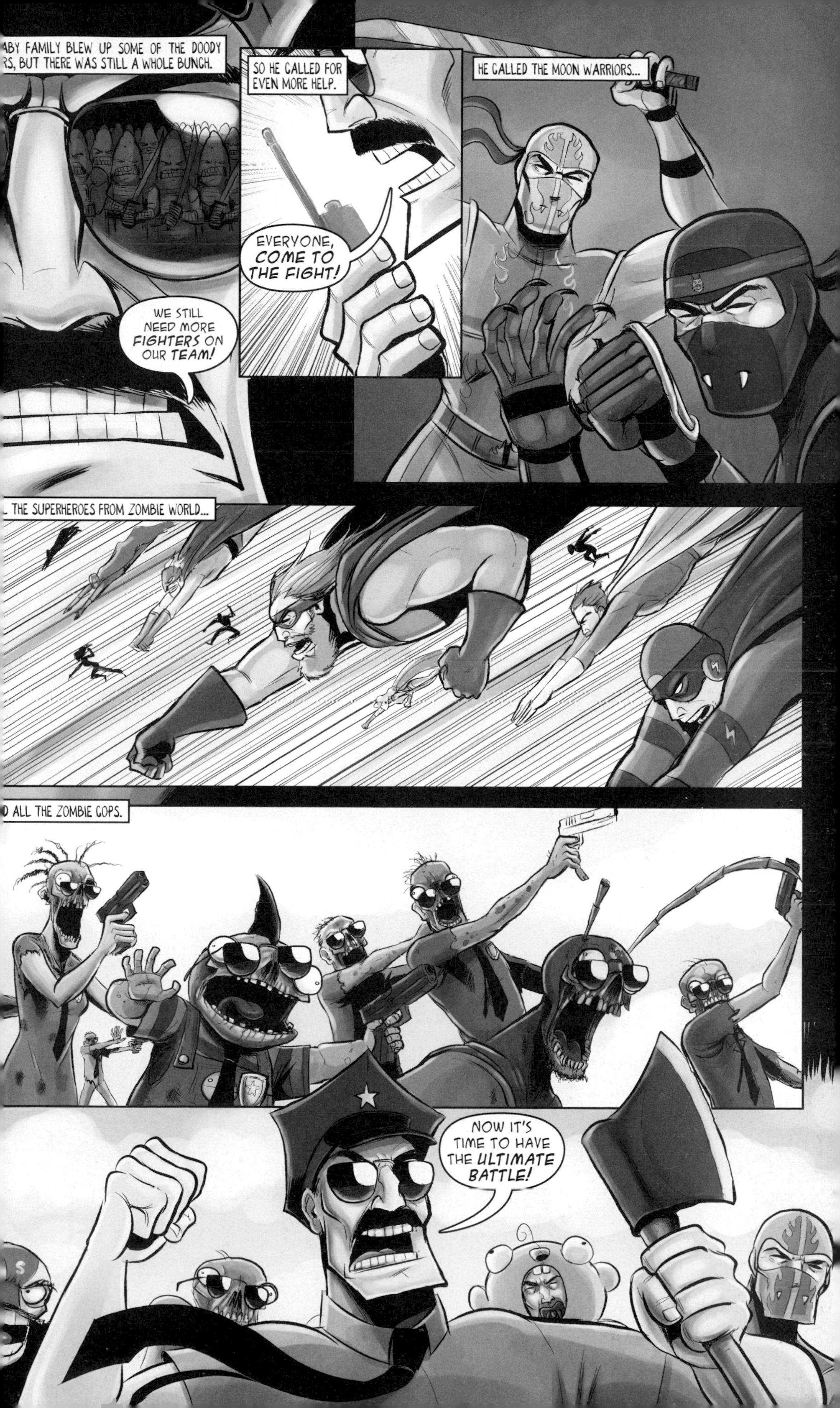

ABY FAMILY BLEW UP SOME OF THE DOODY
RS, BUT THERE WAS STILL A WHOLE BUNCH.
WE STILL NEED MORE FIGHTERS ON OUR TEAM!
SO HE CALLED FOR EVEN MORE HELP.
EVERYONE, COME TO THE FIGHT!
HE CALLED THE MOON WARRIORS...
L THE SUPERHEROES FROM ZOMBIE WORLD...
D ALL THE ZOMBIE COPS.
NOW IT'S TIME TO HAVE THE ULTIMATE BATTLE!

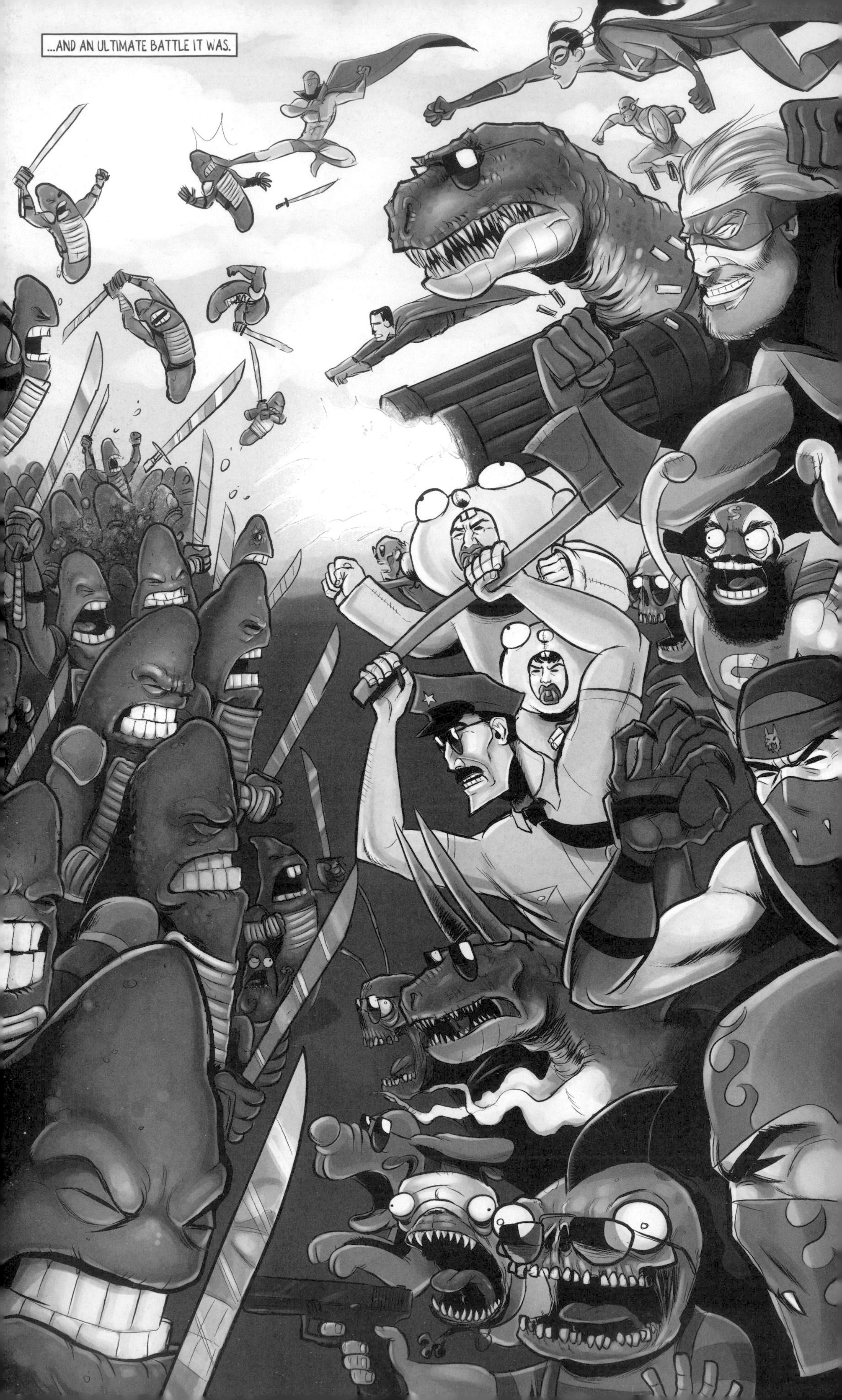
...AND AN ULTIMATE BATTLE IT WAS.

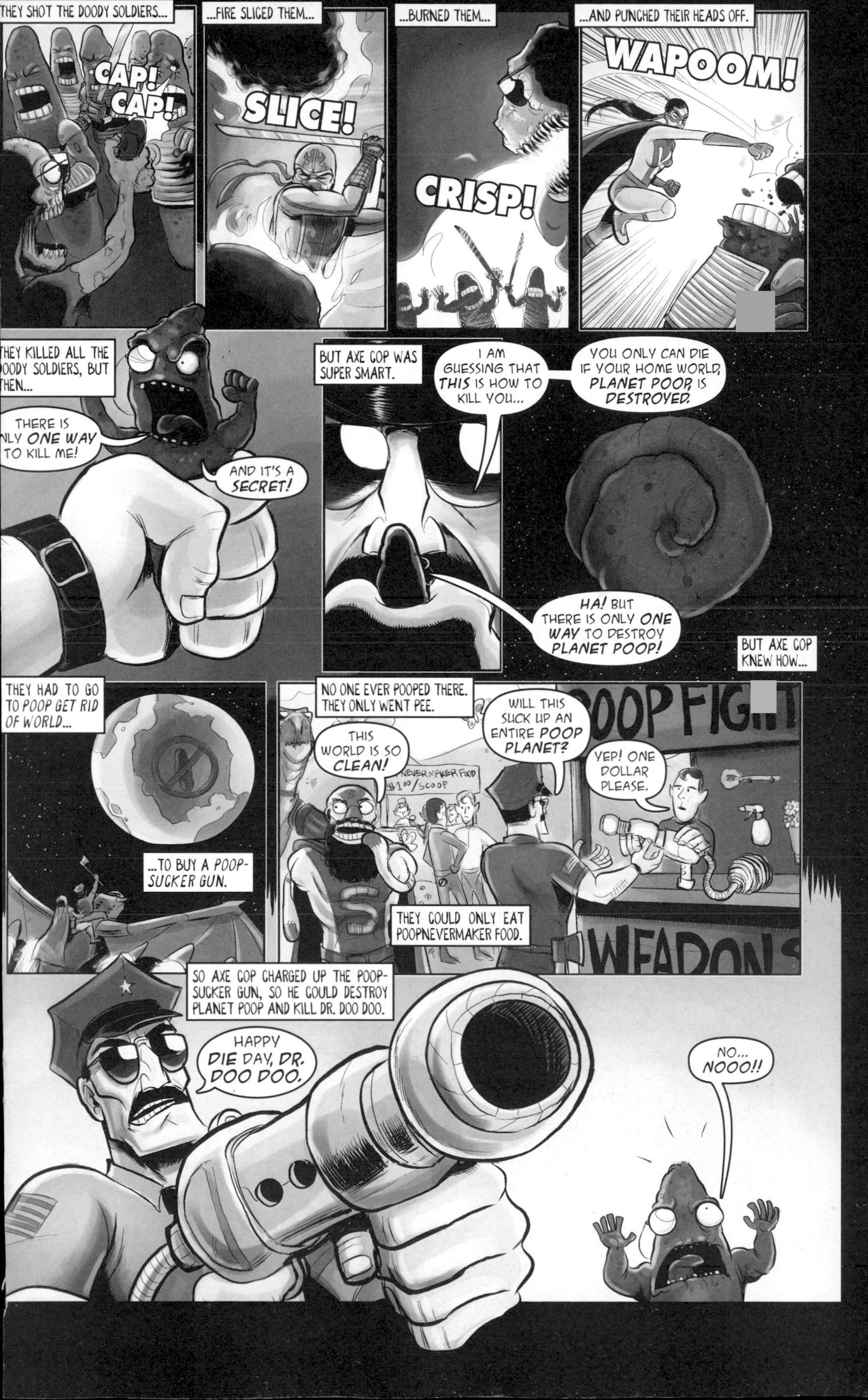
THEY SHOT THE DOODY SOLDIERS...
CAP! CAP!
...FIRE SLICED THEM...
SLICE!
...BURNED THEM...
CRISP!
...AND PUNCHED THEIR HEADS OFF.
WAPOOM!
HEY KILLED ALL THE OODY SOLDIERS, BUT HEN...
THERE IS NLY ONE WAY TO KILL ME!
AND IT'S A SECRET!
BUT AXE COP WAS SUPER SMART.
I AM GUESSING THAT THIS IS HOW TO KILL YOU...
YOU ONLY CAN DIE IF YOUR HOME WORLD, PLANET POOP, IS DESTROYED.
HA! BUT THERE IS ONLY ONE WAY TO DESTROY PLANET POOP!
BUT AXE COP KNEW HOW...
THEY HAD TO GO TO POOP GET RID OF WORLD...
...TO BUY A POOP-SUCKER GUN.
NO ONE EVER POOPED THERE. THEY ONLY WENT PEE.
THIS WORLD IS SO CLEAN!
NEVERMAKER FOOD $1.00/SCOOP
WILL THIS SUCK UP AN ENTIRE POOP PLANET?
YEP! ONE DOLLAR PLEASE.
THEY COULD ONLY EAT POOPNEVERMAKER FOOD.
SO AXE COP CHARGED UP THE POOP-SUCKER GUN, SO HE COULD DESTROY PLANET POOP AND KILL DR. DOO DOO.
HAPPY DIE DAY, DR. DOO DOO.
NO... NOOO!!

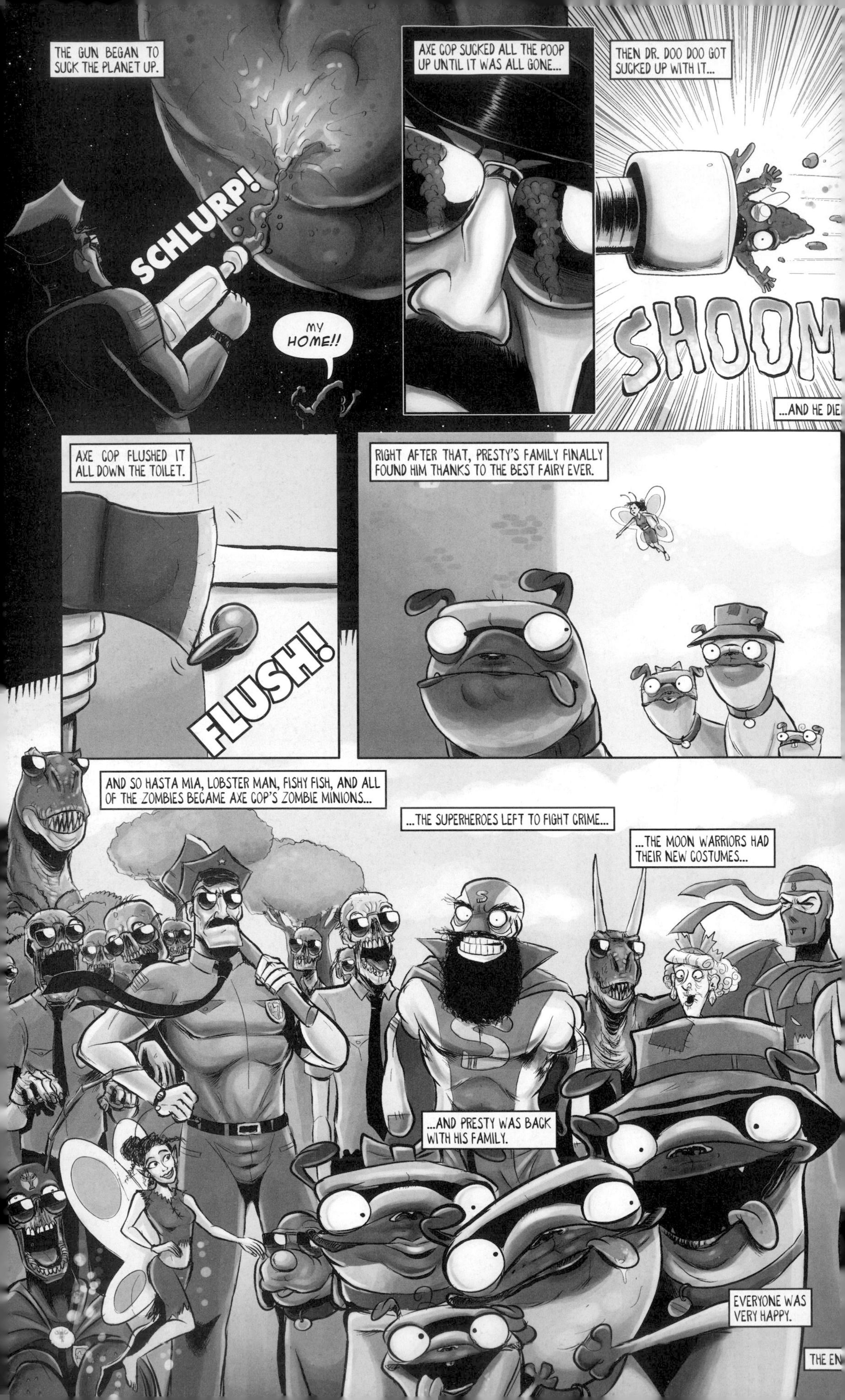
THE GUN BEGAN TO SUCK THE PLANET UP.
SCHLURP!
MY HOME!!
AXE COP SUCKED ALL THE POOP UP UNTIL IT WAS ALL GONE...
THEN DR. DOO DOO GOT SUCKED UP WITH IT...
SHOOM
...AND HE DIE
AXE COP FLUSHED IT ALL DOWN THE TOILET.
FLUSH!
RIGHT AFTER THAT, PRESTY'S FAMILY FINALLY FOUND HIM THANKS TO THE BEST FAIRY EVER.
AND SO HASTA MIA, LOBSTER MAN, FISHY FISH, AND ALL OF THE ZOMBIES BECAME AXE COP'S ZOMBIE MINIONS...
...THE SUPERHEROES LEFT TO FIGHT CRIME...
...THE MOON WARRIORS HAD THEIR NEW COSTUMES...
...AND PRESTY WAS BACK WITH HIS FAMILY.
EVERYONE WAS VERY HAPPY.
THE EN

[MA]LACHAI NICOLLE is a five-year-old boy genius from Washington with a heart of gold who [lov]es making up stories where the bad guys get destroyed and the good guys win. He loves [rob]ots, ninjas, dinosaurs, unicorns, and superheroes.

[ETH]AN NICOLLE is from a small town in Oregon. With no formal training in art, he first self-[pub]lished his own comics in high school. After working on obscure comic books like *Creep* [and *Puppet Terrors*, and his own debut graphic novel, *The Weevil*, Nicolle's humor series [*Chu*mble Spuzz was picked up by Slave Labor Graphics (*Johnny the Homicidal Maniac, Milk [and Cheese*). The series gave him the honor of being a special guest at the Alternative Press [Exp]o in 2008, and he was nominated for an Eisner Award for Best Humor Publication in 2009.

[Eth]an and Malachai would like to thank: Our dad, Tom, and our moms, Deela and Diane. Our sisters, Megan and [Caro]lyn, and our brothers, Noah and Isaiah. Doug and Angie TenNapel, Anthony and Amy Munoz, Caryn and Lou Walter, [Pete]r McHugh, Eddie Gamarra, Nate Matteson, Mark and Elon Freedman, Shawna Gore, Mike Richardson and everyone [at D]ark Horse Comics, Dave DeAndrea, Jay M. Johar, Daniel McGuffey, Dylan Marvin, Tony Laughton, Donald Lim, Glen [Turn]ey, Scott Fedor, Maurice LaMarche, Bob Souer, Lee Gordon, Marcus Irvine, STEPDAD, Carl Sondrol, comicsalliance.com, [Tom] Welch, Jason McElhinney, Jason Porath, James Kennison, John Steinklauber, Kevin Murphy, Bill Corbett, Mike Nelson, [Rob] Gemm and everyone else at Riff Trax, Sean McGowan, Eric Branscum, Steven Wesley Guiles, Katherine Garner, Jefferey [Row]land and everyone at Topatoco, Chris Hastings, Dan Vado and everyone at SLG, Ryan Agadoni, Josh Kenfield, Paul and [Sto]rm, Simon Pegg, Hilary McNaughton, Adam Bentley, all our guest-episode contributors, everyone in the forum and on [Face]book, and pretty much everyone who reads *Axe Cop*!

The Gallery

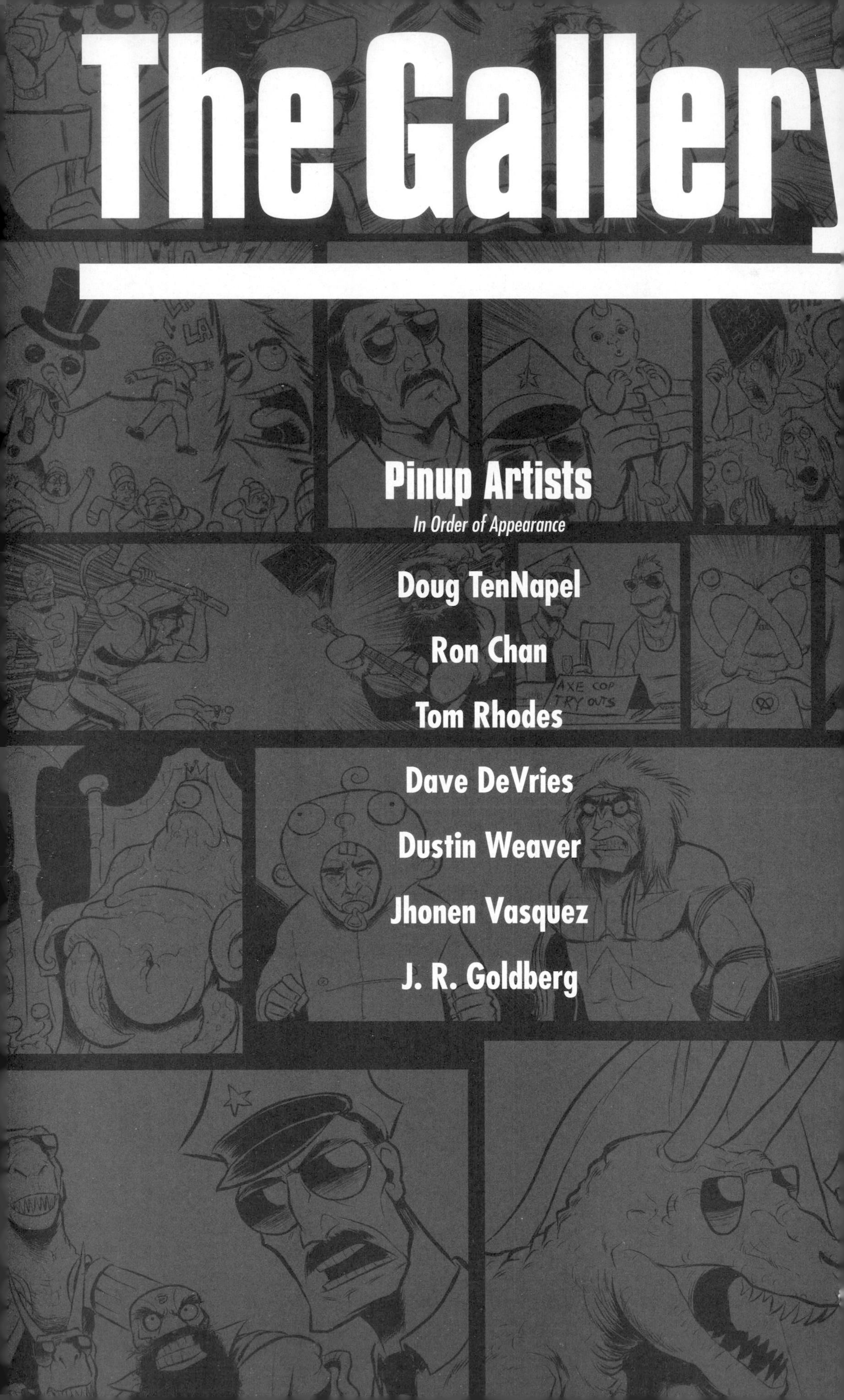
AXE COP
TRY OUTS

Pinup Artists

In Order of Appearance

Doug TenNapel

Ron Chan

Tom Rhodes

Dave DeVries

Dustin Weaver

Jhonen Vasquez

J. R. Goldberg

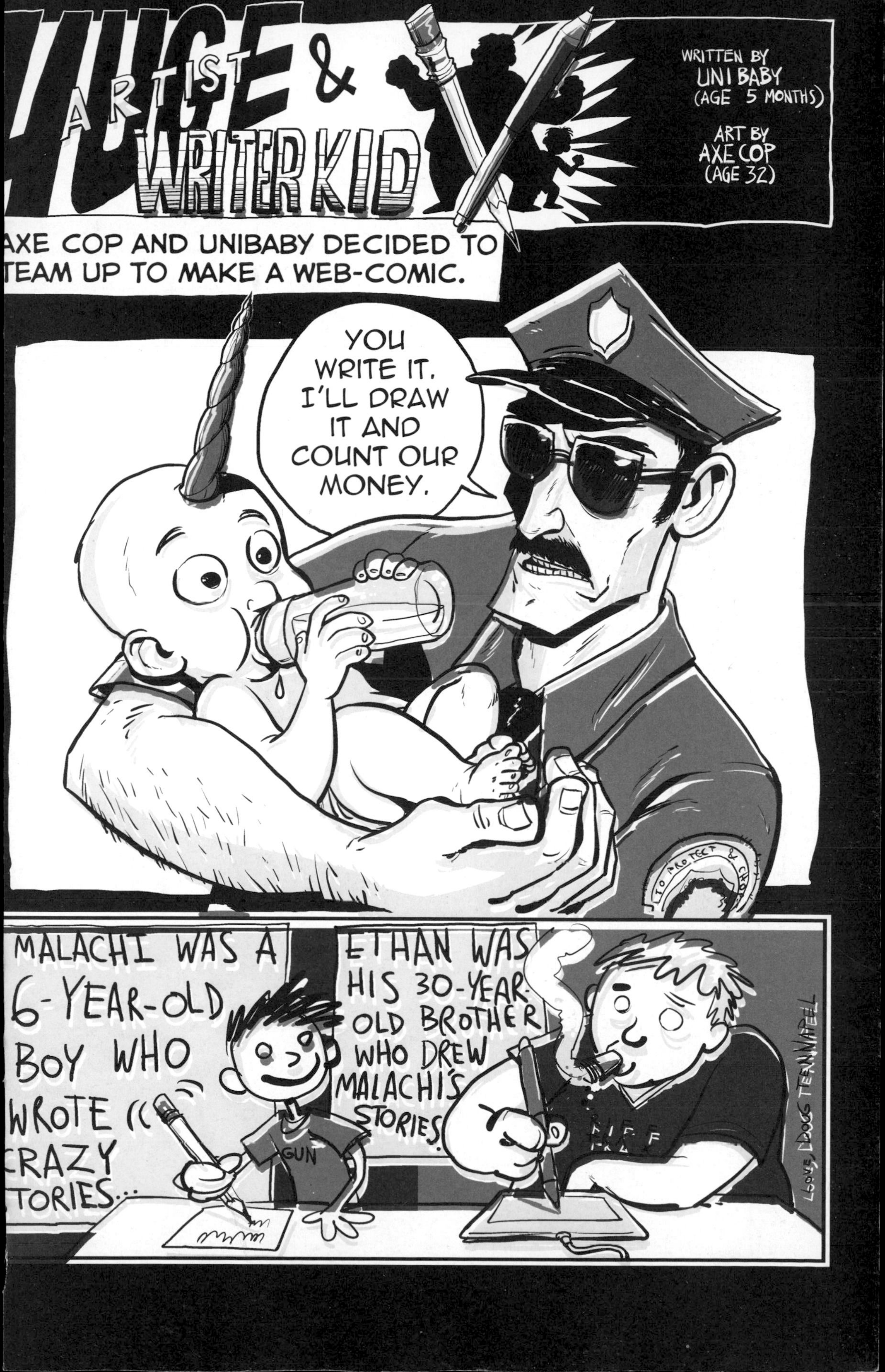
HUGE ARTIST & WRITER KID
WRITTEN BY UNI BABY (AGE 5 MONTHS)
ART BY AXE COP (AGE 32)
AXE COP AND UNIBABY DECIDED TO TEAM UP TO MAKE A WEB-COMIC.
YOU WRITE IT. I'LL DRAW IT AND COUNT OUR MONEY.
TO PROTECT & CHOP
MALACHI WAS A 6-YEAR-OLD BOY WHO WROTE CRAZY STORIES...
ETHAN WAS HIS 30-YEAR-OLD BROTHER WHO DREW MALACHI'S STORIES.
GUN
LOVE, DOUG TEN NAPEL

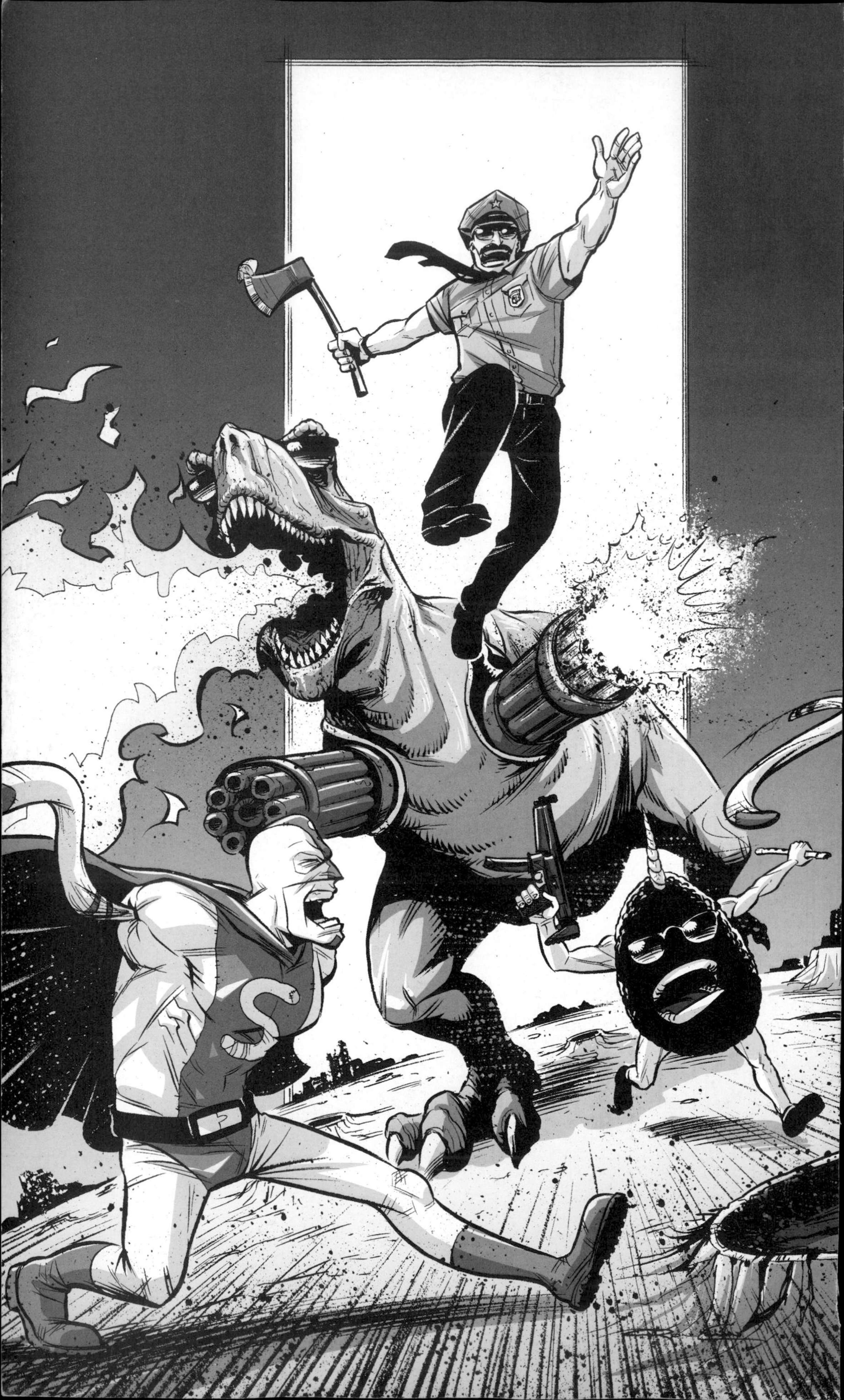

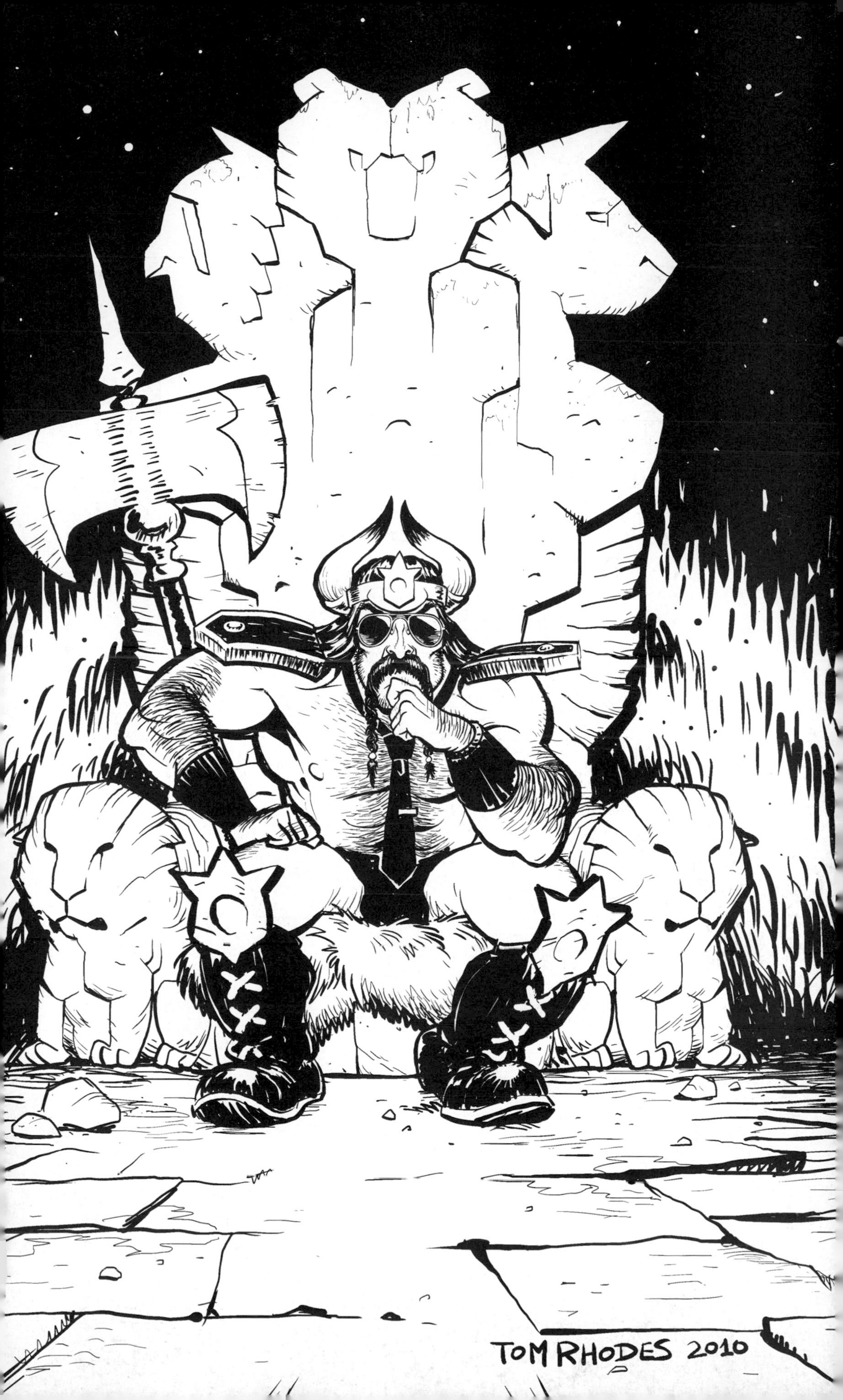
TOM RHODES 2010

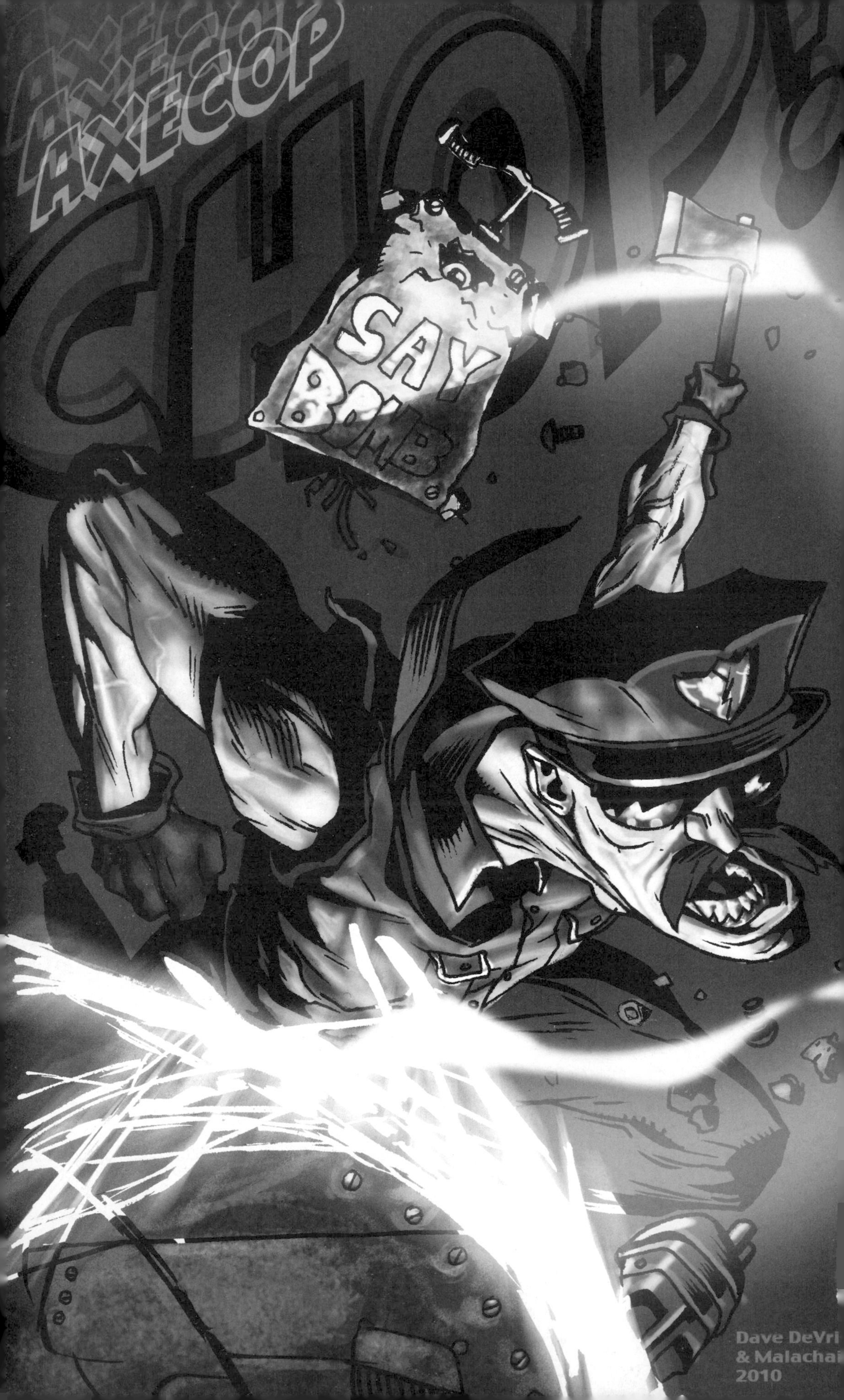
AXE COP
CHOP!
SAY BOMB
Dave DeVri
& Malachai
2010

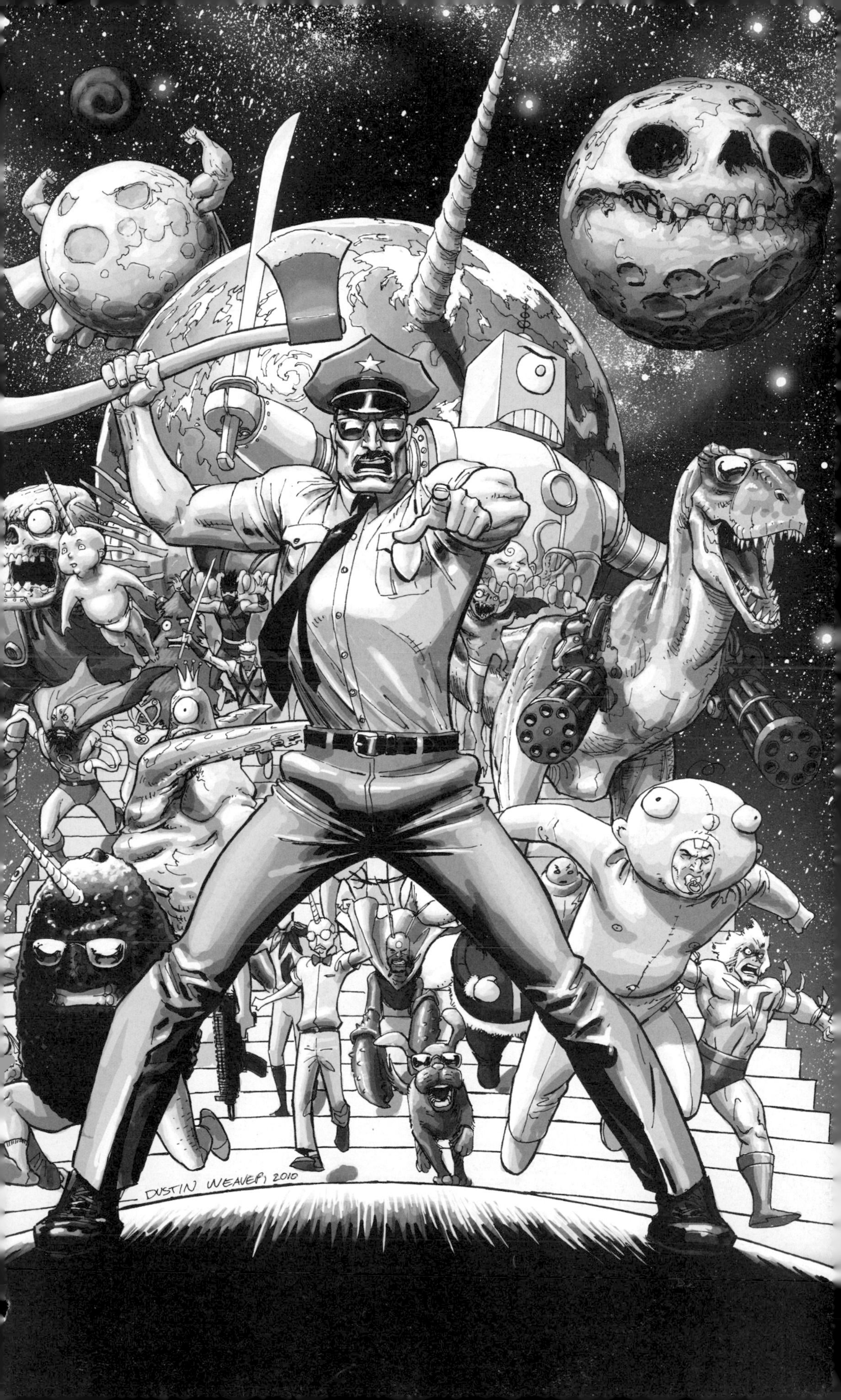
DUSTIN WEAVER, 2010

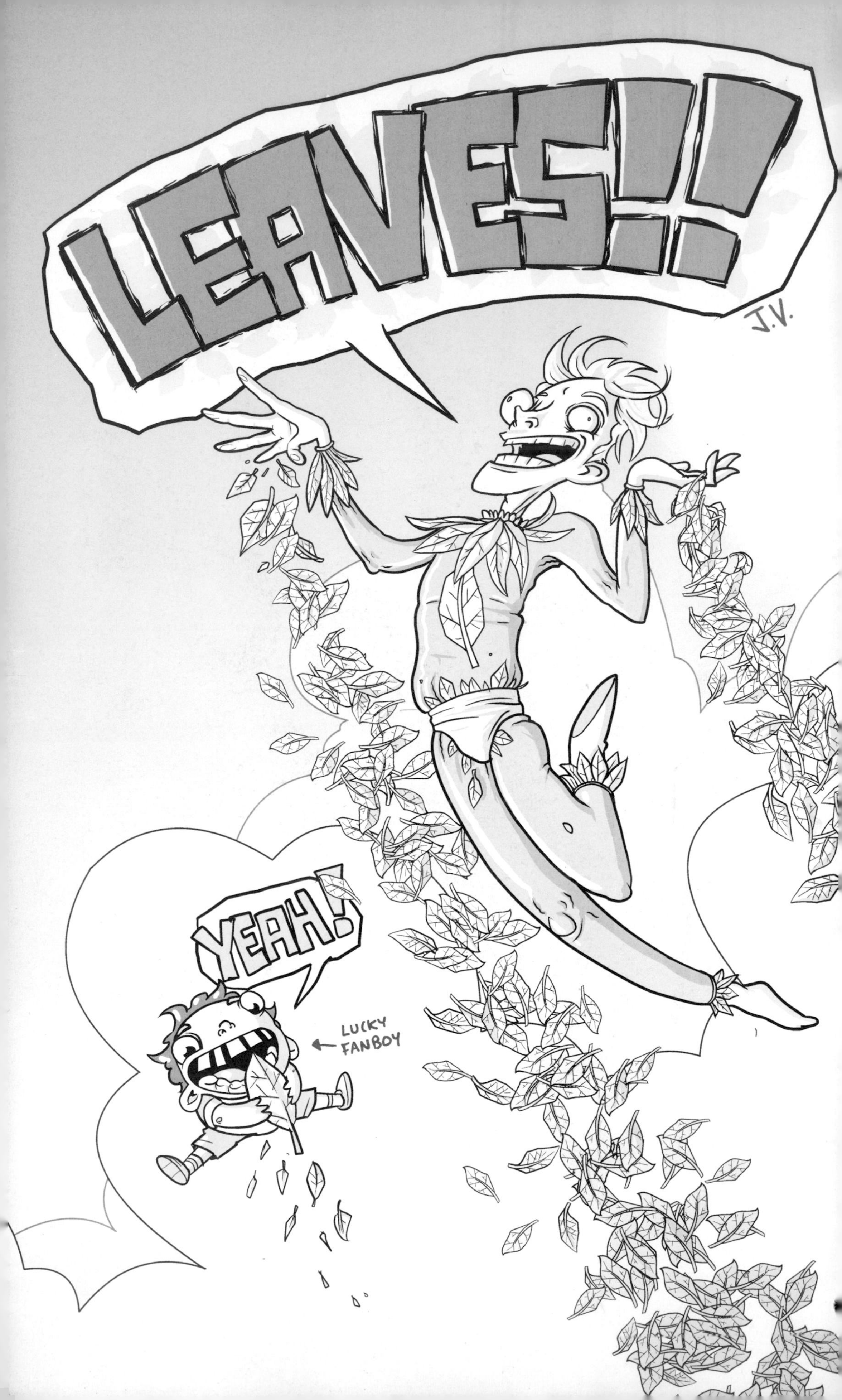
LEAVES!!!
J.V.
YEAH!
LUCKY FANBOY

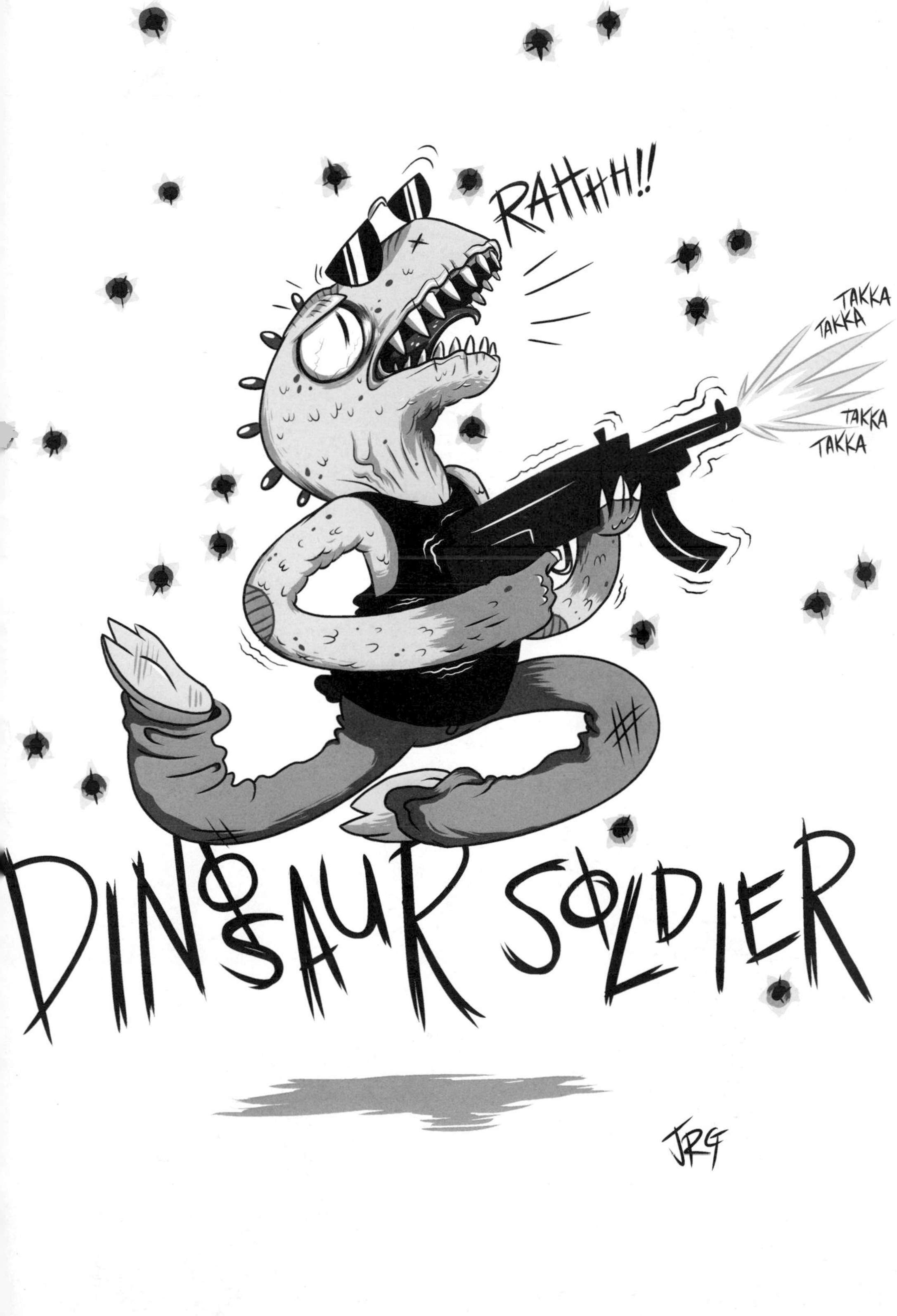
RAHHHH!!
TAKKA
TAKKA
TAKKA
TAKKA
DINOSAUR SOLDIER
JRG

Looking for something new to read?

CHECK OUT THESE ALL-AGES TITLES FROM DARK HORSE BOOKS!

兎用心棒 USAGI YOJIMBO™

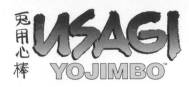

Join Usagi Yojimbo in his hare-raising adventures of life and death. Watch as he faces assassins, medicine peddlers, bat ninjas, and more, in this twenty-volumes-and-counting epic! This is a story of honor and adventure, a masterful adaptation of samurai legend to sequential art. Dark Horse is proud to present this Eisner award–winning and internationally acclaimed tour de force by master storyteller Stan Sakai!

Sock Monkey™

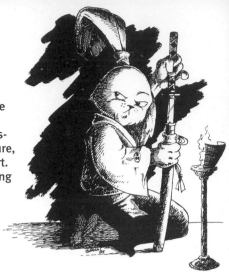

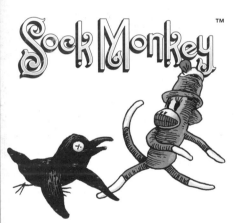

Just how much trouble can a toy animal really cause? Find out in this funny, unsettling, and utterly endearing series written and drawn by Tony Millionaire! Follow along with mischievous sock monkey Uncle Gabby and bumbling bird Drinky Crow as they try to find a home for a shrunken head, try their hands at matchmaking, hunt salamanders and butterflies, tackle home repairs face off against creatures from the deep, and try to get to heaven. Delights! Happy endings and random destruction are guaranteed! Check out any of the amazing Sock Monkey stories already out and about, or hop on board for the latest Sock Monkey yarn, *The Inches Incident*.

CHICKENHARE™

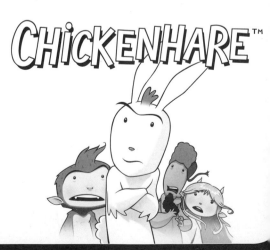

What do you get when you cross a chicken with a hare? The funniest, most exciting all-ages graphic novels of all time! Chickenhare and his turtle friend Abe find themselves on their way to be sold to Klaus—an insane taxidermist with a penchant for unique animals! With the help of two mysterious new companions, our fuzzy, feathered, and amphibious heroes might be able to escape, but... where?

Find out more about these and other great Dark Horse all-ages titles at darkhorse.com!

AVAILABLE AT YOUR LOCAL COMICS SHOP OR BOOKSTORE • TO FIND A COMICS SHOP IN YOUR AREA, CALL 1-888-266-4226
For more information or to order direct: •On the web: darkhorse.com •E-mail: mailorder@darkhorse.com •Phone: 1-800-862-0052 Mon.–Fri. 9 A.M. to 5 P.M. Pacific Time.